Sophie Pembroke has been ~~reading~~ and writing romance ever si~~nce~~ ~~reading her first~~ Mills & Boon as part of her ~~English Literature~~ degree at Lancaster University, so getting to write romantic fiction for a living really is a dream come true! Born in Abu Dhabi, Sophie grew up in Wales and now lives in a little Hertfordshire market town with her scientist husband, her incredibly imaginative and creative daughter and her adventurous, adorable little boy. In Sophie's world, happy *is* for ever after, everything stops for tea, and there's always time for one more page…

Incorrigible lover of a happy-ever-after, **Jessica Gilmore** is lucky enough to work for one of London's best-known theatres. Married with one daughter, one fluffy dog and two dog-loathing cats, she can usually be found with her nose in a book. Jessica writes emotional romance with a hint of humour, a splash of sunshine, delicious food—and equally delicious heroes!

Also by Sophie Pembroke

Best Man with Benefits

Dream Destinations miniseries

Their Icelandic Marriage Reunion
Baby Surprise in Costa Rica

Twin Sister Swap miniseries

Cinderella in the Spotlight
Socialite's Nine-Month Secret

Also by Jessica Gilmore

Christmas with His Ballerina
It Started with a Vegas Wedding

The Princess Sister Swap miniseries

Cinderella and the Vicomte
The Princess and the Single Dad

Discover more at millsandboon.co.uk.

CHRISTMAS BRIDE'S
STAND-IN GROOM

SOPHIE PEMBROKE

MISS RIGHT
ALL ALONG

JESSICA GILMORE

MILLS & BOON

First published in Great Britain 2024
by Mills & Boon, an imprint of HarperCollins*Publishers* Ltd,
1 London Bridge Street, London, SE1 9GF

www.harpercollins.co.uk

HarperCollins*Publishers*, Macken House, 39/40 Mayor Street Upper,
Dublin 1, D01 C9W8, Ireland

Christmas Bride's Stand-In Groom © 2024 Sophie Pembroke

Miss Right All Along © 2024 Jessica Gilmore

ISBN: 978-0-263-32142-5

11/24

MIX
Paper | Supporting
responsible forestry
FSC™ C007454

This book contains FSC™ certified paper
and other controlled sources to ensure responsible forest management.

For more information visit www.harpercollins.co.uk/green.

Printed and Bound in the UK using 100% Renewable Electricity
at CPI Group (UK) Ltd, Croydon, CR0 4YY

CHRISTMAS BRIDE'S STAND-IN GROOM

SOPHIE PEMBROKE

MILLS & BOON

To Jess, for saying yes to this duet!

CHAPTER ONE

MILLIE MYLES SAT back in her seat and laughed obligingly at the right moments in the best man's speech. Giles Fairfax was born to play the best man, really. He had the breeding, the training… Giles was polished, appropriate, wildly handsome in his morning suit, and his speech was going down well—the right proportion of laughs to groans and embarrassed blushes from the groom. Even she had laughed, against her will. He was *annoyingly* good at this.

Of course he'd always been annoyingly good at lots of things. Or sometimes just annoying. Even though they hadn't been in the same room since they were about eighteen—not an accident—Millie still had plenty of memories of Giles Fairfax before that, and stories from her best friend Charlie about his successes since, to hold against him.

Because Charlie was also *his* best friend. Giles and Millie had been competing for Number One Best Friend status since they were about twelve. Childish? Yes. Was Millie still determined to win? Absolutely.

Before Giles came on the scene, it had been just her and Charlie. And since they'd become actual adults she'd managed to arrange things so that it still felt that way, most of the time—even if she knew Charlie and Giles got together often in her absence.

It had been something of a shock to see Giles Fairfax all grown up—no gangling eighteen-year-old youth any longer, but a broad-shouldered, confident and—damn it all—incredibly handsome thirty-year-old man. Before she'd realised who he was, she had to admit to even indulging in an appreciative look or two from behind.

Not that she'd ever do anything about it. Physical attraction was nothing compared to actual compatibility at a soul level. Millie had no interest in playing around with passion—she'd tried that before, and knew all too well where it led. She didn't want a guy who oozed charisma and charm—at least until he got bored with her in bed. No, next time she got involved with a man it would be a proper, grown-up relationship, based not on mutual desire, but on mutual beliefs and respect.

Was that really so much to ask?

Up at the top table, Giles still held the crowd in the palm of his hand. He told tales of mischievous university days at Oxford, which his audience all related to. Most of the guests had been to one or other of the elite English boarding schools beforehand, and after university gone on to work in the City, or the law, or medicine.

Millie was pretty sure she was the only state-educated florist in the bunch. She'd never felt more out of place in her life, and that was really saying something.

Up at the top table, Giles had paused for a laugh, smiling easily—until he looked over in her direction and, just for a second, caught her gaze. The smile fell away, and there was something else in his expression—something she couldn't quite read and didn't want to understand.

She looked down and focussed on the floral display in the centre of the table—one of those she'd spent all the night before reworking, because the bride had changed her mind about what she wanted—*again*—at the last moment.

She'd known Giles for more than half her life now, and even if they hadn't spent time together in over a decade her opinion of him hadn't changed in all those years. He was the quintessential posh boy, from a family with money, land and a title, gliding through life on other people's efforts and only ever putting on a show instead of being a real person.

It was that last part that made him different from the man she'd come to this wedding with. Their mutual best friend Charlie might have the land and the money, and the family title one day, but he knew what it was to work for it. When times—and renovation costs—had got tough, his family had turned their inherited good fortune into a thriving business that employed a lot of local people and small businesses. Giles's family, as far as she knew, had just pulled up their drawbridge and enjoyed their good fortune.

Her gaze moved to the bride, icily beautiful at the top table, and she squeezed her date's hand. Beside her, Charlie had a fixed smile on his face—a 'society smile' she called it. Because he sure as hell wasn't smiling inside. She knew that much.

The love of his life was marrying another man, and she'd never been as furious at anyone as she was at Octavia Sinclair right now. Even her almost two-decades-long annoyance with Giles faded into insignificance next to what Octavia had done to Charlie.

'You doing okay?' she murmured to Charlie, as Giles wound up the best man's speech with a heartfelt ending and received a round of applause that went on for a while.

'Of course,' Charlie said, clearly lying. 'Why wouldn't I be? I'm here with the most beautiful—and wonderful—woman in the room.'

The smile he gave her as he said the last bit was, at least, a real one, but Millie wondered if she should have cut him off from the champagne a little earlier.

'Seriously, Mills. Thank you for coming with me. Hanging out with you today has made it all a little bit more bearable.'

She leaned in and rested her head against his shoulder. 'I wouldn't be anywhere else.'

It wasn't strictly true. Attending a high society wedding with the sort of people Charlie had grown up with wasn't exactly her idea of a good time. But Charlie needed her. So of course she'd said yes when he'd asked her to attend the wedding. Even if Octavia's nose had wrinkled slightly when she realised that her ex-boyfriend was bringing her florist as his date.

It had meant that she could watch the fruits of her labours today, though. The glorious riot of autumnal colours she'd carefully arranged into an arch that the bride and groom had stood under for the ceremony. The trailing bouquet of honey and golden hues that the bride had discarded somewhere already. The turning leaves and blousy roses in the rustic-but-polished table decorations. It was nice to see her work being enjoyed. Octavia had wanted to wow everyone with the flowers, and Millie was pretty sure she'd pulled that off.

Usually she was gone before the guests arrived, so it made a nice change to see things through to the end.

Charlie reached for the champagne bottle again, and Millie began calculating how hard it would be to actually carry him out to the taxi at midnight. She was glad she'd decided to stick to just one small glass for the toasts. She needed her wits about her today. Besides, she needed to get used to cutting out alcohol.

There were black-tied waiters moving around the room with coffee pots, so she smiled hopefully at the nearest one and he made his way over, filling both their cups. Millie thanked him profusely—she was going to need the caffeine.

Something else you'll have to give up if you want to get pregnant.

The thought burst, uninvited, into her mind, and she dropped her teaspoon into her saucer with a clatter.

Charlie looked up, concerned. 'Okay?'

'Fine!' She beamed back at him. Today wasn't about her problems, it was about his. 'How are you doing?'

Charlie gave a small half-shrug, and an attempt at a smile. 'It is what it is.'

Oh, how she hated that phrase. The idea of lying down and accepting things. She wanted to *change* the stuff that made her miserable, or angry, or whatever.

She supposed there really wasn't very much Charlie could do about Octavia marrying another man, though. Or the fact that Octavia had been a stone-cold bitch since the first day Millie met her—not that Charlie had ever really seen that.

Millie was well aware that her perspective on the world—and especially on *Charlie's* rarefied and prosperous world—was from a different angle to his. She hadn't grown up in the splendour of Howard Hall, or at boarding school, attending society events with the same people with the same world view every season. Her parents didn't have a wardrobe of black-tie outfits ready for any occasion, or a cook on hand to cater and staff to serve when they hosted.

She'd grown up in the gatehouse at the hall, with a mother who *was* that cook and a father who'd cared for the gardens and grounds before he died. Charlie had been her first play-mate, her childhood best friend since he was four and she was three, and even after he'd been shipped off to boarding school for most of the year. Even after he'd met Giles there, and she'd suddenly had to share best friend status with an aloof and difficult boy she didn't know.

The point was, Charlie knew her better than anyone, and she knew who he was behind the society smile.

But she'd never really been part of his world the way Giles had. That had given him an advantage in the Best Friend Battle.

She'd watched those Howard Hall parties and grand occasions from behind the bushes, seen Charlie trotted out in a miniature suit to match his father's to make nice with his parents' friends and acquaintances. She'd stared with wide eyes as she took in what seemed to be a fairytale world—at least until one of her parents had found her and dragged her home to bed.

She shook the memories away. Here, now, she was an invited guest at the society wedding of the year, on the arm of one of the most eligible bachelors in the country—Charles St Clare Howard, heir to the title Baron Howard, which had links back to the Normans. None of the guests here knew that she was only attending for moral support in the role of childhood best friend. For all they knew she *belonged* here, and Charlie was wildly, madly in love with her. Maybe he was planning to propose. They could be thinking of starting a family—

Don't think about it, Mills.

Not today. Today wasn't a day for thinking about her problems—it was for distracting Charlie from his.

Which would be easier if the bride wasn't now bearing down on them in her designer wedding gown, feathers ruffling along the train and her icy beauty on full display.

'*There* you are,' she said, as if Millie hadn't been sitting in her assigned place on the seating plan for the last several hours. 'I need you to fix my bouquet.'

Millie got to her feet. 'What happened to it?'

Octavia shrugged delicate shoulders. 'No idea. But it looks uneven, and it needs to be *perfect* before I toss it later. Come on!'

Of course Octavia needed her flowers to look perfect before she threw and probably destroyed them for the cameras. Millie cast an apologetic look at Charlie, whom Octavia hadn't even acknowledged, and then followed her.

It was a reminder that, really, she was only staff. Just in case she'd been getting any ideas above her station.

Giles Fairfax had heard, often from ex-girlfriends, the phrase 'always the bridesmaid, never the bride'. But he'd never come across the idea of 'always the best man, never the groom'.

All the same, that seemed to be his lot in life. Octavia and Layton's wedding was the third time he'd been best man this year alone. Honestly, he was running out of material.

He suspected he was just a safe pair of hands. In the circles he ran in—or had done growing up, at least—everyone had a large group of friends, but close, best friends were less of a thing. And so, when prospective grooms started falling, one by one, they looked around for who was most likely to keep a wedding day calm, on track, and not humiliate them in his toast.

He did also have a bit of a reputation for organising some spectacular stag dos by now, so that might play into it, too.

It suited Giles well enough. It wasn't as if he had any intention of ever getting married himself anyway, but seeing so many other people's weddings up close and in all their bickering glory would have put him off if he did.

Not to mention what the grooms tended to get up to on the stag weekends.

He'd been conflicted about saying yes to this one, though. As much as he liked Layton, his opinion of Octavia was rather less positive. Not least because of the man she'd just left slumped at a table on the outer edges of the room, watching her sashay away in her wedding gown.

Or maybe he was watching the woman beside her...just a little bit. The dark-haired woman in the sage-green dress, helping the bride fix her bouquet. She had curves where Octavia had angles, was dark where the bride was icy blonde, and soft where she was sharp. If he didn't know the wicked tongue and disapproving stare she'd turn on him, Giles would be doing more than looking.

The moment he'd caught her gaze during his speech he'd felt the undeniable spark of attraction that usually boded very well for his evening. Except it was *Millie*, so it had confused more than excited him. And, of course, she'd looked instantly away. Clearly her opinion of him hadn't changed with the passage of time.

He hadn't seen Millie Myles in over a decade, but he had to admit he didn't remember that zing of chemistry between them when they were teenagers. More a zing of irritation and annoyance. But now… Now she was utterly gorgeous, and she walked with a confidence in herself she'd definitely never had at eighteen. He could absolutely understand Charlie asking her to this wedding as his date…except for the fact that until now Charlie had never given any indication that he saw Millie Myles as anything but his *other* childhood best friend.

Not that friendship was a competition, really. Except somehow it always had been for Giles and Millie. They'd battled over being the most important person in the world to Charlie—and somehow, in the process, let him fall into Octavia's clutches instead.

In all honesty, Giles was glad Charlie had Millie beside him today—especially since Giles himself had too many other duties to keep a close eye on him. Obviously he'd never admit as much to Millie herself, or even to Charlie. That wasn't how the dynamic between the three of them worked, and he could see no good reason to change it now.

Giles slipped into the now empty seat beside Charlie to check in on his friend, noting the empty bottle of champagne and full coffee cup in front of him.

'How's it going?'

It seemed an inadequate question. The real one was something more like, *Is your heart torn apart inside you, watch-*

*ing the woman you love marry another? How the hell are
you still sitting upright? Why did you even agree to come?*

But they didn't ask those sorts of questions in his circles.

'Oh, Giles.' Charlie plastered on a smile that Giles didn't
believe for a moment. 'It's been a lovely day. Great speech,
by the way. You must be an old hand at this by now.'

'Just practising for when you ask me to be *your* best man.'
Giles tilted his head towards where Millie was fussing with
Octavia's bouquet, while the bride watched her like a hawk.
'Although since you brought *Millie* as your date to your ex's
wedding, I guess that's still a way off?'

It occurred to Giles that if Charlie ever looked up and realised that Millie was a beautiful woman, and a thousand
times better than Octavia, he'd probably promptly fall in love
with her. And that would mean that Millie would *definitely*
win the battle over Charlie they'd been engaged in since they
were about twelve.

Maybe he should just let her. 'She did grow up well,
though, I have to admit,' he said, staring over at Millie again.
Probably it was just that long-lasting feud that made something inside him clench at the idea of Millie marrying Charlie.

'I notice *you* didn't bring a date, even though you're best
man.' It was a clumsy attempt to change the subject on Charlie's part, but Giles went along with it.

'I never do—you know that.'

He had no intention of getting married—ever—and he
was always worried about any of his casual hook-ups getting ideas if he brought them to something as meaningful as
a wedding. There was just something about the atmosphere
at these things.

Giles looked back over at Millie. At her gently curving
body, the dark hair falling over her shoulders, the slightly ir-
ritated look on her face as Octavia bossed her around. Was

she getting ideas? Did she want more than friendship from Charlie after all these years?

He wouldn't put it past her. And if Millie finally wanted to change their relationship, it might just wake Charlie up from his Octavia obsession.

If that happened… Well. Giles would just have to work very hard at being happy for his best friend.

And start working on his next best man's speech.

He decided to test his theory.

'So, if you two are just friends, as always, and I don't have a date—'

'No.' Charlie interrupted him before he could even get the thought out.

Yeah, they're still just friends. Not buying it.

'Why not?' Giles raised his eyebrows in innocent query. 'It's not like we're strangers hooking up at a wedding. We've known each other for ever, and we're not the same bickering teenagers we were back then. Although maybe we were just trying to hide a deeper attraction…'

'Because…she's not your type,' Charlie tried.

Looking at the way Millie had grown into her curves, and her confidence, Giles had to disagree.

'Oh, I think she looks *exactly* my type.'

Gorgeous and confident and curvy and *luscious*. He'd only said it to needle Charlie into admitting his feelings—but that didn't mean it wasn't true. If they'd met now, for the first time, Giles knew he would have been interested in getting to know Millie better. For a night, at least. But God, what a night… If she channelled all that passion she'd managed to bring to their teenage fights into his bed, it would be *explosively* good.

Hell. He *really* wanted Millie Myles. That was new.

'Absolutely not.' Charlie's voice was, if anything, even firmer this time. 'Millie is…she's my oldest friend.'

'Because I'm your *best* friend,' Giles put in, automatically. It was a reflex born of years of feeling he was competing with Millie for that title, he supposed.

'And I know that she is looking for commitment—for a real happy-ever-after and true love and a family—everything you go out of your way to avoid,' Charlie finished. 'So, no. She is not your type.'

Giles shuddered at the very idea. Time to let the fantasy go.

Yes, one night with Millie Myles would be something spectacular, he was sure. But he didn't mess around with women looking to settle down.

'Fair enough, then.' He looked between Charlie and Millie again and smiled. Well, if he couldn't have her... 'If only there was someone else here who wants the same things she does...'

Charlie took his meaning at last and rolled his eyes. 'Go away, now. She's coming back, and I don't want you to get tempted and abandon reason.'

Giles laughed and stood up, nodding politely at Millie and Octavia as he headed for the bar, and trying not to notice how attractive the confused little frown line between Millie's eyebrows was.

Charlie was right—she really wasn't his type. Which was a shame. But maybe he'd be best man again sooner than he thought, if he was reading the signs right.

CHAPTER TWO

CHARLIE WAS GROWING more and more morose as the evening wore on. Millie had given up trying to ration the champagne, and instead settled for trying to distract him. She scanned the dance floor for something, or someone, to talk about—but got immediately distracted by the sight of Giles Fairfax dancing with one of the bridesmaids.

Damn him. Couldn't he even be bad at dancing?

It wouldn't bother her so much, except that every time she glanced his way she got that funny feeling in the pit of her stomach—the sort she'd used to get when her junior school crush walked past her desk. Which was ridiculous, given that she was a grown woman now, and certainly not interested in Giles Fairfax in a childish crush way or any other.

It didn't help that he caught her looking every single time, either.

She glanced away, but not before Giles had caught her gaze and smiled, low and warm, then whispered something in his dance partner's ear. Probably mocking her. That would be about right.

Charlie reached for his glass again, and she got back to the task in hand. Distraction. Which, at a wedding, meant gossip.

'Those two definitely had an argument before the wedding.' Millie nodded towards the couple dancing past them. 'They were glaring at each other in the church.'

'Were they?' Charlie sounded surprised. 'I didn't notice.'

'Because you were staring at the bride.'

'True.'

Charlie leaned against her, as they both gazed around the room.

'I think she was hoping he'd propose before now,' he said, after a moment. 'They've been dating long enough.'

'How long is "long enough"?' Millie asked absently.

She'd dated her ex, Tom, for three years and they'd never got close. She'd assumed they were just too young, until the day she'd found him in bed with his work colleague. Apparently the passion had faded between them and he needed to get his kicks elsewhere.

Obviously she knew, intellectually, she was better off without him—and that she'd learned an important lesson from his betrayal: not to trust good sex and mutual attraction to turn into a lasting relationship. But it was still depressing to realise now that he might have been her best chance at the future she wanted.

God help me if that's *the case.*

Charlie shrugged. 'I don't know. Octavia and I were together for years—'

'Except you broke up every six months or so,' Millie pointed out.

'That might have been the problem.' His glass still hung precariously from his fingers, but he never spilled a drop.

'Not the only problem,' Millie said. 'She was also awful to you, and the whole relationship was toxic, and I wanted better for you because I love you and you're one of my very favourite people.'

'And you're one of mine.'

He gave her a sloppy hug, and she felt tears prick her eyes. She really should have said no to that last glass of wine.

'You know, I don't think I'll ever get married now,' Charlie went on, still staring morosely over at where Octavia was dancing with a group of her bridesmaids—minus the one who was still snuggled up against Giles's shoulder. Not that she was watching them. 'I think Octavia was my one shot. If I couldn't make it work with her...' He shook his head. 'Except I have to, somehow. There's the estate. The title. The entail. My family expect—no, they *need* me to marry and carry on the line. But how can I? She was my one true love. How can I marry someone else?'

'I don't believe that.' Millie stopped watching Giles and reached over to take Charlie's hands in hers. 'I know it hurts now, but...you have to have faith. I thought that Tom was my one shot—'

'And you haven't dated anyone seriously since. Remind me how this is supposed to convince me?'

Millie sighed. The man had a point.

'I guess *I* just have to have faith,' she said. 'I saw the doctor the other day and—'

'Is everything okay?' Suddenly Charlie's full attention was on her, his eyes wide with concern. 'What did they say.'

'Nothing like that,' she assured him. 'But I'd been having some tests for...well, women's stuff. And it turns out that my fertility is declining a lot faster than is usual for someone in their late twenties. They reckon that if I want to start a family I need to either freeze my eggs and hope, or get started now.'

Charlie let out a long breath. 'I'm sorry. I know how much having a family means to you.'

Her whole life it had only been her, her mum and her dad. No extended family, no cousins or siblings. Then her dad had died when she was fifteen, and it had become just her and mum. One day, it would just be her.

Millie had always imagined a large family...grandkids for her mum to spoil, a loving husband there to share the load. Now...it seemed that dream might already be over before it had started.

'What are you going to do?' Charlie asked.

'Find someone to fall madly in love with me in the next forty-eight hours and marry them after a whirlwind court-ship, settle down and have kids as soon as possible, and live happily ever after?'

It was a joke. Of course it was a joke.

It was just also what she wanted most in the world.

Charlie was still looking at her. She sighed.

'I guess I'll look into getting my remaining eggs frozen. Hope that things work out later.' She shrugged. 'Not many other options, are there?'

Charlie looked thoughtful. 'Maybe *we* should just get mar-ried. Could solve a lot of problems.'

Millie laughed. 'Can you imagine? My mum would be over the moon.'

'So would mine.' The music changed to something faster, more upbeat, and he held out a hand to her. 'Come on. If we have to do this wedding, let's at least do it properly and get a good boogie in.'

The best man dancing with the bride was probably one of those things that was on a checklist of 'must-haves for the perfect wedding day' somewhere—certainly Giles had been roped into it at all the other weddings he'd attended recently. Sometimes the bride in question used the dance to berate him for the hungover state of the groom at the church, other times to thank him for keeping the stag do under control.

Octavia, however, didn't seem interested in talking to him at all while they moved to the music. Stiff in his arms, she stared over his shoulder, so Giles tried to manoeuvre them so he could figure out what she was looking at.

Oh, of course. Charlie was dancing with Millie just be-hind them.

Giles had never tried to understand what kept Octavia and

Charlie together—and then apart and then together again—over the years. He'd just figured that love was unfathomable. They weren't good for each other, though—that was clear to anyone with eyes.

And if Charlie and *Millie* really could find happiness together, maybe he should start rooting for them. Instead of imagining a different world in which *he* was the one taking Millie home tonight.

It really was a peculiar change of pace to find himself wanting to spend time with her, rather than avoid her completely.

'They make a nice couple, don't you think?' He only said it to needle Octavia, and was rewarded by a scowl.

'I just can't believe he brought my *florist* to the wedding as his date!' she snapped back.

'You know full well that they're very old friends.'

Octavia rolled her eyes. 'Yes, well… Sometimes the friends we make in our youth aren't supposed to follow us through to adulthood.'

Despite her words, Octavia had managed to manoeuvre them closer to the other couple and, before Giles realised what she was doing, the bride slipped out of his arms and cut in between Charlie and Millie, saying, 'Bride's prerogative.'

Which left Giles and Millie standing staring at each other. Alone. In the past, Giles had gone out of his way to avoid moments like this. But today was a rather different sort of day, and he was discovering all sorts of new emotions about Millie Myles, so after a second, he offered her his arm. 'May *I* have this dance?'

She shrugged, looking as surprised as he felt. 'Sure.'

He wondered if she sensed it, too—the way things had changed between them. Maybe it was just meeting again as adults, as whole people who had more in their lives than a feud over who could be a better friend to Charlie. A chance to see each other in a new light.

Whatever it was, Giles had to admit it had him off balance.

Being attracted to a woman wasn't exactly new ground for him—usually he'd take them home or he wouldn't, but either way he wouldn't think about them again. Wanting a woman he couldn't have wasn't familiar, but still not outside the realm of his experience.

Finding himself so passionately wanting a woman he'd always hated was definitely new, though.

The band had changed tempo again, to a slow, crowd-pleasing old standard. Giles wondered if Octavia had personally approved the set list and had known this was coming up next. He wouldn't put it past her.

'She still can't quite take her claws out of him, can she?' Millie said softly, unknowingly echoing his own thoughts as they watched Charlie dance with the bride.

'She's always wanted to have her cake and eat it,' Giles said. 'Actually, I think she wants the whole bakery.'

Millie gave him a small flash of a smile. That was definitely new, too. Before, she'd always scowled at him.

'You don't sound very approving. And yet you agreed to be her husband's best man. What were you thinking, Giles?'

He shifted his arms slightly, bringing her in a little closer. It was easier to dance that way, that was all. Nothing to do with the way she felt against his body. Warm and soft and… She'd asked a question, hadn't she?

'Oh, I'm basically a best man for hire these days,' Giles admitted. 'A safe pair of hands. I won't let the groom get *too* wasted before the wedding, but I'll make sure he has enough fun that he doesn't feel he missed out. I give a good speech, and mothers-in-law love me. This is my third wedding this year.'

'I should have known that wearing a suit and tie and being charming would end up being your ultimate skill set.'

She laughed, and he felt it reverberate inside his chest. She was taking him over, and he couldn't help but imagine how much closer they *could* be.

'You know me,' he said, making it sound easy and care-less, even though it felt anything but. And even though it wasn't true. She *didn't* know him. He'd made sure she—and the rest of the world—never did. Except for Charlie. Charlie was an exception—for both of them, he suspected.

Another reason he had to stop noticing the way her breasts brushed against his shirt. She wasn't for him. And she could never know the truth.

Giles played the part, the game, and smiled and charmed, but he never let on that underneath it all he was fighting tooth and nail. Nobody saw his struggles—with his family, his finances, his own sense of fairness—because he didn't put them on show, and nobody looked too deep. They knew his name, his family, and that was all they needed to know to make their assumptions about who he was.

He wasn't about to let Millie Myles know any different. But she was distracting him with her closeness. With the chemistry between them that had taken him by such surprise.

Maybe it was because she *didn't* play the game. She prob-ably didn't even know what the game was.

If he'd never met her before today Giles would have known that Millie didn't belong to the same sort of society that he—and almost every other guest in the room—had grown up in. Not because she didn't look the part, or because she'd done anything particular to give it away. But because of that laugh.

It was too honest, too real, to belong in his world.

His world was filled with fake smiles and polite amuse-ment. With saying one thing, then turning around and saying the opposite to the next person. Everyone played the game, played the room, and said or heard what would get them where they wanted to be. They traded favours, not jokes.

But Millie laughed as if she found him funny, rather than because she was buttering him up for something. It was strangely refreshing. And probably the result of the excellent champagne Octavia was serving, because she'd definitely never found him funny before.

'You should set up a website offering your best man services,' she said. 'I'd recommend you to my brides.'

'Octavia said you were responsible for the incredible wedding flowers. I knew you were a florist, but this…it's really great, Millie.' He could give her a compliment. That wasn't *flirting*, exactly. Just a sign that they were adults now, not bickering teens.

Millie snorted. Something else none of the young ladies he'd grown up with would ever do in company. Well, not his company, anyway.

'You mean she told you she couldn't believe Charlie brought the florist to her wedding as his date.'

'You heard her?' Normally Octavia was more discreet with her catty comments, but maybe a florist didn't deserve discretion in her eyes.

'Just a guess.'

She glanced over to where they'd last seen Charlie and Octavia, but either they'd got swept away to the other side of the dance floor, or Charlie had made a rapid escape from the clutches of his ex. Either way, apparently Giles's fate was always to be dancing with someone who was looking for someone else.

All things considered, that was probably for the best. Weddings gave people ideas, and God forbid he—the eternal bachelor—start getting any.

He'd seen what wedded bliss did to people, especially in

his family, and he had no desire to propagate that misery down to another generation, thank you.

'I'm hoping that Charlie will be asking for my services next, now he's clearly over Octavia,' he said, raising an eyebrow at her suggestively.

'Charlie? Oh, we're not... I'm not here as his *date*, Giles. Well, I am. But not *that* sort of date. You know it's not like that between us.'

'I know... I know. You've always been just friends,' Giles said, to stop her rambling. 'I just thought... I know you and I haven't always got along, but honestly...? It's so nice to see him with someone who actually *likes* him, for a change. He deserves to be happy. And aren't all the best relationships ones that are founded in friendship? Come on, Millie. You can't tell me you've never even *thought* about it.'

Just because *Giles* had no intention of marriage, he still wanted that happiness for his friends. And Charlie, he knew, *wanted* all the things that Giles hoped to cast aside. The wife, the kids, the family, the estate and the title carrying on in perpetuity.

And if Charlie got together with Millie, maybe Giles could stop thinking about her this way. She'd be firmly off limits then, and Giles would never, ever mess with his best friend's girl.

'He *does* deserve that,' Millie said quietly. Then she looked up at him with a sad smile. 'My mum always says that marrying her best friend was the best decision she ever made. She still says it now, even though Dad's been gone for years.'

'I'm sorry.'

Giles could tell from the sudden glassiness of her eyes that the loss still hurt. He remembered the day he'd died; Giles had been visiting Charlie for the summer, like he often did, and he'd made one of his usual digs at Millie...and Charlie had yelled at him. The only time he'd ever done it. Giles had run and hid in the orchard, and it had been hours later that Charlie came and explained what was going on.

Now, Millie just shrugged, which made her lose time with the music, and Giles tightened his arm around her waist to get them back on track. It pressed her even closer against him, and he swallowed as he tried to ignore the sensation.

Get it together, Fairfax. She's talking about her dead father, for God's sake.

'It's been a long time,' Millie said. 'But Charlie has been a good friend to me—and to you. His whole family have. I knew today would be hard for him, and I wanted to be here to support him. Even if it is wildly obvious to everyone else that I don't really belong here.'

'I wouldn't say "wildly obvious"…'

Except it was. Not because of Millie, exactly. Just because everyone else in this room knew each other—had been coming to events like this, where the guest list was almost exactly the same, for ever. There were a few other outliers—not to mention the American contingent—but he'd heard a few people asking who the woman on Charles Howard's arm was.

'Just not as obvious as Layton's crowd.'

She laughed. 'That's true. Maybe I should affect an American accent. *Whaddaya reckon?*' she asked, in the most outrageous Southern drawl he'd ever heard, surprising a laugh from him.

'Perfect,' he said. Then he sobered. 'You know, it really was good of you to come for Charlie today.' He knew she must feel uncomfortable attending as a guest, rather than a supplier—and Octavia clearly hadn't done anything to ease that feeling. But she'd come anyway. 'I'm glad he has you in his corner. Especially since I had other duties.'

The music came to a close and she stepped out of his arms. 'So am I. And now I'd better go and track him down. Thanks for the dance.'

She turned and walked away, her sage-green dress swishing around her legs as her hips swayed, and Giles found he couldn't help but watch her go.

Somehow, the room felt a little colder without her in his arms.

Swallowing hard, he shook the feeling away, and turned to find out when the bride and groom intended to cut the cake. He had best man duties to attend to.

The invitation Charlie had shown her had said 'carriages at midnight', and so, as the clock struck twelve, right on cue a fleet of taxis arrived outside Octavia's ancestral home to ferry the guests away again.

Charlie had sunk at least a couple of drinks at the bar since their dance, and Millie had to admit to another glass of wine or three, too, so they wrapped their arms around each other as they made their way down the stone steps at the front of the manor towards a cab.

Thankfully, Charlie's own sprawling family home, Howard Hall, wasn't far away—Charlie and Octavia's families were actually neighbours, although the size of the estates meant it still wasn't a safely walkable distance home at this time of night.

Or after quite so much to drink.

She glanced back over her shoulder as they waited for their cab driver to pull up and open the door. On the steps she saw Giles, watching them. He raised a half-full champagne flute in her direction and smiled.

Millie looked away. Today had been complicated and difficult enough without throwing Giles Fairfax into the mix. She definitely wasn't going to spend any time thinking about how surprisingly lovely it had felt to have Giles's arms around her as they danced, or that it might have been the first time in history when they'd actually managed to talk and joke without sniping at each other. Much.

And she *definitely* wasn't dwelling on that feeling in the pit of her stomach. Or the sparks she felt between them every time their gazes met.

'Come on,' she told Charlie as she helped him into the car. 'Time to go.'

Today had just been far too weird for her to handle any longer. She and Giles had even *agreed* about something—even if that something was Charlie.

'Are you going to come home with me tonight?' Charlie asked into her shoulder, as the cab bumped its way along the endless driveway. 'Or wake up your mum?'

That was a no-brainer. 'I'll stay with you.'

It was what they'd done all through their late teens and early twenties, whenever they were both home and fancied a night out. Inevitably Millie would end up staying with Charlie rather than waking up her mum by stumbling into the tiny gatehouse cottage in the early hours of the morning.

It all felt so familiar—setting up the daybed in the living room area of Charlie's suite, pouring pint glasses of water and finding paracetamol for the morning, then curling up together under all the blankets and cushions to debrief the night. They might have been home from university for the Christmas holidays, still twenty and clueless.

Howard Hall still belonged to Charlie's family, free and clear, but large portions of it—the most showy, oversized areas—were mostly just used for events these days. The family had claimed the East Wing for their own, however, and modernised and done it up tastefully. Charlie's suite there was still four times the size of her own flat above Holly and Ivy, the florist shop that she ran, and that was before she even took the communal spaces in the wing into account.

There were spare rooms, too, but she'd always preferred to stay with Charlie than use them.

Now, she curled up on the daybed, wrapped in a cashmere throw and leaning against cushions that had probably cost more than her actual bed at home, watching Charlie pour them one last nightcap.

'I think that went about as well as it could be expected to, don't you?' he said, weaving slightly as he crossed the room towards her.

She took her drink and held it to one side as he dropped, heaving himself onto the mattress next to her.

'I give them six months,' she said loyally. 'A year, tops.'

'You're probably right.' Charlie took a long sip of his drink. 'What do you think it is? The secret to an actual happy relationship, I mean.'

Ah, so they'd reached the philosophical portion of the evening. 'Well, my mum always said the secret was marrying your best friend,' she said, remembering the conversation she'd had with Giles while they danced.

He'd been a good dancer. And he seemed to really care about Charlie.

That was probably the only reason she was still thinking about him. Still imagining his arms around her.

'Going by that rule, I should probably marry you.' Charlie looked up at her with bleary eyes, smiling as he spoke.

Millie laughed, because of course he was joking.

Except…

'Giles thinks we should get married, too,' she said.

Was that proof that, whatever sparks she'd felt between them, he had felt nothing? Why else would he have suggested she and Charlie could be a match? Oh, God, he'd probably guessed that she was having some highly inappropriate and never-to-be-repeated crush-like feelings about him and been trying to let her down gently.

And she'd thought she'd got through the wedding without experiencing utter humiliation. Looked like she'd relaxed too soon on that front… Who knew what else she'd realise or remember when she sobered up fully?

'Did he, now? Interesting.'

Something about Charlie's voice made her suspicious. He never could hide anything when he was drunk. And if Giles had said anything to him about her, she needed to know now. For damage control purposes.

'Interesting how?'

'Just that he said something similar to me,' Charlie replied. 'I was warning him off you at the time.'

That burned more than she'd thought it would. It wasn't like she'd planned on *doing* anything about her crush, but it still hurt to know that Charlie disapproved. And she could guess exactly why.

'Because I'm not good enough?'

'Because you're far *too* good.' Charlie grabbed her hand—the one not holding her drink—and squeezed it tight. 'You're one of the best people I know, and you deserve everything you want in this world. And you want a family, and a happy-ever-after—and we both know that is the last thing that Giles wants.'

Of course it was. Even if this stupid feeling in her stomach outlasted the hangover she was bound to have tomorrow, it didn't matter. She'd never do anything about it for plenty of reasons. Starting with how attraction didn't lead to lasting relationships, and that was what she needed if she wanted to start a family. Then there was the fact that compatibility of goals and dreams mattered far more to her than passion. And Giles, as Charlie pointed out, didn't want the things she did.

'But *you* do,' Millie said.

His words had taken that burning feeling of not being enough and turned it into the sort of warmth that filled her chest and made her feel loved. And with that warmth came a realisation. One that she felt in the moment could change her whole life.

'You want the same things I do—to get married, be happy, have a family to carry on your name and title.'

Her gaze met his before he leaned back, just a fraction, and for a moment something hung in the air between them.

Something with potential.

It wasn't romance, or the sort of love that poets wrote about. It wasn't even close to the frisson she'd felt when she'd looked into Giles's eyes as they danced, or the way her blood had hummed as she'd been pressed against him.

It wasn't passion. But that was good. Passion never lasted.

Instead, it was something that made her feel safe and cherished.

And that was more important than passion. Wasn't it?

'*We* should get married.'

Millie honestly couldn't say for sure which one of them spoke the words first. The idea was just there, fully formed, in the room with them, and neither of them could ignore it.

She could marry her best friend, have the family she longed for, despite her failing fertility, and she'd never have to worry about anything like bad first dates or walking home alone at night again.

Millie had never thought she was the sort of woman who wanted to be looked after—she'd certainly never considered marrying for money or status. But marrying a man she loved, even if not romantically, so that they could take care of *each other*…

Now, that was the kind of plan she could get behind.

Of course, she was also kind of drunk. And so was he. She could never hold him to anything he agreed to after a day like today. And there was a chance this was utterly insane. She'd never, ever thought about Charlie that way. But then, she'd never thought about Giles and imagined him kissing her until today, either.

Oh, boy, she was definitely drunk if she was admitting that—even in her head.

Charlie opened his mouth to speak again, and she pressed a finger to his lips. 'Let's… We need to sleep on this. Sober up. Think things through. We'll talk about it in the morning.'

'And if we still think it's a good idea in the cold light of day?' Charlie asked.

'Then we'll start wedding planning.'

CHAPTER THREE

GILES'S PHONE RANG just as he was ushering the last—and most drunken—of the wedding guests into the remaining taxis. He ignored it.

Up ahead, he saw Charlie and Millie climbing into a cab, arms around each other and both giggling. Something inside his chest ached at the sight, and his brain helpfully reminded him how good she had felt in his arms.

If she was a different woman, or he was a different man, maybe things would be going differently this night. But they weren't, and they wouldn't. However tempting the idea might be.

He shook the thought away. Far better for her to be with Charlie tonight. And at least it seemed that they had enjoyed the day. Octavia, meanwhile, was stamping her feet some-where behind him, but he was choosing to ignore it.

For a minute or two Giles enjoyed the stillness of the night, watching the last of the revellers leave.

Then his phone rang again.

Reaching into his pocket, he saw that he already had three missed calls, all from the same unknown number. The one that was calling now.

Well, that boded well…

He swiped to answer. 'Giles Fairfax.'

'Gilly! Oh, good, I've caught you.'

Only one person called him Gilly—and got away with it.

Barely. And only one person would sound so upbeat about calling him repeatedly at gone midnight.

'Rebekah. What's happened? What do you need?'

His sister only ever called him if there was a problem, after all.

'Oh, just a tiny thing. I seem to be locked out of the house again. Do you think you could bring your spare set of keys over and let me in?'

Her tone was too light, too artificially inconsequential for him to believe that was all it was.

Besides, this had happened before.

'Where's Marc? Where are the kids, for that matter?'

He already knew the answer. But he was damned if he was going to go over there again without her saying it.

'Oh, they're inside. But they're asleep. It's late, you know. I don't want to wake them.'

But you'll wake me.

Not that he'd been asleep this time, but he knew from past experience that it wouldn't have mattered if he had been.

'I'm on my way.' He hung up.

Lucky for Rebekah that he'd only had the one glass of champagne to toast with at this wedding and made it last all night. Plus his car was parked in the garage around the back. He hadn't even taken his overnight bag into the room assigned to him here, after spending last night at a local hotel with the groom.

He grabbed his tailcoat and keys and headed for the garage.

His already sour mood—it was never fun being the only sober person at a wedding—sank further. What was he doing, standing up beside Layton and all his other friends, watching them sign themselves up for a life of misery or causing one for someone else? He'd thought he could believe in the magic of love for others, even if not for himself, but with every wedding that passed it became harder.

His parents hadn't exactly started him off with the best example, he supposed. Despite loathing each other openly for his entire childhood, still neither one of them would leave and risk losing the lifestyle they'd grown accustomed to. The same way they wouldn't leave the ancient pile of Fairfax Lodge, even as it fell apart around their ears.

They liked the trappings of aristocracy—the house, the title, the invitations, the society. But they'd do nothing to keep up their entitlement to it. Charlie's family, realising times and fortunes had changed, had leveraged their land, turned their property into a flourishing events business— not just providing lots of local employment but also using at least some of their staggering profits to benefit the people and the area around them.

Giles's parents would do nothing of the sort. They wanted the life they'd been born into without making any acknowledgment that the world they'd started in no longer really existed.

The home that Rebekah shared with her husband—a large, Georgian house in an acre or two of land—was thankfully no more than a forty-minute drive from Octavia's family estate. Giles's car crunched up the gravel drive, its headlights flashing off the bricks and the gardens, before landing on his sister, sitting shivering on the doorstep. With a sigh, Giles killed the engine and stepped out of the car.

'What was it this time?' he asked as he approached, his keys in hand.

'I must have just left them in another bag,' Rebekah said, unconvincingly. 'And you know how the kids need their sleep.'

Giles kept hold of the keys even as she tried to take them. 'Bekah. It's late. I've had a long day and driven all the way over here. So don't mess me about. What was it this time?'

'He didn't want me to go out.' Her shoulders slumped as

she spoke. 'He doesn't approve of the other mothers at the village school, but Benjy isn't old enough for boarding school yet, whatever he says, so I *have* to see them. And I didn't want to offend them by not going tonight, or Benjy will be ostracised, won't he?'

She looked up at him with wide eyes, looking for absolution, but it wasn't his to give. More than that, she shouldn't need it.

'He took your keys again?'

She nodded. 'And you know how he'll be if I wake him up. So I called you.'

Giles nodded. 'Right.'

Anger coiled in his stomach. This wasn't the first time he'd been called out to let his sister into her own home because his brother-in-law had taken her keys in protest at her going out.

She'd never call him if there was another way out—he knew that much.

'How do you think he'll react if *I* wake him up?'

Rebekah's eyes widened even further. 'Gilly, no! We've talked about this. You might not approve of my marriage, but it's not your business, or your place to judge me for it.'

'I'm not judging you. I'm judging him.'

And he did. Regularly. Rebekah seemed to have echoed their parents' marriage, more or less directly, and she still chose to live it out every day.

'Well, don't,' she snapped. 'This is my choice. I chose him, and this house, and this life and my family. And I'm not going to give it up just because he was in a bad mood about me going out tonight.'

She grabbed the keys from his hand and opened the door, before handing them back again.

'Thank you for coming out here,' she said, as she slipped inside. 'Goodnight, Giles.'

And there he was, left on his sister's doorstep in the middle of the night, feeling frustrated and impotent and hating marriage more than ever.

If he ever believed that his brother-in-law's behaviour had gone further—if he hurt her or the kids, or cut Rebekah off from her friends and family, or controlled her finances—he'd have grounds to step in. If she ever asked him to get her out, he'd do it in a heartbeat.

But instead she seemed content to defy her husband, then call Giles to let her into her own home. To argue, loudly, when she and Marc were alone—but put on a happy face in front of the children and company.

She chose to stay. For the same reasons, he assumed, that his parents clung on to a life long gone. For appearances. For the lifestyle they all wanted.

No wonder he'd decided to swear off both love and marriage early on. Theirs was a legacy he wanted to cut short here and now.

From nowhere, a memory of Charlie and Millie with their arms around each other, laughing, came to his mind. Millie's words quickly followed.

'My mum always says that marrying her best friend was the best decision she ever made.'

Maybe if he'd ever had a friend like that—one who loved him through everything…who supported him as he supported them…one he could love—maybe then he'd feel differently.

But he didn't. He wouldn't even know where to start.

Charlie and Millie had fallen into each other's lives and hearts effortlessly. He'd always been an extra, a spare part, getting in their way, not quite sure how to find his own place. Always battling to matter to Charlie against the unbreakable bond he had with the girl next door. And he'd certainly never found his own Millie.

Love, it seemed, had never been an issue in his family.

Love was not required, only an appropriate partner. Love wasn't something his family had taught him anything about.

Giles had had enough of the whole damn lot of them.

But, since Octavia's estate would be locked up by now, his London flat was too far to drive to at this time of night, and Rebekah clearly had no intention of antagonising her husband further by inviting him to stay, it seemed he'd have to deal with at least two more family members before he left again for the city.

Easing back into the car, he turned over the engine and headed for his parents' crumbling ancestral pile.

Millie's head throbbed and her tongue seemed to have doubled in size. But somewhere she could smell coffee brewing. And…and was that bacon? Bacon could fix a lot of ills, in her experience.

She experimented with opening her eyes and, having successfully achieved that, sat up and took a long gulp of the water in the pint glass beside her daybed.

The previous evening's activities and conversations trickled back into her consciousness.

Octavia being ridiculous about her bouquet and stealing Charlie for a dance.

Dancing with Giles. God, practically *lusting* after Giles Fairfax, of all possible people. She hoped he hadn't noticed. She'd never live that humiliation down. Giles had already witnessed one humiliation of hers in the past, and she wasn't keen to add to it.

What else? Drinking some more with Charlie, and coming back to his place to sleep it off, and…

What had happened then? She felt sure there was something more.

The room swam into focus and she blinked in the direction of the kitchen area of the suite. Charlie stood barefoot at the stove, frying bacon, the coffee machine whirring beside him. She shuffled out of bed, glad she always left a pair of pyjamas in his bottom drawer for nights such as last night. She'd made it halfway across the room before a memory from the previous evening hit her. Hard.

'Did we agree to get married last night?'

Charlie turned slowly to face her, his own face tired and a little grey. At least she wasn't the only one suffering.

'That is entirely possible, yes,' he replied. 'Coffee?'

'God, yes, please. In a bucket, if possible.'

The coffee was served, of course, in perfectly matching china mugs. Charlie sat opposite her at the small kitchen table and they stared at each other.

It felt as if they were each waiting for the other to laugh and say how ridiculous the idea was. And part of Millie wanted to do exactly that.

I mean, how did I get from dancing with Giles Fairfax to agreeing to marry Charlie?

Except…

Was it so ridiculous? Really?

She loved Charlie. She trusted Charlie. He made her laugh, and she was pretty sure they could make each other happy. That was more than a lot of people went into a marriage with, wasn't it?

For a moment, another flash of memory lit up her brain. A memory of dancing with Giles the night before, and how she'd felt as if her body knew his—knew how it would move against hers. The spark of… Attraction wasn't a strong enough word. The *want* that had flooded her from just being close to him had been something she wasn't sure she'd ever experienced before. Let alone with someone she'd basically disliked for the better part of twenty years.

But that was just lust—and probably champagne. Sexual attraction was easy—she'd had plenty of that with Tom at the start, and look how that had ended up. The passion had faded, and they'd slowly realised they had nothing else in common—but not before *he'd* realised he could have that passion with other women he hooked up with through dating apps.

She'd thought he would be her for ever person, even though he'd never talked about marriage. Now she knew she'd had a lucky escape. But it still hurt that she'd wasted so much time on someone who could treat her that way, who rated lust above love. Especially now that she knew her ovaries didn't have that kind of time to waste.

No, passion *definitely* wasn't a sign of anything.

But friendship was.

'We'd need to have rules,' she said, before she could change her mind. 'If we decided to go ahead with it, I mean.'

Charlie's eyebrows flew up as he took another sip of coffee. 'You want to?'

'I think it's not the worst idea the two of us have ever had when drunk.'

'No, that's still breaking in to see the new baby piglets on Mr Grange's farm when we were on our way home from the pub that night.' He shuddered. 'I still have nightmares about Momma Pig chasing us.'

'Agreed. This is definitely a better idea than that was.'

'But rules?' Charlie asked. 'What are you thinking?'

From the expression on his face, Millie knew he was already thinking his own way through the plan, spotting potential pitfalls and areas for which they'd need to have agreements in place.

'If the idea is to get married to have a family and be happy, we need to agree what that looks like for each of us,' she said, thinking it through as she spoke. 'Like fidelity.'

Charlie nodded vigorously. He knew how she felt about Tom's betrayal—and she knew how Octavia's cheating had almost broken him.

'Absolutely. If we're married, we're married. Properly and faithfully and all that. I don't want one of those marriages of convenience where it's all just for the name and the status, and secretly they're both carrying on with someone else on the side.'

Millie shuddered at the idea. 'Definitely not. So if we do this, we do it properly. The minute we say "I do" we're exclusive. What about sex?'

She tried, for a fleeting second, to imagine her and Charlie in bed together, and failed. All her brain would give her was images of Giles bloody Fairfax, which was *not* helpful.

What was the problem? Charlie was gorgeous, and she was sure any sex he had was good and fulfilling for both parties. It was just… he'd been her friend for too long for her to see him that way.

She'd have to get over that if they were getting married.

Sex with Charlie. Huh…

'My understanding is it's kind of essential for the having of children,' Charlie replied flippantly.

'Not necessarily.' Millie swallowed as she remembered her doctor's words. 'It might be that my fertility issues mean we need medical help anyway. There are options if you don't want…' She trailed off. She couldn't quite add *me*.

'That's not… It's not that I don't want…'

God, how were they going to do this if they couldn't even talk about it?

'I don't want a sexless marriage,' Charlie finished finally. 'If you're okay with that?'

'Yes. Of course.' She didn't want that either. Even if the idea of her and Charlie in bed together still felt…alien.

Just because sex wasn't the number one priority in a marriage for her, it didn't mean she didn't want it. Should she be worried that the idea of sleeping with Charlie put her on edge? She certainly hadn't had that problem dancing with

Giles the night before—something she was definitely blaming on the champagne.

Is it weird that it's never come up before?

All those years of friendship, nights spent together, her sleeping on that daybed. Was it strange that they'd never fallen into bed together before?

Of course before there had always been Octavia—or Tom, or someone else. Had they ever even been single at the same time before? She couldn't remember.

'So we're going to get married?' Even as she said it, she wasn't sure if it was a question or a statement.

'Great!'

Charlie smiled at her. She couldn't tell if it was the hangover or the subject matter that made it look...not quite right.

'That's... I mean... Happiest man alive and all that.'

'Charlie.' She reached over to take his hand. 'Keep being honest with me, okay?'

It was the only way they were going to get through this.

'I will make you a good husband,' he told her, suddenly serious. 'And a good father to our children. I think we can have a good marriage, Mills.'

And that was all she'd ever wanted. Wasn't it?

'Thank you.'

Suddenly, Charlie was all business. 'So, next steps. I guess we tell people. Time being of the essence baby-wise and all that.'

'Yes, I guess we do.'

She was going to have to tell her mother. She'd be thrilled, she was sure. But once Jessica Myles had the news, *everyone* would know, and there'd be no going back.

'Okay, then. There's a post-wedding meet-up at the pub. Let's start with Tabby and Giles.'

Giles. Of course Charlie was going to ask Giles to be his best man, just as Giles had predicted.

Millie couldn't help but be just the tiniest bit annoyed that this meant Giles had been right. On the other hand, she was going to get to spend the rest of her life with Charlie at her side. That meant that she'd won the endless battle of the best friends, didn't it?

And it was just as well she'd decided to put that sudden, ridiculous, out-of-the-blue crush on Giles out of her head. Because once she and Charlie were married, the chances were he'd be back in her life in a way he hadn't been since they were teenagers.

As a friend.

No more inappropriate thoughts at all, she told herself, firmly.

She couldn't afford them. Not if she was going to be Charlie's wife.

Giles woke up in his childhood bedroom, not hungover, but also not well rested. He'd spent the night tossing and turning as he thought over what he should have said to his sister, what he would say to his parents that morning, and everything else he'd ever done wrong in his life.

When he had slept, he'd dreamt of dancing. He hadn't been able to see his partner's face, because every time he'd tried to look she'd moved another step out of his reach, until he'd been dancing entirely alone.

Which, he reminded himself on waking, was only for the best.

His parents were already seated around the chilly breakfast table, eating cold eggs and burnt bacon, when he made his way to the dining room. Mrs Harper, the woman from the village who had sourly and unhappily been keeping the house ticking over and his parents fed for the last decade or more, scowled at him as he sat down, before stomping off towards the kitchen. If he was lucky, there might be some toast on its way.

'Giles. We weren't expecting you last night, were we?' His mother gave him an assessing look over her teacup.

'I was in the area,' he said vaguely. 'It was late. Seemed safer to stay here than risk driving back to London tired.'

'And here we were thinking you might have come to see your loving parents.' The edge in his father's voice was unmissable. 'Perhaps even take responsibility for this crumbling pile and the family fortunes. All this will be yours one day soon, you do realise!'

Quentin Fairfax flung his arms wide, the action violent enough to knock the arm of the chair next to him from its precarious hold on to the wooden chair-back and send it clattering to the ground.

'This whole place is falling apart,' Mrs Harper muttered as she reappeared, a plate of almost black toast in her hand.

'I'm not stopping long.' Giles looked at the toast and decided that there would be somewhere to stop for breakfast on his way home.

'You never do,' his mother said under her breath, and sent a glare at his father.

'Oh, and that's my fault, is it?' His father shoved his chair back and got to his feet. 'Of course it is. Everything always is, isn't it? No money? My fault. Never mind that our son has millions at his disposal and chooses to spend it elsewhere.'

'Well, maybe if you were a little more welcoming,' his mother shot back.

Giles looked between them and then stood up. They probably wouldn't even notice him leaving.

It took him no time at all to gather his things and get them back in the car. His mother caught up to him just as he slammed the boot.

'It really would help if you could just see to extending

our allowance a little bit.' She wrapped her cardigan tighter around her. 'Your father would like to spend some money doing up the dining hall, for when we're entertaining.'

Of course he would.

His parents had no interest in learning how Giles had earned his money—the careful study, the networking and cultivating of working relationships with people in the field he wanted to be in, the stepping stones of jobs in the property investment company his mentor had owned, not to mention nearly a decade of working every hour God sent to be in the right position to take over the company when his mentor retired. That had made his career. His real money had come from studying the markets to learn about investing himself and taking the right kind of chances—not that he planned to tell his parents that part.

He wondered idly what Millie would make of all that if he told her. He knew what she thought of him—that he'd lucked out into a do-nothing job that paid well and lived off his inherited wealth the rest of the time. That was what he wanted people to believe, he supposed. In his circles there was something almost shameful about having to work hard for a living.

But Giles, despite his family name and advantages, had built his career himself. He'd earned his money himself. And he was damned if he was going to let his father fritter it away as if it were his right, without ever even asking where it came from.

He rested his hands on the door of his car and sighed. If he looked out to the east, he could see the village associated with the lands of the big manor house his parents still called home. A village they were supposed to look after and take care of, historically.

Supposed to being the most important words there.

'Wouldn't he rather use the money for fixing the roof? Or setting up a business to make the lodge self-financing instead of a giant money pit? Or even rebuilding the village hall after the fire last summer?' Giles couldn't help the edge in his voice.

'As I understand it, you've already taken care of the village hall,' his mother snapped back. 'You'll give *them* money, but not your own parents—'

'Because when Dad says "entertaining" he means more poker games, or buying more overpriced antiques he can't afford from friends who know he has no knowledge about these things.'

There was no way that Quentin Fairfax would change at this point in his life. For as long as Giles could remember his father had been spending money they didn't have on things they didn't need—then begging and borrowing for the essentials.

These days Giles paid for the essentials. But he wouldn't pay for any more.

He'd wait his father out. And when the lodge was his… Well…

Maybe then things would finally change.

God, he hoped so.

'I'll see you soon,' he told his mother, and drove away without looking back at her disapproving face in the rear-view mirror.

His phone rang as he pulled out onto the main road, already looking forward to returning to London. He connected the hands-free and answered.

'Giles? Are you still around, or have you gone back to London already?' Charlie's voice sounded tinny through the speakers.

'I'm still here,' he said. 'Just. What do you need?'

'Uh…could you come to The Fox and Duchess? Millie and I have something to ask you…'

CHAPTER FOUR

MILLIE HAD HOPED that the post-wedding meet-up at The Fox and Duchess would be small, and quiet—partly to facilitate her hangover recovery, but mostly because she and Charlie had a lot to talk about and she'd prefer not to have an audience. But this, like so many things lately, did not go to plan.

'The place is heaving!' Charlie pushed through the doors into the pub itself. 'See if you can grab us a table? I'll check they're still serving Sunday lunch.'

Millie made her way through the crowd, noting that the few remaining outside tables were also full. September was almost over, but some warmth still lingered here.

She didn't see the bride or groom—presumably they were already off on their honeymoon. But she spotted Charlie's sister Tabitha, holding court across the room with several of her friends, and waved.

Tabitha gave her a knowing look that suggested she knew exactly where Millie had spent last night. Charlie's sister had never bought their 'just friends' spiel.

Now they were about to prove her right.

She didn't admit to herself that she was looking for one face in particular until she realised he wasn't there. Charlie had called Giles on the way and asked him to meet them— she'd been right, he wanted to ask him to be best man. She should probably think about bridesmaids, too. There were so many things she suddenly had to think about.

She was getting *married*.

They hadn't told their families yet. Too many other things to work out first. But Charlie had assured her that, with all his best man experience, Giles would be able to help them make a plan to tackle it all. Millie wasn't convinced that best men were all that involved in planning anything more than the stag night, but he was their best option.

Well, no. The best option would be Tabitha, who worked in the family events business and had overseen hundreds of weddings, Millie was sure. But she also knew that the moment Tabitha was involved her wedding would suddenly be The Event of the Year, and that really wasn't what she wanted. Giles was more likely to just guide them through the basics.

But Giles wasn't there yet. And, as she slipped into a tiny corner table just as the occupants were putting their coats on, Millie had to admit she was a little relieved about that. She still wasn't sure how much her sudden crush on him had been obvious at the wedding, and how embarrassed she should be.

Something tugged at her attention and she looked up, barely even surprised when she realised that Giles had entered the pub and was scanning the room, looking for them. His gaze caught hers and locked, and once again she felt that strange connection she'd tried to ignore on the dance floor.

'Millie. Charlie at the bar?' Giles slid into the seat opposite her, leaving the extra chair on the side for Charlie. 'He asked me to meet you guys here.'

'I know.' Millie swallowed. 'He… Well, he'll explain when he gets here.'

She could see the curiosity in Giles's eyes, but he didn't press. He gave her a small, tight smile, but he didn't mention the night before at all. Maybe he really hadn't noticed. That would be something.

Charlie had told her he'd warned Giles off her, but she

was certain that was just Giles winding Charlie up. This was further proof.

'Giles! You made it.' Charlie swept up to the table and deposited drinks between them. 'Thanks so much for coming.'

Giles broke away from Millie's gaze to smile at Charlie. 'Of course! So, what's so urgent it couldn't wait until next time we meet up in London? I *had* planned to try and avoid this shindig altogether, now the bride's out of the country and can't order me about any more.'

'Well…' Charlie glanced nervously at Millie and reached out to take her hand. But before he could get any further, another figure barged up to their table.

'Charlie! And Giles! The old gang back together!'

Millie's jaw tightened as she recognised Ronan, an old schoolfriend of Charlie's—not one she'd ever liked.

Charlie, meanwhile, liked everybody. 'Ronan! Good to see you, buddy. You weren't at the wedding yesterday, were you?'

'Not me, mate. I don't reach Octavia's exacting standards. But I wanted to come and catch up with you all anyway.' Ronan lowered his tone, although he still spoke loudly enough for the whole pub to hear. 'And to see how you're coping, of course. Can't be easy…watching the love of your life marrying another. Bet you went home and had a little cry last night, didn't you?'

That was Ronan all over—pretending to be friends and then needling in the back, digging and cutting and causing pain. And Millie couldn't bear it.

'Actually, he went home with me.' She placed a hand over Charlie's and smiled up at him in what she hoped was a loving fiancée way. 'You see, we just got engaged last night.'

Giles managed to swallow the mouthful of his pint rather than spitting it out at Millie's announcement—which he was calling a win.

Married? Millie and Charlie? Now?

Yes, he'd hinted at it to them both the night before—even as he'd flirted with Millie while they danced. But he hadn't expected them to go from not-a-couple to *engaged* in the space of twelve hours. Hadn't they heard of dating?

He considered the idea that Millie was only saying it to annoy Ronan, but Charlie was nodding. And in the hushed silence that followed he saw Tabitha streaking across the room towards them, wide eyed.

'What?' She slammed to a halt beside their table. 'Did I just hear that right? Have you two *finally* got your heads out of your—?'

'Tabby,' Charlie interrupted, but she carried on regardless.

'Out of your you-know-whats and decided to do something about the *obvious* fact that the two of you are in love with each other?'

Charlie and Millie exchanged a look, and Giles realised he was holding his breath, waiting for an answer.

'If you're asking if we're engaged to be married,' Charlie said slowly. 'Then the answer is yes.'

Tabitha's squeal almost burst Giles's eardrums. He wasn't sure he'd mind. He'd quite like to be deaf at this point, then he wouldn't have to hear this news.

I should be happy for them. This is perfect for both of them. Hell, I even suggested it.

So why did it feel as if his stomach had sunk through the floor the moment Millie said the words?

'This is just *perfect!*' Tabitha leaned over to hug Millie, then Charlie, then Millie again. 'And you must be the best man again Giles, then?' She hugged him, too, then stepped back to give him an appraising look. She leaned in to stage whisper, 'Millie, if you're in need of a maid of honour, I definitely wouldn't mind standing up with him. Or not standing up, if you get my meaning.'

'*Tabby.*'

Charlie looked genuinely pained by his sister's antics. Giles wondered how long she'd been in the pub.

'No, you see, the *reason* it's perfect is that we've just had a cancellation for a Christmas Eve wedding up at the house!' Tabby bounced on her toes as she clasped her hands together in genuine joy. 'Because you *are* getting married at the house, right?'

'Oh, of course…' Millie said, sounding uncertain.

Giles was almost certain she'd never even thought about it.

'And Millie! You've always wanted a Christmas wedding, haven't you?'

'I have?'

She seemed even more uncertain about that. Giles suspected that *Tabby* had always wanted Millie to have a Christmas wedding, which wasn't quite the same thing.

'Of course! With your colouring, jewel tones and a winter theme will be *perfect* for you.' Tabby clapped her hands again. 'I'm going to go up to the office and book you in now, before anyone else can steal your date. Mum and Dad are going to be so excited!'

She hurried off, presumably to spread the news like a slightly tipsy town crier in a floral dress. Her brother chased after her, presumably to temper exactly what she was going to tell their parents.

Most people watched them go.

Giles watched Millie.

'A Christmas wedding, huh?' he asked.

'Apparently.' She smiled, but the slightly blindsided look Tabby's announcement had given her didn't fade. 'I mean, I thought we were talking about next year, but actually… Christmas will be perfect.'

'Once you find the person you want to spend the rest of

your life with you want the rest of your life to start right away—that sort of thing? Very *When Harry met Sally.*

As was the proof that perhaps men and women couldn't be just friends after all. He and Millie had certainly never managed it.

But they'd have to now, if she was marrying Charlie.

Except last night they'd both denied there was anything more than friendship between them. And now they were getting married? It all seemed rather…sudden.

Even though he'd kept those thoughts to himself, Millie had obviously intuited that he was thinking them.

'I know this must be a bit of a surprise.' She bit her lower lip. 'To be honest, it came as a bit of a surprise to us, too.'

'You didn't fancy dating first?' He said it as a joke, although it wasn't…not really. 'Most people do.'

'I guess we realised that, actually, we'd been dating for years,' she said with a smile. 'We go out together, we spend quiet nights in together, we talk every day and we're always each other's plus one for things these days.'

'That sounds like a great friendship,' Giles said cautiously. 'But marriage is a little bit more.'

'Is it?' She raised her eyebrows questioningly. 'Surely friendship is the basis of any good marriage.'

'But what about…?' He wasn't going to say sex. He wasn't going to be That Guy, who brought everything down to its basest level.

But at the same time…what *about* sex?

Friendship was one thing—he had friends; he knew that. Maybe not as close and as caring as Charlie and Millie had always been, but still. He had friends. And he didn't want to sleep with any of them.

'Passion,' he finished, the memory of holding her in his arms as they danced returning with a vengeance.

'You mean sex?'

Her cheeks flushed a deeper pink as she said it. He had to admit, it was adorable.

'Do you really think that's the most important thing in a marriage?'

'No,' he admitted.

He'd never asked his sister and brother-in-law or his parents about their sex life, but even if it was good their clashing personalities and expectations still made them miserable. It wasn't that he couldn't see Millie's point...

'But it does matter.'

He wasn't going to get married. But if he was, he would want it to be to someone he had a physical connection with. Someone who could turn him on with a glance...who he wanted to touch all the time.

He met Millie's gaze and felt his body start to warm, so he looked away again. Fast.

'Charlie and I...' Millie glanced down at the table, her cheeks redder than ever. 'We've never been single at the same time before, so we never had time to explore that side of things. Until now.'

Suddenly it all made sense to Giles.

This was all his fault.

He'd got them thinking about each other in a romantic light at the wedding yesterday, then sent them off tipsy together, and they'd promptly acted on his suggestion and fallen into bed together.

And apparently that physical connection he wanted was so strong between them that they'd decided to cut out the faffing around of dating and just get married straight away.

Millie was right. They already had one of the strongest friendships he knew. They knew each other inside out. Add in a fantastic sex life and, really, what else was there? They probably had the best shot at a happy marriage of anyone he'd ever met.

And if a small part of him wished that, now they were adults instead of bickering teens, he'd had a shot with Millie before they figured that out…? Well, he was going to shout that down. Because he couldn't give Millie the happy-ever-after life she wanted anyway, and she and Charlie both deserved this.

'I'm happy for you both,' he said.

And he almost completely meant it.

Millie should have known that as soon as Tabby had heard the news the rest of the family would, too and they'd be summoned up to Howard Hall. At least she'd had a little time to practise being convincingly in love with Charlie beforehand. She was *almost* sure that Giles had bought it.

After all, it made sense. That was why they were doing it.

But it mattered, suddenly, to Millie that people believed they were doing it for the right reasons—and she knew that, as solid as the reasons she and Charlie had were to them, other people might not agree.

Other people like her mum.

'Millie!' Jessica Myles was waiting on the steps of Howard Hall, her arms spread wide, ready to welcome her daughter to what would, after her marriage, be her new home.

Oh, God. I hadn't thought about that.

Howard Hall was *enormous.* And historic. And imposing. It was one thing to stay there in Charlie's rooms now and then. But to *live* there?

'I can't believe it!' Her mum was still hugging her. Tightly. 'We always hoped… But obviously the heart wants what the heart wants. You never really know. And Charlie has always been so sweet to you… I'm so happy for you! I just wish your father was here to see it.'

'Me too, Mum.'

That was easy to agree with. The rest…

Nobody—in her family or Charlie's—had ever said out loud that they thought the two of them should be more than friends. But, from the way Charlie's parents were beaming down at them from the front door, it seemed she might just be enough of a better option than Charlie not marrying at all for everyone to be happy.

Even if she never *really* felt she belonged, her children would, and that was what mattered.

Children. She was going to have a family with her best friend. That was what she needed to focus on here.

They were all ushered inside, where Millie was welcomed with hugs from all the members of Charlie's family and sherry was poured all round. Millie tried to keep her hungover stomach in order as she smiled and accepted hers.

'To Charlie and Millie!'

The toast echoed around the room and Millie's head pounded as their drunken idea took full form.

'What happened to Giles?' Charlie asked, as everyone talked at once about their wedding plans. 'I never got around to asking him to be best man.'

'He stayed to settle up at the bar,' she said. 'For us and for Tabby and Liberty. You kind of ran off in a hurry.'

'That's why he's going to be best man,' Charlie said, with a grin. 'He's good at taking care of things like that.'

'Now, Millie, have you thought about your wedding gown yet?' Lady Howard asked.

Charlie's Aunt Felicity burst in before Millie could answer.

'She should wear Mother's! Although it might need to be let out a bit,' she added, eyeing Millie as if she was one of her prized horses.

'No way,' Tabby said, shaking her head in a way that just reminded Millie of how her own head still ached. 'Millie's going to want something new—something *her*. Ooh, can I come wedding dress shopping with you? We can have our own *Say Yes To The Dress* moment!'

'Maybe…' Millie hedged.

'What about the ring?' Charlie's father asked. 'You didn't ask for the family one to propose with.'

Millie's heart clenched. Did they suspect? Had they all figured out that this wasn't a love match? She wanted them to believe it was real. It made it easier for her to pretend it was, too.

'Because Mother is still wearing it,' Charlie pointed out drily. 'And I want Millie to have a ring that *she* loves, so we'll pick one out together.'

He squeezed her hand as he said it, and it should have made her feel reassured. Loved. Instead it just reminded her that buying a ring was one more thing to do before their Christmas Eve wedding date.

Oh, God. How was she even going to do it all? She had her own floristry business to run, and it wasn't as if Christmas was a quiet time of year, with all the wreaths and garlands and the festive flower workshops she ran from her little shop.

She just wanted to be *married*. This whole wedding business was just getting in the way.

Luckily, everyone else seemed to be happy to get on with organising it without her. The planning conversation was now exclusively between Tabby and their mothers, with Aunt Felicity adding an occasional unhelpful comment. Charlie's father was beckoning him over towards the drinks cabinet, so Millie took the opportunity to escape for a moment.

'I'll go see if Giles is here yet,' she murmured, before slipping out into the hall.

As soon as she was certain she wasn't being followed, she darted towards the front door and out into the crisp autumn air.

She hadn't really planned to look for Giles—that had just

been a convenient excuse to escape the suffocating air in that room. But as she stood with her back against the ancient door she saw him making his way up the long driveway on foot. He must have left his car at the pub, she realised. It was quicker to walk between Howard Hall and The Fox and Duchess than to drive, given the twisty Norfolk roads, and there was a shortcut over the fields that she and Charlie had been exploiting since they were teenagers.

She knew the moment he spotted her, because there was a slight hitch in his steps, and she felt her heart give a double beat before he carried on towards her.

'Running away already?' Giles asked, pausing as he approached the bottom of the steps.

Millie smiled and shook her head. 'Just needed some air. Hangover.'

'Right.' Giles tilted his head as he studied her. 'They can be a bit much, I know. Families.'

'I love Charlie's family,' she objected. 'And my own mum is in there, too.'

'Still.' He shrugged. 'People get crazy about weddings. Don't feel you have to give in to everything they want. It's your special day, after all. You and Charlie love each other, and you get to choose how you share that with your guests.'

'Is that your accumulated best man wisdom?' she asked.

'Basically. That and don't forget that a wedding is only one day. A marriage is the rest of your life.'

Somehow he managed to make the words sound like a ball and chain, clamping around her ankle.

'That's the idea,' she said, as brightly as she could. 'Come on. There's sherry inside.'

Even the wedding planning conversations were more appealing than this.

CHAPTER FIVE

It wasn't that Millie was trying not to think about her impending wedding. But it *was* surprisingly easy to push it to the back of her mind when she was engrossed in her work. Back in her little florist shop in a small village outside London, somewhere between the capital and Howard Hall in Norfolk, where she belonged.

At least until her phone rang and she saw Charlie's name on the screen, and she felt her chest tighten.

Normally they'd text each other through the day, but the last week had been silent between them. As if they were both still processing the momentous change in their relationship that was coming.

But now Charlie was calling.

She swiped to answer. 'Hey.'

'Hey, is this a bad time?'

It was weird how he still sounded just like her best friend, not her fiancé.

'No, no. I'm just designing the colours for that pitch—you know the big corporate event I mentioned?'

Back when things were normal.

'How's it going?' Charlie asked.

'Hmm, not quite there. It feels a little brassy at the moment. They want glamour, but classy glamour—diamonds not rhinestones, you know?'

And it didn't help that she kept getting distracted, thinking about her own wedding flowers—if she could figure out what she wanted for them, everything else would fall into place.

'Do they want Christmassy colours?'

'Yes, but not traditional. So red and white are out, which makes things tricky. I'll get there. I've just been distracted.'

From the brief silence that followed, he knew exactly by what.

'We've just had the weekly meeting and there's an opportunity to let out Glenmere Castle for a couple of months, starting now,' he said, after a moment.

Millie blinked at the abrupt change in topic. 'Erm…that's good.' She'd lost track of quite how many properties Charlie's family owned and ran. That was probably something else she should figure out before they got married.

'For a film shoot. Liberty is the location manager—you know, Tabby's friend. She's had a crisis. A flood or something. Anyway, we're stepping in and offering her the venue.'

He was babbling. That was never a good sign.

'Okay…' She waited. Eventually he'd tell her what was really going on.

'Anyway, we're not quite set up for letting yet. Still snagging and so on. So the only way we could agree is if one of us is on site for the shoot.'

Or maybe he didn't need to tell her. She could already tell exactly what was coming next.

'By "one of us" you mean you?'

He was going to Scotland. Now. Leaving her here to deal with…everything else.

'I know the timing is horrible…'

Was she supposed to laugh or cry at this? She wasn't sure.

'We are supposed to be getting married in less than three months, Charlie, and are you seriously telling me you are heading off to Scotland for the entire duration, with everything still to plan?'

'Is this our first marital disagreement?'

If it was an attempt at a joke, it was a bad one. She could practically hear him wincing.

'Mum and Tabby seem to have everything in hand...'

That was what made her feelings start to boil over. Charlie was delegating their *wedding* to his mother and sister.

'But this is *our* wedding! I don't want to be steamrollered by your family. It might not be the most traditional of set-ups, but that doesn't mean it shouldn't be meaningful...personal. If things go the way we plan, then this will be the only wedding either of us have.'

There was a pause, and when Charlie spoke again there were no more excuses. 'I'm sorry, Millie. I'm an arse. I didn't think. You're right. I'll tell Tabby we can't accommodate the booking after all...'

Her anger faded in an instant.

'Is that the alternative?' She sighed. 'I don't want you to lose out. I'm being silly. It's just a little overwhelming, you know?'

'I really do,' Charlie said, with feeling. 'Look, Giles is around. How about I get him to stand in for me on any wedding-related business? I'll be at the end of the phone whenever you need a decision, and he can be there for all the tastings and whatnot, so that you're not alone and at my family's mercy. He's my best man after all. Let's make him earn it.'

'Giles. Right.'

Ideal. Just what she needed. But she could hardly tell Charlie that, could she? Either he'd think she was holding on to a childhood grudge, or she'd have to admit that she'd had some entirely *non*-childish thoughts about him since they'd danced together at Octavia's wedding.

'If I was marrying anyone else I would want you, obviously, but I think juggling the roles of best woman and bride is too much, don't you?' Charlie joked.

She laughed. 'True! Look, of course you should go. I'll manage. No one is indispensable—not even the groom.'

'That's what Mum and Tabby think. They think I am completely surplus to requirements.'

He didn't sound as if he minded too much.

'They're just excited for us. It's nice.'

At least, that was what she kept telling herself.

'It is.'

Another pause. Millie could hear the wind in the trees down the line. He must be outside.

'Are you?' he asked suddenly.

'Am I what?'

'Excited for us?'

Millie considered her answer. She wasn't going to start lying to her best friend—her future husband—now. That wouldn't bode well for marriage, would it?

Finally, she said, 'I'm excited to get started with our lives. I kind of wish we could fast forward through the engagement and wedding part, though.'

'We could fly to Vegas tonight.'

She almost believed he meant it.

'Is that what you want?' she asked.

It was Charlie's turn to fall silent for a long moment. Then, 'Mother would never forgive me—nor would yours. And I know better than to upset the cook. Look, Millie...'

'Mmm?'

'I'm going to be gone for a while.'

'I know.'

Where was he going with this?

'I meant what I said about fidelity, but we're not actually married yet. So, look, what happens in Vegas stays in Vegas. I'm fine with that.'

Vegas? What?

'Charlie, what on *earth* are you babbling about? I thought we decided not to go to Vegas?'

'I mean, if you want a final fling or two, or whatever, before you say *I do,* then you should go for it. Sow those wild oats, as my grandfather used to say.'

Wild oats. Really?

'A final fling? Charlie, I have never had a fling in my life!'

And it was definitely not a good thing that the first person she thought of when she said those words was Giles Fairfax, of all people.

This was why passion was dangerous. She might be attracted to Giles, but that kind of chemistry only led to heartbreak when it wore off. She needed something more long term than a passing fancy.

'So maybe you should, while you can,' Charlie said, a little too eagerly for her liking.

'Hang on, is this about you?' Her voice sharpened. 'Are *you* having regrets? Do *you* want to be sowing oats?'

'Me? No. I'll be in the wilds of Scotland.'

'With an entire film crew and no doubt several eligible actresses. It's not as if you'll be a hermit in a bothy,' she pointed out. 'I'm sure there will be enough women for several flings. An entire magic porridge pot of wild oats.'

'I didn't mean it like that… I'm not interested in actresses or anyone. Honestly, Mills, this isn't me saying I want to sleep with someone before settling down with you. I've never actually had a fling either.'

Of course he hadn't. It had always been Octavia for him. And now it was her.

'Then maybe you *should* do some sowing, too. Maybe you're right. We are about to commit to each other for life. Maybe we should…oh, I don't know…not go out there *looking* for a fling, but not feel guilty if the opportunity comes up. Argh! I can't believe I just said that—but do I mean it?'

She thought. Probably. But she *definitely* wasn't thinking about Giles as she said it. He, of all people, was not an option.

'Okay, then. This is weird. Isn't this weird?'

'A little,' she admitted. 'But we've always been able to talk about anything before. I think it's important we still do. And I think, with you gone for two months or so and the wedding so close, you're right. This is our last time to…you know… act on pure attraction rather than being sensible.'

'Millie Myles. Are you saying you're not attracted to me?'

And there, of course, was the biggest concern she had about this whole thing. She'd just never thought of Charlie that way.

But that's a good thing. I'm looking for a marriage that lasts, *and that means it can't be based on passion.*

She and Charlie had something better than that. And she had to have faith that the rest would come—at least enough for them to be content with it. Deep, real respect and love was far more important than sex.

'I'm working on it.'

She laughed, but it didn't feel funny. Loving Charlie was easy. It was everything else that was a leap of faith.

'We'll get there,' he promised. 'Okay, let me break the glad news to Giles…'

Millie's chest tightened again. 'You're going to tell *Giles* that we're allowed to sleep with someone else while we're engaged?'

'No! He believes he has played Cupid, and who I am to dissuade him? I'm going to let him know that his best man duties have expanded somewhat. You're okay with that? I know you and he can be a little off, but he's a good sort when you get to know him.'

'Yes. Of course. Look… I'd better go—this colour scheme won't resolve itself. Bye, Charlie.'

She hung up before she could hear his answer.

Then she looked at the designs she'd been working on, put her head on her arms and groaned.

Planning a wedding with Giles Fairfax. This was going to be a disaster.

It was easy enough, back in London, for Giles to put the events of Octavia's wedding and the days that had followed from his head. Well, mostly.

Charlie had asked him to be best man, as expected—but, given that Tabby and the mothers of the bride and groom seemed to have all the wedding planning in hand, and Charlie didn't want an extravagant stag do, it seemed likely that all Giles would need to do was show up on the day with the rings, an appropriate speech, and a willingness to usher difficult relatives into place with a charming smile.

He could do all that standing on his head by this point.

No, Charlie's Christmas Eve wedding looked to be the easiest one he'd had to take part in yet.

Even if the idea of him marrying *Millie* still made something in his chest tighten if he thought about it for too long...

So Giles happily threw himself back into his old life— into work and drinks with colleagues, business dinners and early-morning breakfast meetings, and nothing even slightly wedding-related.

Until Charlie called and told him he had a little addition to his best man duties.

'I'm sorry, what?' Giles must have heard him wrong. That was the only possible explanation here. 'You need me to... what?'

'Help Millie with the wedding.'

Charlie was on hands-free in his car, and Giles could hear the traffic and the wind whistling by outside.

'I've got to go to Scotland for the next ten weeks or so, to oversee a production up at Glenmere. For insurance reasons. Can't get out of it. But I don't want Millie to be left to Tabby's tender care when it comes to all the wedding planning either. So could you just…help out? If she needs it?'

'You're going to Scotland for over two months. Right before your wedding.' Giles still wasn't quite sure he was hearing this right. 'And Millie is okay with this?'

There was a telling silence on the other end before Charlie replied, 'She understands. It's the family business. There's no one else who can do it.'

'Still…' Giles couldn't imagine any of the other brides he'd known going along with this plan.

'Besides, you know that my input is the least important. It'll be Millie and Tabby and our mothers organising the whole thing, anyway.'

'Right…'

There was something odd here, but Giles couldn't put his finger on quite what it was. Charlie *was* unnaturally dedicated to the family business. And, God knew, Giles understood work commitments that were impossible to get out of—another reason, if he needed one, why a long-lasting relationship wasn't on the cards for him.

'So what do you need *me* to do?'

If the women were taking charge, surely he was surplus to requirements?

'Just…be there for Millie.'

Charlie sounded faintly guilty, Giles realised. Well, good. So he should. Not for putting this on him, but for abandoning Millie right now.

'Don't let Tabby and the others steamroller her into a wedding she doesn't want. I want… I really want this to be her perfect day.'

'Not yours?' Giles asked.

'If it's perfect for her, it's perfect for me. Just make sure she gets everything she wants, right?'

Ah, so this was how Charlie was salving his conscience over leaving—throwing money at the problem. Giles could relate. Even if, with his own family, he'd chosen the opposite path.

'I'll do everything I can,' he promised. 'Send me her contact details so I can get in touch.'

After they'd hung up, Giles tried to throw himself back into his work, but his focus was shot, and his assistants had already left, so he decided to call it a night. Checking his phone, he saw a new contact card from Charlie, that had Millie's phone number, email and address.

Holly and Ivy Florists

Her shop. He'd never visited it before, but the address showed it was in a village outside London, off to the northeast. Probably in the commuter belt, but still only an hour or so from Charlie's home, Howard Hall, in Norfolk.

He wondered if she'd keep it after the wedding, or if she'd throw her floral talents into the Howard family business.

Maybe he'd ask her.

Maybe he'd ask her how she felt about her fiancé disappearing right before their wedding while he was at it. Try to smooth the ground for Charlie there.

Before he could second-guess himself, he grabbed his car keys and headed down to the office's underground car park. He'd made a promise to his best friend and he intended to keep it.

Weddings, it turned out, were bigger business than Millie had thought.

Oh, she'd done enough wedding flowers in her time to know how extravagant they could get, how expensive, and how utterly obsessed some people could become with planning the perfect wedding. She'd seen the beautiful venues, the stunning gowns, the fabulous catering, the three different photographers and the videographer all trying not to get in each other's shots.

But what she hadn't realised was just how many decisions there were to make.

She'd visited her local library and taken out a couple of wedding planning books, as well as bookmarking the top websites recommended in all the wedding magazines Tabitha had handed her before she'd left Howard Hall. Every single one of them promised to give her the *only* checklist she needed to plan her wedding—except every checklist had different things on it. And that was even before she got to the email she'd received from Tabby the moment she'd returned home to her little flat above the florist's shop in the village of Wendon Stye.

Now, as she sighed at the stack of wedding-related publications sitting on her tiny coffee table, she pulled the email up again on her phone.

Hi Millie!
Just checking in about the first things we need to sort for the wedding. Numbers are obviously the big one, so I'm attaching the guest list from our side. You know Charlie will never do it, but you'll need to check with him about friends and colleagues he wants to invite in addition to these, so you can add your lot on, too and we'll see how it all shakes out.

The attached guest list had almost given her a heart attack. There were almost two hundred names on it, before she and Charlie even talked about who *they* wanted there.

But that wasn't the end of the email.

Let me know when you want to go dress shopping—I've got some great contacts who can find or design you something truly unique, even in our condensed timeframe. And I know you'll want to take care of the flowers, but let's talk about your colour scheme soon, so I can start sourcing the other decorations and tableware, etc.

I'm also attaching our usual list of recommended suppliers for music for the ceremony and bands for the evening. Oh, and our current seasonal menus, although these will change once we get the Christmas menus confirmed. We'll arrange a date for you to come up and do the tasting for that, and the wine…

I've block-booked as much local accommodation as I can for now, so guests can reserve what they need when they confirm their acceptance. Other things—like timings for the day and plans for the evening, etc.—can wait a little while, but not too long as we'll want to put details on the invitations.

Oh, speaking of which! Here are a couple of examples from stationers we've used recently for you to take a look at. Classic and refined, of course.

I think that's all for now! Can't wait to get started.

Love

Tabby x

PS Here's the wedding checklist I give to all our Howard Hall brides. The only list you'll need!

Tabby's checklist, Millie noted, had twice as many items on it as any of the other ones she'd found. She'd printed it out on the office printer downstairs and almost run out of paper.

With a sigh, she slumped back down onto her sofa and dropped her phone onto the cushions. She'd have to start going through it all soon, but right now it just felt too overwhelming.

If only Charlie was there to do it with her. Then they could laugh at all these ridiculous requirements, and how they didn't care about any of this stuff, telling each other it was just another hoop to jump through before they could get on with what they actually wanted to do—living a happy family life together, as best friends.

But Charlie was away in Scotland, overseeing Liberty's movie at Glenmere Castle, and wouldn't be back until right before the wedding. It was unavoidable, he'd assured her, but that didn't stop her worrying. Did he regret their decision to marry? Was he looking for a way out already?

If he was, she needed him to tell her now—before she fell down Tabby's wedding-planning rabbit hole.

So she asked—outright. That was another advantage of marrying her best friend rather than a romantic partner. She had no qualms about confronting him about things because he couldn't break her heart. Although he could take away her future...and if he was going to do it she'd rather he do it now than later.

But Charlie assured her he was still all in.

'This is what I want, Mills,' he said firmly. 'That isn't going to change. But I just need... I need to be in Scotland right now. I promise you I'll be back.'

And she trusted him, so she knew he would be.

Just not in time to do any of this damn wedding planning.

Downstairs, the doorbell rang, and she frowned. The shop had been closed for hours, and there was no flower-arranging workshop scheduled for tonight. She hadn't ordered any takeaway, and Charlie was in Scotland.

Millie had literally no idea who else might be calling on her here at the shop.

Pulling a fluffy cardigan over her pyjamas, she plodded down the creaky wooden stairs in her slippers and peered out through a gap in the closed blinds.

A tall figure stood outside, wearing a long, black woollen coat, a mobile phone clamped to his ear.

In her cardigan pocket, her own phone started to ring.

The man turned as she fumbled to answer it, the sound of her sleigh bell ringtone obviously sounding through the glass.

It's October now. That's nearly *Christmas, right? Sleigh bells are totally acceptable.*

He smirked, and his features came into focus.

Giles Fairfax.

What the hell was he doing here?

Ending the call, she yanked open the door. 'We're closed, you realise?'

'This isn't a business visit.'

Giles stepped inside and she shuffled backwards out of his way, leaving him to shut the door and lock it again behind him.

'Charlie sent me to help.'

'Of course he did.'

When Charlie had said that Giles would help, she'd assumed it would be with things like addressing invitations or something. Not showing up at her flat unannounced one evening when she was already in her pyjamas.

Charlie didn't trust her to organise this wedding, so he'd sent his best man to babysit her. Because Giles, of course, knew everything there was to know about society weddings. He'd been born into that world and, by all accounts, had spent far more time involved in making them happen for his friends over the last few years than anyone else they knew.

It made perfect sense. It also made acid rise in her throat and caused her to want to throw things.

'Okay, from that glower I'm guessing that this is not a welcome intervention?' Giles pulled a bottle of Prosecco from behind his back. 'Does this help? I realised I hadn't actually bought you an engagement present yet.'

'It's a start,' Millie allowed.

Then she sighed. He'd obviously travelled up after work, since he was still wearing his suit—and, while it wasn't a *very* long drive, it still took a lot to get Giles and his sort to leave the capital, in her experience. And, since he'd already enjoyed the sight of her in her fuzzy slippers and pyjamas combo, there wasn't much point sending him away.

Also, if she knew Giles Fairfax at all—which she didn't, much, but she knew enough men like him—the Prosecco would be of the highest quality. And she really could do with a glass.

'Oh, all right then,' she said. 'Come on up to Wedding Planning Central.'

CHAPTER SIX

GILES HADN'T EVER visited the village of Wendon Stye before tonight, but from what he'd seen driving through it in the falling darkness it was much like many picturesque English villages outside the M25. With a grassy area in the centre with the war memorial, a church rather larger than he suspected the current congregation warranted, some thatched and beamed cottages in the centre, and lots more recently built terraced and semi-detached houses radiating outwards on the new estates.

Millie's florist shop, Holly and Ivy, had a prime position on the small high street, between boutique interiors shops and organic cafés. Clearly Wendon Stye was catering to high-earning professionals and their families—the ones who'd moved out of London when they started having kids, but with one or both parents still commuting the hour or so back in, to be able to afford to live there or pay school fees.

It was a village for families.

Giles had wrapped his coat tighter around himself and hoped no local curtain twitchers would notice how much he didn't belong there.

Millie, when she had appeared to let him in, had looked both surprised and annoyed to see him. Not counting Octavia's wedding and the following day, Giles hadn't seen Millie more than a handful of times since he and Charlie had left school. He'd stopped visiting for a week every summer holiday. And he'd certainly never seen her in pyjamas with fuzzy pink slippers on her feet.

Not that it mattered. He still felt that same surge of attraction he'd discovered while dancing with her at the wedding, even knowing how incredibly inappropriate it was. Hopefully she didn't notice the way he kept a Victorian-era-level respectable distance between them. It was just that he couldn't shake the worry that if his hand brushed against her skin there might be actual sparks.

The shop was in darkness as she led him through it, although the scent of flowers and fresh greenery still filled the air, and he saw the occasional holly berry gleaming red in the flashes of light from the streetlamp outside. He followed Millie through a back door behind the counter, then up a staircase that creaked as badly as the one at Fairfax Manor, to a bijou flat above the shop.

He'd never really imagined where Millie might live, but if he had, he suspected he wouldn't have included quite so many cushions and throws in his vision. Every inch of the bright, sunny yellow sofa seemed to be covered with them, almost running into the deep pile rug that filled most of the wooden floor.

The small coffee table in front of the sofa—the only table there was space for in the whole living area—was also covered, this time in bridal magazines, printouts from wedding websites and invitation samples.

'Wedding planning going well, then?'

'Wedding planning is…' Millie sighed. 'Give me the Prosecco.' She headed for the kitchen area he could just see through an open door, calling back over her shoulder, 'You can sit! Just…move things.'

Giles considered his options, then shifted a stack of magazines from the armchair next to the sofa onto the floor beside the coffee table and sat. By the time Millie returned with a champagne flute full of Prosecco for him, he was already flicking through the checklist he'd spotted on top of the magazines.

'Tabby's work, I assume?' He waved the checklist at her.

'Oh, yeah. Apparently a lot more goes into planning a wedding than I ever imagined.'

Millie dropped down into a small gap between cushions and paperwork on the sofa, her own glass in hand.

'Looks like it.'

The checklist ran to several pages, and was ordered into different sections by headings in a curly font. Each item had a heart-shaped check box next to it.

He tossed the list back on the table. 'This is why Charlie sent me, you realise?'

Okay, maybe *sent* was a little strong, but he'd asked him to help, and this was the only way Giles could think of to do that. Besides, looking at the wedding chaos that had taken over Millie's home, he hadn't arrived a moment too soon.

'He didn't want Tabby to take over your wedding and strong-arm you into things you don't want. He trusts *you* to organise your wedding, not his sister. So I'm here to help you do that.'

Millie's shoulders seemed to straighten a little at that. 'That's really why he sent you?'

'Why else?'

She gave a small shrug, but he read sentences into it.

'You thought he didn't trust you to organise a society wedding on your own, didn't you?' he realised.

'It's not entirely ridiculous,' Millie said. 'It's not like I have a lot of experience with this sort of thing. Unlike you.'

It was funny, Giles thought. Ever since he'd met Charlie, back at school, he'd heard about his best friend Millie. The brave, funny, unstoppable Millie. The one person who meant more to Charlie than anyone—except possibly his actual family.

As a child, he'd been jealous of her before he'd even met her. She held a place in Charlie's life that he could never touch. And a place in the world that he couldn't imagine.

He didn't know how much of the Millie of his imagination was real, but back then he'd assumed she had everything that he didn't. She was part of Charlie's happy home life, with its successful family, and buildings that weren't crumbling around them, and parents who didn't argue all the time. He knew, sort of, that she wasn't *really* a part of it—that she lived in the gatehouse and her own parents worked for Charlie's. But as a young boy that distinction hadn't been as clear as it had become when he grew up. If anything, it had just added to his impression that Millie had both the freedom and the acceptance that he never expected to have.

It had been a year or so into his friendship with Charlie before his first invitation to Howard Hall, during the summer break. Even then, he'd been unsure about visiting—because to do so would require him to invite Charlie to Fairfax Manor in return, and he'd already known he couldn't do *that*. And until that first visit Millie had remained the perfect friend, who had a relationship with Charlie that he'd always wanted.

Giles was ashamed to admit he'd hated her a little then.

By the time they'd met, that view had been fairly in-grained. Most of the time he'd kept his distance—and she'd kept hers during his visits, too. When they *had* met, they'd clashed—often spectacularly.

Soon enough he'd realised how imperfect her position was—and the huge advantages his own life had given him, even if they didn't always feel that way. But he'd never expected to feel *sorry* for Millie until this very moment. Seeing her so uncertain about her own place in the world made him want to tear down anyone and any thing that made her feel that way. To turn a mirror on her and show her what *he* saw. A gorgeous, kind, incredible woman.

He was man enough to admit that now. Because they weren't vying to be Charlie's best friend any longer. That battle was over—she was his fiancée, going to be his wife, and Giles would still be his best friend and that was enough for him.

Maybe they could *all* be friends. He hoped so.

And it started here, with him helping her with this wedding, just as Charlie had asked.

He could do that.

He just couldn't let himself get distracted by how absurdly cute she looked with her hair piled on top of her head and an oversized cardigan wrapped around her. Or how much he *still* wanted to peel that cardigan off her and find out what was underneath…

Not what you're here for, Fairfax.

'This is *your* wedding,' he said firmly. 'Yours and Charlie's. Everything else—tradition, society's expectations, keeping other people happy—that has to come afterwards. Make sure you've got what you really want—the things that matter to you and Charlie—and *then* let Tabby in to add her own sparkle to the things that don't matter so much to you.'

Millie blinked at him with obvious surprise. 'That's…actually really good advice.'

'Of course it is.' Giles was only *slightly* offended. 'Weddings are just like business negotiations, really. You have to know what matters to you before you go into the room. Unless you're a real Bridezilla—and I'm not suggesting you are,' he added quickly. 'But unless you are, then there's no real point or need in micromanaging every single aspect of the day. Pick a general vibe, decide what matters, and let the rest go.'

'I can…do that?'

Millie waved a hand at the stack of wedding information

that seemed to be breeding on her coffee table. Giles could swear there was already more there than when he'd arrived.

'These all seem to say that the perfect wedding is all in the details, and Tabby's checklist is twenty gazillion pages long, and—'

Giles reached over and put his hands on her shoulders. He was relieved that the sparks stayed away—even if his blood seemed to warm, just at being close to her. Her breath hitched, too, but he suspected that had more to do with wedding panic than his proximity.

'Breathe. Honestly. It's just a wedding—just one day. The marriage is what matters. The wedding day…? It can be anything you want. So… What matters most to you?'

'Well, the flowers, obviously. And the groom! But I've got those two things covered. After that…'

He pulled back as she bit her bottom lip, her brow furrowed as she thought. It was hard, suddenly, to remember that he'd once been so envious of this woman, whom his imagination had built up to be perfect and in control.

Suddenly Millie smiled, and it felt as if the whole room lit up.

'Cake,' she said decisively. 'I want a really incredible cake.'

Giles returned her grin and pulled out one of the invitation samples to start a new list on the back.

'Then that's where we'll start. With cake.'

Millie hadn't expected Giles to actually be any help when he arrived on her doorstep that evening, but to her surprise, by the time he left at just after midnight, they had a comprehensive list of things she cared about for the wedding, another email listing things she could delegate mostly to Tabby and her mother, and an appointment for a cake-tasting in a few weeks' time at a bakery owned by a friend of Giles's sister, who had been delighted to squeeze them in.

They'd also finished the bottle of Prosecco. But, since he was driving and had refused more than the one small glass he'd started with, Millie had to admit that was mostly her.

It was also probably why she'd hugged him as he left.

She hadn't meant to, but he'd just been so *unexpectedly* helpful and kind she hadn't been able to help herself.

It had absolutely nothing at all to do with wanting to feel his body against hers again, because she wasn't that sort of woman. Wild oats be damned.

He'd coughed awkwardly at her thanks, told her it was nothing, and then left to drive back to London—which probably meant that their next interaction would be as awkward as all the ones they'd had before Octavia's wedding.

But at least there would be cake.

And so, this Saturday lunchtime, she waited outside the shop nervously for Giles to pick her up.

It had meant leaving Holly and Ivy in the capable hands of her assistant for the afternoon, but Kayla had sworn she was up to the responsibility and—well, Millie supposed she'd have to start letting her look after things solo sooner rather than later.

Once she was married…

One thing at a time. Let's deal with the cake first.

Giles's car was, as she'd imagined it would be, sleek, high-powered and probably incredibly expensive—just like the man himself. He pulled away from the kerb before she'd even finished buckling herself in, barely managing to grunt hello.

Which was good, really. Because he looked even more damn attractive when he was glowering. But she didn't need that kind of energy in her life, so it was easier than usual to remind herself that chemistry was not what she needed in a relationship.

'Well, you're in a good mood,' she said, as they sped out of the village.

'I had a visit with my sister,' Giles replied. 'It's never good for my temperament—or my temper.'

Millie frowned. She hadn't even known he *had* a sister until he'd mentioned her friend with the bakery. 'She didn't like it that we were going to her friend's bakery for a cake?'

He glanced over briefly, frowning before returning his attention to the road. 'Why would she care about that?'

'Because you said… Never mind.'

Clearly he wasn't in a mood to talk about anything—and, really, his relationship with his sister was none of her business, anyway. The only thing they had in common right now was getting this wedding organised in Charlie's absence.

Once she'd said 'I do' to Charlie, she and Giles would probably go back to being disapproving acquaintances with nothing but Charlie in common. Which was for the best.

It was definitely for the best. Even if she wasn't sure she should be having to spend so much time reminding herself of that fact.

The rest of the drive was mostly silent, until they pulled into the village where the bakery was located—about halfway between Millie's home and Charlie's, which was convenient.

'I don't get on with her husband,' Giles said suddenly.

It took Millie a moment to cast her mind back and figure out what he was talking about.

'I should have stopped her marrying him,' he said.

'I don't think you can have that kind of sway over anyone else's life, Giles,' Millie said, with a rueful smile. 'Not even your sister's.'

'Maybe not.' He opened the car door. 'But I still should have tried harder.'

Millie followed him, frowning. She wasn't used to any of Charlie's schoolfriends *really* taking responsibility for their actions—let alone for things that weren't even their responsibility to feel guilty over.

Maybe this was part of Charlie's plan. He'd always wanted her and Giles to be better friends—actually, to be even vaguely friendly towards each other at all. She wouldn't put it past him to have engineered a situation in which they'd have to actually get to know each other and get over all their preconceived notions about the other before the wedding. She knew well enough that after all these years Giles was as much a part of Charlie's life as she was, and she could understand him not wanting a lifetime of them sniping at each other in his future.

The bakery—called Cherry On Top, according to the swirly lettered sign—was pink and sweet and it smelled fantastic. It was also warm inside, compared to the cooling late-afternoon air. They were almost into November already, and Millie could smell the colder weather coming in the air.

'Giles!' A petite blonde woman stepped out from behind the counter, beaming as she wrapped Giles into a huge hug. 'I couldn't believe it when Rebekah told me!' She turned to Millie. 'And you must be the fiancée! It's so exciting to meet you. We were starting to think that Giles would *never* get serious about anybody—and now here you are, choosing a cake!'

Millie's eyes widened as she looked at the woman in horror. 'Oh, no! That's not—'

'Tuppence, I'm not the groom,' Giles said calmly. 'My friend Charlie is. But he's away on business, so I'm here as part of my best man duties.'

Tuppence's face fell, and she pouted at him as she stepped back from Millie. 'I should have known it was too good to be true.'

'Yes, you should,' Giles replied with a grim smile. 'I thought you knew me better than that.'

Tuppence shrugged. 'What can I say? I'm a romantic. And when Rebekah told me you needed a wedding cake tasting session… Well, I thought that maybe you'd *finally* got over that whole "never getting married" phase.'

'It's not a phase.' Giles's response sounded like one he'd given often over the years.

'I take it this is a conversation you two have had before?' Millie observed.

It really was surprising how much she was learning about Charlie's other best friend today. And they hadn't even got to his taste in cakes yet.

She'd never really thought of Giles as a person apart from Charlie before. It was weird…

Giles rolled his eyes. 'Tuppence here has been my sister's best friend since before I was even born. She thinks that gives her the right to pass judgement on my life choices.'

'Make better choices and I won't have to,' Tuppence said, smiling widely. 'But we're not here for you and your disastrous outlook on life today. We're here for cake! So, Millie, right? Let's have a cup of tea and talk about what you're looking for, shall we?'

Tuppence led them through to a side room off the main bakery counter, where a bistro-style table was set up beside a long counter with cake stands on it, each loaded with a different sort of cake. She motioned Millie and Giles to take a seat, and moments later joined them, carrying a tray with a teapot and three cups and saucers on it, which she placed between them on the table.

'So,' she said, as the tea brewed in the pot, 'tell me about your wedding, Millie. And your groom! What sort of things do you like? Dislike? What's your theme? Your colours? That sort of thing.'

'Um…' This should be easy. She'd known Charlie almost her whole life. She knew his likes and dislikes almost as well as her own. But having to act as the *owner* or guardian of those likes and dislikes just felt…weird.

'It's a Christmas Eve wedding,' Giles put in for her. 'It'll be at Howard Hall, of course—Tabby is doing a lot of the organising—but I think Millie and Charlie are hoping to rein her in on a few things. And Millie is a florist, so she's organising the flowers. In fact, she has sketches...'

He nudged her arm, and Millie reached into her bag for the sketches she'd brought, suddenly on firmer ground. Flowers were something she could talk about.

'I thought, since it's Christmas, we'd go with the classic deep green foliage with accents of red and white—although not together, of course.'

'Of course,' Tuppence agreed, nodding sagely.

Giles, meanwhile, looked baffled. 'Why not together?'

'It's unlucky,' Millie explained. 'Supposed to symbolise death.'

'And you believe that?' He raised his eyebrows incredulously.

'No,' Millie admitted. 'But I guarantee that someone on Tabby and Lady Howard's vast invitation list will, and they're bound to mention it. Loudly. It's just easier to avoid it all together. So, white flowers for the service at the family chapel, and for the buttonholes and bouquets, but a jolly red for the table centrepieces and decorations in the reception hall.'

'Sounds perfect.' Tuppence beamed. 'And these sketches are glorious! I love the wooden bases for the centrepieces.'

Millie shrugged. 'It's probably a bit rustic for Tabby, but when she started talking about deep green being perfect for my complexion, suddenly all I could picture was a winter forest in the snow and... Well, this is where I ended up.'

'It's beautiful,' Tuppence said firmly. 'And I've got some fantastic ideas already for how we can echo this on the cake! But first...let's talk flavours.'

'And taste some, I hope,' Giles added. 'I skipped lunch.'

Tuppence laughed. 'I promise you, you will not be hungry by the time we've finished here.'

Tuppence had been right—Giles certainly wasn't hungry by the time they left the bakery. They'd tasted types of cakes that he hadn't even known existed, flavours he hadn't dreamed of—and they were all delicious. Tuppence definitely knew what she was doing.

And yet as they left—Millie having chosen something both tasteful and tasty that he was almost certain nobody could object to on the grounds of wedding superstition or anything else—he found himself craving something savoury. All that sugar had left his teeth aching and his stomach rebelling.

'I know this sounds ridiculous,' he said, as he swerved Millie away from the car, 'but I need chips. Come on, let's check out the local pub.'

'I'm so glad you said that.' Millie grinned up at him. 'All that sugar has left me a little queasy. I need salt.'

The local pub—The Bell—was more or less exactly as Giles had expected. Scrubbed wood tables, menus clipped to tiny wooden boards, tasteful fairy lights strung around the beams and a small fir tree trimmed in gold in a pot by the door, advertising their Christmas menu.

They grabbed a table by the fire, and ordered chips at the bar.

'So. Tuppence is lovely...' Millie said, in that sort of leading way Rebekah always did when she was saying one thing but meaning another. 'She seemed disappointed about your determination not to marry, though...'

Oh, so that was it. Millie had reached her *I'm so happily loved up I want everyone else to be as happy as I am* stage. He supposed it was inevitable, but he'd hoped he might be able to avoid it for a bit longer. Not least because it was hard to imagine wanting anyone else when he was still remembering holding her body against his as they danced.

'Tuppence is very happily engaged to her girlfriend,' he said, nipping *that* idea in the bud.

'Oh.' Millie looked genuinely disappointed for a moment, before rallying as their chips arrived. 'Still, how can you be so certain you never want to get married? Maybe you just haven't—'

'Met the right person yet?' He reached for the vinegar and doused his bowl liberally. 'Trust me—I'm sure. It's not about the person.'

She gave him an odd look as she sprinkled salt on her chips. 'I'm pretty sure that's *exactly* what marriage is about, Giles.'

They swapped condiments, and he was surprised to see she added just as much vinegar to her bowl as he had. Usually people accused him of drowning his chips. His mother said it was 'positively common'. Which might or might not have been why he started doing it; now he just liked the taste.

'Not for me.'

It wasn't something he liked to explain, but when Millie just kept looking at him, waiting as she ate her chips, he knew she wasn't going to give up without more of an explanation.

'I just… Marriage isn't something that goes well in my family. And I have no reason to believe that I'd be any better at it. So I think it's better for everyone if I just…don't.'

'You said you don't get on with your sister's husband,' she said, eyeing him carefully. 'What about your parents?'

'I don't really get on with either of them, either.' He said it half as a joke, even though it was perfectly truthful.

She didn't laugh.

'I *meant* how do they feel about you swearing off marriage? I mean, Charlie's parents have been on at him about marrying and continuing the family name, providing heirs and that sort of thing for *years*, now.' She stopped suddenly, her cheeks pink in the firelight. 'Not that that's why he's marrying *me*, or anything.'

Giles laughed. 'I never thought it was. If that was the case, he'd have done it years ago.'

The idea that Charlie might only be marrying Millie to keep his parents happy was absurd. He watched as she smiled shyly at him and thought that he could list five or six reasons to marry Millie right off the top of his head, if he had to.

For *Charlie* to marry her, anyway. Obviously. Marriage wasn't what he thought about when he looked at Millie. That was definitely something less…respectable.

But Charlie had merely come around to seeing what was right in front of him all along—like in all those Christmas romcoms Rebekah liked to pretend she didn't watch, but blubbed at every time.

Truly, it was the time of year for miracles, and all that. Or it would be by the time the wedding rolled around.

'And in answer to your question… I have both a niece and a nephew. What is left of our family estate can carry on perfectly well without me when I'm gone.'

Not the name, though; Rebekah had taken her husband's name when she married, and the children had his name, too. Something else he didn't deserve, but that was the way of the world.

What his brother-in-law *did* have, though, was money. As did Giles. His niece and nephew would never have to worry about making ends meet—and that would be far easier for them if he got rid of the money pit of the house first.

Millie gave him a curious look. 'What's left of your family estate? Is it crumbling into the sea or something?'

'It might as well be.' He reached for another chip—hot and salty and tangy with vinegar—and focussed on the taste in his mouth to distract him from the feelings that the subject made swirl around his chest. 'The house is falling apart, the land is poorly maintained, and my parents won't do anything to change that.'

'Oh. I'm sorry. I didn't... I didn't realise.'

There was a confused frown between her eyebrows, as if she were readjusting her view of the world in light of this new information.

He gave her what he hoped was a reassuring smile. 'No reason why you should.'

He hadn't intended to get into a discussion of his family's net worth, but if they were going to be spending time together planning her wedding, he supposed it was inevitable that they get to know each other better than they'd ever bothered to in the past.

'Fortunately, my personal wealth is intact. It's only the estate that's going to the dogs.'

The little frown line deepened. Giles was horrified to discover he found it *cute*.

'That's why I... I mean, Charlie always says that you're richer than any of them these days. So why don't you—?' She broke off. 'I'm sorry. It's none of my business.'

She was right; it wasn't her business. And normally Giles would take the way out—change the subject to something less likely to make him want to drink. But for some reason he didn't want her to think worse of him than she always had. Because things were different now from back when they'd both been competing for Charlie's friendship and happily loathing each other behind his back.

God help him, he wanted Charlie's bride to *like* him. Because if she didn't she'd have the power to cut him out of his best friend's life, and he wasn't sure he could take that.

Charlie was the only thing that had made boarding school—even university—bearable. He didn't want to lose that friendship. Even if it meant telling Millie the truths he usually tried to keep close to his chest.

'You don't understand why I don't just bail out my parents and pay for the estate repairs and so on?' He gave a wry smile. 'Neither do they.'

'But you have a reason.' Millie gazed at him steadily. 'And I'd wager it's a good one. You don't have to explain it to me.'

He blinked in surprise. Whatever he'd expected from her, it wasn't this blind and trusting acceptance. More likely, he'd have predicted suspicion and scepticism.

He wondered if this was what Charlie saw in her eyes every time she smiled at him. If so, he couldn't believe it had taken his friend this long to propose.

'I didn't expect you to have such faith in me,' he said carefully. 'I'm almost certain you never used to.'

Millie gave a small shrug and reached for another chip. 'That was years ago. I figure if Charlie has kept you around all this time, he must see something in you I didn't. Besides…'

She bit her lip, and Giles found he couldn't look away from where her white teeth pressed against the pink flesh.

'Besides?'

'You're here,' she said, looking down at the table. 'I know Charlie would be here, doing all this, if he could, but since he's had to go away…you've really stepped up to help me, and I appreciate that. You could have easily just called and asked if I needed anything, then accepted my answer when I said I was fine. But you didn't. And… Well, that tells me a lot about you that I didn't know before.'

Suddenly a hot anger filled his chest—with himself, for hating this woman for so long, but mostly with Charlie, for leaving her when she needed him. For forcing her to make do with Giles instead—a man so unsuited for the task that it had to be seen to be believed.

Charlie should be here, not him. If only because when Millie looked up with those sparkling, hopeful eyes, her lips slightly parted, Charlie could kiss her and Giles couldn't.

Not that he wanted to. Okay, fine. He wanted to. He'd wanted to do a lot more than kiss her since Octavia's wedding. But he *wouldn't*—and that was what mattered. Wasn't it?

Surely this ridiculous attraction would pass soon. Before the wedding, ideally.

But what if it *didn't*?

At first, he'd assumed his sudden passion had been brought about by her looking gorgeous at the wedding, and weddings being the sort of occasion when he usually pulled women. After that, maybe he'd felt a bit of a 'one that got away' thing for her. And then he guessed he'd just been feeling sorry for her after Charlie absconded.

But what if it was more than that?

What if he spent the rest of his life wishing he could kiss Millie Myles? Not because she looked good in a dress, or because he couldn't have her, but because of the woman she was.

Because of how he felt about her.

Oh, hell.

'Anyway, since you *are* here…'

Oblivious to the internal confusion that had set Giles's world in a spin, Millie smiled and carried on talking.

'I promised Tabby and Charlie's mother that I'd head up to Howard Hall the weekend after next to finalise some arrangements for the venue. Do you think you could come with me? Help me stand my ground so I don't end up with gold-encrusted beef for the wedding breakfast, or something.'

He laughed, despite himself. 'I don't think Tabby would waste gold on the guests. More likely she'll have found some crown or other for you to wear with the antique family veil.'

Millie groaned. 'Oh, God, the dress… That's a whole different argument I need to have with them. They don't seem to realise that there isn't a chance of me fitting into any of their family heirloom gowns. I'm hoping I can just get away with ordering one from some website in China…'

The idea of Millie in a wedding gown—antique or otherwise—seemed about ready to short-circuit his brain. He hoped to God she had other people to take her dress shopping—he was fairly sure Tabby wouldn't let *that* responsibility get delegated to him.

But Millie was waiting for an answer.

In light of what he'd just realised—quite how much he wanted to kiss his best friend's fiancée, and not just to get her into bed, but just *because*—he knew he should say no. He was busy…had work commitments he couldn't get out of just like Charlie. She'd buy it and never know the difference.

And yet when he opened his mouth to reply, the words that came out were, 'Sure. I'll pick you up on my way.'

CHAPTER SEVEN

GILES WAS QUIET on their drive up to Howard Hall, a couple of weeks later. Millie had hoped to talk about the things she needed to stay firm on, but all attempts at conversation had been met with non-conversational grunts or hums.

'Late night last night?' she asked eventually.

She'd never seen Giles hungover, but she assumed this was what it looked like.

He gave her a wan smile. 'No. Just a long week. At work.'

'Right.'

She had no reason to disbelieve him, but she couldn't shake the feeling he wasn't telling her something. Instead of pressing him further, she shifted in her seat and stared out of her window at the passing countryside instead.

She hadn't pressed him on his family the other night in the pub, either. Maybe she should have, because curiosity had been eating her up ever since. In the moment it had seemed more important to show him that she trusted him—or at least was beginning to trust him, as Charlie's other oldest friend—than to get all the gossip. But Millie had to admit she did have a bit of a weakness for... Not gossip. *Understanding* people.

She wanted to *understand* Giles. As a... Well, as a friend, she supposed.

As an outsider in Charlie's world, she knew there were myriad things she'd never understand about the life high-society people lived, even if she was expected to join it. She'd never been to boarding school, or to Oxford. Nor even skiing, as it happened.

In the same way that Charlie would never understand about having to budget down to the penny for the weekly food shop, or knowing that a bad month at the shop could be the difference between paying her rent or not, she'd never fully understand his upbringing—or Giles's either.

But she wanted to at least try.

Maybe if she knew him better as a person she'd move past the ridiculous crush that had had her blushing when he opened the car door for her, or when his hand brushed hers over a bowl of chips.

She'd given in to her curiosity on a video call with Charlie earlier in the week. Once they'd got through the wedding update, she'd mentioned her conversation with Giles about his family.

'What *is* the deal with him and his parents?' she'd asked, trying to sound casual.

Charlie had raised his eyebrows. 'Since when do you care about Giles Fairfax's life?'

'Since you left him to be my wedding planner,' she'd replied pointedly.

But Charlie hadn't caved. 'It's not my story to tell.'

So Giles remained as much of a mystery to her as ever. Aloof and secretive, and today silent and grumpy. But he was still here and, quite aside from the fact that looking at his handsome profile was always fun, she was grateful for the company.

Doubly glad, in fact, once they reached Howard Hall.

Tabby and Lady Howard were surprised to see Giles accompanying her, that much was clear on their arrival, but they took it in their stride, like everything else.

Millie wasn't sure if that was an aristocratic thing, or a trait bred from running events at their many properties, but

either way it worked for her. Giles had merely explained that
Charlie had asked him to stand in for some things while he
was away, and everyone had nodded, as if that was a perfectly normal thing for a best man to do.

But he proved she'd been right to ask him to come within
the first twenty minutes.

As they all sat down in the front parlour, with tea and
cakes, Tabby pulled out a clipboard with a familiar-looking
list on it and said, 'So, Millie, have you had a chance to look
at the guest list I sent over? How many names do you think
you're going to want to add?'

'Um…'

They hadn't even talked about money, she realised. Charlie had told her right at the start not to worry about it—that
he'd cover everything, or his family would—but Millie knew
that by normal social convention it should be her family paying. She knew her mum would feel awkward about not being
able to do that. Hell, she felt awkward about not paying for
it herself in this day and age. Why should they be relying on
their parents to fund it anyway?

Except that she'd put everything she had saved into the
shop, and Charlie's career *was* the family business, so…

'I… I still need to check with Charlie about exactly who
he wants to invite—you know how busy he's been up in
Scotland.'

In truth, she had no idea how busy Charlie had been, or
what he'd been doing, because all their conversations had
been about the wedding rather than anything else in their
lives. But it worked as an excuse now, because she hadn't
known how to raise the question of the guest list with him.
The one time she'd mentioned it, he'd just said that his mother
and Tabby would know who to invite.

And, since that was sort of the problem, it hadn't really
helped at all.

She glanced sideways at Giles, who appeared to be concentrating all his attention on a small iced cake.

'I do know that we were thinking that…with it being Christmas Eve and all, and people wanting to spend time with their families…maybe it would be best to keep the guest list…well, small?'

That sounded okay, didn't it? It was concern for others that was making her say that, rather than not wanting a couple of hundred of the Howards' random society acquaintances sharing the most important day of her life.

'We thought exactly the same,' Tabby said, leaning forward with a smile. 'That's why we pared down the list before we sent it to you!'

'Two hundred is "pared down"?' The words blurted out of her before she could stop them.

Tabby and her mother shared a knowing smile.

'Millie, darling, I know this is a lot for you,' Lady Howard said. 'But a wedding in our family—and in our home—is bigger than perhaps the events you're used to. To *not* invite certain people would be a serious faux pas.'

'But, as you say, maybe some of them will be busy on Christmas Eve,' Tabby added. But she didn't sound as if she believed it.

Millie shot a hopeless look at Giles. 'I just think… Charlie and I were planning something…small. Intimate. Personal.'

'It will be personal!' Tabby assured her, happily ignoring the other attributes Millie had been hoping for. 'I've got so many ideas for how we can make the whole thing really *feel* like the love you and Charlie share. Look!'

She pulled out another folder, this one filled with samples and colours and vision boards, and Millie felt the whole room go a little swimmy around her.

She couldn't do this. She couldn't marry into this family—into their expectations and their society. Except if she wanted the family she'd always dreamed of, and to give that family to her best friend, too, she had to.

She'd be happy married to Charlie—she knew that. She just had to survive the wedding planning first.

'Back to the guest list for a moment,' Giles said, and all three women looked at him in surprise.

It was the first time he'd commented on anything wedding-related since they'd arrived. Millie suspected that Tabby and Lady Howard had assumed he was only there under duress, and mostly for the food and to play chauffeur.

Millie hadn't been sure herself.

But now he seemed completely engaged in the conversation.

'I think Millie's right. Charlie really wants it to be an exclusive gathering. No photos sold to the press or a social media frenzy. I know you want to show off the venue, of course, but I think showcasing it as a truly private, exclusive wedding location would be even more effective. Not to mention it adds a certain cachet to the whole occasion.' He sat back in his chair. 'Obviously there'll be some people who need to be there, and some you'll want there. But if you keep the list small those people will feel truly special and appreciated, too. Keep if really...refined.'

This time the look that Tabby shared with her mother was more speculative. Considering, even.

Millie felt something akin to hope start to rise inside her chest and sent Giles a grateful smile. He looked away.

'A smaller guest list would mean we could do something truly ambitious with the menu,' Tabby said thoughtfully. 'Maybe even a full festive tasting menu with wine pairings.'

'And we could use more of the rooms before and after the service,' Lady Howard added. 'Yes, it *could* work.'

'Let me go and speak with Chef.' Tabby jumped up from her chair. 'He's preparing food for us to taste already, but he should also have supplies for the tasting menu on hand, for the trial run of next weekend's event, so it shouldn't be difficult to set it up. You two carry on here.'

And then she was gone, leaving Millie alone with her future mother-in-law.

No, not alone. Giles was still there.

But she wasn't sure how much there was that he could do when Lady Howard fixed her with a steely look and said, 'Now, Millie. Let's talk gowns and rings while we're waiting.'

Giles had done his best on the guest list thing, but he knew when he was beaten. Lady Howard's expression told him that she and Millie would be discussing wedding dresses and rings with or without him—and without him sounded definitely preferable.

He shot Millie an apologetic look as he slipped out of the room, phone in hand, as if it had silently buzzed with an incoming call. From the betrayed look on Millie's face, she knew it hadn't.

Outside, the air was turning wintry already—cold and grey, with a slight haze hanging over the fields. Giles leaned against the ancient stone of Howard Hall and swiped across his phone to place a call.

'How's it going?' Charlie asked, the minute he answered.

'I think we've managed to persuade your mother and sister to keep the guest list under a thousand or so. But you may now have a twelve-course tasting menu wedding breakfast as a result.'

Charlie groaned. 'Is Millie okay?'

'Your mother is currently talking to her about wedding gowns and heirloom rings.'

No point sugar-coating it. He imagined Millie would be calling her fiancé later to share the misery anyway. Might as well give his friend a heads-up for what was in store.

'I should be there.' Guilt sounded heavy in Charlie's voice.

'Trust me, I would definitely rather you were here than me,' Giles said. 'And I'm sure Millie would, too.' He paused, wondering whether to add the next bit. Then he decided that he and Charlie hadn't stayed best friends for so long by not saying what needed to be said. 'Why aren't you?'

'This movie…up here in Scotland. I need to be here. For the…antiques…insurance purposes. You know?'

'Right. Insurance.'

It wasn't that Giles thought Charlie was lying. It was just… Surely he could have got away for a day or two, to do this with Millie?

And it wasn't that Giles minded standing in. If he was honest with himself, he was enjoying it all a lot more than he'd imagined he would—and he knew a lot of that came from just getting to spend time with Millie. But he hated seeing her so lost without Charlie there.

He knew he could never really be a replacement for their mutual best friend.

'Tell Millie I'm really sorry she's having to do this alone,' said Charlie. Then there was a commotion on the other end of the line. 'Sorry, I'm going to have to go.'

The line went dead, just as he heard Charlie shouting 'Liberty!' as he walked away.

Yeah, maybe Charlie would rather be here than in Scotland. But it didn't change the fact that he wasn't.

With a sigh, Giles turned and headed back inside—only to crash into Tabby in the hall.

'*There* you are. Come on! We're menu-tasting. Chef is cooking *everything*. I hope you're hungry!'

His stomach growled in response. 'Apparently so. Lead on!'

At least there were *some* good things about his additional best man duties.

Even if it meant helping Millie get married to their mutual best friend and ignoring the guilt he felt about imagining what they could be doing if she *wasn't* marrying another man...

Four hours later, Millie was so full she didn't think she could stand. 'You're going to have to roll me out to the car,' she told Giles, after they'd made their goodbyes to Tabby and Lady Howard. 'I don't think I can see my feet any more.'

The food had been delicious—all of it—and there would have been no way Millie could have decided between all the fantastic options alone. Luckily, the other three diners had had plenty of opinions, so mostly Millie's job had been to agree with them. By the end of the tasting session they'd had a menu of seven small courses that would apparently be perfect for the Christmas Eve wedding.

'I thought your mother was the cook at Howard Hall.' Giles opened the car door for her. 'The man cooking today didn't look a thing like you.'

She rolled her eyes as she collapsed into the passenger seat. 'Mum is the *family* cook. They have a whole kitchen and a pseudo celebrity chef for events. And besides, Mum's mostly retired these days anyway.'

She felt a pang of guilt as she looked down the long driveway in the direction of the small gatehouse where she'd grown up—and where her mother still lived.

She should have invited Mum to the tasting today. Wasn't that what parents of the bride were supposed to do? It was only that, as much as the Howards had always made them feel a part of the family...they weren't. They were staff. And she knew her mother felt that.

Yes, Jessica Myles had been excited, supportive—delighted, even, when they'd announced the engagement. But as they'd sipped sherry with the Howards that day she'd watched as her mum grew silent, fading into the background as Charlie's family took over with their wedding plans and expectations.

Millie and her mother couldn't contribute financially to the wedding. She didn't even have a father to give her away—although she'd already told Charlie *and* Tabby, in no uncertain terms, that her mother would be doing that, and neither of them had dared to argue with her about it.

But now the wedding plans were continuing apace, and she hadn't even thought to invite her mum.

As Giles pulled away from Howard Hall and started down the driveway he glanced over at her. 'Do you want to stop and see your mum before we head back?'

She jerked her head round to stare at him in shock. 'How did you know I was thinking about her?'

He shrugged. 'You're kind of an open book, you know. Easy to read.'

Except she wasn't. Because if she was he'd already know that this wedding wasn't quite the love match she'd been telling everyone it was.

And *that* was the real reason she'd been avoiding her mum. She knew Millie better than anyone—better, even, than Charlie. If anyone was going to guess, it was Jessica Myles.

But, oh, she wanted her mum to believe that her little girl was marrying for true love. That this really was the fairytale ending everyone kept saying it was.

She swallowed. She'd just have to be a better actress, then, wouldn't she?

'Yeah, if you don't mind. I'd like to stop in if we have time.'

'At your service, milady,' Giles said, and pulled over at the gatehouse.

Her mum was surprised to see them—that much was clear.

'Millie! I didn't know you were visiting. Is Charlie home, then?'

Her gaze darted towards Giles, then back to Millie, looking for an answer to the unspoken question of what she was doing there with her fiancé's best man.

'No, he's still in Scotland.'

Millie stripped off her winter coat and hung it on one of the hooks by the door, just as she'd done every day throughout her childhood. In fact, under the normal-height hooks were a series of brightly coloured plastic ones at varying heights, which her father had put up for her to use as she grew. Neither she nor her mum had ever had the heart to take them down.

'I had to come and meet with Tabby and Lady Howard about some arrangements and the menu. Giles agreed to come and help me avoid being steamrollered.'

'And how did that go?'

Her mum raised an eyebrow as Millie unwound her scarf and moved out of the way for Giles to add his own smart, tailored wool coat to the hooks.

'Is it still your wedding or is it Tabby's now?'

Millie laughed. 'Still mine—just about. They had this ridiculous guest list, but Giles persuaded them to tone it down.'

'In exchange for an equally excessive tasting menu,' Giles added. 'But I've always preferred food to people, so that works for me.'

Millie's mum laughed at that. She realised her mother had probably never spent any time with Giles before—even Millie hadn't really, so why would her mum? But she already had her arm through his, leading him through to the little sitting room and promising to put the kettle on in a moment since, even if they *were* still full from the tasting, there was always room for tea.

She felt a pang in her chest as she watched them go, both joking and laughing. It should be Charlie here with her and her mum—her actual fiancé joking about wedding plans. Not the stand-in Charlie had sent because she needed back-up.

Not for the first time since she and Charlie had cooked up their plan, a wave of uncertainty rushed through her. Was she crazy to be doing this? Did the fact that Charlie was to be hundreds of miles away for basically their entire engagement mean he was getting cold feet? He swore not, whenever they spoke on the phone, and she'd always been able to tell when he was lying before. But still the doubt lingered.

And she had to admit spending time with Giles wasn't helping with that. Oh, it wasn't that she imagined for a moment she could have the kind of future she wanted with Giles, but that was her mind talking. Her body definitely had other ideas.

Lucky that she'd learnt that passion wasn't to be trusted, really.

I can trust Giles, though.

The thought caught her by surprise—mostly because she realised it was true. Somehow her childhood enemy had become the one person she trusted to help her navigate her way through this whole wedding chaos. She *almost* wished she could tell him the truth.

In the lounge, she swept her fingers over a delicate, crocheted blanket in shades of grey and white that her mother had hung over the back of one of the upright dining chairs at the tiny table in the bay window. It was unfinished, obviously a work in progress, and just as obviously intended for a baby.

'Mrs Pratchett in the village…her daughter is expecting. Doesn't want to find out the sex—or isn't telling if she has—and she's gone for an all-neutral nursery, which seems to mean grey and white.' Her mum looked with dissatisfaction at the blanket. 'Not the colours I would have chosen for a baby—you want joyous colours for that, and grey always feels a bit depressing, don't you think? But grey's what they want, so grey is what they're getting—it's their baby, after all, not mine. And I think it'll be pretty enough when it's finished.'

'It's beautiful.'

The words choked her; she could feel her eyes pricking and her throat swelling. Oh, God, she really couldn't cry over a baby blanket. Then her mum would definitely know something was wrong—and the last thing she wanted to do was tell her about her fertility issues and have her guessing the real reason she was marrying Charlie. She'd be so disappointed in her, for not holding out for the sort of true love she and Millie's dad had once had.

But Jessica Myles only smiled and squeezed her shoulder. 'Maybe I'll be making one for you and Charlie before too long. Not grey, though,' she added, as a warning.

Millie laughed, and was pleased it didn't come out too soggy. 'Definitely not grey, Mum. I promise.'

'Good.' One last squeeze of the shoulder, and she moved away towards the kitchen. 'Come on. I've set Giles to laying the tea tray. Let's see how he's got on.'

It was several hours later—after many cups of tea and even a round or two of cheese on toast, when the effects of the tasting menu wore off—before Millie and Giles left the gatehouse.

'Safe travels home,' Jessica told Giles, as he went to warm up the car.

He gave her a mock salute in return, before disappearing into the darkness and leaving Millie alone with her mum.

'He's not like the rest of Charlie's old schoolfriends, is he?' Jessica mused. 'I remember the state they used to leave the house in when his parents went away and they'd have a party. Maybe he was the same as the rest of them back then, but he at least seems to have grown up—which is more than you can say for some of them.' She gave a satisfied nod. 'Charlie chose well for his best man. I'm glad he's here to help you out while Charlie's away.'

'Me too,' Millie replied, surprised to realise how much she meant it. 'He's been great, actually. And I wasn't expecting that.'

If anything, she'd expected Giles to treat her as a burden, or as if he was doing her a massive favour—which he was—and to expect constant gratitude in return. Instead, he'd just been there, quietly doing exactly what she needed even when she wasn't sure quite what that was. Like coming to visit her mum. He'd known that was what she needed even before she had.

But there were some wedding-related things he simply couldn't do. Or at least things that she wouldn't feel comfortable asking him to do.

'Mum, are you free to go down to London one day in the next couple of weeks?' Millie asked.

'I can be,' Jessica replied. 'What for?'

'Well, if I'm not going to try to squeeze into one of the Howard wedding gowns…we're going to need to go dress shopping.'

CHAPTER EIGHT

LONDON WAS READY for Christmas. Never mind that it was only November, the city wasn't waiting. The lights were up and sparkling, the air smelled of roasting chestnuts and hot chocolate, people in shops were wearing Santa hats, and the whole city was absolutely rammed with people.

Giles hated London at this time of year.

Normally, he'd do everything he could to avoid having to come into the centre of London during November or December. His offices in the City weren't nearly so bad.

But Charlie hadn't made it home for his appointment at the jewellers to choose a ring. So here he was, getting ready to meet Millie again and play the part of stand-in groom once more.

It was getting to be a problem, he admitted to himself as he sipped a coffee at the window bar of an overheated and over-crowded coffee shop near where she'd asked to meet him. Just as well that in a month or so Charlie would be back, they'd get married, and he could get on with his life away from them.

Okay, not totally away. Charlie was still his best friend, and Millie was certainly becoming something. But he wouldn't have to be in their pockets the whole time, at their beck and call, with their wedding the most important thing in his life.

If he wanted, he could stay away for weeks on end.

Except then he wouldn't see Millie. And the idea of that…

Well, this was why it was becoming a problem.

He *liked* his best friend's fiancée.

Liked as in it was getting harder and harder to imagine never kissing her. Not seeing her, talking to her regularly. Not being the person she turned to for things.

And that was *definitely* a problem.

Chemistry and attraction was one thing—he could handle that. What he wasn't used to was just wanting to be near another person this way. Thank God she *was* marrying someone else, or he might actually have to stop and examine what the feeling meant, and that couldn't end well.

It didn't matter, anyway. He couldn't do anything about it—wouldn't even let on about his feelings if he could help it, because that wouldn't be fair to anyone. Millie was engaged to Charlie, and he didn't want to do anything that could possibly disrupt that.

Not least because they were such a perfect fit. They both wanted the same things—marriage, family, the fairytale. Things that Giles categorically did *not* want. So it would be utterly unfair for him to say anything and add even the smallest smidgen of uncertainty into the proceedings.

If he were a humbler man, he'd doubt that anything he said or did could possibly shake the love Charlie and Millie shared. And long term he was sure that was true. But right now…in the moment…

Millie was anxious about the wedding—that much was obvious—and Charlie being away wasn't helping her confidence either. More than that…sometimes she looked at him, too. Oh, she looked away again, fast, but he still saw it—hoped for it, even. Those brief moments when he caught her considering as she watched him. Wondering, maybe, what it would be like to kiss him—the same way *he* wondered about her.

He shook his head and took another sip of coffee. It was

pointless dwelling on it. Millie was marrying Charlie and nothing was going to change that—he wouldn't let it. She was just having pre-wedding jitters, and he wasn't going to be the bastard who took advantage of that.

So, instead, he drained the rest of his coffee and got to his feet, escaping the roasting coffee shop for the crisp, cool November air outside. Millie had been shopping with her mother that morning, and had asked him to meet her at their last shop and go on to the jewellers, which was nearby.

Apparently, Charlie had sent in an order for their wedding rings, but he wanted Millie to choose her own engagement ring. Which made sense—apart from the bit where *Giles* was the one shopping for it with her.

Still, once they left the shop he'd keep hold of the wedding rings, in his capacity as best man, and she'd be wearing the engagement ring. Maybe a huge freaking diamond on her left hand would help him get it through his thick head that she was not for him.

He could only hope.

Except the shop where Millie had asked him to meet her was a wedding dress boutique. And she was running late.

Giles pushed open the door and stepped inside to see Millie draped in ivory satin, looking like a goddess in an off-the-shoulder gown. And any words he might have intended to say to announce his arrival disappeared.

'Giles!'

She looked flustered at his arrival—maybe even as flustered as he felt seeing her in a wedding gown—for all that she'd asked him to come.

'Now, now… It's bad luck for the groom to see the bride in her dress before the wedding day!'

The boutique owner approached him with an incongruous fan in her hand—one he suspected she was about to hit him with, before Jessica laughed and said, 'Oh, that's not the groom. It's the best man.'

Millie, bright red, had bustled away behind some screens to a changing area, but her voice carried back into the room.

'Besides, I'm not sure that's the dress. I like it, but…' She trailed off.

'You looked amazing in it,' Giles said—hopefully helpfully. 'But I didn't see the others.'

'They all looked beautiful,' Jessica said loyally. 'But that last one was something special.'

Too damn right it was.

'I'm just not sure…'

Millie emerged from behind the screened-off area of the changing rooms, this time dressed in her more usual jeans and a warm, snowflake-patterned jumper. Giles cursed inwardly as he realised he still wanted to strip that woollen layer off her every bit as much as he had the ivory gown.

'Well, there aren't very many dress shops that can get you *any* wedding dress ready and perfectly fitted before Christmas Eve,' the boutique owner said. 'If it weren't for the fact that Tabitha asked me personally… Anyway… I wouldn't leave it too late.'

'I won't,' Millie promised. 'I'll go through the photos Mum took and make a decision tonight, then I'll be in touch tomorrow. Thank you so much for your help.'

They said their goodbyes to Jessica, who assured them she would be fine catching the train back after 'a bit of a mooch around the shops' on the lookout for Christmas presents.

Giles personally couldn't think of anything worse.

Or at least he thought he couldn't. Until they reached the jeweller's shop.

Collecting the rings Charlie had ordered was an easy enough job. The owner—who had been supplying fine jewellery to the Howard family for decades, possibly centuries—checked his ID against the name and details Charlie had supplied, nodded, and went to retrieve the bands from a safe, leaving his assistant to keep a beady eye on Giles and Millie as they perused engagement rings.

'They're all so *expensive*,' Millie whispered to him as she stared at the trays of sparkling diamonds.

The assistant took a step closer, apparently not reassured that they belonged in such a fine establishment. Giles expected it had something to do with the fluffy snowflakes on Millie's jumper, which he was trying very hard not to find adorable.

'Do you have any idea what sort of thing you're looking for?' he asked.

Millie's eyes only widened.

'Well, did you and Charlie discuss a style? Or even a budget?'

'Not really,' Millie admitted.

Giles was beginning to wonder if the pair of them had discussed *anything* about this wedding before Charlie hightailed it to Scotland.

'He just said that he wanted me to choose something that felt like *me*, no matter what it cost.'

She gave a sheepish but besotted smile, and Giles felt his jaw tense.

'He knew I didn't like the idea of wearing one of the family rings, beautiful as they are. They're too fancy for me—and totally impractical for my work.'

He hadn't considered how rings might impact her floristry career. He supposed having huge, valuable gems that could get caught on delicate petals or, worse, lost in buckets of water, was not a great idea.

'Okay, let's start over here, then,' he suggested, pointing at a display of more modern rings, many with lower profile settings.

He stood back, hands in his pockets, as she considered the offerings. But then one ring caught his eye, and he just knew it would be perfect.

'What about this one?'

The words were out before he could stop himself—something that seemed to be becoming a problem around her. But the way her eyes lit up when she saw the ring he was suggesting made it all worthwhile.

'Oh, wow, that's *perfect*,' she breathed.

It was gold, which would match the wedding bands Charlie had ordered, but instead of the usual diamond a bright green emerald sat in the wide band. The band itself had two tiny rubies inset on either side. The emerald matched her eyes, Giles thought, not to mention the greenery she worked with every day. And the rubies made him think of the holly she'd insisted had to feature in her bouquet.

Giles motioned to the shop assistant and got him to open the case, then plucked the ring from its cushioned case. 'Hold out your hand.'

'It'll probably need resizing,' Millie told him, even as she gave him her hand. 'I have chubby fingers. But still— Oh!'

She broke off as he slid the ring onto the third finger of her left hand. It fitted perfectly, nestled in position as if it had always been there.

As if he had always been the person who was fated to put it there.

Not my fiancée. I don't want *a fiancée,* he reminded himself fiercely in his head.

It didn't help. Something hot and possessive and primal was coursing through his body, and the only thing that was stopping him from kissing her was the memory of his best friend, at one time his *only* friend, and the knowledge that he could never, ever betray Charlie.

However much his body begged him to.

He couldn't do that to Charlie.

And he couldn't make Millie promises he couldn't keep.

Giles looked up to her face and in the same movement she looked away from the ring and met his gaze. 'This is the one?' he whispered.

She swallowed, then nodded.

Giles turned back to the shop owner, who had returned with the wedding bands from the safe and was beaming at them, as if overcome by the romance of it all.

He wondered if the shopkeeper realised that he wasn't the groom.

'We'll take it.'

Giles pulled out his credit card. Charlie had told him to use his line of credit at the shop, but that would only hold things up. At least that was the excuse he made to himself for insisting on paying for the ring personally.

'Now.'

He had to get out of there—fast. Even if it meant seeing that ring on Millie's hand for the rest of the day.

Millie had a problem. And she was starting to think that she wasn't the only one suffering from it.

There was no good reason for Giles to drive her home after ring-shopping; she was perfectly capable of taking the train. But when he'd offered, she'd accepted. And when they'd arrived it had only seemed polite to invite him in—even if that meant he was now helping her stuff invitations into envelopes while the remains of their takeaway curry sat on her kitchen counter.

There was also no good explanation for the way her heart had seemed to thump twice as hard as she'd watched Giles slide her engagement ring onto her left hand. The ring that he'd spotted and chosen as the perfect ring for her. The exact ring she would have chosen for herself if she'd seen it first.

The ring she still wore now, symbolising her intention to marry another man.

There was no reason for her to feel suddenly wobbly about that decision. She'd spent so much of the past month imagining her future life with Charlie—a contented, comfortable existence with a man she loved, not in the passionate way that faded with time, but in the sort of way that lasted for ever. *That* was what she wanted. So there really was no reason to feel wobbly. At all.

But sitting there in the candlelight with Giles, sticking stamps on wedding invitations, she did.

And she'd think she was alone in that feeling except for five things.

Exhibit A: The look on his face when he'd seen her in a wedding dress.

Exhibit B: The aforementioned way he'd chosen her dream engagement ring.

Exhibit C: The fact he'd *paid* for it himself.

Exhibit D: How both driving her home and getting a takeaway had been his idea.

Exhibit E: The fact he was willingly stuffing envelopes with her instead of…whatever he usually did with his evenings in London.

Probably something involving svelte, rich society blondes and cocktails she didn't even know the names of.

This wasn't usual behaviour for any of Charlie's friends. Even taking into account that Charlie had asked him to help her out, surely this had to be above and beyond?

In her past encounters with Charlie's friends, the most any of them had wanted from her was a quick grope at a party or a one-night stand after the pub. They'd certainly never wanted to be *friends* with the likes of her. Charlie didn't know, but she'd heard more than one of them mocking him for being friends with 'the help'—never mind that she'd never actually worked at Howard Hall. She wasn't their type, and that much was obvious in every look they gave her and every word they spoke to her.

'Good enough to bed, but not good enough to wed.'

That was what her mother had said—a warning when Millie had first been invited to one of Charlie's parties up at the hall.

'You watch yourself around them boys. Stay close to Charlie. He's different. He'll look after you.'

And he had. He still was. He was marrying her, for heaven's sake.

And she was repaying him by lusting after his best friend.

Because that was what it was, of course. Just lust. She'd developed a stupid crush on Giles Fairfax when they'd danced together at Octavia's wedding and now it just wouldn't quit. But it had to eventually, didn't it? It was just chemistry, just passion, not anything real.

It was only based on the way he looked at her, the way he anticipated her needs, the way he wasn't at all the man she'd expected him to be—and probably something to do with the way he raised his eyebrows at her and smiled.

Or the way she couldn't close her eyes without imagining his hands on her waist, sweeping up over her body even as his lips worked their way down...

She opened her eyes again. Quickly. Before Giles noticed she was fantasising about him even as he sat right opposite her. She *really* didn't want him figuring that out. Because a crush was all it was—all it could be. Even if she *wasn't* engaged to Charlie, Giles wasn't interested in the kind of future that she wanted. So what was the point of even considering it? Not that she *was* considering it, of course. But if she had been it would be pointless, that was all.

She didn't want a future filled with uncertainty, always waiting for the other shoe to drop when her husband grew bored of her, when the passion faded. She wanted the certainty of a solid marriage based on friendship. With Charlie.

She just wished she didn't feel as if she was trying to convince herself of that all of a sudden.

Millie reached out for the next envelope in a rushed, jerking movement—and realised too late that Giles was doing the same. Her fingers brushed against the back of his hand, and she heard him take a sharp breath before yanking his hand away.

'Sorry. Bride first.'

God, even his voice sounded affected by her touch—suddenly lower, more gravelly than usual. As she imagined it might sound in bed.

Not that she'd imagined that.

At all.

Much.

Millie shoved the next invitation into the relevant envelope and hoped that whoever the recipient was didn't mind theirs being a little crumpled. Hopefully they'd blame it on the Royal Mail.

This was ridiculous. And none of it would be happening if Charlie was here.

She blinked, her brain stalling on the thought.

Did Charlie know this would happen?

'Millie?'

From the way Giles said her name, she thought it wasn't the first time he'd spoken.

'You okay?'

'Yes. Of course.' She dropped the invitation and jumped to her feet. 'I was just going to make…tea. Decaf tea. Because it's late. Do you want one?'

'Sure,' Giles said, with a shrug.

But she felt his eyes on her as she walked away to hide in the kitchen, and when she glanced back there was a frown line between his eyebrows.

He knew something was up. Which was fair—because it was mostly his fault.

Except it was *Charlie's* words, or the memory of them, that had sent her world spinning.

'I meant what I said about fidelity, but we're not actually married yet. So, look, what happens in Vegas stays in Vegas. I'm fine with that. I mean, if you want a final fling or two, or whatever, before you say I do, *then you should go for it. Sow those wild oats, as my grandfather used to say.'*

At the time, she'd almost dismissed the idea completely—rolled her eyes and told him to go to a strip club, or whatever, for his stag and get it all out of his system. She trusted Charlie—once they were married he'd be faithful, and before then he'd be careful. She hadn't really considered that his theory might apply to her, too. After all, she'd gone plenty long enough without sex since Tom—and, really, it wasn't as if Charlie wasn't objectively gorgeous. Assuming they had *any* compatibility at all, sex with him wouldn't be a hardship, and besides, she'd rather have Charlie and a cup of tea and a good conversation than mind-blowing sex every night.

She'd been *sure* of that. Which was why she was now so confused by the fact she couldn't stop imagining Giles Fairfax naked.

Naked and inside her, to be precise.

Naked and inside her, holding her hands down on the mattress as he moved above her, her legs wrapped around his waist as she arched her back to get closer to him, her whole body trembling with the feel of his skin against hers…

It was incredibly distracting.

Had Charlie suspected? Oh, maybe not that she'd develop this crush on her best man. But that their impending nuptials would send her a little sex-crazy, perhaps. Was he having the same problem up in Scotland?

It felt like something she should be able to discuss with her best friend—but at the same time something incredibly weird to talk to her fiancé about.

But they *had* agreed not to feel guilty if the opportunity for a last fling presented itself. So why was she feeling so guilty about even contemplating one?

Because it's Giles.

Giles, who would always be in their life. Giles, who had been her competition for so many years. Giles, who had stepped up and taken on everything Charlie had run out on in planning this wedding.

When Charlie had suggested the whole 'last fling' thing, she hadn't worried, because she'd been so sure that neither of them could want anybody else more than they wanted the future they planned together. There was no risk of anything turning serious, because Charlie's heart still belonged to Octavia, and she wanted security far more than passion.

Giles was passion. But he was also the one who'd been there for her over the weeks since Charlie had left for Scotland. The man she was getting to know in her fiancé's absence was so much more than passion.

And this was more than a crush.

That was the problem.

The tea brewed, she carried two mugs back through to the living room and plonked one on the coffee table. Giles swiped a pile of invitations out of the way just in time, as a small wave of tea escaped over the top of the mug. Millie dived for a cloth to clean it up, before slumping back down onto the sofa and staring balefully at the remaining envelopes, still unaddressed and unstamped.

If ever there was something to silence the libido, it had to be putting wedding invitations into envelopes.

And yet here Giles was, dutifully helping without a single complaint. Even though Tabby had said that the printers they used could have done the mailing, using the designer's files and some fancy mail-merge tech. Millie was the one who'd insisted on doing it by hand—partly because that felt more real, somehow, and partly to make sure that Tabby hadn't slipped any names back onto the guest list.

'You really didn't have to come and help me with this tonight,' she said.

Giles shrugged as he stuffed another envelope. 'Honestly? I didn't have anything better to do. And I promised Charlie—'

'I think this goes above and beyond best man duties,' Millie broke in. 'It's making me feel bad. Isn't there anything I could do to help you in return?'

'Actually, there is one thing.'

Giles looked up and met her gaze, and the sudden flare of heat between them caught her unaware. God, he could ask her for anything in this moment and she'd probably say yes. She wondered if he knew that.

She moistened her lips. 'Anything.'

She had to admit she wasn't expecting his reply to be, 'Go toy shopping with me.'

Her mind stuttered, drawn to a place it really shouldn't be going. A place where it was already spending too much time.

'For my niece and nephew,' he clarified, looking back down at the envelope in his hand. 'I never have any idea what to buy them for Christmas, and somehow I feel like you'll be much better at it than I would. Maybe we could go next week? Or the week after that? If there aren't too many wedding things you need to be doing.'

Actual toys. For actual children.

Right.

Mind out of the gutter, Myles.

'Sure,' she said, far more brightly than she felt. 'I can do that! Uh, I'll check the shop rota and let you know when works.'

After all, the man needed help. If that meant she got to spend a little more time lusting after his broad shoulders and handsome face before she got married, that was a cross she was willing to bear.

But that was all. She was putting this whole thing firmly back in its crush box.

Because she really couldn't let it be anything more.

Piccadilly Circus during the Christmas shopping season was, predictably, like Piccadilly Circus. Which was to say manic and chaotic, full of people who didn't quite know where they were going, and not somewhere Giles would ever choose to be if it weren't for the fact that he'd made plans to meet Millie here.

God, he was pathetic. And so far gone over a woman he couldn't dream of touching that it was ridiculous. He'd even started bargaining with himself…promising himself that as long as he didn't touch her, or tell her how he felt, he could just look and soak in the brightness that seemed to surround her, as much as possible between now and the wedding.

He knew he'd have to stop doing even that much once Charlie was back. He'd guess what was going on in Giles's head in a heartbeat. Even if he wasn't willing to admit it to himself.

This had been so much easier when he'd just wanted to sleep with her.

Giles shoved his hands in the pockets of his black wool coat and wished he'd remembered to bring gloves. Or a scarf. He wasn't really used to being outside in this sort of temperature these days. Used to be he and Charlie would be rowing, or playing rugby, or even hiking, no matter what the weather.

These days he hardly seemed to leave his office, his car or his apartment. The closest he'd got to nature in a while was the greenery in Millie's shop.

Maybe he should consider moving out to a village, too. Closer to the countryside. Fresh air.

But closer to his parents, potentially, too. And no one to share it with.

Maybe he'd stay where he was.

Just as he was stamping his feet to keep some blood circulating in them he saw a berry-red bobble hat emerge from the tube station, and Millie's beaming smile follow right after. And suddenly he didn't feel so cold, or so annoyed, nor frustrated by the tourists any longer.

'Are you ready for this?' Millie bounced on her toes as she stood in front of him, gloved hands clasped by her stomach. 'The world's oldest and possibly largest toy shop, right before Christmas? It's going to be an experience!'

'Hmm...' Giles replied, noncommittally. 'You realise it would have been closer if we'd met at Oxford Circus?'

Millie shrugged. 'I know. But I just love the walk up Regent Street. And we can end up on Oxford Street to see the lights!'

'I suppose we can.'

Why wasn't he surprised that she'd thought this through? Somehow, Millie managed to make things an *experience*, rather than a chore. He already felt his mood lifting—and was surprisingly annoyed by it.

Regent Street was, he had to admit, beautiful in the late-afternoon winter light. The sun was already sinking behind the pale stone of the crescent, and the twinkly overhead Christmas lights were coming on. And walking beside Millie, watching her joy in the moment, made him feel almost joyous, too.

He could just keep walking with her, commenting on the

city at Christmas, all night. But before very long he saw the
red awnings of Hamleys stretching out over the pavement,
beckoning in toy-shoppers from far and wide.

They stopped in front of the store and stared up at it together.

Seven floors of toys. Seven floors of people Christmas
shopping. What on earth had he been thinking?

'We can hold hands if you're scared,' Millie said drily.

'Terrified,' he admitted. 'But I'm pretending to be brave
in front of you.'

She laughed. 'I really wouldn't bother. I like you scared—
it makes you more human. Come on.'

Suddenly she grabbed his hand in her own gloved one and
pulled him past the shop assistants demonstrating the latest
toys, dragging him towards the escalator.

'I'm assuming you don't want to go the boring stuffed toy
route?' she said, as they rose up to the next floor. 'So, what
are the kids into? How old are they, again?'

'Benjy is seven and Lily is nine,' he said, glad he'd checked
their ages with his sister by text while he was waiting for Millie. 'Lily likes…craft stuff, I think? And Benjy…'

He had no idea. He only knew about the crafts because
last time he'd visited—well, last time he'd visited when the
kids were awake—he'd been presented with some sort of
card decorated with curled paper and glue that had stuck to
his jacket.

'Is seven,' Millie finished for him. 'So he would probably
want *everything* in this shop.'

'Probably,' he agreed, with a chuckle. 'So, where do we
start?'

'At the top!' Millie tugged him towards the next escalator.
'We start at the top and work our way down. Okay?'

'Sure.' Giles shrugged.

What else could he say?

Millie took over from there. They enjoyed the trains going around and around an elaborate track, considered the models and drones as they moved down the store, pausing for a while at the remote-control vehicles. Giles might have chased her around with one of the display models, until one of the shop assistants stepped in, but she got her own back with the army of talking cuddly bear creatures she set on him.

The arts and crafts section on the third floor furnished him with a whole armful of things for Lily—from colour-changing pens to stamps to pastels, and plenty of paper to use them on. He also placed an order for an easel to be delivered later.

They continued down to examine the board games, before heading back up again to purchase the remote-control car he'd really wanted for Benjy from the start.

'You can drive it with him on Christmas morning!'

Millie sounded so excited at the prospect that he didn't have the heart to tell her he probably wouldn't actually see the children on the day. They'd be with Rebekah's husband's family, as always.

Laden down with bags, they finally left Hamleys and continued to walk up towards Oxford Street. By now dark had fallen fully and the Christmas lights sparkled brightly overhead, lighting up the skies with festive wonder.

Normally Giles would walk under them, head down, barely noticing their sparkle. With Millie holding on to his arm, that wasn't even an option.

He saw every light, every joyous moment, reflected in her eyes.

He swallowed and looked away.

This was more than a problem. This was a disaster.

He wanted his best friend's fiancée. And not only couldn't he have her, he *shouldn't*. Everything she wanted from her future was the opposite to what he needed.

When he thought about it that way, it really was just as well she was engaged to someone else. And to the one person he could never dream of betraying at that. Charlie would give her the future she wanted. What could he possibly offer her?

Four and a half weeks until the wedding. And he already knew every second of them was going to be unbearable.

'Okay?' Millie squeezed his arm and smiled up at him.

He smiled back before he could stop himself. 'Just fine,' he lied.

He was always fine. That was how he got by.

And he'd get through this, too.

Just four and a half more weeks.

CHAPTER NINE

THE WREATH-MAKING WORKSHOP she ran every year in the back room of Holly and Ivy was Millie's favourite festive activity outside of Christmas week itself. She wasn't a huge fan of Christmas shopping—toy shopping with Giles had been an exception to that rule—and while she enjoyed a Christmas advert, or receiving her first card, it was the wreath-making workshop in early December that always made her start to feel properly Christmassy.

Greenery and berries and chicken wire and bows were neatly gathered in vases and piles on each table, and Millie had the coffee maker brewing and pastries from the local bakery on hand for everyone. This year, she had more people signed up than ever, and the tables with supplies reached from the back room into the shop itself to accommodate everybody.

And that was before the extra walk-in arrived...just before she was due to open the doors to her paid-up participants.

The shadow at the door grabbed her attention—although until she got closer she assumed it was someone early for the workshop. When she saw who it really was, she yanked the door open and beckoned him inside, out of the cold.

'Giles! I wasn't expecting you today, was I?' She had to admit, with everything that was going on with wedding prep and the business, she wasn't *quite* as on top of her calendar the way she'd like to be.

He gave her a forgiving smile. 'I was just passing. Tabby asked me to drop these off for you.'

She took the large padded envelope from his hand and opened it. 'You've been up at Howard Hall?'

'I was up that way, sorting some things at my family estate. I dropped by to give her a rundown on the wedding stuff, since she wouldn't stop texting me—apparently you've stopped replying?' Giles sniffed. 'Is that coffee?'

'Mmm, help yourself.' She motioned towards the coffee machine. 'I was *going* to reply, but I've just been so busy getting ready for today's wreath-making workshop. Want to join in?'

It was an impulse to ask him—a foolish one, really. But she'd had one last-minute cancellation-due-to-illness email that morning so there was space…just about. And now he was here she was sort of loath to let him just go again, before they'd even talked or anything.

When had she got so dependent on having him around? She wasn't sure, but she had to admit that it had happened. And, as much as she knew it was a terrible idea with Charlie away, it felt good to have him on her side.

And *by* her side, too.

'Wreath-making?' Giles frowned a little, but then shrugged and said, 'Sure.'

'Great.'

They did a little awkward dance—him making and then drinking coffee, while she finished setting up for the workshop—until the other participants arrived. After that she was too busy running the show—tweaking chicken wire, arranging berries and advising people on leaf placement—to worry too much about Giles. She was barely even surprised, when she stopped by his station, to see that he'd turned out a more than serviceable wreath. He seemed to be competent at almost everything he turned his hand to.

It was more of a turn-on than she cared to admit.

Everything Giles Fairfax did these days seemed to turn her on, though. She could hardly believe she'd come to this, given the animosity between them as teens, but there it was. She *wanted* him—every single inch of him—pressed up against her. As often as possible…

Wait. What was she meant to be doing? Right, wreath workshop.

Focus, Myles.

'Okay, so if you take one of the stems with berries on…'

Even when it was over, and her happy students were leaving with their wreaths, chatting and possibly heading over to the pub, by the sound of things, Giles didn't leave. Instead, he stayed to help her clear up, sweeping up clippings and bits of ribbon efficiently.

Millie found herself watching him rather than doing her own chores, mesmerised by the way the muscles in his forearms flexed as he worked. How his hair flopped over his forehead and he flipped it out of the way. The way he carefully moved his own wreath to clear underneath it. How he'd taken the workshop utterly seriously, despite the fact she was almost certain it wasn't how he'd choose to spend his day off.

But he'd come, and he'd stayed anyway. Why?

Why was he doing all this? Could it really be just because of his promise to Charlie?

She tried to convince herself that it was. That he was just a really, really good friend. That she was imagining the way she caught him watching her sometimes. Those times she only caught him because she was already watching him.

And again and again that last conversation with Charlie kept returning to haunt her. His assurances that if she needed to let loose a little before the wedding he was fine with that.

She wasn't sure she was, though.

But maybe she was just being prudish about this. Maybe if she got this crush out of her system somehow, she'd be able to settle down to the future she'd chosen with Charlie. Passion wasn't love, after all—and it certainly wasn't for ever. She *knew* that.

But passion was definitely what she wanted with Giles. She could barely think about anything else these days. It would scare her, if it were anyone else. But she knew she could trust Giles. And it wasn't as if he could break her heart if everything was on her terms—she'd be the one walking away to marry another man.

She didn't want to go into marriage with any regrets. And Giles had already told her flat that he had no interest in the kind of future she wanted, so anything between them could only be casual.

A pre-wedding fling.

Would that be so terrible?

Of course it would mean admitting the truth to Giles. Telling him everything. She wasn't sure *that* was what Charlie had had in mind when he'd given her the out for 'a fling before the ring'.

But if it was the only way to shake these feelings—this uncertain *wanting* that kept her awake at night, that had her thinking more about Giles's arms around her than her wedding planning… Charlie was her best friend. He'd understand.

Wouldn't he?

Would Giles, though? Would he despise her for marrying without love in the traditional, romantic sense, anyway? She knew how he felt about marriage. Wasn't she just proving him right? That it was all transactional, anyway?

Would he put those feelings aside if it meant they could give in to the pressure building between them?

She supposed there was only one way to find out.

* * *

'I think we're done.'

Giles leant the broom against the wall and turned to find Millie by the door, staring at him. When he caught her, she turned away and locked the door.

What was happening here?

'Don't I need to leave through that?' He spoke lightly, hoping to cover his uncertainty.

'Later.'

Millie's voice didn't even sound like hers. It was rougher, and filled with a sort of fearful excitement he didn't know what to make of.

'I need to talk to you about something first. Want a cup of tea before you go?'

Okay, tea. That was good. If something was really wrong she'd be offering him alcohol. But he couldn't shake the feeling that something wasn't quite right, either. That something was about to change, dramatically, and all he could do was sit back and let it happen.

'Sure.'

He handed her the broom and watched as she put it away in a cupboard, then followed her up the stairs to her little flat—a place that was becoming far more familiar to him than it probably should.

Soon, mugs in hand, they were both perched on opposite sides of her coffee table and Giles was waiting for her to start. Millie, meanwhile, was chewing so violently on her lower lip that he was afraid she might do permanent damage.

'So?' he asked. 'What did you want to talk to me about? Is it to do with the wedding?'

'In a way,' Millie replied. 'I mean, yes. Completely, in some ways. And in others…' She looked down at her mug.

Well, that cleared everything right up. He was going to

have to get a Millie translator in here at this rate. Her babbling was endearing, but not exactly informative.

'You realise you're not making a lot of sense here?' he said, gently.

She looked down again. 'I know. I just… This is kind of hard to say. So…be patient with me?'

'Of course.' He sat back, his mind whirring with possibilities. 'Take your time.'

He wasn't even sure what he hoped she'd say. If he wanted this to be about…well, about them, or not. Confirmation that he wasn't the only one feeling this way would be nice, but on the other hand it would only open up a whole different box of problems.

She loved Charlie. She was marrying Charlie.

And he was never getting married at all.

So what good would it do anyway?

Whatever he was expecting, it wasn't what she started with.

'I saw the doctor a few months ago, and he gave me some…unexpected news.'

Giles's heart clenched, and in that moment he'd have done anything—*anything*—to make sure she was okay. But all he could actually do was reach across the divide between them and take her hand.

'What news?'

'My fertility is declining—fast. And I've always wanted a family. I was an only child, and I want…more. I found out just before Octavia's wedding.'

'Just before you got engaged to Charlie.'

He trusted Millie, and believed she was a good person— possibly the best person he'd met since Charlie. But he couldn't ignore that coincidence of timing.

'Does he know?'

She nodded. 'I told him that night. And he told me that,

with Octavia Mrs Layton Stone now, he couldn't see himself ever finding someone else to marry. Except he needs to, because of the estate and the family name and everything.'

Things were becoming horribly clear—in a way that Giles really wished they wouldn't.

'So you put the moves on him? Convinced him to marry *you* so you can have your family?' He pulled away. 'Did you ever love him at all? Is this the culmination of decades-long unrequited love, or are you just taking advantage of my best friend in his weakest moment?'

She recoiled as if he'd slapped her. 'Is that what you think of me?'

Giles closed his eyes and pressed his hands to them, his mug of tea forgotten on the coffee table. 'No,' he admitted. 'It's not. Not at all. But I just don't understand where this is going.'

'Then stop accusing me of things and start listening,' she said sharply. 'You've always listened before. Don't ruin it now.'

He nodded, and stayed silent.

The story of how Millie and Charlie's engagement had come to be flowed over him, and he knew he'd be processing it for hours, even days to come. But for now, only one part really stood out.

'You lied to me. You *both* lied to me.'

'Not really.'

Millie's face was drawn, tired and strained in a way he'd never seen before—not even when she'd been arguing with Tabby about wedding guest lists.

'We *do* love each other. It might not be the kind of romantic love you read about in books, but it's real and it's ours. We love and care for each other more than anyone else in the world, and we've decided to spend our lives together, to have a family together, and to live in happy, friendly harmony to-gether. What's wrong with that?'

She made it sound reasonable, and he had to admit that they probably had a stronger base to work from than most married couples he'd stood up with in the past few years. Certainly more than any in his own family.

But still…

'What about passion? Attraction, at least? You're going to have to get those babies somehow, you realise?'

He just couldn't imagine someone as vibrantly alive as Millie living without the kind of passion she deserved in her life.

'We know. We've discussed it.'

She sat so primly on her chair that he couldn't help but wonder how, exactly, those discussions had gone.

'And?'

'Once we're married, we will be…intimate. And only with each other. This isn't going to be one of those fake marriages where they both pretend to be in love but actually have other partners on the side. Once we say *I do* we're both all in. He'll be the only man I ever sleep with.'

There was something about the way she said it… Or per-haps it was in the way she met his gaze as she spoke. Or how she leaned a little closer across the table, maybe.

Whatever it was, the room suddenly felt smaller. Warmer. The air was heavy with a tension he couldn't quite under-stand—until he thought back over her words.

'Once we're married… Once we say I do…'

'What about *before* the wedding?'

The words were out before he could fully consider what it meant for him to be saying them. Where they could lead.

Where he even wanted them to lead.

'Charlie has made it clear that until the wedding, if either of us have something we need to…to get out of our systems, say, then we should do that.'

She wasn't meeting his gaze any longer. She was staring down at her hands to avoid looking at him.

And suddenly, finally, Giles understood why she'd brought him to her flat tonight.

He just wasn't quite sure yet what he was going to do about it.

Millie didn't like the way Giles was looking at her. As if something had changed in her appearance and he was trying to figure out what. Or as if he wasn't sure she was the person he'd thought she was.

He was re-evaluating everything he knew about her—she could tell. And she didn't know how he would feel once he'd finished.

There was nothing she could do about it. She'd put her cards on the table, and now she had to wait. She'd been honest—more honest than she was really comfortable with. Now she had to wait and see if he'd be honest in return.

She figured he had three options.

One, he'd thank her for telling him, pretend it had no personal impact on him, finish his tea and leave.

Two, he'd say he understood, and admit to the draw between them, but then remind her that Charlie was his best friend and they'd be seeing each other in that capacity for the rest of their lives once she and Charlie were married, and he didn't want to complicate that for them all.

Three… Well, three was the one she was placing all her hopes on.

If she were honest, she expected him to go for Two, though. He'd always been straight with her, and she couldn't imagine he'd try to pretend that her feelings were all one-sided.

Unless they really were and she'd read this all wrong…

Oh, God, *why* wasn't he talking yet? She'd had time to reason all this out in her brain and he hadn't even said a word yet!

Finally, *finally* his mouth opened. Then closed again. Then he spoke.

'I… I'm not sure what to say to that, if I'm honest. In some ways it explains a lot. I mean, the way you two went from friends to fiancés overnight… I kind of worried about that a bit. And I'm glad I *do* know. But in other ways…it doesn't really change anything at all.'

'Doesn't change anything?' Millie felt her hopes sinking as she repeated his words.

'Because Charlie is my best friend. My one and only constant for the last God knows how many years. And I can't… Millie, I can't do anything to ruin that. No matter how tempting it might be.'

His gaze met hers and her breath caught in her chest. 'But it is…tempting?'

Giles looked away and swore quietly. When he looked up at her again Millie saw an intensity in his eyes she'd never seen in him before. Heat flooded across her body at having that focus all on her.

'Millie, if you think for a moment that I haven't spent every day since the wedding holding back from telling you how much I want you…all the bloody time…then you are sorely mistaken.'

Oh, God. It wasn't just her. It really was both of them. She hadn't imagined the electricity between them. Or the heat that was flooding her body at his words.

Now the only question was what they were going to do about it.

Giles thought he'd made up his mind. But Millie didn't think he'd thought through all the possibilities just yet.

'What if it didn't have to ruin anything?'

* * *

Millie's voice was breathy and low, and Giles's blood pounded at the sound of it. At the possibility in it. At what it might mean for both of them.

He should leave.

He should have left already.

But wild horses couldn't have dragged him from this place right now.

He swallowed. 'What are you suggesting?'

Millie leaned closer over the coffee table and Giles was torn between pulling away, and saving his sanity, and moving in closer and giving himself everything he wanted.

'I want my future with Charlie. I want a secure and stable and loving family with lots of kids. I could take or leave the big house and the family line, but I can't deny that the security of the money is good. But that's not why I'm doing this. I'm marrying him for the family it will give me—and to give him what he needs to live his life the way he wants, too. He's my best friend and we're going to be happy together.'

'Okay. But none of that is explaining how something between you and me wouldn't ruin it,' Giles admitted.

'Because you *don't* want any of those things,' Millie pointed out. 'Nothing between us could ever become serious enough to endanger the plans Charlie and I have made. We couldn't fall in love and call off the wedding because that goes against everything you want, and I could never love someone who doesn't want the same things as me.'

'Okay, so what are you suggesting?'

Giles's head was spinning with all the contradictions. She didn't love Charlie, but she loved the idea of marrying him. She *desired* Giles, it seemed, but not the life *he* wanted. So what *did* she want, really?

'A pre-wedding fling,' she said bluntly. 'No expectations, no *feelings*, even. Just…scratching an itch.'

'No, really, stop…you're embarrassing me with your flattery,' he replied in a monotone.

Millie rolled her eyes. 'You know what I mean. You don't love me. You don't *want* to love me. And nothing that happens between us is going to change your feelings about marriage, is it?'

'No.'

That much, at least, he was sure about. Everything else seemed to be shifting sands.

'And I want my future with Charlie too much to risk it by engaging in anything more than a fling with you,' she said simply. 'But… I can't ignore this feeling between us, either. I've tried—trust me, I've tried.'

'So have I,' he admitted.

'I know that passion…chemistry…doesn't equal love or for ever. It's just sex. It's far safer than love. So I figure the best thing to do is to get it out of our systems before the wedding,' Millie explained. 'I mean, it would only be worse if we kept on feeling this way *after* I was married, wouldn't it?'

'That's true.'

He was certain there was a flaw in her logic somewhere, but he was struggling to see it right now. Was that because she was right or just because he was hypnotised by her eyes.

'I haven't… Since I broke up with my last boyfriend—and that was a while ago—I haven't been with anyone. I might even have forgotten how, it's been so long. And it would be… useful to have a reminder before I get married.'

'So this is purely practical?'

He raised an eyebrow at her and she blushed, shaking her head a little.

'No. It's not. I just… I want this. I want to settle down and have the life I've planned with Charlie. But I also want *you*. I want to enjoy these last weeks before the wedding, and I want to see where this connection leads. Don't you?'

Her eyes shone with determination as she met his gaze, and he could see the fire behind them. The passion.

And, God, he wanted to taste it. Taste her.

Giles didn't have it in him to deny it any longer.

So, instead of answering, he leant forward and captured her lips with his own.

CHAPTER TEN

MILLIE WOKE UP ALONE.

To be fair, she'd gone to bed alone, too. After that kiss she'd had expectations—high ones, given the way that just the press of Giles's lips against hers had made her entire body tingle. She'd thought—hoped—that they'd moved past the awkward conversation part now that she'd bared her soul and exposed her biggest secret, and could move on to the much more fun, physical part.

But it had turned out that Giles had other ideas about what happened next.

He'd pulled away and rested his forehead against hers, his breath coming as fast as her own. 'As much as I want to take this further, I also think we need to be careful.'

'And what does being "careful" mean?' she'd asked, hoping it was a question of contraception rather than anything more serious.

She'd needed him. Now she'd finally admitted how much, she *really* hadn't wanted to wait.

But she'd been disappointed.

'It means we take tonight to be sure,' he'd replied. 'This has moved fast—for me, at least. An hour ago I thought you were madly, passionately in love with Charlie, remember? This whole…arrangement is a lot to digest. So we take tonight to make sure we're both certain about this. And in the morning we can lay some ground rules, if we're still both sure.'

It had been so much like the night she and Charlie had first had the idea of getting married… She couldn't exactly say no—not when she knew he was right.

So she'd given him blankets and pillows for the sofa and retreated to her own bed, frustrated and confused and wondering what the morning would bring.

And now it was here.

They were *supposed* to be visiting the Christmas markets in the nearby town, to search for wedding favours that would satisfy both her *and* Tabby's tastes, but Millie had a feeling that they weren't going to be top priority for the day.

That went to the conversation they really, really needed to have.

She slipped out of bed and into the bathroom next door, so she could at least clean her teeth and sort her hair before facing him. What if he'd come to his senses and decided the whole thing was crazy?

She *knew* it was crazy. But *she* was going crazy not having him, so it still seemed like the lesser of two evils. This was what passion did to a person—and why she wasn't going to base her whole future on it. But the next few weeks? That… that she wanted. With Giles.

Huh. She'd slept on it, like he'd asked, and she still wanted this. This last chance to cut loose—with him—before marriage.

But he'd also wanted her to think about rules, so she considered that as she brushed her teeth, and by the time she emerged into the lounge she had a pretty good idea of what she needed from this arrangement.

She found Giles sitting warily on her sofa, wearing boxers and a thin T-shirt, two cups of tea in front of him.

'I heard you get up,' he said, by way of explanation.

From the way he was watching her—as if he expected her to dart away and run off down the stairs at any moment—he thought she had changed her mind. Or he had. She guessed it was time to find out which.

'I've been thinking,' she said. 'Like you told me to.'

'And you've changed your mind?'

She shook her head. 'I've figured out how this needs to work, to make sure it doesn't ruin anything.'

He pushed her tea towards her as she sat town. 'Tell me. Because I've been thinking all night and…'

He did look tired. Like, bone-tired and worn out.

'And?'

'And I'm scared, Millie. I want this—want *you*—badly. I can admit that. But this is exactly why I stay away from serious relationships. I can't… My life, my plans, will only work if I'm only worrying about myself. I can't add another person into the mix.'

'You don't need to,' she reassured him. 'I am absolutely not your problem, okay? Look, here's what I was thinking. We need ground rules—you were right about that—and these are mine. This is a last-ditch fling for me—nothing more. It is all over when Charlie gets home…before we head up for the wedding. No one gets attached and we stay friends afterwards—that one really matters, because against all my best efforts I actually *like* you now you're not an idiot teenage boy any more, and I don't want to lose you as a friend.'

He looked slightly poleaxed at that, but smiled a little shyly and said, 'Okay…'

'This is the big one, though,' she went on. 'Nobody knows. I don't want anyone thinking that my marriage to Charlie isn't true love in the traditional way—especially not his parents or my mother or Tabby. So we keep this secret. Can you do that?'

Giles reached across the table and took her hand in his, keeping his gaze fixed on her own. Millie couldn't help but recognise how different this felt from her similar conversation with Charlie just a couple of months ago.

With Charlie she'd felt safe and secure, even if she'd been a little nervous, because he was her best friend and she knew he'd never hurt her. She'd looked into his eyes and felt comforted and comfortable, too.

With Giles… She met his gaze and her whole body felt on edge, sparking as if electricity was racing through her blood. This wasn't comfortable—it was terrifying.

But exciting, too.

'I can do that,' Giles said, his voice low. 'And your rules are my rules, too. Everything I decided during the night.'

'Then it seems like we're in sync on this.'

On more than this, she was willing to bet, if only he'd kiss her again.

'We are,' he said.

She wasn't sure which of them moved first, but suddenly there was no coffee table between them—no distance at all, in fact—and she was in his arms, kissing him again, and it felt even better than it had the night before.

Eventually, they pulled apart again.

'So, we have a deal, then?' she asked breathlessly.

'An arrangement,' Giles countered. 'Just until Charlie comes home.'

'Exactly. And in that case… I think the Christmas markets can wait, don't you?'

Even getting to the bedroom seemed like an insurmountable challenge. But taking Millie for the first time on her sofa, with one or other of them banging into the coffee table, wasn't a great plan. Giles decided that compromise was the way forward, stripping her pyjama top slowly from her as she lay back on the sofa, and taking his time savouring every inch he uncovered one by one.

She squirmed a little under him as he kissed his way up her ribcage. 'Tickles?'

'Mmm.' Millie looked down at him with hooded eyes. 'But in a good way. Don't stop.'

'I really wasn't planning to.' His next kiss brushed the underside of her breast, and this time she shuddered rather than squirmed. 'Definitely not now…'

Another inch or so and he'd uncovered the rosy tips of her nipples—first the right, then the left—taking them each in his mouth in turn, delighting in the way she arched up to meet him, and how they hardened even more under his tongue.

This—this was what he needed. What he'd been wanting since Millie Myles had come back into his life again and they'd danced at the wedding. The chance to get to know her—completely. The last two months of wedding planning had introduced him to her mind, her personality, in a way years of competing over Charlie's friendship never had. And now, finally, he had the chance to get to know her body, too. He didn't intend to waste a moment of it.

'Giles…'

The sound of his name on her lips, the desperate way her hips canted up to meet his—all conspired to force him into action.

But he made himself take his time.

He did finish taking off her pyjamas, though, stripping the top from her shoulders before sliding the pyjama pants down her shapely legs. He had to pause, to take a moment to regain control as all that bare flesh came into view, though. Then he pulled off his own T-shirt and got to work.

This time he started lower, parting her thighs and kneeling between them, kissing his way up to her core, desperate to know, to taste, to feel this most secret part of her. She tensed under him for just a moment and he stopped, waiting for her to relax again or ask him to stop.

When she did neither, he risked a glance up and found her watching him. 'Do you want this?' he asked.

Her throat bobbed as she swallowed, then finally she said, 'More than I can remember wanting anything, right now.'

And that was all the answer he needed.

Millie felt every muscle in her body clench as Giles's tongue swept over her, and she reached down to tangle her fingers in his hair—not to hold him there, but to be part of what he was doing. To show him how *much* she was part of this, too.

It wasn't something he was doing *to* her.

It was something they were doing together.

Together, they'd fallen into this. And now Millie knew she wouldn't be able to bear being apart from him again until they had to say goodbye for good.

She was going to suck every single moment of pleasure, of togetherness, from this fling before she started her real life again.

Then Giles shifted slightly, changed the angle of his tongue on her body, and every rational thought flew from her brain. She didn't have thoughts any longer, only feelings. Senses… Senses that felt as if they were about to spark and catch fire if she couldn't—

Her orgasm burst through her in waves of electric beauty, and she swore she actually saw coloured lights behind her eyes.

It had *definitely* never been likc that with any of her exes.

It'll probably never be like that with Charlie, either.

The thought brought her down faster than she'd have liked. She pushed it away. That was why she was going to make the most of this time now. And who knew? If she learned enough about what made her explode like that, maybe she'd be able to teach her new husband one day, even if the thought of that conversation made her squirm.

Funny how she'd always thought she and Charlie could talk about anything. But *this?* She wasn't sure.

Giles rested his cheek against her stomach and gazed up at her. 'Did I lose you?'

'No. God, no. I just…needed a minute.' She reached down to trace a finger along his shoulder. 'And now I've had it… do you want to try this in an actual bed?'

'Sounds good to me.'

In an instant he was on his feet, yanking her up from the sofa and pulling her close against him. He still wore his boxers, but nothing else, and she could feel him hard and hot and *big* through the fabric.

'God, I want you,' she breathed, her brain not bothering to filter the words before they reached her mouth.

She'd expected a smug smirk in response, but instead Giles looked serious, and dipped his head to press a hard, fast kiss to her lips.

'Not half as much as I want you right now. Watching you fall apart like that… Millie…'

She swallowed. 'Bedroom. Now.'

She didn't want to talk. They'd done talking…done getting to know each other.

All she wanted to do now was feel. And make the most of having this man in her bed and her arms before she had to say goodbye.

Eventually, they made it out to the Christmas markets.

The town they'd chosen—less than an hour's drive from Millie's little village—clearly made a big deal about Christmas, and it was probably a good boost to the economy, too, since the place was buzzing even in the fading late-afternoon sunlight.

Bright white lights were strung across narrow cobbled streets, with cosy-looking shops decorated for the season peeking out from under ancient roofs and between wooden beams. In the market square, stalls that looked like miniature log cabins had been set up in a horseshoe shape, selling everything from glass ornaments and hand-carved nutcrackers to Santa hats and sleigh bells.

The open end of the horseshoe led to the local pub, which seemed to be doing a roaring trade in spiced cider, mulled wine and cones of chips eaten straight from the paper with plenty of salt and vinegar. Just the smell was making Giles's mouth water.

They hadn't exactly stopped to eat much that morning. Or at lunchtime. They'd had other priorities. And Giles was not regretting those choices.

Holding Millie in his arms, kissing her, feeling her skin against his own, his body claiming hers... He'd choose that over and over again if he could. Especially knowing that their time alone together was limited, and growing shorter all the time. In just a few short weeks the wedding would be upon them and they'd go back to being friends, so for now he'd take advantage of every moment they had.

'Do you know anyone in this town?' he asked softly.

'Nope,' Millie replied. 'Not a soul.'

'In that case...' He took her gloved hand in his own, holding it tightly as they perused the stalls.

Holding hands with a woman wasn't something he usually craved, or even liked, but it was different with Millie. Probably because he knew this was his only chance.

Together they studied the festive fare on offer, considering its suitability as table presents or favours for the wedding guests. Giles suspected they were cutting it rather fine on finding the right thing, but since Millie and Tabby had been disagreeing on the matter almost since the engagement had been announced, he was keen to help Millie find something she liked, so she didn't have to give in to Tabby and go with her preferred supplier of...whatever the hell it was Charlie's sister wanted on the tables. Giles had to admit he'd given up on listening to the particulars a few weeks before.

'What do you think of these?' Millie asked, as they paused at one of the log cabin stalls. 'I think they could work.'

Giles studied the hand-carved decorations. Despite being made from wood, they were delicate as the snowflakes they depicted, each tied on a dark red or green ribbon, and looking for all the world as if they might fall from the leaden sky above.

'I think they're perfect,' he agreed. 'Now let's see if they have enough of the things…'

Luckily they did—just. Millie bought up more or less the whole stock—making the artist's day in the process—and sent a photo to Tabby, presenting the whole thing as a *fait accompli*. Hopefully Charlie's sister would like them as much as Millie and Giles did, but really, it wasn't *actually* her wedding anyway.

Giles stopped halfway through packing the carefully wrapped snowflakes into a bag.

Of course it wasn't *his* wedding, either.

For a moment there he'd forgotten. He'd got so caught up in the wedding planning, in helping and supporting Millie, that he'd actually *forgotten* he wasn't the groom here—only the best man.

He finished packing the bag and stepped away, clutching it safely, leaving Millie to finish chatting with the artist. He needed space and air. He needed to breathe—and to think.

Because it wasn't just the wedding planning, was it? It was being with Millie. Not just in the way they had been that morning—naked and entwined. But spending time with her. Talking and laughing with her. Listening to her points of view and having her listen to his.

He'd never had a friendship or a relationship like this before. If this was how things were for her and Charlie, no wonder his best friend had jumped at the chance to marry Millie. If marriage could be like this…

But it couldn't. Not for him.

'You okay with those?' Millie appeared beside him, pink-cheeked and smiling, gesturing towards the bag of snow-flakes. 'I can take them.'

He clutched the bag closer and shook his head. 'Come on. If we're done shopping, let's go and get some of those chips and some spiced cider.'

'I am never going to disagree with that plan,' Millie said cheerfully.

She bounded off in the direction of the pub and Giles followed more slowly, still thinking.

He'd never told Millie quite why he was so opposed to the idea of marriage. But for the first time he wanted to.

If he could only figure out how.

CHAPTER ELEVEN

MILLIE WASN'T SURE what had changed while they were at the Christmas markets, but something definitely had. Either Giles secretly really hated the wedding favours they'd chosen, or he was having second thoughts about their arrangement.

He'd been subdued over chips and spiced cider, but the atmosphere in the pub had made up for that—and really, they'd hardly been able to hear each other talk anyway, so she hadn't thought much of it.

But he'd been silent for almost all of the journey home, and when she'd mentioned that they couldn't be too far from his own family home a line had settled between his eyebrows that hadn't gone away for the rest of the drive.

Was *that* it? Something to do with his parents or his sister distracting him? She'd like to think so, but she wasn't convinced. He hadn't even *looked* at her on the drive back to her flat above the shop.

He'd followed her up the stairs, though—that was something. She'd half expected him to say goodbye at the door and drive back to London, even though it was getting late.

By the time she'd put her key in the door she'd convinced herself that he'd decided the whole fling idea was a mistake and she'd never get to kiss him again. Let alone feel him moving inside her, his lips over every inch of her body…which, after everything she'd experienced that morning, would be a crying shame.

And, actually, she wasn't going to let him make that decision without talking to her about it. They'd *both* set the rules they were playing by. They *both* got to decide when they changed.

The door opened and she stepped inside, turning around immediately to confront him. But before she was able to get a word out he'd spun her around, backing her up against the closing door, his mouth on hers.

The warmth of her anger rapidly transformed into a passionate heat, flooding her senses and making her skin tingle. She waited for him to say something—maybe about how he'd been imagining this all the way home, and that was why he'd seemed so focussed—but he didn't. He didn't say anything at all.

His mouth never left hers as his hands roamed up under the wool of her knitted dress, her coat falling from her shoulders as he pushed the dress up and over her head, breaking their kiss just long enough to leave her in bra and tights.

'God, you're gorgeous,' he murmured, before kissing her again.

Was this really what he'd been thinking about on the drive home? She was sure she hadn't been imagining his bad mood...

'Giles... Giles!' she said against his mouth, and he pulled back, resting his forehead against hers.

'Do you want me to stop?'

His voice was low, full of wanting, and Millie's body knew her answer even before her mind did.

'God, no.'

'Then less talking, more touching.'

He kissed her again, his fingers already unclasping her bra behind her back.

Maybe they could talk later. Right now, she had far more important things to concentrate on.

She slid her fingers under his own clothes, and lost herself in the feel of his skin instead.

* * *

Later—quite a lot later—Millie rested her head on his chest, glad they'd finally made it to her bed at last, and asked, 'So... what was all that about?'

He looked down at her with an eyebrow raised. 'I think I was fairly clear on that matter at the time. I wanted you. Badly. And it seemed you rather returned the feeling...?'

'Oh, I definitely did,' she confirmed, her body still happily tingling. 'It was just...sudden. In the car, I thought there was something wrong—I even thought you might be about to call the whole thing off. Then, when we got back—'

Giles's arm tightened around her. 'Quite the opposite. I'm just...very aware of how little time we have together. And I want to make the most of it.'

'Me too.'

She was excited for her new life with Charlie—of course she was. But she couldn't deny that saying goodbye to this... with Giles...was going to be hard. Even if it *was* only a fling. Still, they had a few weeks. Probably the chemistry would have worn off by then, and Giles would have grown bored and be ready to leave anyway.

'So...is that what you were frowning about in the car?'

Giles sighed. Then, unexpectedly, he released her from his arms and sat up against the headboard. Confused, she followed suit, and he pulled her back in against his shoulder, drawing the duvet up over them both for warmth.

'I was thinking about my parents,' he admitted. 'And my sister. And...well, marriage.'

That was *not* what Millie had been expecting.

'Marriage?' The word came out a little squeaky.

'You asked me once, do you remember? Why I'm so against the idea of marriage?'

'Yeah, I remember.'

She hadn't ever really expected him to answer, though.

She'd assumed it was just the usual reasons. Not wanting to be tied down, loving freedom more than security, being scared of commitment. Or always wanting the next high—the excitement and passion that came with a new relationship without having to worry about what happened when it became stale and old because he'd already have moved on. Heaven knew she'd met enough men suffering from the same affliction—Tom being a case in point.

'That's what I was thinking of in the car. How as much as I'm enjoying being with you, and how under other circumstances this could be something more than it is, it can't. Because of them.'

This wasn't what Millie had expected at all. She could hear the pain in his voice as he spoke, the frustration. And for almost the first time she let herself wonder about the what ifs.

What if Giles *didn't* hate the idea of marriage and children?

What if she didn't have to get married *now* if she wanted a baby?

What if Charlie didn't need her to marry him, too?

But that way madness lay. Because the world was the way the world was, and they could only live in it, not change it. Not fundamentals like that.

So instead she listened.

'Tell me,' she said, shifting against his shoulder so she could watch his face as he spoke.

'My parents...theirs was a marriage of...inconvenience, I guess. Obviously I wasn't around then, but from the stories I've heard my dad fell for my mum pretty hard, but it seems the attraction was mostly physical. His parents *definitely* didn't approve, because she wasn't from their usual society set. You know how that goes.'

Millie did know. The fact that she'd been so welcomed by Charlie's family probably had a lot more to do with being the least awful option compared to Octavia than any actual pleasure in her humble upbringing. The fact that she'd at least grown up *at* Howard Hall, more or less, meant that she understood how things there worked, which she supposed was a bonus.

'My mum got pregnant, and back then and there that meant they had to get married. She was thrilled—and so was her family. I mean, she'd taken a step up in life. But they didn't know each other very well—not as well as you need to in order to get married, anyway. They had my sister and...well, it soon became clear that my mother loved the house and the title and the money more than she loved my father. And he... I don't think he loved anything at all—except maybe showing off.'

'Showing off?' Millie asked.

Giles shrugged the shoulder she wasn't leaning on. 'Best as I can figure, anyway. He spends money like it's nothing, and always on flashy things—things that say *I have a lot of money* to anyone watching. You know how they always say that the richest people *don't* flaunt their wealth? Well, by the time my dad inherited the title the estate was already in trouble. He's been pretending to be the rich lord of the manor his ancestors were ever since.'

'I bet your mum was pretty angry when she figured that out,' Millie guessed.

'I imagine she was, too,' Giles agreed. 'But they've never mentioned it. They like to keep up appearances...pretend that all is normal.'

'That sounds...unhelpful.'

'It is.' Giles sighed. 'Very.'

'So...how do they manage, then? Do they rent out the house for events, like Charlie's family?'

The way Charlie told it, his family had been on the verge of ruin—which she suspected meant a very different thing to that sphere of society than to most people—or at least of having to sell off a lot of land or property until his parents found a way to turn the family legacy into a business opportunity.

'Oh, they would never.' Giles sounded bitter about that. 'Trust me, I've tried to persuade them. But for them, they can't understand the point of being titled if it doesn't entitle them to exactly the kind of life they want. And that doesn't involve working. Instead, my father invests money he doesn't have in schemes that are never going to work, and then expects me to pick up the bill when it all inevitably ends in disaster. Or when the roof starts caving in. Or any other time they're a little short, to be honest.'

'And do you? Pay, I mean?' Millie asked.

'I used to.'

Giles shifted his body further down the headboard, and turned them so they were facing each other, heads on pillows. It felt intimate, secret, in a way that went further than any of the passion they had shared.

'When I first started working I had dreams of using my salary to rebuild my family's fortunes. To save the legacy that looked so much in danger.'

'What changed?'

'It's more what *didn't* change,' Giles replied. 'My parents. They took the money happily enough, but they still wouldn't let me do anything new with the house or the land. They weren't willing to *do* anything except complain about the state of the house and ask for more money. And eventually...'

'You cut them off?'

'Yes.' Guilt hovered behind his eyes as he studied her face, obviously waiting for her reaction.

'I don't blame you,' she said easily. 'Helping people is one thing. But you don't have to mortgage your own life for them.'

Even in the darkness of the bedroom she saw the surprise on his face before he kissed her. And she wondered how many times he'd been told he was selfish or ungrateful for making that choice. How much guilt he'd been made to feel.

She wished it was as simple as kissing that away.

Giles hadn't expected Millie to react the same way his parents and even his sister had to his decision to cut them off, but he hadn't dared to hope for such easy acceptance, either.

'They made you feel guilty about that, didn't they?' she asked, pulling away from the kiss.

'Yeah,' he admitted. 'They told me I was betraying the family name, our ancestors, the people who relied on our family and estate for work...everyone.'

And even though he *knew* that wasn't true—aside from anything else, he *did* still support a lot of the village and projects around the estate to provide employment for locals and such—it *felt* true.

'I'm sorry.' Millie ran a hand up his arm, warm comfort pouring out of her the way it always did. 'I still don't understand what any of this has to do with *you* getting married, though.'

He tried to find the words to explain.

'My parents' marriage was miserable—is *still* miserable and always will be. But my mum won't leave because the cachet of being Lady Fairfax is too great...even if the financial and everyday reality is so awful. Growing up watching them, I knew I could never put myself in a position like that. And then my sister Rebekah got married...'

He'd only been a teenager at the time, but he still remembered standing in the church, hoping against hope that someone would speak out when the vicar prompted anyone who knew of reasons why they shouldn't marry to do so.

Nobody had.

'That was even worse, somehow. She'd grown up in the same house I did—seen the same consequences I had every day—and yet she'd still… Her husband is not a good man. But he blinded her with charm and money and she believed herself passionately in love with him. Once they were married, he started to show his real character.'

'Why does she stay?' Millie asked.

Giles sighed. 'They have two kids—you helped me buy presents for them, remember? They're his heirs and she won't risk losing them. But it's not just that. She's told me flat that she's not willing to give up the lifestyle that her marriage affords her.'

And *that* was the part Giles didn't understand.

When he'd been at school, he'd always been conscious of how precarious his own financial situation was compared to the other boys. Of what had been sold from the family estate to keep up appearances and send him there. He'd asked, once, if he couldn't go to the state school in the nearest town instead—and been so roundly rebuffed that he'd never asked again.

He hadn't understood then and he didn't now. Appearances didn't matter more than *reality*. Not to him, anyhow.

Millie snuggled a little closer and he felt her warmth against his bare skin. *This* was real. It might not be all it could be, and it certainly wasn't for ever, but right now he and Millie were real.

Even if her marriage wouldn't be.

Evidently her thoughts were running on similar lines, because she asked, 'Do you think I'm doing the same thing with Charlie?'

'Not entirely,' he said slowly. 'You genuinely do love and know each other, and your motives are less mercenary.'

'But apart from that…' She trailed off, and neither of them finished the sentence.

Because the truth was, yes. He did think it was the same thing, even with those caveats.

'So that's your parents and your sister,' Millie said, bringing the conversation back. 'What about you? Is it just their bad examples putting you off? Because I could counter that with plenty of better ones. My parents, for example.'

Giles shut his eyes. 'It's not just them. I mean…a lot of it is. I don't want to carry on the family tradition of being miserable in marriage just for the look of the thing. And if I married and had kids now, I'd owe it to *them* to save the house, the estate. To give my parents all the money they ask for. And that…'

It wasn't selfishness or greed that kept him from paying them any more. It was the feeling that to do so would be agreeing with them—that the appearance mattered more than the truth, that they deserved to sit around and have others pay their way just by virtue of birth or marriage.

Maybe when they were gone and he could sell the estate, or make it profitable somehow, he would think again. But right now…

'You can't do that,' Millie said softly, and he knew that somehow she understood. 'Not even for true love.'

Her words caught him in the heart. And, although he hadn't meant to, he found himself telling her the *other* reason he would never marry.

'I thought once that maybe I could,' he admitted. 'There was a woman… Sienna. Back when I'd just left university, and before I started making my own money. I loved her, and I thought she loved me, and I was close to choosing a ring when I overheard her in conversation with her sister and realised that I was just a means to an end for her. That she'd picked me to "fall in love with" because I met her criteria.'

Millie winced. 'Ouch. What did you do?'

'I told her about my family's financial troubles and watched her walk away.'

It had hurt at the time. It still did a little. But the lesson it had taught him was far more valuable to him than any relationship could be.

'So, marriage really is firmly off the cards for you,' Millie said. 'I can understand that.'

'Maybe one day that will change. But not while my parents are alive, I expect.'

It was a horrible admission to make. But Giles knew there was a worse one in his heart.

He was in love with Millie.

Despite all his best efforts to deny it, Giles at least tried to be honest with himself—to face reality instead of the illusion.

If he could marry anyone in this world it would be Millie. But he couldn't. Not when he couldn't give her everything she wanted—and not when it would destroy his own efforts to rebalance his family's impact on the world.

So instead he held her close, and didn't mention the fact that in just another few weeks she would be marrying someone else.

CHAPTER TWELVE

IT WAS TIME.

The past few months had been surreal—first planning her wedding with the best man rather than the groom, and then, for the last few weeks, falling into bed with him. But now the plan would get back on track. Her future was about to start.

Because Charlie had come home.

She and Giles had already agreed that the previous evening was to be their last night together. He hadn't even stayed overnight, for once, leaving just as the church bells chimed midnight.

She'd wrapped herself up in her duvet and walked him to the door of her flat, kissing him one last time—deep and hard—before she watched him walk away, down the stairs and through the shop, listening for the door locking behind him.

Then—and only then—had she cried.

She'd held the tears back during their final bout of love-making, even when Giles had held her closer than ever and whispered words she hadn't quite been able to hear against her skin. But as he'd left her for the last time she'd let them fall in acknowledgment of all they'd lost.

In another world, maybe there would have been a future for them. A future in which she could have let herself fall in love with him and hoped that he could love her, too. That they could be something more than great sex and incredible chemistry. More than the friends they were destined to be from now on.

But here and now she knew it couldn't work. She wanted marriage and a family *now*, while she still could—and that was something Giles absolutely would not and could not give her. It went against who he was in his soul. And since that was what she loved about him—

No. Not loved. Admired. Liked. Respected in a friend.

Definitely not love.

She wouldn't let herself love Giles that way when she knew she still didn't love Charlie as anything more than a friend. She didn't and couldn't want him the way she wanted Giles. Not when she still had to see him as a family friend for the rest of her life.

Millie hadn't slept much last night.

Eventually she'd got up in the pre-dawn darkness and sat with a cup of tea, preparing for the day ahead. In just a few hours Giles would be there to pick her up for the drive up to Norfolk together—as friends. She'd packed already, over the past couple of days, and her suitcase in the corner of her bedroom had been a constant reminder to both of them that their time was nearly up.

She needed the distraction of busyness, of wedding preparations—something to help her focus on the future ahead of her, not on what she'd had to give up. But everything all seemed to be done already.

Her dress had been sent ahead and was waiting for her at her mother's house. Her engagement ring was on her finger. Her hair and make-up would be done there by professionals, so she'd just packed her usual products. With the wedding being on Christmas Eve, they planned to stay and spend the festive season with their families before thinking about a honeymoon, or something similar, so she'd packed her every day clothes as well.

Would they be acceptable to wear when she was Charlie's wife? Well, if not, she was sure Tabby would take her shopping for more appropriate clothes.

What else?

She pulled up the packing checklist on her phone, squinting at the screen as she mentally checked off items.

Toothbrush, yes.

Toothpaste, yes.

Moisturiser, yes.

Tampons, yes.

Hairbrush, yes.

Wait.

Tampons…

She'd packed them, sure. But shouldn't she have needed them *before*?

Closing the checklist, she pulled up her cycle tracking app instead, realising immediately that she hadn't looked at it in a while. About five weeks, in fact.

Because she hadn't needed to track anything.

She was late.

Almost five days late.

She blinked at the screen a few more times.

It could be wedding stress—it almost certainly *was* wedding stress, given her fertility issues and the fact that she and Giles had used protection. But still…

As she sat in the darkness, waiting for the man who was no longer her lover but the father of her hypothetical child to take her to her wedding to another man, Millie felt a tear slip down her cheek. The careful structure of lies and excuses she'd built over the last few weeks was starting to crack at last.

Millie was quiet on the drive up to Howard Hall. Subdued, even. Giles tried not to spend too much time looking at her instead of the road, but it was hard to shake the idea that there was something wrong.

Or maybe he was just projecting.

Saying goodbye to her the night before had been the hardest thing he'd ever done—right up until he'd come back this morning and tried to act normally around her. Friendly, but nothing more. No casual touches…no kiss pressed to the side of her head…no secret smiles that promised more later.

Just friends.

Yeah, *that* had been the hardest thing.

Or it had been until *now*, when he had to watch her in obvious distress, not knowing how much he was allowed to say or do to help her.

Maybe it was just the stress of the impending wedding getting to her. It was entirely possible—probable, even—that her low mood had nothing at all to do with him. She had a lot on her mind, after all.

That was what he told himself all the way along the long, straight road that led them into the depths of Norfolk.

Right up until the point when he saw the first tear roll down Millie's cheek.

He pulled over on the side of the road, killed the engine and unbuckled his seatbelt as he turned to her.

'What is it? What's the matter?'

There was panic in his voice; he could hear it himself, as well as see it reflected in Millie's eyes. But she didn't answer.

'Is it the wedding? Have you changed your mind?' he pressed. 'Because, Millie, I swear to God if you want out I will get you out. I'll turn the car around now, take you home, then come back and sort everything. I'll be the bad guy. Whatever you need, I can do it.'

He wasn't even sure himself what he wanted her answer to be. It wasn't as if he was asking her to choose him over

Charlie. He wasn't an option—he couldn't give her the life she wanted. He wanted her to be happy. That was all.

But whatever answer he expected from her, it wasn't the one he got.

'I'm late.'

He blinked, trying to process the two tiny words. And as they finally swirled into making sense in his head, the world around them seemed to stop cold.

'You're *pregnant*?'

He wished he hadn't sounded quite so incredulous. But they'd been careful. And wasn't the whole point of her getting married to Charlie the fact that she probably *couldn't* get pregnant easily?

'Almost certainly not,' Millie admitted. 'But…there's a chance. And I can't marry Charlie tomorrow if I'm pregnant with your baby, can I? So I have to…check. But the pharmacy in the village opened late today, so I couldn't get a test, and now I'll have to find somewhere to get one when we get to Howard Hall, and I—'

Giles grabbed her hands, holding them to his chest, very aware that it was the first time he'd touched her since they'd said goodbye the night before.

'There's a town at the next junction. I'll pull off there and get you a test. We'll stop at a café or something for some proper breakfast and you can take it. *Then* we'll talk about what happens next—okay?'

She nodded mutely.

Giles knew he should leave it there, but everything inside him told him that he couldn't.

So he pressed a small kiss to her knuckles and murmured, 'It's going to be okay, sweetheart. One way or another. I promise.'

It wasn't a promise that was really his to give. He knew that. But he couldn't stop himself. He wanted to make things right for her—to take responsibility. After all, if she *was* pregnant it was at least half his doing.

Exactly *how* he'd make it right... Well, he didn't know yet. But for the first time since he'd left her flat the night before the tightness that had taken up residence in his chest started to loosen and he could breathe again.

That had to mean something, didn't it?

The test was negative.

That shouldn't have been a surprise—Millie knew how low her chances of conceiving naturally were. And yet...she *was* surprised.

When she'd realised her period was late, she'd sort of assumed it must be a sign from the universe, telling her to take a different path. But apparently the universe wasn't watching. Or it was, and it was rooting for her and Charlie.

Which was what she should be doing, too.

Giles certainly was. She'd never seen a man so relieved by a negative pregnancy test. Well, she didn't actually have any other men or tests to compare it to, but still... He'd been pretty damn relieved.

'Let's go and get you married, then,' he'd said, smiling.

And off they'd driven to Howard Hall, leaving the remains of their breakfast and a generous tip behind on the café table.

And now here they were...sitting in his car in the driveway of Howard Hall, about to head in.

'You're ready?' Giles asked, not looking at her.

'As I'll ever be,' she responded.

Not the most ringing endorsement of a wedding ever, she supposed. But honest, at least.

'Then let's go.'

She risked one last glance at him and thought, just for a second, that she saw a hint of the same pain she felt in his eyes. But it was gone in a flash and there was Charlie—safe, wonderful, loyal Charlie—waiting for her on the stairs.

Millie pushed down any last, lingering thoughts about what might have been and walked towards him, only half hearing Giles behind her, saying that he'd see them at the rehearsal dinner.

'Everything okay?' Charlie murmured as they hugged.

'It's all going to be fine now,' Millie replied.

And she almost believed it.

Up until the point when Charlie left her alone in what was apparently going to be her new rooms and she burst into tears for everything that might have been and never could be.

Giles resisted the urge to go and get blind drunk—but only just.

He also resisted the urges that followed, like dominos in a line. First, to go and find Millie and tell her that he was wrong, that he loved her, that she shouldn't marry Charlie and instead they should just carry on exactly the way they'd been, except she'd get none of the future she wanted, but he'd be happy so that was fine, wasn't it?

The other urge was even less useful—the desire to head down to the gatehouse and bare his soul to Millie's mother. He'd only met the woman once, but he already knew she'd be more sympathetic and helpful than his own parents.

But Millie didn't want her mum to know she wasn't marrying for true love, so that option was out, too.

As a last resort, he went for a walk around the extensive Howard Hall gardens—despite the fact that all the flowers were dead because it was winter—and tried to make sense of the rollercoaster of emotions he'd experienced that day.

First, there had been the pain of leaving Millie, knowing he'd never hold her, have her the way he had again. That had hurt maybe more than he'd expected, but he'd at least expected it.

The pregnancy scare had come out of nowhere.

Could he even call it a scare, when he'd only known about it for an hour before they saw that negative test? Millie must have sat with it for longer, and a pregnancy was a longed-for thing for her. Even if he wasn't the ideal father, given the circumstances, she must have wanted it at least a little bit.

And he...he didn't. He *didn't*. He didn't want to have to explain to his best friend how he'd got his fiancée pregnant. He didn't want to put Millie in that position either. He didn't want to have to row back on all his years of campaigning to use his family estate for the wider good, to end the entitlement of his ancestors instead of just blindly handing it on to the next generation. He didn't want to tie himself into a family he didn't want just because of one mistake. That would surely be the worst thing he could do to Millie and any child—to make them both miserable for ever just because of a failure of contraception. Just like his parents had done.

He would have done it, though, he realised. If she'd been pregnant, and if what she'd wanted was marriage, he would have done it. For her. Because he loved her and he couldn't bear to hurt her any more than he already had done.

But she didn't love him. And even if she grew to love him it was hardly an auspicious start, was it? If they were forced to marry under those circumstances, it would only increase their chances of resentment and bitterness in the future, leading down that inevitable path to a marriage like his parents', or his sister's. One that would poison every beautiful moment he and Millie had ever shared.

He couldn't have taken that. So he was glad she wasn't pregnant.

Except...

He wouldn't admit it to anyone else—hell, he could barely

admit it to himself—but for a brief, fleeting second when he'd heard the words 'I'm late' he'd pictured it. Millie, round with his baby, beaming up at him—not in a wedding dress, but *his* all the same.

And for that brief, fleeting, blink-and-you'd-miss-it second, he'd *wanted* it.

But it wasn't his to want. He'd known that when they'd started their fling, and he couldn't forget it now. Millie had chosen the life she wanted, and it wasn't the life he wanted. And she'd chosen it for Charlie's sake as much as for herself—for a man who was the closest thing he'd ever have to a brother.

He wouldn't ruin that for either of them.

That future wasn't in the cards for him, and that was a *good* thing.

He just had to keep reminding himself of that.

Grimly determined to do just that, Giles stomped back inside Howard Hall to the room he'd been assigned to get ready for the wedding rehearsal and associated dinner that night.

Not for me. Not for me.

Chanting the words in his head seemed to help as he watched Millie, smiling and practically glowing with happiness, beside Charlie at the top of the table. The rehearsal dinner was being held in the formal dining room of Howard Hall—a space too small for tomorrow's wedding breakfast, but still vast enough to host everyone staying at the house the night before the wedding.

Just an hour or so before he'd stood beside Charlie in the tiny family chapel on the estate as they'd rehearsed their lines for the following day. He'd listened carefully and nodded when the vicar had told him at which point he'd hand over the rings, and pushed away the memory of sliding Millie's engagement ring onto her finger. He hadn't been able to stop himself looking away when Charlie had bent his head to place a chaste kiss against Millie's lips, on the vicar's orders.

It was good that there had been a rehearsal, he told himself now, as he pushed a piece of chicken around his plate. He'd needed the practice. To rehearse smiling and looking happy as Charlie and Millie pledged their troth to each other. To manage to make polite conversation with his table neighbours even as he felt his heart was cracking in two.

He'd made it through the rehearsal. He'd make it through the real thing, too.

As they finished up their desserts Millie got to her feet, and Giles braced himself all over again. He'd helped her pick out the dress she was wearing tonight—a deep, emerald-green silk that swept across her curves elegantly. The perfect dress for the future lady of the manor.

She tapped a fork against the side of her glass and the room fell silent. On either side of her, Charlie and her mum were beaming up at her—approving, happy and loving. With a smile, she started to speak—confident and clear, and with no sign at all of the stressful morning she'd had, thanks to him.

He should never have started anything with her. He'd known it was wrong at the time, for all that they apparently had Charlie's blessing. It was wrong to start something he couldn't finish. Millie wasn't the sort of woman he could mess around with.

He should have known he'd end up with a broken heart.

He was only half listening to her speech—thanking her fiancé and family and such—until he heard his own name.

'Finally, I want to say a special thank-you to Charlie's best friend and best man, Giles. When Charlie's work dragged him away, Giles stepped up and helped me organise all sorts of wedding-related things—from invitations to flowers and rings. And I can tell you he can now put together a pretty impressive festive wreath, too!'

That got a laugh, and he didn't even mind that it was at his expense.

'Seriously, though. Thank you, Giles, for everything.'

She looked right at him as she said it, and he raised his glass to toast her in response. When she sat down again, he knew it was really, truly over. His part in her life was over.

She had her dream, and she was marrying the man who could give it to her.

Just like he'd told her to.

CHAPTER THIRTEEN

THE REHEARSAL DINNER was over. All the guests had retired to their rooms, to rest up for the day ahead tomorrow. Millie had told her mum she didn't need her to stay with her, and she'd even managed to send Tabby away, too. She was alone. And she was too nervous to rest.

But she had a feeling that someone else—just one person in the world—would be feeling the same tonight.

Slipping out through the back door of Howard Hall without being seen was tricky—the huge house seemed to be full of people preparing for the wedding—but she managed it... just. With her big coat wrapped over her pyjamas, and her feet in thick socks under someone else's wellies that she'd found in the boot room, she sneaked outside and shut the door silently behind her.

The night was dark, lit only by the pale lights from the windows of Howard Hall, but Millie knew her path well. Once she was out of sight of the house she pulled out her phone to use the torch, tramping through the woods behind the gardens until the stone walls of the ruined folly came into view.

She smiled as another figure stood as she approached, a bottle of champagne in his hand.

'Millie?'

'Who else?' She took the last few steps and dropped to sit on the wall beside Charlie. 'Did you bring a second glass for me?'

'I didn't even bring one for me.'

Charlie took a gulp from the neck of the bottle, then handed it over to Millie, who copied the movement before passing it back.

'I wasn't really expecting company.'

'Why not?' Millie tucked her feet up onto the wall so her knees were her under her chin, her arms wrapped around them. 'We always used to meet here as kids. And teens, for that matter.'

'Yeah, but…everything's different now, isn't it?'

'I suppose.' It *felt* different, that was for sure. 'But if we're really getting married tomorrow I don't *want* it to be different. I want it to be like it always was between us. Don't you?'

'*If* we're getting married?' Charlie raised his eyebrows at her. 'Having doubts?'

'No,' she said quickly. 'Why? Are you?'

'Of course not.'

They sat in silence for a moment. Then Charlie said, 'So… Giles. He really was a help? I know you two haven't always got on so well, and I really did feel bad about having to go away and leave it all to you two, but—'

'No. He was great. He… I couldn't have done it all without him.'

'Good.' Charlie gave her a speculative look. 'Only…the way he was watching you at the dinner, I wondered if maybe something had happened between you two?'

Groaning, Millie sank her forehead to her knees. 'Were we that obvious?'

'You weren't,' Charlie replied. 'But he was. To me, anyway.'

'I'm sorry. We didn't mean for it to happen. It was just—'

What? Convenient? Inevitable because they were spending time together? A last fling before the ring, just as she'd said it would be?

But Millie knew in her heart it wasn't any of those things. Not by the end.

She loved him. But that didn't matter because he didn't want the things she did, and he was too damn stubborn to give up on what *he* wanted either.

'It's fine.' Charlie brushed away her apologies. 'We both agreed that if we wanted to have a last few weeks of freedom we should. And at least it was with Giles. I don't have to worry about his stealing you away and marrying you before I can!'

'Right...' She stole a glance across at her fiancé. 'What about you? Did you find someone to...to sow those last wild oats with in Scotland, while you were away?'

Even in the moonlight she could see the dark red flush flooding his cheeks.

Grinning, she shifted to face him. 'You did! Who was she?'

Charlie looked awkward, and his words sounded strangely formal as he explained about his unexpected, unintended Scottish fling.

'But it's done now,' he finished, his expression suddenly sobering. 'And I'm here. I'm committed to you, Mills. I won't let you down. I promise.'

'I know.'

Octavia had been Charlie's one true love and, if Millie was honest, she was beginning to suspect that maybe Giles had been hers. But if neither of them could have that heartbreaking, frustrating version of love, at least they could have *this*. Marrying her best friend wasn't a second choice—it was a sensible one. And she knew he needed it as much as she did. She wouldn't let him down either.

She reached for the bottle and toasted him with it. 'To us,' she said, before drinking.

With a soft smile, Charlie took it back and drank, too. 'To us.'

* * *

Giles had important best man duties to be doing this morning—he knew that. But the wedding wasn't until the afternoon, and it wasn't as if he'd slept much after the rehearsal dinner, anyway. So, very early on Christmas Eve, he crept away from Howard Hall and drove to his sister Rebekah's house to play Santa.

After all, he wouldn't want the gifts he and Millie had chosen so carefully to get forgotten. And seeing them sitting in the corner of his room was only reminding him of the time they'd spent together, anyway.

Rebekah was surprised to see him, that much was obvious, but she ushered him in anyway. The kids, clearly already in a Christmas Eve frenzy of excitement, came thundering down the main staircase, narrowly avoiding dislodging the carefully wound garland on the banister and crashing into the eight-foot colour-coordinated tree at the bottom.

'Uncle Giles!' his niece cried, with a gratifying amount of excitement in her voice.

'Have you brought us presents?' her younger brother asked, with the same excitement but more mercenary meaning.

He laughed. 'As it happens, I have.'

'Let's go through and have coffee while they open them,' Rebekah suggested.

Settled in Rebekah's meticulously designed and decorated morning room—a family space off the modern kitchen in a glass extension at the back of the much older house that looked out over the extensive gardens beyond—he let his sister pour them both strong, black coffees as they watched the kids rip the paper off their gifts.

'Unexpectedly thoughtful this year,' Rebekah said, not unkindly. 'New girlfriend?'

The kids hugged him in thanks, then both ran off to play with their early presents.

Rebekah, however, was still waiting for an answer.

'Not exactly,' he hedged. 'I did have a friend to help me shop…'

'A friend?' The disbelief in his sister's voice was palpable.

'It's complicated.'

'Isn't it always?'

Not this *complicated*, he thought, but didn't say.

How could he possibly explain that he was playing best man at the wedding of the woman he loved later that day?

'Marc not here?' he asked, in an attempt to change the subject.

Rebekah shook her head. 'Working in London, so he stayed at the flat there last night—well, the last few nights. He'll be back in time to see the kids open their stockings in the morning, I'm sure.

'Right.'

Giles didn't comment. He had a million things he *wanted* to say, but he'd said them all to his sister before and it had only driven them further apart. Today, of all days, he couldn't face another fight.

But she gave him a sideways look all the same. 'I know what you're thinking.'

'I didn't say anything.'

'You didn't have to.' She sighed. 'I know you don't understand it, Gilly. Honestly, some days I don't either. But I made my bed and I'm damned if I'll let anyone else lie in it. Like you said, love—marriage—is complicated. But when you get right down to it I love my kids more than the world, so I will stay here in this house and get to be with them every single day.'

'And when they're grown up?'

This was the closest she'd ever come to admitting that she might be unhappy in her marriage. And, while he didn't necessarily agree with her logic, he couldn't exactly refute it either.

'Then we'll see,' she said simply.

They sat in silence for a long moment, Rebekah swirling her coffee around in her cup.

Then, out of nowhere, she said, 'I had another choice, you know. Another love, I mean. Stronger, even. It came too late, of course—I was already engaged. Still, I know it could have been… But it would have meant giving up *everything*. Marc had the money, the social standing—we were invited everywhere as a couple…we *mattered*. Paul… He had none of that, and no hope of getting it either. I'd have been ostracised by friends and family for leaving Marc, too. And, like I said, this was years ago. When things were good with Marc. When I still had hope for what my marriage could be…the life we might live together. And so I let it pass by. I just… I didn't realise how much of myself I'd lose, married to Marc instead.'

Giles reached over and grabbed her hands, gripping them tight. 'You know that if you are ever ready to leave I will get you out. No questions, no fuss. You just call.'

'I know.' She gave him a watery smile. 'Maybe one day. But not yet.'

He studied her face for another long moment, then nodded, releasing her hands. She hadn't given up yet, even if he couldn't see from the outside what she was fighting for. The life she'd built, the future she expected, he supposed. It was hard to give up those dreams, those convictions.

He knew that, didn't he? His convictions might be the opposite of hers, but they were every bit as strongly held.

Still, when he left he was still picturing his sister's face, and praying that Millie and Charlie wouldn't be having the same regrets in ten years' time.

* * *

Millie hadn't wanted a whole party of bridesmaids to troop after her down the tiny aisle of the family chapel, all dressed in identical dresses with matching hairstyles. She'd debated long and hard about who to ask, but in the end she'd kept it simple. Tabby would stand up with her as her adult brides-maid, and they'd pop pretty velvet party dresses on her cous-in's two small daughters and call it good.

But despite the bridesmaid streamlining it still felt as if the world and his wife were in her suite at Howard Hall on this, the morning of the wedding. What with her mum, Tabby, her cousin supervising her daughters *and* the hair stylist and make-up artist, it was getting a little crowded.

Millie gravitated towards the window, staring out at the frosty wonderland of the Howard Hall gardens outside, won-dering if she could open one of the sash windows and suck in a lungful or two of crisp, fresh air.

'This is the suite we always provide for brides at Howard Hall.' Tabby eyed the space critically. 'Maybe we need to put some more mirrors in here for them.'

'I'm sure that would help,' Millie replied, thinking of how hundreds more reflections of people would actually make her feel even more trapped.

Tabby gave her a sharp look. 'Are you okay?'

Millie swallowed. 'Fine. Just a bit…overwhelmed.'

'Of course.'

With an understanding smile and a few soft words some-how Tabby managed to herd everyone out of the room—well, everyone except Millie's mum, which was just right.

'*Are* you okay, sweetheart?' Jessica Myles wrapped an arm around Millie's shoulders where she stood at the win-dow, being careful not to crease the beautiful wedding dress they'd chosen together.

'I'm fine,' Millie replied quickly.

But it was a lie, and from the way her mum hesitated and watched her, she knew it, too.

With a last squeeze of her shoulder, Jessica stepped away from her side, only to lean against the windowsill in front of her. Millie met her gaze, then looked away again—fast. The gleam in her mother's eye was all too knowing, as if it saw right into her heart. There were things in there she definitely didn't want her mum to see—especially today.

But all Jessica said was, 'You look so beautiful, sweetheart. The dress is perfect, and so are you. Charlie is going to be blown away.' There was a catch in her voice, and then... 'Your dad would be so proud of you, you know. Oh, not just for this—not for marrying a Howard. For who you are and everything you've done. The wonderful woman you've grown into.'

Tears pricked behind Millie's eyes. 'I hope so.'

'I *know* so.' Jessica reached out and ran a palm down Millie's arm. 'I wish, more than anything, that he was here today to see you...to walk you down the aisle.'

'So do I,' Millie admitted. 'But... I'm glad that *you* get to do that, too.'

Jessica nodded. 'One thing I do know... If he was here, he'd want to ask you one last time. Are you sure about this? About marrying Charlie? Because it's still not too late—'

'Why wouldn't I be sure?' Millie tried for a confident smile. 'I'm marrying my best friend—just like you did when you married Dad. Isn't that what you always said I should look for in a husband? Someone who was my best friend, like Dad was for you?'

'Yes. I did say that.' Jessica looked away, out of the window, perhaps hoping that if she looked hard enough she might even see her late husband out there amongst the frosty greenery. 'And it still holds. But Millie...that wasn't *all* he was. Friendship matters, but in a marriage you need a partner. Someone who will always be there for you—be fundamentally on your side even when you disagree about the details. Someone you can trust to always come through for you.'

'Charlie has always come through for me.'

Except the part where he ran off to Scotland and left her to organise their wedding.

'Charlie has been a very, very good friend to you,' Jessica agreed. 'But I wasn't finished. Trust runs deeper than just friendship. You need someone you can trust with your *passion*. With your body…your soul. You need someone you can connect with on a physical level.'

Millie looked away. This was *not* the sort of conversation she usually had with her mother.

But Jessica grabbed her hands. 'I *know* we don't talk about these things—I always trusted that you had your female friends to talk about sex and such with, beyond the essential basics of consent and safety. But, Millie, this *matters*. Yes, I told you to marry someone who could be your best friend—but I'd be doing you a disservice if I told you that was all there was to it. Marriage is more than friendship. It's passion. It's *love*—bone-deep and part of your soul. The part that connects you when you make love, make *life*. And if Charlie isn't that for you—if you're not that for *him*—and if there's someone else who could be—'

She broke off as Millie looked up to meet her gaze.

'How did you know?' Millie asked in a whisper.

Jessica smiled. 'I saw you two together, remember?'

That had been long before anything had ever happened between her and Giles, but apparently it didn't matter. It had still been there between them…waiting.

It still was, even though they'd said goodbye.

She was starting to think it always would be.

Millie swallowed. 'I need to talk to Charlie. I need to talk to—'

'Giles,' her mum finished for her.

And Millie nodded, suddenly ashamed of letting things get this far, and yet at the same time knowing it didn't really change anything.

Because she wasn't willing to give up her dream of a family, and she knew that Giles didn't want that. But she wasn't willing to settle for anything less than she'd found with Giles now she knew it was possible. Maybe it wouldn't be with him, but if she'd found it once she could find it again— couldn't she?

She'd freeze her eggs. She'd look into adoption—or fostering, even. She'd take her chances and design her own life, full of passion and love and friendship.

But she couldn't marry Charlie.

CHAPTER FOURTEEN

CHARLIE'S HANDS WERE SHAKING. And Giles was pretty sure the groom hadn't had a drink that morning, or even much the night before, so he assumed it had to be nerves. Stress, even.

It was getting hard to pretend he didn't know why.

Charlie gripped hold of the windowsill in front of him, his knuckles white as he stared out at the driveway and the approach to Howard Hall, watching the guests arrive, and Giles knew he had to say something.

'Charlie… Millie told me about why the two of you decided to get married so fast.'

His best friend looked back at him over his shoulder. 'The way she tells it, that's not the only thing the two of you shared while I was away.'

Giles looked away. 'I didn't know she… She said that you told her to have a last fling, if she wanted.'

Charlie's laugh was hollow. 'I did, God help me. I thought it would help us both reconcile ourselves to marriage.'

Which Giles took to mean that Millie wasn't the only one to take advantage of that agreement. He wondered who Charlie had found up in Scotland.

It didn't matter now, though. What mattered was Charlie and Millie and whether they should get married at all. Because from the grey sheen on Charlie's face, he was having second thoughts.

It'll break Millie if he doesn't go through with it.

Giles frowned at the thought. Would it? Would it, really?

Millie was stronger than that. Stronger than he'd ever given her credit for. And probably stronger than even Charlie knew.

If that test hadn't been negative Giles had no doubt that Millie would have walked in here, owned up to everything, called off the wedding and then gone out and been the most kick-ass single mum in the world if he hadn't been willing to stand with her.

Except he would have been. He'd have been right there at her side if she'd needed him. But that wasn't the way the dice had fallen.

Still…

'If you're having second thoughts about this wedding, you need to tell Millie,' Giles told his friend.

Because walking away on their wedding day would hurt Millie, for sure. But marrying her and making them both miserable because it wasn't what he really wanted…? That would be the one thing that *would* destroy her.

He couldn't watch Millie and Charlie end up like his sister and her husband. He loved them *both* too much for that.

'I'm *not* having second thoughts,' Charlie snapped back, too vehemently for Giles to believe him.

He spun round to face Giles, his hand no longer shaking as he spoke, emphasising his points with a pointing finger.

'Millie is one of the best people I know, and I love her. She needs this, and I'd never let her down like that. She wants a family, a happy-ever-after, and if no one else is going to give it to her then I'm damn well going to make sure she gets it—because she deserves *everything*.'

'I know,' Giles said quietly. Because she really did.

And he'd give anything to be the one to give it to her.

Anything? his mind asked.

Would he give up his preconceived ideas about marriage?

His beliefs about the right thing to do with his family legacy? His bitter revenge against his parents?

Because that was what it would take, right?

Charlie's eyes narrowed as he watched him. 'And what about you, Giles? So quick with the advice for others, but what do *you* want? I thought it really was just a fling before the ring between you and Millie, like we agreed. But looking at you now, I'm not so sure.'

Giles felt the blood drain from his face. 'I'll stay away once you're married, Charlie. You know I'd never betray you that way. Millie and I ended everything before we came here. You know I can't give her what she wants.'

'But you wish you could, don't you?'

Charlie's words hit too close to his own thoughts, and Giles stepped back, turning away to fuss with the tray of button-holes Millie had sent up.

White roses with dark green sprigs of leaves. Just like they'd planned.

Oh, God, he'd helped plan this entire day, and in the process he'd almost forgotten it wasn't his wedding.

'You're here asking what *I* want, but have you thought about what *you* want?' Charlie took a step closer, into Giles's space, forcing him to look up at him. 'Or have you spent so long focussing on what you *don't* want—on *not* falling in love, *not* getting married, *not* ending up like your parents or your sister, or chained to a money pit of a house because of history and society and expectations—that you've forgotten to even *think* about what *you* want?'

The words hit home, and they hit deep.

Because there was a moment when he'd let those thoughts of what *he* wanted in.

When he'd thought Millie might be carrying his child and against the odds…against everything he'd thought he believed in, every conviction he had…he'd wanted it. He'd wanted

Millie and their child and that damn happy-ever-after that he hadn't even *believed* in until he'd fallen in love with her. Maybe not right now—he wasn't fool enough to think that he could overturn his whole belief system and understanding of the world overnight. But someday.

And for ever.

God, he'd *never* thought he'd want for ever.

He turned to Charlie, knowing his mouth was gaping open and unsure what to do about it. He had no words.

Charlie had been his best friend for most of his life. He'd helped form him into the person he was—helped him see that there was another way to live in the world than the one his parents had chosen. That he could live a life of contribution and creation rather than entitlement and acceptance. He'd helped him become a man he was proud to be.

A man who could fall more deeply in love than he'd ever imagined, as it turned out.

Charlie was his best friend and he'd betrayed him. And yet somehow he was still smiling.

'So. When exactly did you fall in love with my fiancée?' Charlie asked. 'And just what are you going to do about it?'

Millie raced down the stairs of Howard Hall, hoping she was early enough to catch Charlie before he headed to the chapel and to avoid the guests arriving early for a welcome drink before the service.

She recoiled as she hit a wall of sound—people in hats and fancy outfits were everywhere, and the levels of gossip and chatter were epic. She spotted Tabby in her bridesmaid's dress, ushering people into one of the many reception rooms, but she couldn't see the best man anywhere.

She did see her groom.

Charlie waded through the crowd, against the tide of people heading in the opposite direction, and grabbed hold of the bottom of the banister. 'Want to get out of here for a moment?'

Millie nodded enthusiastically, and before she knew it he'd whisked her back up the stairs and into a tiny side room—or was it a cupboard?—she'd never noticed before, halfway up the staircase. There were racks of fur coats against one wall, and for a moment Millie wondered if Charlie was suggesting they run away to Narnia.

It didn't sound like such a bad idea right now. Except, given her outfit—and what she was about to do—she'd probably be cast as the White Witch.

'You aren't supposed to see me in my wedding dress before the ceremony,' she said, looking down at her wide white skirts, and seeing only Giles's face when he'd walked into the dress shop.

'I think that only counts if the wedding is actually going to take place.'

Charlie's voice was soft—kind, even—and when she looked up at him there was no anger in his face. If anything, she thought she saw…relief.

'Is it?' he asked.

'I… I don't think it can. I'm sorry, Charlie. I can't marry you.'

Just saying the words lifted a weight from her shoulders that she knew, if she'd gone through with the wedding, would have broken her down eventually. Walking away from Charlie was hard. But not as impossible as it would have been to be married to him, knowing she was in love with someone else.

'Because you're in love with Giles.'

It wasn't a question, more a statement of fact. And, actually…was Charlie *smiling*?

'You're not…angry?'

Millie knew others would be. Everyone who'd come all

this way on Christmas Eve. And Tabby had put all that into the wedding. Not to mention the money…

But Charlie shook his head. 'I'm not angry. I'm… Honestly, right at this moment, I'm not sure what I am. Except your best friend. I'll always be that.'

She smiled up at him, reaching out to grip his hand tight, trying to convey all the love and gratitude she had for him and his place in her life in just that gesture.

She loved him—deeply. But, looking up at him now, she didn't know how she'd ever believed she could be his wife.

'How did we end up here?' Millie asked. 'I mean…really?'

Charlie shrugged helplessly, then wrapped his arms around her and pulled her into a hug. 'I think we both wanted to make each other happy. And maybe we would have done. But it would only ever have been a sort of…'

'Contentment.' Millie finished for him when he trailed off. 'We'd have been content, I think. Except now we both know there's something more out there, and it's hard to settle for contentment after that.'

'It is.' Charlie placed a kiss to the top of her head, then stepped away. 'So I think we'd both better get out there and demand what we *really* want from life. Don't you?'

Millie slipped out of the closet, surprised to find the hall below already empty. Where had everybody gone? Then she spotted the grandfather clock. It was time for the ceremony.

They'd all gone to the chapel.

Leaving Charlie behind—he'd offered to go with her, but she'd insisted she be the one to do it—she padded down the stairs, hiking up her wedding dress so she didn't trip over it, and ran out through the front door towards the family chapel.

Frost crunched underfoot as she ran across the grass. The chapel wasn't far, but she shivered as the cold air hit her bare arms all the same. As she approached, she could see her mum and Tabby waiting just outside, and she saw the panic on Tabby's face. Of course. Charlie wasn't there. And his sister wouldn't want to have to break the news to his bride.

She tried to smile to reassure them, but then she heard a voice—one that her heart recognised as well as her ears.

'Don't worry,' she murmured to Tabby and her mum as she continued towards the voice. 'I've got this part covered. But there is something I need you to do, Tabby.'

She filled Charlie's sister in on what they needed from her as quickly as she could. Now she'd started on this path she was impatient to reach its end.

'But—' Tabby started, but Jessica placed a hand on her arm and nodded to Millie.

'You go on, love,' her mum said.

And Millie paused just long enough to place a kiss on her cheek and whisper, 'Thanks, Mum.'

The heavy wooden door of the chapel opened easily under her hands and swung closed behind her, Tabby and Jessica having slipped inside in her wake. Millie ignored the crowds of people and focussed on Giles, standing by the altar, trying to reassure people.

'If you could all be patient for just a few more moments…' Giles was saying, as the door banged shut.

The chapel fell silent as all the guests turned to watch Millie walk down the aisle. At the front, the string quartet started playing her processional music—until Tabby appeared from the side of the chapel to shush them.

But Millie kept her gaze on Giles, who stared right back. One hand darted out to indicate the empty space beside him, where Charlie should be standing, but Millie merely smiled serenely.

Everything was going to be fine. Oh, maybe not immediately—she was pretty sure that untangling this mess was going to take some work. But she knew Charlie would probably face the worst of it, having to explain everything to his parents and all their friends.

The only people here whose opinion Millie really cared about were on her side—her mum, Charlie and, she hoped, Giles. Even Tabby would come round eventually, she was sure.

Everything was going to be all right now.

No, better than all right.

She was going to make her future *glorious*.

Millie reached the front of the chapel. Giles stepped aside with a confused look on his face. Then she turned to face the crowd and began to speak.

CHAPTER FIFTEEN

GILES HAD NO idea what was happening.

He knew that Charlie was having doubts about the wedding, and hoped that his friend had gone to talk to Millie about it while Giles stalled at the chapel. But now here was Millie, walking down the aisle alone to where Giles stood, without her groom beside him.

Had Charlie found her?

Had they talked?

What was she feeling right now?

Whatever it was, it didn't look as if it was clenching at her heart the way his own anxiety and concern and hope were his.

Millie smiled beatifically out at the crowd of gawping congregants, clasped her hands in front of her, where her bouquet should be, and began to talk.

'Thank you all so much for coming out on such a cold and frosty morning to support Charlie and I today. Unfortunately, I have to tell you that there won't be a wedding today. Charlie and I have decided that, much as we love and adore each other as best friends, and always will, that friendship isn't enough to sustain decades of marriage together.'

A murmur was going around the crowd now. Giles wondered where Charlie was…whether Millie had asked him to let her do this. He thought she probably had. He wouldn't have left her alone otherwise.

Except he hadn't left her alone, had he? Charlie would have known that Giles would be here, standing right beside her.

Maybe that was why he wasn't there. He was giving Giles his chance to stand up and do the right thing.

And finally Giles thought he might even know what that was.

'But, while there isn't a wedding today, it *is* still Christmas Eve, and I know the Howard family are still excited to celebrate the season with you all up at the house. After all, life, love and friendship should *always* be celebrated, don't you think?'

At a look from Millie, the string quartet burst into action again, playing a rousing chorus of 'We Wish You a Merry Christmas', while Tabby and Jessica opened the chapel doors wide and began ushering guests back to the hall. A few stopped to offer their condolences to Millie as they passed, but every time she shook her head and told them that this was the best for everyone, and she'd rather keep Charlie as her best friend than her future ex-husband—a line that got at least a few polite laughs.

Giles suspected they all thought she was just putting on a brave face. But he knew her better than that, and knew she was telling the truth.

More than that, she was glowing. With happiness, or anticipation, or hope—or something else he couldn't even identify but hoped she'd explain.

Then, as the last guest left the chapel and the door closed behind them, she turned to him—with all that hope and happiness on full, glowing display—and smiled.

And Giles's heart began to soar.

Telling a crowd of society's finest, who'd traipsed out to Norfolk on Christmas Eve to see a society wedding, that there wasn't going to *be* a wedding was easy.

Telling the man left behind that it was because she was in love with him was going to be much harder.

Or so she thought.

Millie turned to find Giles watching her cautiously, a very small smile dancing around his lips.

'You changed your mind, then?' he asked.

'We both did, I think,' Millie replied. 'But mostly it didn't seem right for me to marry Charlie when I was in love with someone else.'

The slight, sharp intake of breath she heard was probably because of the cold. He *had* to know she loved him by now, didn't he?

'Millie, I—'

She knew what he was going to say, so she cut him off before he could start.

'Giles, look… I know we agreed that this would only ever be a fling. That you hate the idea of marriage and children and all that. I can understand why—even if I don't agree with you—but I'm in love with you anyway. I'm in love with the way you look at me, the way you touch me, the way you think of me and care for me. It makes me want to do the same for you. You've taught me what I want from love. And even if you can't ever give it to me, I'm not willing to settle for anything less now I know what love can be.'

She stared at him with defiant, wide eyes and waited for his response. Because this was it. This was the moment when she knew which way her future would go.

But Giles didn't say anything. Instead, he lurched forward and wrapped her into his arms, kissing her hard and deep.

As answers went, Millie had definitely been predicting worse. But just as she was settling into the kiss he pulled back again, resting his forehead against hers as he stared into her eyes. His arms were still tight around her waist, and Millie felt as if he might never, ever let her go.

And she was fine with that.

'You know I love you, too, don't you?' His words were harsh, desperate. 'You have to know that?'

'I… I hoped,' Millie replied. 'I wouldn't say *knew*. And I definitely didn't think you'd admit it.'

His eyes fluttered closed as he gave her a rueful smile. 'I know. I… Love, commitment, marriage—it all felt like a trap to me. Just another angle on the legacy and expectation my parents placed on me from birth, because of the title and the crumbling estate and everything that was coming to me when my father dies. It was as if, if I ever fell in love and married, they'd have me at last. Because of course I'd have to save the estate for my wife and kids. I was scared… Not of the work, but of becoming like them. Of turning into what they've become. Hating each other but never able to leave. I couldn't—'

'I know,' Millie whispered. 'I understand.'

'I don't think you do,' he said. 'Because the thing I've realised is…you'd never let that happen. *You're* not like them. You're…magical, Millie, to me. The way you see the world, the way you live in it… You'd never be like them, and so *I* would never be like them. When you told me you might be pregnant… I think my heart stopped, just for a moment. And I realised afterwards that it wasn't fear that did that. It was longing. I *wanted* that life with you. I wanted any reason at all to stop you marrying Charlie and choose me instead. I wanted an excuse to put all my old beliefs behind me, and I thought that might be it.'

'You…want that?'

Millie fought back the hopeful feeling swelling inside her—just in case. She needed to hear him say it. Not just that he'd have taken the excuse if it presented itself—he needed to *want* it.

'With me?'

'I want...'

Giles looked up at the ceiling of the chapel and she watched his Adam's apple bob as he swallowed.

'Millie. I love you. I want you in my life for ever. I want a *future* with you—one I thought I could never want. But... I know how much you want kids right now, and why you need to do it now, and I can't... I can't promise to be good at any of this. I might need some time to adjust, but you don't *have* time and—'

She reached up to take his face in her hands and stopped him talking with a kiss.

'I'll freeze my eggs. Or we'll look into adoption when we're ready. We have options,' she said. 'What I want most of all is a loving, supportive relationship and a family—however that comes to pass. And I know you can be all that for me. I can wait while we figure out what that looks like. If that's what you want, too.'

'It is.' His words were fervent and his kiss possessive. 'God, Millie, it's what I want more than I've ever wanted anything.'

'Me too,' she admitted in a whisper. 'I never imagined... back when you were Charlie's annoying schoolfriend...that we could end up here. But I'm so glad we did.'

Giles smiled, and kissed her lightly again. 'Looks like the best man won, after all.'

She groaned at the joke, then wrapped an arm around his waist to lead him back up the aisle and out of the chapel into the frosty morning.

'Come on,' she said. 'Tabby and Mum will be going wild with curiosity up at the house. And I want to check in on Charlie, help him figure out what *he's* going to do now.'

'I think Charlie will be fine,' Giles said. 'But whatever he does next, I guarantee he won't be as happy as me. No man on earth could be right now.'

'And you thought you couldn't be a husband,' Millie said fondly. 'Keep talking like that and you'll do just fine.'

Giles laughed, and with their arms wrapped around each other they headed up to Howard Hall to find their best friend and start their new life. Together.

* * * * *

Look out for the next story in the
Blame It on the Mistletoe duet

Miss Right All Along
by Jessica Gilmore

And if you enjoyed this story,
check out these other great reads from
Sophie Pembroke

Socialite's Nine-Month Secret
Cinderella in the Spotlight
Best Man with Benefits

All available now!

MISS RIGHT
ALL ALONG

JESSICA GILMORE

MILLS & BOON

For Katy,
thank you for asking me to be part of this duet.

I always love working with you.

CHAPTER ONE

'I AM SURE she asked for this song on purpose.' Charlie took a swig of his champagne and casually looked away from the dance floor. He was *not* going to give the bride the satisfaction of seeing him staring. Of seeing him display any emotion apart from showing that he was having a perfectly marvellous time, thank you very much.

Millie Myles, his best friend and long-suffering date, looked up from her own glass. A glass she had been staring into like it might hold the answer to many of life's problems. It was an outlook Charlie shared, tonight at least, but not one Millie usually took, and she was unlikely to be devastated by the wedding of society beauty Octavia Sinclair—and Charlie's long-term on/off girlfriend—to tech bro billionaire Layton Stone. The opposite in fact.

'We are never ever getting back together?' Millie grinned. 'I doubt the *whole* playlist has been designed to humiliate you, but with this song you might have a point. Ignore it, just look at me and pretend you're having a good time. That's what I am here for. That, moral support and to make sure you didn't do anything stupid during the vows.'

'Your hand on my knee was very helpful at the *persons here present* bit, thanks, but unneeded, honestly. I have humiliated myself in front of Octavia Sinclair for the last time. Octavia Stone I suppose she is now.' He took another swig. 'At least the champagne is good.'

'Too good.' Millie grabbed the bottle from the middle of the table and refilled both their glasses. 'Let's do a toast. Here's to being young, free and single...' There was an edge to her voice he couldn't quite decipher. It was a while since she had split up with Tom, but Charlie hadn't seen any signs that she was craving a new relationship; her floristry business was doing so well it seemed to take up all her energy. No wonder, she was *really* talented. Look at how she'd transformed the rather gloomy stone great hall belonging to Octavia's parents with her clever use of colour, her gorgeous designs and decorations.

'Does thirty count as young still?' Charlie asked doubtfully. 'According to my parents it's the *high time you settled down and thought about your responsibilities to the estate* age. Not much young and free there.'

'What responsibilities? You could hardly do more for the ancestral home, Charlie. You live there, work there...'

'And apparently I need to settle down and supply the next generation of overlords and worker bees.'

'Ah, that kind of responsibility.'

Charlie picked up his glass, dangling it by the stem. 'The problem is where do I start with the whole marriage and kids thing? I've only ever been serious about one woman and she's the one on the dance floor in the long white dress. You know, I always thought that one day Octavia and I would stop all the breaking up and dramatics, get married and live reasonably happily ever after.'

Millie raised an eyebrow so expressive it could have starred in its own video. 'Optimistic much? Seriously, take away the drama and what really was there, Charlie?'

'It wasn't all bad,' he protested. 'Far from it. We spent fourteen years together, on and off.'

'Mostly off,' Millie muttered and he nudged her.

'She's not just the drama queen and society queen bee everyone thinks she is. She has a really sensitive side, she just hides it from most people...'

'Which is why she's weaponizing Taylor Swift at her wedding?'

'Good point well made.' Charlie took another swig. This champagne really *was* going down a little too well. But then it wasn't every day a man had to sit by and watch his first and only love, his *ex-fiancée*, say 'I do' to another man.

He sighed. He'd been one half of the golden couple that had been Octavia and Charlie since his mid-teens and it took some getting used to the fact that they were absolutely and utterly finally over. In many ways the drama of their relationship had been an addiction. He knew it was bad for him and there was no happy outcome and yet he had kept on returning to her anyway.

But no more. The last break-up was the final one and it was time he moved on into whatever—or whoever—his future held. Millie thought so, his other best friend Giles thought so, his little sister Tabitha thought so, hell, even the family dog had a firm opinion on the matter. Octavia herself had clearly and publicly moved on, hence the expensive designer white dress and huge glittering rock on her left hand. In a way he envied her, her seamless transition to Layton. Charlie had no idea how to go about dating someone different after so many years with one person. All he knew was that he wanted his future drama-free. A sedate, adult relationship where disagreements were talked out and compromises reached and no one ever threw an engagement ring into a river.

'Those two definitely had an argument before the wedding.' Millie nodded at the couple dancing past them. 'They were glaring at each other in the church.'

'Were they? I didn't notice.'

'Because you were staring at the bride.'

'True,' he conceded. Although not so much in hope she would call the wedding off, as so many people here no doubt thought, but in hope watching her say 'I do' meant he could finally close this very long, drawn-out chapter.

Hugo and Charity, instead of glaring, were now wrapped around each other and kissing passionately. Charlie leaned against Millie. Bless her for trying to distract him. Again. He really needed to make more of an effort to be a more amusing companion; after all, he knew that she often found society affairs difficult, too conscious that she was the daughter of a cook and a gardener, here as Charlie's friend not in her own right. Which was, of course, utter nonsense. Millie was worth twice every other person here, with the exception of his sister Tabitha and Giles. Actually, scratch that, bloody Giles was acting as Layton's best man after all, just Tabby then.

He glanced over at his sister. Tabby was laughing as she chatted to her best friend Liberty, who looked up and met his gaze, her own a concerned query. Was everyone here waiting for him to do something drastic? They'd be disappointed if so. All Charlie intended to do was sample as much of the free champagne as possible and survive the day with his dignity intact. He smiled at her reassuringly and then looked away quickly. Once, long ago, he'd put Liberty in an awkward position, one right between him and Octavia, and that night still prickled at his conscience. She'd been far too young, just eighteen, and things had never been the same between them since, their easy, almost familial relationship, turned awkward and polite. If Tabby knew, about the kiss, about the way he had just walked away, about the way he had never mentioned it again or apologised, she would, if not kill him, maim him—she had always been very protective of Liberty. And he would deserve it.

So best not to even notice let alone think about how beautiful Liberty looked tonight. Charlie turned his attention firmly back to Millie, leaning in and lowering his voice as Hugo and Charity stopped close to their table, still snogging, hands groping places that really didn't need to be groped in public. 'I think she was hoping he'd propose before now. They've been dating long enough.'

'How long is long enough?'

Charlie shrugged. 'I don't know. Octavia and I were together for years...'

'Except you broke up every six months or so,' Millie pointed out.

'That might have been the problem.'

'Not the only problem,' Millie said. 'She was also awful to you, and the whole relationship was toxic, and I wanted better for you because I love you and you're one of my very favourite people.'

Why couldn't he be in love with *Millie*? She was his best friend, the kindest, the funniest, the most talented woman he knew. He pulled her in for a hug. 'And you're one of mine. You know, I don't think I'll ever get married now. I think Octavia was my one shot. If I couldn't make it work with her...' He shook his head. 'Except I have to, somehow. There's the estate. The title. The entail. My family expect—no, they need me to marry and carry on the line. But how can I? She was my one true love. How can I marry someone else?' Oh no, he had definitely drunk too much. He was getting morose and sentimental not to mention repetitive. One day he would be that man in the corner of the bar telling every unwary stranger who got too close about the one who got away. Even though he knew better, had known better for a long time.

'I don't believe that.' Millie took his hands in hers. 'I know it hurts now, but you have to have faith. I thought that Tom was my one shot…'

'And you haven't dated anyone seriously since. Remind me how this is supposed to convince me?'

'I guess *I* just have to have faith,' she said. 'I saw the doctor the other day and…'

She had *what*? Suddenly he felt a lot more sober. Was this why she had been so quiet over the last few days, lapsing into thought, not really listening or chatting on as usual? 'Is everything okay? What did they say?' He couldn't hide his worry and she squeezed his hand.

'Nothing like that,' she assured him. 'But I'd been having some tests for, well, women's stuff. And it turns out that my fertility is declining a lot faster than is usual for someone in their late twenties. They reckon that if I want to start a family, well, I need to either freeze my eggs and hope, or get started now.'

Charlie let out a long breath. 'I'm sorry. I know how much having a family means to you.' Millie had always talked about having lots of children. An only child herself, she craved noise and bustle and laughter. And if anyone would make a wonderful mother it was her. Life really was bloody unfair sometimes. 'What are you going to do?'

'Find someone to fall madly in love with me in the

next forty-eight hours and marry them after a whirlwind courtship, settle down and have kids as soon as possible and live happily ever after?' she said wryly. 'I guess I'll look into getting my remaining eggs frozen. Hope that things work out later.' She shrugged. 'Not many other options, are there?'

'Maybe *we* should just get married,' Charlie suggested. 'Could solve a lot of problems.'

Millie laughed. 'Can you imagine? My mum would be over the moon.'

'So would mine.' He got to his feet and held out his hand. 'Come on. If we have to wedding, let's at least wedding properly and get a good boogie in.'

He'd been joking of course, when he had suggested they get married, but as he dragged her onto the dance floor he couldn't help wishing again that they *could* fall in love. It would certainly solve both of their problems.

'This might be the worst wedding I have ever been to,' Liberty Gray whispered as she held her glass up in what was, to her at least, a mocking toast to the bride and groom. 'Just ridiculously ostentatious and so self-important.'

'You're only saying that because a, you hate weddings in general and b, because you despise Octavia,' her best friend Tabitha whispered back. 'I mean, it's fair. I despise Octavia even more than you. And I haven't exactly warmed to the groom either.'

'Has he had excessive Botox do you think? Maybe he suffers that thing our teachers used to warn us about; you know, don't pull faces in case the wind changes? No one's face can be that taut naturally surely?'

'With his money if it *was* Botox then surely it would

be a better job? Besides, he's the same age as Charlie and *he's* not resorted to fillers yet.' Tabby giggled, looking over at the next table. 'Poor Charlie. He's doing very well. I can't imagine why on earth he accepted the invitation. No one would blame him for swerving.'

'How long were he and Octavia engaged for?' As if she didn't know.

'In total two years but of course they had at least one of their many breaks during that time. You know, I accepted the invitation just to make sure she really did get well and truly married off and any threat to Charlie was finally over.'

If Liberty was being very honest with herself then she would admit that she had accepted Tabby's pleas to be her plus-one for exactly the same reason. Not that she still had any feelings for Charlie—or Charles St Clare Howard as he was more formally known, the future Baron Howard, heir to a historic title, stately home and huge estate—she had grown out of them *long* ago. A schoolgirl crush, nothing more. But she was glad he was no longer in any danger of marrying Octavia. She wouldn't wish that fate on her worst enemy.

Despite herself she glanced over at Tabby's brother again. He had clearly had a glass or two of champagne too many, his blue eyes a little too glazed, his dark hair a little too ruffled, his tie slightly askew as he leaned against the pretty, curvy girl next to him, laughing as she whispered in his ear. Something that felt a lot like jealousy shot through her and she quickly dampened it down. Charlie Howard was a free agent, he could cosy up to whoever he chose.

Tabby followed her gaze and grimaced. 'Looks like Charlie is going for the drowning his sorrows option,' she said. 'Thank goodness Millie is keeping an eye on him. Don't they look good together? We always hoped that they would end up falling for each other, but Charlie has never been that sensible, or maybe Millie is *too* sensible to get tangled up with him in that way. She did the flowers and say what you want about Octavia and I usually do, but even I have to admit she has exquisite taste. Doesn't it all look marvellous?'

'Yes,' Liberty conceded. It did. The great hall was decked out in autumnal colours, warm golds and oranges softening the austere grey. And Octavia of course looked stunning, her rather sharp, cool angular beauty the perfect framing for the designer wedding dress—her second of the day so far. Her green eyes glittered with triumph and why not? She was marrying one of the richest and most successful men of their generation. He on the other hand looked like he was adding a rare object to his collection, his gaze possessive rather than loving and proud.

'I'm glad Millie is here, especially as Giles is best man. I have no idea what he's thinking agreeing to be part of the wedding party,' Tabby continued, throwing a disdainful look up at the top table. 'He's *Charlie's* best friend, apart from Millie obviously. I didn't even think he knew Layton that well.'

'Another way of sticking it to Charlie? It's not enough that Octavia is marrying someone else, he has to witness it, you are invited too, his childhood best friend has to do the flowers, his best mate is the best man. Is she just trying to hurt him, or do you think all this is a desperate plea for him to ride to her rescue?'

'You and I both know that Octavia Sinclair is quite capable of rescuing herself. I just hope that this shows Charlie once and for all that he is better off without her.'

'Me too,' Liberty agreed.

But two hours later it seemed unlikely that their wish would come true any time soon. What was Octavia thinking, cutting into Charlie's dance with Millie and insisting he dance with her? Had the woman no heart? Liberty took a sip of her wine and glared at the busy dance floor as Octavia threw her head back and laughed at something Charlie said, an intimate smile on her pouting mouth, looking up at him from under her lashes, a look Liberty had spent far too many teenage years trying to replicate without success.

Charlie's smile on the other hand looked forced, his posture tense, and Liberty's heart squeezed. The man might be a fool wasting his teenage years and all his twenties on a woman as mercurial and dramatic as Octavia, but she knew Charlie had truly loved her, had seen depths in her that nobody else had. Maybe he had been fooling himself, or maybe Octavia really did have a secret side she had only shown to him. But today she was behaving true to form, trying to reel him back in even though she had literally just married someone else.

Well, it might be her wedding day but that didn't mean everything had to go her way.

Before she had time to think through her actions, Liberty strode onto the dance floor, wishing she had bought a pair of flats as her feet protested the movement, and tapped Octavia on the shoulder.

'Mind if I cut in?' she asked sweetly.

The momentary look of shock and anger was so vitriolic that Liberty nearly took a step back before Octavia clearly remembered where she was and smiled.

'Of course, I've monopolised you for too long, Charlie darling.' She couldn't just leave it there, leaning in to press a lingering kiss on his cheek before sashaying away without a backwards glance.

'You don't have to dance with me,' Liberty said quickly. 'I just thought you might need a rescue.'

Close up she could see that Charlie was both more and less drunk than she had imagined.

'I would love to dance with you,' he said with an exaggerated bow. 'Shall we?' He held out a hand and she took it, flushing as his fingers closed around hers.

'Having fun, Liberty?' he asked as he whirled her into the middle of the dance floor. Charlie was an excellent dancer, she hadn't forgotten that, even though she hadn't danced with him since New Year's Eve eight years ago. A night she both tried to relive and forget in equal measure. Did he remember at all? She suspected so. He'd been a little distant with her ever since then, polite and friendly enough, but he had avoided ever being alone with her. Liberty's gaze dropped to his mouth and despite herself she couldn't help remembering how he tasted, how he had felt, how his kiss had been everything her romantic eighteen-year-old heart had wanted it to be. How she might have let things progress if Octavia hadn't shown up unexpectedly. How Charlie had left her with just one apologetic backwards look. How they had never spoken about it again. How she had tried to forget it and yet, despite several actual relationships since, that kiss was still the one she thought about when she couldn't sleep at night.

Eighteen-year-old her had been a romantic fool. Luckily twenty-six-year-old her was much more sensible.

With a start she realised that Charlie was still waiting for an answer. What was the question again? Ah yes, was she having fun. 'Not really,' she said honestly and after a startled look he let out a shout of laughter.

'Me neither,' he said. 'Tell me, are you nursing a broken heart too?' His tone was self-mocking. 'Champagne is an excellent cure if so.'

'No broken heart, I just don't like big over the top weddings.'

'Don't let Tabby let you hear you say that,' he warned. 'Where would the Howard family be without huge weddings and glitzy parties? The more excess the better is our new family motto.'

Liberty laughed. 'Tabby knows how I feel, it doesn't mean I don't admire what you do.' The Howard family had taken their portfolio of expensive to maintain houses, castles and lodges and created a hugely successful events and location business, supplying the backdrops for myriad films, TV programmes and photo shoots as well as organising luxury and glamorous weddings and parties.

'So, tell me Liberty Gray, what kind of wedding would you want?'

'I'm not sure marriage is for me. It always seems like hope over common sense, most end in divorce anyway.'

Charlie laughed. 'So cynical, so young.'

Not cynical, experienced. Her family were single-handedly responsible for most of the divorce statistics, after all. 'Just being practical,' she retorted. 'But in the unlikely event I did succumb then I would want it to be small, intimate, something real. If I ever *did* get married, I want it to be forever.'

'Me too.' Their gazes caught and held, his smile rueful. 'I've had enough drama and ups and downs to last me a lifetime. I suspect you are the same.'

'I don't know how my mother had the energy to organise a big extravaganza for her fourth wedding or my father to think that the fifth might be the one to succeed, you know.' She was the only product of her mother's second marriage and her father's third, born into a dysfunctional theatre dynasty with a family tree so complicated it required pages of footnotes to figure it out. No wonder she had always been happier to spend her holidays with Tabitha. Howard Hall might be imposing and impressive, but the family were warm and welcoming and Liberty had always felt wanted there, something that wasn't always the case in the revolving door of her stepfamilies.

'Here's to real, Liberty.' Charlie had manoeuvred her back to his table where he picked up his glass of half-drunk champagne and held it up to her in a toast. 'To real and happy ever afters, whatever they may be.'

'Whatever they may be,' she echoed, toasting him back. For one moment as she looked into his still glazed blue eyes Liberty felt that old pull, a renewing of the crush that had kept her navigating towards Charlie during the years he had known her only as his kid sister's friend. But there were no happy ever afters for her where Charlie Howard was concerned. If she ever gave her heart away again—and that was a big if—next time it would be to someone who truly wanted it.

CHAPTER TWO

IT WAS A relief to get away from the wedding and back to Charlie's apartment in his Norfolk home. Howard Hall wasn't the oldest of the family houses, but it was the largest and most imposing thanks to the numerous bedrooms, drawing rooms, a ballroom, billiards room, library and all the other essential spaces for the landed gentry to rule their small fiefdoms from. Now, most of the house was let out for events and filming, the family occupying the East Wing, but Charlie's rooms were still more spacious than most people's entire houses and comfortably furnished with a mixture of priceless antiques and modern furniture.

'Nightcap?' he asked Millie who had collapsed onto a daybed where, according to family legend, at least one princess had once nursed a headache.

'Please.'

He took out two crystal glasses and filled them with ice before adding a generous splash of cognac and then another before handing one to Millie.

'I think that went about as well as it could be expected to, don't you?' He grabbed his own glass and settled next to her. After all, he hadn't disgraced himself. In fact, he had even been the one to break off the dance with Octavia thanks to Liberty.

Despite his best intentions it had been impossible to ignore how beautiful Liberty had looked, her green silk dress clinging to slim curves, her hair autumn red. Maybe he should have told her so. But the memory of how he had once taken advantage of the younger girl's evident then-crush on him still made him squirm. Really, he owed her an apology although he doubted she even remembered; after all, she must have hundreds of men dangling after her.

Charlie grimaced. That wasn't as comforting a thought as it should have been.

'I give them six months. A year, tops.' Millie recalled him to the here and now. The wedding. Octavia was a married woman. For now at least.

But one thing he knew for absolute sure. She might be married for a week, a month or a year, but he was done. No more reunions, no more break-ups, no more drama. She'd made her choice and he'd made his and he chose a future where he was happy. Whatever that meant.

Charlie sipped his cognac. 'You're probably right. What do you think it is? The secret to an actual, happy relationship, I mean.'

'Well, my mum always said the secret was marrying your best friend.'

He leaned against her. 'Going by that rule, I should probably marry you.'

'Giles thought we should get married, too.'

Giles *what?* It was one thing for his friend to offer unwanted advice to Charlie but he had no right where Millie was concerned. And what was with Giles's sudden interest in Millie anyway? It wasn't as if he'd never met her before.

Charlie couldn't help feeling protective—after all, he

knew his two best friends inside out. Charlie knew Millie's type and Giles was definitely not it thanks to his allergy to marriage and serious relationships. Giles was the epitome of no strings whilst all Millie wanted to be was tangled in all the strings. Besides, selfishly, it was bad enough that the two of them had never got on. The last thing he needed was to be in the middle of a fling gone wrong.

'Did he now?' he bit out. 'Interesting.'

Millie looked up at him. 'Interesting how?'

'Just that he said something similar to me. I was warning him off you at the time,' he added grimly.

'Because I'm not good enough?' Millie sounded hurt and Charlie cursed himself for a tactless drunken fool.

'Because you're far *too* good.' Charlie squeezed her hand in apology. 'You're one of the best people I know, and you deserve everything you want in this world. And you want a family, and a happy ever after—and we both know that is the last thing that Giles wants.'

'But you do. You want the same things I do—to get married, be happy, have a family to carry on your name and title.'

Charlie leaned back and thought about it. He had to get married for the sake of the estate and the title, true, but actually he wanted more than that. He wanted to be with someone who genuinely liked him and who he liked. Someone who wanted to build a life with him, not keep tearing it down.

Someone like the woman sitting next to him. His oldest and best friend. Charlie looked at Millie who returned his gaze with equal speculation. *Millie.* He loved her, more than anyone apart from his family. No, she *was* family. He knew her inside out just as she knew him.

And he wanted her to have everything she desired. The babies she yearned for. Security, respect. He could give her all of that.

'*We* should get married.'

Had he said it, or had she?

It didn't matter, it was an amazing idea and Charlie was about to tell her so when she pressed a finger to his lips. 'Let's…we need to sleep on this. Sober up. Think things through. We'll talk about it in the morning.'

'And if we still think it's a good idea in the cold light of day?'

'Then we'll start wedding planning.'

Despite the copious amounts of alcohol—or maybe because of it—Charlie didn't sleep well. Every time he tried to sleep he saw Octavia, glittering triumphantly, Liberty laughing up at him—and Millie. His beautiful, adorable, clever, warm friend. She would make someone the perfect wife. Could that person be *him*? Should it? What would it mean for their friendship?

One thing he did know was that if they did go ahead, he would have to be in their marriage one hundred per cent; he didn't think either of them would be comfortable with a halfway house, and Millie deserved nothing less than his full commitment. Theirs might not be a traditional romantic love but he did love her, too much to hurt her in any way. Could he do it? Say goodbye to passion and romance? He thought so. It wasn't as if either had served him well in the past, after all. Besides, he was thirty. He needed to grow up anyway and didn't all normal relationships settle down eventually? No one could keep up the romance forever. And just yesterday he'd been thinking how much he yearned for calm in his life, for a marriage based on liking and respect. The kind of marriage he and Millie could enjoy.

Eventually Charlie gave up attempting to sleep and got himself and his hangover up, heading to the large combined kitchen, dining and living room to make some much-needed coffee and breakfast. The coffee had just brewed and the bacon started to crisp when he heard footsteps padding in.

'Did we agree to get married last night?' He had never heard Millie sound so tentative.

He turned to face her. She was wearing a pair of the pyjamas she had left at his apartment the last time she had stayed over, her hair bundled up, her face as tired and grey as he suspected his was. Millie. Familiar, comforting.

'That is entirely possible, yes,' he replied. 'Coffee?'

'God, yes, please. In a bucket, if possible.'

'Coming up, take a seat.'

He handed her a coffee, grabbed his and sat at the kitchen table opposite her. The silence stretched on and on. They *never* had uncomfortable silences. Was this an omen? A sign that one of them needed to point out that this whole idea was ludicrous? But he couldn't quite bring himself to speak. Last night he had decided to choose stability and happiness over drama and uncertainty. It felt like both those things were in his grasp.

True, if Millie hadn't told him about her fertility issues then he wouldn't even consider marrying her. She was still so young; she should have years to find a man she loved the way a woman should love her husband, but those years had been taken from her. Time was no longer on her side, and he could do something about that.

'We'd need to have rules,' she said suddenly. 'If we decided to go ahead with it, I mean.'

So, she was seriously considering it. Charlie tried to figure out how he really felt about their drunken idea becoming reality, but the queasiness and the thumping in his head made introspection difficult. 'You want to?'

'I think it's not the worst idea the two of us have ever had when drunk.' Every word sounded careful.

'No, that's still breaking in to see the new baby piglets on Mr Grange's farm when we were on our way home from the pub that night. I still have nightmares about Momma Pig chasing us.'

She smiled as he had intended, the heavy air lifting somewhat. 'Agreed. This is definitely a better idea than that was.'

'But rules? What are you thinking?' Setting ground rules seemed sensible. People so often jumped into marriage with their expectations unaired, with no idea what the other partner hoped for. Look at Liberty's parents, serial romantics with devastating consequences for the children and partners they discarded in their search for happiness.

Better not to think about Liberty right now. Or actually maybe it was better to remember her and how relationship dramas could end up hurting innocent people. That would never happen with Millie, surely, not when they had honesty and openness and integrity on their side.

'If the idea is to get married to have a family, and be happy, we need to agree what that looks like to each of us. Like fidelity.'

Fidelity. They had both been cheated on and they had both been heartbroken by the deception. 'Absolutely. If we're married, we're married. Properly and faithfully

and all that. I don't want one of those marriages of convenience where it's all just for the name and the status
and secretly they're both carrying on with someone else
on the side.' He knew plenty of people in those kinds of
marriages. Each to their own and all that but it wasn't
for him. He wanted a partnership. Like his parents. They
might argue and disagree and drive each other crazy but
they respected each other too.

'Definitely not. So if we do this, we do it properly. The
minute we say "I do" we're exclusive. What about sex?'

Sex. Charlie swallowed. He had never thought of Millie in a sexual way, not even as teens. She was gorgeous,
obviously, but even so… He defaulted to joking. 'My
understanding is it's kind of essential for the having of
the children.'

'Not necessarily.' Millie looked as uncomfortable as
he felt. 'It might be that my fertility issues mean that
we need medical help anyway. There are options, if you
don't want…'

Damn it. He was making his best friend feel like she
wasn't desirable. And of course she was! She was beautiful! Look how Giles had been transfixed by her last
night. It's just *he* had never desired her, which from a
friendship point of view was just as well, but marriage
changed everything. 'That's not… It's not that I don't
want… I don't want a sexless marriage. If you're okay
with that?' He didn't think any sentence ever had been
more uncomfortable to say.

'Yes. Of course.'

That was that then. If they did this, they would have
sex. Which would be fine of course. Eventually. They
would have plenty of time to get used to the idea anyway.

Millie clearly needed to think about starting a family sooner rather than later but a wedding took time to plan.

Millie set her cup down. 'So we're going to get married?' It was half question, half statement.

'Great!' He tried to smile at her. 'That's, I mean, happiest man alive and all that.'

'Charlie,' she said, reaching over to take his hand. 'Keep being honest with me, okay?'

'I will make you a good husband,' he told her. That was honest, he absolutely would do everything in his power to. 'A good father to our children. I think we can have a good marriage, Mills.' There was no reason why not, they had everything going for them, love, liking, understanding, compatibility. In fact, the more his head cleared and he could think, the more this seemed like a good idea.

'Thank you.'

'So, next steps. I guess we tell people. Time being of the essence baby wise and all that.'

'Yes, I guess we do.'

'Okay then. There's a post-wedding meet up at the pub. Let's start with Tabby and Giles. And then we can let the family know. Actually, we just need to tell Tabs. She'll spread the news quicker than a viral video.'

Once they told people, once it was out there, there would be no going back. Charlie had one failed engagement under his belt, he did *not* want two, but that was okay. He had an opportunity for a new start; he would be a fool to jeopardise that in any way.

Liberty had thought she would never drink again and yet here she was in a pub, surrounded by a lot of the same crowd she had been with yesterday, a gin and tonic untouched on the table in front of her. Tabby was clearly not suffering in the same way; her drink was almost finished as she flirted with a man in red trousers and a tweed blazer who Liberty knew she had absolutely zero interest in. But then to Tabby, flirting was as natural as breathing.

Charlie was at a nearby table alongside Millie and Giles. Liberty didn't want to be as aware of him as she was, to be shamelessly eavesdropping on the table, to notice how Charlie seemed nervous, looking at Millie constantly.

'Charlie! And Giles. The old gang back together!' A raucous voice cut through the noise.

Tabby broke off from flirting to glance over at her brother's table, eyes narrowed. 'Ugh, what's Ronan doing here? Total creep. Remember when he suggested we have a threesome? Pig. We were barely sixteen.'

'Did you ever tell Charlie?'

'If I told Charlie every time one of his drunken school friends came on to me, he would have done nothing but get into fights. I got my revenge. Itching powder and some STD rumours took care of him.' Tabby smiled and took another gulp of her rapidly disappearing drink. 'Is my brother actually going to say hi at any point?'

'Ronan! Good to see you, buddy. You weren't at the wedding yesterday, were you?' Charlie was saying.

'Not me, mate. I don't reach Octavia's exacting standards, but I wanted to come catch up with you all anyway. And to see how you were coping, of course. Can't be easy, watching the love of your life marrying another. Bet you went home and had a little cry last night, didn't you?'

'Ugh, I hate him,' Tabby hissed. 'Itching powder is too good for him. I want to chop his testicles off with a spoon.' She half got to her feet but before she could say anything, Millie spoke, her voice loud and clear.

'Actually, he went home with me.'

What? Had Liberty misheard? She glanced at Tabby whose mouth was hanging open in utter shock.

'You see,' Millie continued, 'we just got engaged last night.'

Charlie was *engaged*? To *Millie*?

'What?' Tabby whispered and before Liberty could stop her, her friend was on her feet and barrelling over to her brother at warp speed.

'WHAT?!' Well, that was a lot louder. They had probably heard her on Mars. 'Did I just hear that right? Have you two *finally* got your heads out of your—'

'Tabby.' Charlie looked embarrassed. Liberty watched him carefully. Millie was flushed and obviously still angry with Ronan, Charlie uncomfortable, Giles as shocked as Tabby. Things didn't seem quite right.

But then, she would think that, wouldn't she?

Oh, good God. She didn't still have feelings for Charlie did she? Hadn't she learned her lesson a long time ago?

He didn't just not see her that way, he didn't really see her at all.

'Your you-know-whats,' Tabby continued at a volume far too loud for the assorted hangovers. 'And decided to do something about the *obvious* fact that the two of you are in love with each other?'

In love? Of course they were in love, look at them. Gorgeous, best friends, the kind of people who knew each other inside out. They clearly belonged together.

'If you're asking if we're engaged to be married,' Charlie said, slowly. 'Then the answer is yes.'

Tabby squealed and Liberty wasn't the only one to wince as several sound barriers were broken.

'This is just *perfect*!' Her friend half fell over the table as she hugged everyone except a still shocked Ronan, managing to flirt with Giles at the same time. In many ways it was impressive how Tabby managed to multitask. 'No, you see the *reason* it's perfect is that we've just had a cancellation for a Christmas Eve wedding up at the house! Because you are getting married at the house, right?'

'Oh, of course?' Millie sounded uncertain. Not that Tabby took any notice, ploughing right on.

'And Millie! You've always wanted a Christmas wedding, haven't you?'

A Christmas wedding did sound very romantic. Not that Liberty was the kind of girl to dream of white tulle and flowers, she had made that clear yesterday. But if she was, then yes, a Christmas wedding would be perfect.

She didn't actually hear Millie answer but Tabitha was clearly taking silence as acquiescence. 'Of course! With your colouring, jewel tones and a winter theme will be *perfect* for you.' Tabby clapped her hands again. 'I'm going to go right up to the office and book you in now, before anyone else can steal your date. Mum and Dad are going to be so excited!'

She rushed back to Liberty.

'Libs! Did you hear? Charlie and Millie are engaged!'

'Yes.' Liberty smiled weakly. 'Congratulations. That's brilliant.'

She caught Charlie's eye and for one moment the whole pub disappeared and she was back in Scotland, in the snow, laughing in the pine forest as he threatened her with a snowball and with a sinking realisation she knew she wasn't over him at all—and he was further away from her than ever.

CHAPTER THREE

One week later

'THAT'S JUST NOT POSSIBLE,' Liberty repeated. Maybe if she said the words multiple times they would be true. 'We have a contract.'

'And *we* have a flood,' the woman at the other end also repeated, probably hoping that if she said the words enough times Liberty would accept them and stop arguing. 'I am really sorry, Ms Gray, but there is no way we can accommodate a film crew right now. The clean-up job will take weeks, the drying out alone...'

'I see. I'm sorry.' Sorry for herself as well as for the harried owner of the gorgeous Scottish castle where *Jingle Bells Highlander* was due to be filmed in just two short weeks. Liberty had costume people, props people, camera people, a ton of fake snow not to mention all the production and directorial staff heading to Scotland over the next fortnight. Permits had been secured, transport booked, storage organised, catering found and she herself had been planning to travel up to Scotland next week to start receiving shipments and making sure everything from catering to production suites were up and running for the first day of shooting. And now she had no venue. And as location manager, that was definitely her problem.

Liberty concluded the phone call, her mind already whirring with alternatives. The good news: one, she still had a couple of weeks to sort somewhere, two, it was autumn which meant the seasonal whirl of Christmas and New Year parties weren't yet in full swing and somewhere might just be free for the eight weeks she needed, three, she had the best contact list in the business. The bad news? She had just a couple of weeks to sort it out, the budget didn't allow for more than one venue which meant she needed a Scottish-looking castle, forests, lochs (or a lake) and a forest all in the one place, and it had to be in the UK because this was where all the permits and the shipping was organised for and oh God, this was an utter disaster.

Deep. Breath. Then contact list.

Ten calls later and she was feeling less than optimistic. In fact, she was positively pessimistic. No one had actually laughed at her, but there had been more than a few sharp intakes of breath, and ten reasons why two weeks' notice for a film crew to take over whichever house and land she had targeted really wasn't sufficient. It didn't help that budgets were tight and although they were paying an adequate amount for a normal let, she couldn't throw money at the problem. Funny how enough dollar signs could melt most problems away.

Liberty ran her eye over her list again. She had exhausted all her Scottish contacts; it was time to move to the rest of Ireland and the UK and hope some sweeping landscape shots and enough fake snow would do the rest.

The trill of her phone interrupted her and she snatched it up eagerly, hoping it was one of her earlier contacts with a change of heart or even better, the original venue telling her the flood hadn't been as bad after all and if they just all brought wellies...

'Libs?'

'Tabby?' Excellent, Tabby had been next on her call list. Not only was she someone who would offer the right amount of sympathy and practicality, but she might know of some solution. After all, the Howards owned a successful venue hire business—it helped when your ancestors had married into and built a nice collection of castles, stately homes and hunting lodges. In fact...she ran through the properties in her head. No, none of them were quite right, apart from Glenmere Castle and the family didn't let that out. Pity.

But much as she wanted to vent to her friend, Tabby only had one topic of conversation right now. Charlie's wedding. And Liberty really didn't need any more details or to hear how perfect Millie was.

In a way she preferred Octavia. At least she could hate Octavia but who could hate Millie?

Liberty had known Millie as long as she had known the Howards. Effortlessly cool, dark-haired, gorgeous curves, always there and yet somehow on the outskirts. Liberty had never really hung out with her, there was the age difference of course, but also Millie wasn't part of Charlie's smart society set and often melted into the background when his school friends were around. But she often saw the pair of them in the local pub deep in conversation, or laughing uncontrollably, or returning from long walks, the family spaniel Dexter at their heels. She had just never seen a *spark* between them. But maybe she just hadn't wanted to.

'You don't know of a nice Highland castle going spare

do you?' Get the ask straight in. That way she could head off any wedding talk.

'What's this one called?

'Jingle Bells Highlander.'

'Let me guess, it's about a grumpy but hot laird?'

'Tick.'

'Who discovers the magic of Christmas…'

'Tick.'

'Through…a winsome orphan?'

'Try again.'

'A Christmas elf?'

'Last go…'

'The love of a good woman?'

'Give that girl a prize. Only there will be no love for anyone if I don't find a venue promptly. None of yours are free and Scottish-looking are they? It's a shame you don't rent out Glenmere Castle. That would be perfect.'

'But we do! At least, we haven't yet, but the restoration is almost finished. We'll be listing it for next year soon.'

'How almost is almost?'

'We just need to sign it off…'

'Tabby, you might have just saved Christmas. Is there any way we can use it? It would be perfect!' It really would be. Even better than the original venue in fact. Grey stone and turreted, Glenmere Castle was the archetypal Scottish castle on the shores of its own small but perfectly formed loch framed by snow-topped mountains and surrounded by pine forests.

'I can't say for definite but I'll ask. We've put in quite a lot of holiday accommodation, done up the cottages and built some lodges and there are the rooms in the castle itself, so we'd be able to manage cast and crew I should think. The village and pub would be delighted, they've been impatient for us to open up more, but obviously we couldn't while Grandma still lived there. She hated the whole events and location business, we couldn't have inflicted it on her at her home.'

'Tab, if you could sort this for me, I will owe you forever.'

'A drink will do. Look, our weekly meeting is this afternoon. I'll ask and get back to you with an answer by the end of the day. Will that work? It's going to be a fab meeting because we get to start wedding planning. I have *all* the ideas, I can't wait to tell Charlie my thoughts about ponies.'

Ponies? Better not to ask. 'You're a lifesaver.' Liberty finished the call, her heart heavy. She should be delighted that Tabitha might have the solution to her problem, but all she felt was flat thanks to the reminder that Charlie was getting married.

What had she expected? That once he was over Octavia he would realise that Liberty was the one for him, and come and lay his heart at her feet? She knew better. Liberty had long accepted that she wasn't the kind of girl anyone put first. Had long known to leave before she was left. To keep her heart safe at all times, even if that meant locking it away.

There was a reason Liberty preferred short, safe relationships, ones where feelings weren't involved. No risk of rejection, no risk of getting hurt.

It was a template that had served her well, kept her safe. And she had no intention of changing it any time soon.

'I know dear Millie will take care of the flowers, but...'

'Mum,' Charlie interrupted firmly. 'This is a planning meeting, for the business, not my wedding.'

'But darling, your wedding is business. Goodness knows you've kept us waiting for long enough.'

'To be fair the boy tried, not his fault the filly shied at the fence,' his aunt Felicity said. 'Let's hope this new gal has more staying power.'

Tabitha always said they should do a reality show about the running of the estate, a fly on the wall documentary about an ancient family grappling with the modern world and that their aunt would be the breakout star, ending up on *Strictly* and in pantos. Charlie suspected she was right.

'Dear Millie is so very reliable,' his mother said with a fond smile. She hadn't looked so happy when he had announced his engagement to Octavia, nor at the restoration of it. A short-lived restoration in the end, one Charlie suspected Octavia had engineered to target Layton. He was the kind of man who would find an engaged woman a much more interesting challenge than one readily available. Especially if said woman was engaged to an old school friend.

He waited for the usual pang but instead he felt…nothing. Good. He owed it to Millie to be happy and present in their marriage. It wasn't as if his family didn't have a long history of marrying for something other than love, for land or alliances, for influence or money. Marrying Millie for an heir, for stability and to make his oldest friend happy were some of the best reasons he could think of.

Only December did feel very *soon*. He'd expected more time to get used to the change in circumstances. But then again, from what Millie said, time wasn't on her side, so maybe it was better this way.

'Okay, to business.' Charlie got the meeting back on track. 'Anything to report from last week's events?'

Although each house and venue employed professional

events staff, the family kept a close eye on every detail, often managing bookings themselves, starting each week with a retrospective of the week before and a look at the week ahead before discussing details of events scheduled further out.

'Before we do that,' Tabitha said. 'I have a request. Liberty urgently needs a venue for her latest film, the one she secured has flooded, and she wondered if she could use Glenmere Castle for a couple of months. It's nearly ready, isn't it?'

'Poor Mother,' Felicity murmured. Charlie didn't know if she was referring to his grandmother's death of the year before or her certain horror at her home being used for commercial purposes. She had never approved of the letting out of the family houses, retiring to Scotland once widowed which meant, in deference to her, the castle had been kept for family use with only the estate cottages used for holiday lets.

'When does she need it exactly?' His mother, the undisputed inspiration and force behind the family business, pulled up the booking calendar, displaying it on the large screen at one end of the conference room so they could all see it. 'We haven't started to market Glenmere yet so it's free any time from the New Year. Rather a coup to have a film shoot for its first booking.'

'Well, that's the thing, she needs it in two weeks but she needs to be on-site pretty much straight away. It does mean income this year and it would be great to showcase it in use as we start to market it, wouldn't it?'

'Two weeks? Impossible. The insurance hasn't been sorted and there is still snagging to do. I'm sorry, Tabby, I would love to help dear Liberty out of course but...'

'Hang on,' Charlie said. 'How much is she talking about, Tabs?'

His sister named a sum and he whistled. It wasn't the most they had ever been offered, true, but they would be foolish to turn it down. 'The Glenmore restoration has been a substantial investment. The income from a whole estate let for two months would be very welcome, especially to the village and pub. I know they enjoyed some uplift from the builders, but they really need those cottages filled as soon as possible and there has been some grumbling that they will miss out on Christmas and Hogmanay trade. Why wait until next year if we have a booking ready to go?'

'But, darling,' his mother said. 'A film crew? You know how a film takes over the whole house. There's Queen Victoria's bed, and the Gainsborough. The insurance will be a nightmare, not to say that we're not set up for *any* visitors let alone a full venue takeover.'

Valid points but not insurmountable. 'I agree, one of us will need to be on-site for the first few weeks, possibly the whole time, but that's no reason not to do it.'

'Not me, point-to-point season will start soon and I need to be getting the horses ready,' Felicity said quickly and Charlie grinned at her. If horses weren't involved his aunt wasn't interested, but she loved Howard Hall and her historical knowledge was invaluable.

'Don't worry, Aunt Flic, I wasn't planning to exile you,' he reassured her, looking hopefully at his sister.

'Sorry, Charlie, but this is my busiest time,' Tabitha said regretfully. 'I want to help Libs, but between autumn weddings, photo shoots and the start of Christmas, not to mention *your* wedding, I have no free time between now and the New Year.' His sister spent much of her time at their double-fronted London Regency town house managing the many events and filming requests for its famous ballroom and perfectly preserved exterior.

'No, I see that. In that case I think it makes sense that I go.' As soon as he said the words Charlie realised it was what he had been hoping for from the moment Tabitha had mentioned the castle. Scotland. Fresh sharp air. Space galore. Time to breathe. Everything was moving so very fast, he needed to get away and process it all.

But, on the other hand, Glenmere Castle, with Liberty, wasn't exactly getting away. Unlike Octavia, Charlie had never enjoyed pulling other people into the middle of the constant soap opera of their relationship. But New Year's Eve eight years ago that was exactly what had happened. He could tell himself that he hadn't expected Octavia to show up at the castle; after all, they had been on one of their many breaks, he could tell himself it was only a kiss, he could tell himself that Liberty had been an adult, but the reality was that he knew she had a schoolgirl crush on him and he had had no business kissing her at all. Just as he had had no business being so aware of her at the wedding last week. No business noticing her in the pub when he was announcing his engagement to another woman. No business thinking of her in any way other than as Tabby's friend.

Maybe he had been too eager to offer to get away after all. But who else was there?

'You?' Tabby said. *'Now?'*

'What about Millie?' his mother asked.

'Apart from Dad, I'm the only person not tied to a venue and I don't think he wants to head to Scotland for the whole of autumn,' he pointed out. Charlie and his father ran the entire family business, and although the events side was a substantial income generator there was a lot more to the Howard Estate. Charlie and his father had to juggle land management, tenants, agricultural schemes, shooting permits, woodland management and conservation as well as investments, stocks and shares and the myriad assets from art and jewellery to land all over the world. The Howard holding was ancient and substantial and Charlie had been bred to run it since he was a child.

'All I need is a laptop really,' he continued. 'Besides, I oversaw a lot of the restoration work at Glenmere so I am probably the best person to launch it. I can troubleshoot issues on-site, make sure no one breaks Queen Victoria's bed and work quite easily. There's a lot to do, final snagging, getting the marketing done, some forestry and estate work I need to look at, I'd have to head up over the autumn anyway even if we didn't agree to let it. You know, even apart from helping Liberty, I think we would be idiots to turn this down.'

'But Charlie, you have a wedding to plan.'

He grinned at his mother. 'Darling, you have made it quite clear that you and Millie have a wedding to plan and my job is to agree to whatever you decide. I can do that just as well from Scotland. Besides, it's just a few hours on the train, I can easily pop down for anything essential.' He nodded at Tabitha. 'Get Liberty to send me the contracts and her timetable and list of requirements today and tell her we'll get back to her as soon as possible.' Charlie pushed away his doubts. Eight years was a long time ago and it was just one kiss. Ridiculous to even remember it really, and it wasn't as if he hadn't seen Liberty since then, she was Tabby's best friend, practically part of the family. Besides, he wasn't planning to head to Scotland for a clandestine fling, it was work and there would be an entire film crew on-site alongside them the whole time. He'd probably barely see Liberty. And of course, most importantly, he was now engaged to Millie.

Scotland in autumn and then on the cusp of winter, what could be nicer? Glenmere, with its air so fresh it almost hurt, roaring fires and mountains. Time away from weddings and all the responsibility that would descend on him when he said *I do*. He had meant his proposal— if you could call their conversation anything so conventional—and genuinely thought marrying Millie was both sensible and right, but it was all happening so quickly, they could both do with some space.

Now all he had to do was let his bride know that he would be leaving her to the tender mercies of his mother and sister.

CHAPTER FOUR

As soon as the meeting finished Charlie headed outside, managing to dodge his mother and Tabby who both had a long list of wedding-related queries for him. He breathed in, glad of the fresh air after the stuffy meeting room. The weather felt more autumnal today as October dawned, crisp and cool, the trees beginning to tinge orange and red.

He headed away from the house towards the ornamental lake, pulling his phone out of his pocket, and then paused, for once not sure how to approach his oldest friend. Usually, Millie messaged several times a day, sending photos or jokes or links to things she'd read she thought he might enjoy, and he did the same back to her. But the last week there had been near radio silence. They needed to get back to their old ease with each other somehow before their rapidly approaching wedding.

It wasn't the being married part that concerned him. He and Millie were totally comfortable together, they had been sharing beds since they were tiny, she knew all his most shameful secrets and proudest moments, his worries and frustrations and hopes and dreams. They would make a fantastic team, just as his parents did. But he had to admit the sex part was preying on his mind. He just didn't see Millie like that and it felt wrong to try and do so, despite their agreement to try and make babies the traditional way. To have a real and active sex life throughout their marriage. Was he naïve to think this could work? He hadn't even kissed her yet, not in the way he would be expected to as the wedding approached—maybe they needed to try and get it over with, just barge through the embarrassment.

Only now he was heading to the opposite end of the country for over two months. With a woman he had been attracted to once before. A woman he was spending far too much time thinking about given his newly engaged status.

Charlie frowned at his phone before finding Millie's name and, before he could overthink things, pressed the call symbol. The phone rang for a couple of rings before she answered.

'Hey.'

'Hey, is this a bad time?'

'No, no. I am just designing the colours for that pitch, you know the big corporate event I mentioned.'

'How's it going?'

'Hmm, not quite there. It feels a little brassy at the moment. They want glamour but classy glamour, diamonds not rhinestones, you know?'

Charlie had helped plan enough weddings and events to know exactly what she meant. 'Do they want Christmassy colours?'

'Yes, but not traditional, so red and white are out which makes things tricky. I'll get there. I've just been distracted.'

He knew how that felt. 'We've just had the weekly meeting and there's an opportunity to let Glenmere Castle for a couple of months starting now.'

He could hear her surprise at the abrupt change in topic. 'Erm, that's good.'

'For a film shoot. Liberty is the location manager, you know, Tabby's friend.' Now why did he feel guilty just saying her name? Charlie winced; he knew why. It was because he could still see the flash of her grey eyes as she stared Octavia down, feel her hand in his as he led her into the dance. See the curve of her full mouth smiling up at him. He had no problem imagining kissing Liberty Gray. As long as he didn't turn fantasy into reality. 'She had a crisis. A flood or something. Anyway, we are stepping in and offering her a venue.'

'Okay.' Her unspoken question came through loud and clear: *why have you called me to tell me this? What's really going on, Charlie?*

'Anyway,' he hurried on. 'We're not quite set up for letting yet. Still snagging and so on and so the only way we could agree is if one of us is on-site for the shoot.'

'By one of us you mean you?' Millie had always known *exactly* what he meant.

'I know the timing is horrible...'

Was that a laugh or a cry? 'We are supposed to be getting married in less than three months, Charlie, and you are seriously telling me you are heading off to Scotland for the entire duration with everything still to plan?'

'Is this our first marital disagreement?' The joke fell flat and he winced. 'Mum and Tabby seem to have everything in hand...'

'But this is *our* wedding! I don't want to be steamrollered by your family. It might not be the most traditional of set-ups but that doesn't mean it shouldn't be meaningful, personal. If things go the way we plan, then this will be the only wedding either of us have.'

She was right, of course she was. 'I'm sorry, Millie. I'm an arse. I didn't think. You're right. I can tell Tabby we can't accommodate the booking after all...' Which meant letting Liberty down and he really didn't want to do that. He still felt like he owed her, for that thought-less kiss, for her rescue at the wedding. But given the way she'd occupied his mind recently, maybe cancelling *was* for the best.

'Is that the alternative?' She sighed. 'I don't want you to lose out. I'm being silly, it's just a little overwhelm-ing, you know?'

'I really do.' Charlie had reached the lake and he started to follow the path round trying to think of a way to balance the different responsibilities. 'Look, Giles is around. How about I get him to stand in for me for any wedding-related business? I'll be at the end of the phone whenever you need a decision, and he can be there for all the tastings and what-nots so that you're not alone and at my family's mercy. He's my best man after all. Let's make him earn it.'

'Giles. Right.' There was something indefinable in her voice. Was it disapproval? The two of them were a little prickly, they always had been; he didn't consider Giles's momentary interest in Millie at the wedding huge prog-ress. But it was one thing for his two best friends to dis-like each other, quite another for his wife and his best friend. Maybe it would be a good thing for them to spend some quality time together.

'If I was marrying anyone else I would want you, ob-viously, but I think juggling best woman and bride is too much, don't you?'

To his relief she laughed, sounding much more like

her old self. 'True! Look, of course you should go. I'll manage, no one is indispensable, not even the groom.'

'That's what Mum and Tabby think. They think I am completely surplus to requirements.'

'They're just excited for us. It's nice.'

'It is.' Charlie sank onto a stone bench and watched a pair of swans glide past, their almost grown-up cygnets not too far behind. He was glad they had decided to pretend to be in love. He wasn't sure his family or Millie's mum would have been quite as enthusiastic if they had known the real reasons behind the wedding. 'Are you?'

'Am I what?'

'Excited for us?'

Millie didn't answer for several seconds. 'I'm excited to get started with our lives. I kind of wish we could fast forward through the engagement and wedding part though.'

'We could fly to Vegas tonight.' He half meant it.

'Is that what you want?'

It was Charlie's turn to fall silent. Was it? Like Millie he would prefer to get on with the marriage now the decision had been made, to get past the awkwardness and the ceremony and just be them, Charlie and Millie. But at the same time he was glad of the respite Scotland offered him. 'Mother would never forgive me—nor would yours. And I know better than to upset the cook.'

He was still watching the swans. Didn't they mate for life? How did they decide which swan was their soulmate? Did they ever regret the decision? Wish they had gone with a different option? He and Millie had decided to get married so impulsively and she had been single for so long, floored by the news about her fertility. He didn't want her to have any regrets. 'Look, Millie...'

'Mmm?'

'I'm going to be gone for a while.'

'I know.'

'I meant what I said about fidelity, but we're not actually married yet. So, look, what happens in Vegas stays in Vegas. I'm fine with that.'

'Charlie, what on *earth* are you babbling about? I thought we decided not to go to Vegas?'

'I mean, if you want a final fling or two or whatever before you say *I do* then you should go for it. Sow those wild oats as my grandfather used to say.' Charlie had never understood what he meant before but now it made some kind of sense. When marriage was about things other than attraction and desire then was it so wrong to allow yourself to feel those things one last time?

'A final fling? Charlie, I have never had a fling in my life!'

'So maybe you should, while you can.'

'Hang on, is this about you?' Her voice sharpened. 'Are *you* having regrets? Do you want to be sowing oats?'

'Me? No. I'll be in the wilds of Scotland.' With Liberty. But he was certainly not planning on sowing anything with her.

'With an entire film crew and no doubt several eligible actresses, it's not as if you'll be a hermit in a bothy,' she pointed out. 'I'm sure there will be enough women for several flings. An entire magic porridge pot of wild oats.'

'I didn't mean it like that…' But he could see why she would think he did and given his recent thoughts he didn't blame her. Millie had always been something of a mind reader where he was concerned. 'I'm not interested in actresses or anyone. Honestly, Mills, this isn't me saying I want to sleep with someone before settling down with you. I've never actually had a fling either.' After all, he had only actually had sex with one woman before.

'Then maybe you *should* do some sowing too. Maybe you're right. We are about to commit to each other for life, maybe we should, oh I don't know, not go out there *looking* for a fling, but not feel guilty if the opportunity comes up. Argh. I can't believe I just said that, but I do mean it.'

'Okay then.' He watched the swans a little longer, turning her words over in his mind. 'This is weird. Isn't this weird?'

'A little. But we've always been able to talk about anything before. I think it's important we still do. And I think with you gone for two months or so and the wedding so close you're right. This is our last time to, you know, act on pure attraction rather than being sensible.'

'Millie Myles. Are you saying you're not attracted to me?'

'I'm working on it.' She laughed but he could hear the truth in her voice—and a tinge of worry. A truth and worry he understood all too well.

'We'll get there. Okay, let me break the glad news to Giles…'

'You're going to tell *Giles* that we are allowed to sleep with someone else while we're engaged?'

'No! He believes he has played Cupid and who am I to dissuade him? I'm going to let him know that his best man duties have expanded somewhat. You're okay with that? I know you and he can be a little off but he's a good sort when you get to know him.'

'Yes. Of course. Look. I better go, this colour scheme won't resolve itself. Bye, Charlie.'

'Bye, Mills.'

He ended the call feeling uneasy. He had a *carte blanche* for a no strings affair if he wanted it, but his marriage to Millie was about stopping the drama and uncertainty that had characterised his relationship with Octavia. He didn't need any last-minute fun, but he was glad he had made it clear Millie was a free woman if she wanted to be. Millie deserved all the love and happiness in the world after all. It was up to him to supply that once the wedding had taken place, but if she did get some fun in before then good for her.

But as he walked back to the house it wasn't Millie he was thinking of but the memory of the heavy fall of red hair down a slender back, the smile in dark grey eyes and the long-ago memory of a kiss in the snow. He hadn't been lying when he had told Millie he wasn't interested in actresses, he wasn't. And he had no right to be attracted to Liberty, especially after what had happened last time they were in Scotland at the same time. He had embroiled her in his messy affairs once before. He respected her far too much to do it again.

Which made spending the next few weeks with her an interesting challenge. No matter that he and Millie had just agreed to a get-out clause, Charlie needed to remember that he was a happily engaged man and any relationship with Liberty Gray was professional only.

'What did they say?'

Liberty snatched up the phone the second she saw Tabby's name flash up, heart hammering. There would still be two weeks of logistical and administrative nightmares if the Howards agreed to rent her the castle, but that she could cope with. Heading back to square one to start her search again was a far more daunting prospect.

'It's a goer!'

Liberty's hand tightened on the phone as she digested her friend's words, unsure if they had been spoken or she had just heard what she wanted to hear. 'It's a goer? Really?'

'Really and truly! Glenmere Castle is yours for as long as you need it.'

'Oh, thank you! I owe you, I owe you all. The biggest hamper you have ever seen will be wending your way this Christmas.'

'No hamper required, we're happy to help. Honestly, Charlie says the sooner we start monetising Glenmere the better, the renovations went a little over budget, I think.'

The sound of Charlie's name made Liberty's heart beat a little faster, a little harder, a little more painfully. For a moment, during that wedding dance, she had felt as if they had connected in some way, and despite her best intentions she'd been aware of a frisson of anticipation when he'd walked into the pub the following day. Anticipation which turned to shock the moment his engagement was so suddenly announced.

Shock because to the best of her admittedly champagne-addled recollections he and Millie hadn't looked loved up in any way at the wedding. Close, friendly, even intimate but not on the verge of being engaged. She'd actually thought there was something between Millie and Giles, which just showed her how off her radar was.

Shock because for a short time her old crush had come rearing back. It had taken several stern talking tos before she had regained her usual equilibrium. Liberty didn't do crushes, she didn't do vulnerability, she didn't do needy. She was independent and self-sufficient and that was the way she liked it, thank you very much.

With an effort she dragged her mind back to her actual job and the myriad things she now needed to organise. 'Great! Okay. Shall I send you the list of what we need, the shooting schedule, crew and cast names, bedroom requirements—can we use the rooms in the castle as well as the cottages? We may need rooms in the village as well...' Her mind was racing, where was her laptop? She needed to make lists, make all the lists.

'Absolutely. Look, I'm on my way back to London so why don't we grab dinner later and have a quick chat about immediate next steps? I know you're busy, Libs, but you have to eat...' as Liberty started to protest. 'I'll grab something and come to you so don't worry about cooking. But then I'll need to hand over to Charlie. I have a really full schedule in London, so much as I would have loved to work with you, I need to stay in town. But Charlie can manage most of his stuff remotely so it makes sense for him to be the family representative on-site.'

'Charlie?' Liberty's mouth was dry. 'On-*site*? But surely with the wedding so close he needs to be in Norfolk, not all the way up in Scotland?'

'To be honest, between me, Mum and Millie there isn't oodles for him to do.' Typical that the bride was at the end of Tabitha's list. 'The estate hasn't been snagged properly yet, you'll be the first to use it, plus we haven't even started to hire the event organiser, or the new general manager let alone train them so one of us really needs to be there. You'll be done by mid-December won't you? He'll be back in plenty of time for the wedding. We've decided on Christmas Eve.'

'Right.' Scotland with Charlie. That was unexpected. Unwelcome. But it would be different to the last time she had been at Glenmere Castle with him. It was autumn, not Hogmanay, she was older and wiser, and this was *purely* professional. Besides, she would be far too busy to even know he was there.

Liberty spent rest of the day organising her tasks into various to-do lists, checking the clock to see when she would be able to call LA and fill in the production company—always better to be able to deliver bad news with a solution in hand. She kept in contact with Tabby who arranged a call with the Howard Estate lawyer to draw up a contract similar to the one Liberty had arranged with the original venue and Liberty reciprocated with several long, involved emails to be sent on to Charlie about timelines, numbers of people and other requirements from electricity supply to parking arrangements—always more complicated when lots of large lorries were involved. At least they wouldn't need trailers, not if they were sleeping on-site, but they would need make-up rooms, a costume fitting room…she created another list.

'Charlie has promised to be in touch asap,' Tabby said as they spoke for the fifth time in an hour. 'He just needed to sort a few things with Millie today and then he is all yours.'

'Great.' Her heart gave a painful thump at the image Charlie being all hers conjured up.

What was *wrong* with her? She had been over Charlie for years! The painful and obvious crush she had had on him before The Kiss (she always thought of it with capitals) had subsided in a wave of humiliation and regret afterwards. Worse, it had cemented everything her family had made clear, that she was destined to always be the one left behind, unwanted daughter and sister…

It was painful to remember that back then she had still hoped that someone would *see* her, really see her, would want her, show her that she was enough. In some ways she should thank Charlie for confirming her worst fears. She'd used the experience to move on, to harden, to promise herself never to allow herself to be so vulnerable again. And she'd kept her promise, dating carefully, for fun only, calling time before anything deeper could emerge, and that strategy had kept her safe. She wouldn't allow anyone in and nothing and nobody could change that. Especially not Charlie Howard.

CHAPTER FIVE

FINALLY, THE LONG day was over. LA had been called, had exploded and then calmed down, new contracts had been sent over and forwarded to LA, details sent to the production company so that the cast and crew could be updated, logistics contacted, transport diverted and Liberty began to breathe again. She needed to head up to Scotland as soon as possible, ideally the next day, which meant packing and buying a train or plane ticket, but she was so tired she couldn't face either just yet. A very hot very deep bath and an equally deep glass of wine were more than deserved.

Only Tabby was due to head over. Liberty's brain hurt and she wasn't sure she was up to any more organising today but her friend had promised food and she *did* need to eat. Liberty opened her fridge to see if she had anything in and could put Tabby off, but the contents were too depressing to contemplate. A limp lettuce, a shrivelled handful of tomatoes, hard cheese, eggs of an indeterminate date. Great. At least she had time for the bath and the wine before Tabby got there.

Her buzzer rang, making her jump as she glanced at the clock. It was seven and Tabby wasn't due for another half an hour. She might be early for the first time in her whole life but it was unlikely.

'Hello?'

'Liberty?' Deep, masculine, familiar. 'It's Charlie, Charlie Howard.'

Charlie Howard was at her flat? Charlie Howard knew where her flat *was*?

'I know you are expecting Tabby but as I am going to be the on-site manager she thought it might be more sensible to cut out the middle woman and speak directly. I haven't had a chance to read all the emails you and Tab sent but we could go over them together now. If that's okay?'

'Um…' Her wine! Her bath! Her stomach grumbled. Her dinner. The dinner Tabby was going to bring. Hopefully the eggs were salvageable after all.

'If it's not presumptuous I bought food, Tabs said she was supposed to be supplying dinner and made it clear I had to step up,' Charlie added and Liberty leaned against the wall in relief as she pressed the button that released the door.

'Dinner is the magic word. Come on up.' She took a quick frantic look around the room, but it was too late to do any tidying now. At least she hadn't got any drying lingerie on display and if he wasn't impressed by the pile of romance novels stacked by the sofa then that was his problem.

She opened her front door and waited at the top of the stairs for him. 'Come in, this is me.'

'Nice place.'

'Thank you. It's not a stately home or anything but I like it.'

Liberty lived in a mansion block in Marylebone, in a two-bedroom first-floor flat with high ceilings, huge sash windows, a non-working fireplace, decent soundproof-

ing and oodles of character. It was also way out of the
budget of a freelance location manager, but her maternal
grandmother, realising how rootless she was as her parents married and remarried, had gifted it to her for her
eighteenth birthday.

'Your inheritance early,' she had said.

Liberty loved her home, the safety it represented,
the sanctuary of it. Now Charlie Howard was here in it,
something she had never expected to happen but admittedly had fantasised about once or twice. Okay, a little
more than that. She tried to see it through his eyes: carefully chosen jewel-coloured sofas and chairs, an eclectic
mix of pictures, plants everywhere—she needed to let
her neighbour know they would need watering earlier
than expected—filled bookshelves, books overspilling
onto the coffee table and floor, a dining table covered
with scrawled pieces of paper and her still-open laptop
in the bay window. The small but functional kitchen was
through a door on the far wall, two double bedrooms and
bathroom further along the narrow hall.

'So,' he said, holding up the paper bag he had brought
with him. 'Food? Do you trust me with your cooker? I
promise I'm safe.'

'Cooker? Oh. Right. Of course, just through there.' She
hadn't expected that Charlie intended to cook but sure
enough, rather than a take-out the bag contained fresh
pasta, vegetables, tomatoes and anchovies. Soon he was
chopping the vegetables with a languid ease that made her
stomach contract. *Stop watching his hands, Liberty.* 'Just
a simple puttanesca,' he said as she handed him some
wine and her ovaries immediately jumped to attention.

'Great. So, what did you want to discuss?' Keep focused on work, that was the way to survive the next few hours, weeks, months.

'How about we wait till we're eating?' Charlie suggested. So much for that strategy. 'How's your father? His last play got great reviews.'

'He's never been happier, apparently. Finally discovered the joy of a work-life balance and being a hands-on dad. Shame it took four starter marriages and six children he was less hands-on with before he had this epiphany.' She tried for dark humour, but knew she hit bitterness instead and Charlie shot her a quick comprehending look.

'It must be a lot having siblings so tiny. I'm not sure how I'd feel if my father suddenly presented me with a bundle of joy at his age.'

'Luckily for me, it's not the first time. I'm used to it. The truth is I don't see much of him, he wasn't that impressed when I decided on a career behind rather than in the spotlights. Not a boost for the family brand, you know? I guess it might be different if I was writing or directing.'

Charlie emptied the diced onion and garlic into the frying pan, the air instantly mouth-wateringly aromatic. 'How about your older siblings, do you see much of any of them? Some of them act, don't they? Obviously Orlando does.' Orlando Gray, her oldest brother on her father's side, had recently been cast in a superhero film which, along with the success of her father's play and his new marriage had thrust her family back into the gossip pages and headlines. Not that they were ever far from them.

'Apart from me all his other grown-up kids are models, actors, reality stars or influencers—*they* love the spotlight like a proper Gray. Truthfully though I see more of them in the headlines or on social media or on TV than in real life. I don't really know them, any of the halves in fact.' Liberty had never thought of any of her seven siblings on her father's side and three on her mother's as anything other than *half*. There was just too much of a distance between them, and not just in age.

'That's a shame.'

She shrugged. 'I guess it doesn't help that I have never really lived with any of them. Dad's oldest two hated my mum and resented me and so *we* don't really talk. I didn't see much of Dad after he split up with Mum, Fleur, his next wife, didn't want me around which means I've never really known their three and, and of course the twins are young enough to be my own kids. And as for Mum's three, not only is there a considerable age gap but I was already at boarding school when Wren was born. I never spent more than half the school holidays at their house and never stay there now so always feel like some kind of distant aunt, not a sister. Some holidays I spent more time with your family.' She sipped her wine pensively. 'It's a shame Mum and Jack didn't have children, if they had they would have been closer to me in age, and Jack would have made sure I was part of the family. He was a great stepdad, I think I was more upset when she split up with him, than with Dad.'

Wow. Where had all *that* come from? Charlie had asked a polite question and she had turned her answer into a Wikipedia page about her family. She gulped another mouthful of wine and grabbed the bottle to refill it. 'More wine?' Although his glass was barely touched while hers was nearly empty. *Keep it together, Liberty. This is a working dinner, not a date.*

'Okay, this feels ready, bowls?' Charlie ladled heaped spoonsful of aromatic pasta into the bowls she dutifully provided and she took them through into the main living and dining space, hurriedly sweeping the piles of notes off the table before setting them down.

If her teenage self could see her now! Tête-à-tête at a table for two with Charlie Howard eating a meal he had cooked for her! Of course, in her teenage fantasies the evening would have ended with some serious snogging on the sofa and so, considering the amount of anchovies, onion and garlic in the pasta, it was probably a good idea that he was safely engaged and the evening was solely about work.

If it had been up to Charlie, he would have headed straight up to Scotland and met Liberty there, not turned up at her house to cook for her, but in the end he couldn't think of a reason to tell Tabby why her idea he swap in for her wouldn't work that wouldn't make her suspicious.

Tabby had always been very protective of her friend. She wasn't the only one, Charlie's whole family had taken Liberty under their wing after that first summer holiday visit when it had become painfully clear how little her parents cared where she was and who she was with. Soon Liberty had become a regular visitor. She often spent Christmas with them, most of the summer holidays. She had her own room at Howard Hall; even now Charlie's mum took her out for a birthday meal every year, met her for cocktails when in town.

If they knew Charlie had allowed her to become em-broiled in his and Octavia's affairs, Tabby and his mother would have found it hard to forgive him. That was fine, he had found it hard to forgive himself; he wasn't sure he ever really had. Being drunk was no excuse. He still couldn't explain it. How Liberty had one minute just been Tabby's friend, part of the furniture—and the next infinitely desirable.

And then he had got back with Octavia and done his best to put that night, and the attraction he had felt for Liberty to one side. Which was why this sudden flaring up of interest was so inexplicable, not to mention horribly timed. He had to go back to seeing her as a long-standing family friend, nothing more.

Although Liberty seemed a little on edge at first, once they started to discuss her requirements and needs for the weeks ahead she started to relax, showing herself to be clear, focused and extremely professional. It shouldn't have been a surprise finding out just how sharp and knowledgeable she was. After all, she had grown up on film sets and backstage in theatres, had acted as a child and teen, but the job she had now wasn't one she could hold through nepotism alone; it required a forensic brain, a lot of spreadsheets and a terrifying amount of health and safety knowledge. Just like running a family estate with land all over the country in fact. Charlie couldn't help but be impressed. And daunted. She had to squeeze several months of planning into just two weeks and it was clear there was a lot of work ahead, no matter how organised she was.

'I am planning to drive up to Scotland tomorrow,' he said at last. 'You are welcome to come with me, unless you have a ticket booked to travel some other way?'

Now why had he offered that? It took over eight hours to drive to Glenmere Castle. A working dinner was one thing, a long journey in close proximity quite another.

'Changing my plane ticket is something I *haven't* got round to doing today,' she said, her smile tired. 'I originally meant to go up early next week, but of course I had already done several site visits. Luckily, I know Glenmere pretty well, but understanding how it will work as a set is very different to staying there as a guest. I need to plan where every van, lorry, cable will go, think about catering, airport pickups. At least it's not too far from the original venue…' Her voice trailed off as she clearly made several mental notes before she focused again. 'I didn't even answer your question. Yes, please. A lift would be amazing.'

Charlie eyed her with concern. She was pale, shadows under her eyes. 'Look, I'll clear up…'

'But you cooked!'

'…while you make a start on packing and then get an early night. I'll pick you up at nine, it's a long journey and I want to get started as soon as possible, but I'm aware you have had a long day already.'

'Nature of the job.' She tried and rather adorably failed to suppress a yawn. 'Early starts and late-night planning sessions are par for the course.'

'That's as may be, but we'll do no more planning tonight. Go on, start packing. I'll let myself out.'

Liberty's eyes narrowed and Charlie could see her considering arguing back before she laughed and capitulated. 'Okay, you're right. An all-nighter will help no one, I need to see what I am dealing with first. Thank you, for dinner and for the lift, and for bailing us out like this. I can't tell you how grateful I am. You have saved the film and my life.'

'I wouldn't want to deprive the world of *Jingle Bell Highlander*.'

'Maybe we could get you a walk-on part,' she suggested, her sly smile showcasing the dimple at the side of her mouth. 'You do have a kilt up there, don't you?'

'Like you I prefer to be firmly behind the scenes. Besides, no thanks required. We're not doing you a favour, this is business.'

'Do you always cook dinner for your business associates?'

'Only when a two-month let is involved.' Charlie stood up and collected their plates. 'Go on, the sooner you get started the sooner you can get some sleep.'

It didn't take long to clear up and Charlie left the flat, after saying goodbye to Liberty through her open bedroom door. She waved absent-mindedly, concentrating on the piles of clothes on her bed with a look of mild concern.

'Don't forget your thermals,' he called as he closed the front door. He half jogged down the stairs with a sense of relief. He could see Liberty and he working well together. She knew the estate and would respect it and the people who lived and worked there, and despite a couple of moments of silence, the evening had felt warm and relaxed. More, he liked her company. She had grown into an assured—and beautiful—woman. If he was single…

No. Even if he was single Liberty Gray was off-limits. Partly because she was his sister's best friend and getting involved with her was the very definition of messy, and partly because he still felt guilty about that kiss all those years ago. She had been too young to be mixed up in his and Octavia's drama and although he could honestly say Octavia had been the last thing on his mind when kissing Liberty, he *had* chosen her over the younger woman. Partly to protect Liberty. Octavia was never kind to women she suspected he was interested in, and he had tried to shield them rather than confront her. One of many things about their shared past that made him uncomfortable. Their relationship had had a script and it simply hadn't occurred to him that he could just rewrite it.

But it had been badly done. The best thing he could do was stop thinking about how expressive Liberty's eyes were and concentrate on the work ahead. And he definitely couldn't think about the clause he and Millie had agreed upon just that day. The last thing he needed to do was drag Liberty into more of his relationship drama, even if it was a new relationship and new drama. Besides, she probably wouldn't even be interested.

But as he switched the light off that night, he couldn't help but think how ironic it was that he should find himself so attracted to Liberty the moment he had agreed to settle down with someone else. But he had made a commitment to Millie and he intended to see it through. She'd promised him a future free of drama, of messy complicated emotions, a future based on respect, friendship and mutual goals. It was exactly what he needed after the rollercoaster of his teens and twenties and he needed to be careful not to jeopardise it. Millie was his best friend and he loved her and those two things were far more important than the rekindling of a spark of attraction that was probably completely one-sided. Professional, friendly and absolutely no flirting. That was the key to getting through the next few weeks.

CHAPTER SIX

THE NEXT DAY Charlie collected Liberty on the dot of nine as arranged and they headed north out of London and onto the A1 to drive all the way up the east of England before hitting Scotland. Liberty was punctual and surprisingly lightly packed. Charlie was used to Octavia and Tabby, who had little in common apart from their tendency to need a huge suitcase for one night away 'just in case' and would have brought half their belongings for a trip this long.

'Got your thermals?' he asked with a grin and she nodded.

'Wellies and my puffer jacket too. I know what it gets like up there.'

'Forecast is gorgeous right now, sunny and fresh, but a lot can change between now and December.'

The traffic was slow heading out of London and Charlie concentrated on the road as Liberty fired up her laptop and immediately started tapping away. 'I might get quite a few calls,' she warned him. 'Will that annoy you?'

'Not at all, just let me know if you need the music turned down.'

'Can I ask even if I'm not on a call?' There was a tantalising glimpse of that dimple again.

'What's wrong with my music?'

'Middle-of-the-road men with guitars? Nothing. It's lovely.'

'Classic nineties indie.'

'Proving my point...'

'Feel free to change the station.'

'No, no, who am I to deprive you of lad rock? You are the driver after all.'

'Too right.' But Charlie found himself flicking through the stations until he found one with more of a mix and left it playing. He knew he was unadventurous with music, Millie teased him about the same thing. 'Okay,' he said once they were safely out of London and he had put the car into cruise control. 'Do you want to talk through where everyone is sleeping?'

'Do you mind? I know you have your own stuff to do.'

'I do but not while driving and, like you say, you haven't been to Glenmere for some time and the renovation means a lot of changes you're not up to speed on.' He paused. 'Obviously this is your gig but I've been giving it some thought.'

'Go on then. I'm poised.' She tapped her keyboard in demonstration.

'It makes sense to put the director in the apartment we have designated for the general manager. It has its own sitting room and study as well as a small kitchen, so they will have everything they need whether they want time alone or private meetings whilst at the centre of everything.'

'Agreed.' Liberty typed quickly. 'Okay, let's do the actors next.'

'How many and do you think they will prefer a cottage or a room in the castle itself? It's all been done up since you last saw it,' he added. 'Everything is redecorated, no more sharing cold bathrooms with half the enamel missing off the bath and power free showers! En suites all round. There are ten guest bedrooms in the castle itself. Guests also get use of the breakfast room, games room and sitting room. Plus there's the library, restaurant and bar which are open to people staying on the estate too. But of course, with a whole estate hire we can be more flexible around who uses what.'

'Let me see.' She ran her finger down her screen as she counted. 'The main parts are the hero and heroine of course, her best friend, the housekeeper, groundsman and the pub owner, the hero's mother and his childhood best friend. There's also his little sister, but she will need a two-bedroom cottage because her mother is chaperoning.' Liberty read through the list again. 'So that's eight, leaving two bedrooms for the assistant director and producer. The rest of management can be in cottages. How many bedrooms does the pub have again?'

'Eight. And we have six cottages and eight new log cabin lodges with thirty-two bedrooms between them. There are also four tree-houses and two new domes on the other side of the loch but if we can avoid using them I would prefer it. The tree-houses are supposed to be all-weather but I want to check them out in more extreme weather before anyone stays there and the domes are really only meant for a night or two, not a long stay. They really are just one room with a screened off bathroom. But we can use them for any visitors I guess. Some of the villagers may be willing to do bed and breakfast as well.'

'Okay, that's forty rooms. We have two make-up artists, two hairstylists, three for costumes, then there's camera, electrics, scenery…' Liberty muttered to herself as she typed furiously. 'I'd rather not have anyone share, but I think we might be in luck if I call on those bed and breakfast rooms. I'll keep a couple spare as well for any visiting producers or other dignitaries, but it's good to know about the domes which sound very intriguing by the way as do the tree-houses. You must have spent a fortune.'

'Fortune is the word,' Charlie said a little ruefully. Glenmere had been the biggest investment the estate had made for years and it had given him more than one sleepless night. 'We did consider just doing the house and cottages and adding all the rest later, but with so many workpeople on site already and so much disruption we just went for it. This film of yours is a godsend to be honest. Everything ran over schedule as well as over budget so we haven't even started marketing as a holiday and event destination yet. This gives me some breathing space to get that started. We might even pull in some of those crucial Christmas and Hogmanay bookings for this year.'

'More than glad it's worked out. We need you just as much, don't forget. Okay, extras can be bussed in and we've been in touch with the Edinburgh agencies, but if we can recruit some regulars locally, I know the producers would prefer that. The downside is not having professionals on set, but the upside is it helps keep locals onside and invested in the film and means fewer costs. Casting calls and training…' She continued to murmur to herself before sitting back with a relieved 'I think that works. I'll send it through to the producer's assistant for a second pair of eyes. I did accommodate him, didn't I? Oh! What about you? Where are you going to go?'

'Family apartment—we kept four bedrooms, a dining kitchen, boot room, sitting room and study in the west turret. I really don't want any strangers in there, we don't let family spaces, but you are of course welcome to a room there if you need one.'

Charlie knew it made sense to make the offer, it sounded as if Liberty didn't have many rooms to spare, and Tabitha would think it odd if he didn't. But Charlie wasn't sure that having her so close was really the wisest move. He was already far too aware of her every shift, the way she muttered to herself when concentrating, her soft throaty laugh, the way she twisted her hair when speaking.

Funny, he had known Liberty Gray for half his life, but he was wondering if he really knew her at all as a woman in her own right, not just as Tabby's BFF, the wide-eyed girl with a crush on him they had both pretended to ignore until the time they didn't.

She wasn't a girl anymore, he reminded himself. Liberty Gray was all grown up.

'So what's the plot of this masterpiece?' he asked, more to distract himself than because he really wanted to know. The first couple of times he had worked on film sets in one of his venues he had been fascinated but if familiarity didn't breed contempt, it did breed a lack of curiosity. It turned out filming meant a lot of waiting around.

Liberty turned to him. 'So, first thing, these films can appear formulaic and easy to mock but you know what? They bring a lot of pleasure to a lot of people. They're not as easy to write or act in as they seem.'

Charlie recalled the pile of romance novels he'd noted on Liberty's floor. She had eclectic and wide-ranging tastes; there had also been a good amount of crime, fantasy and other bestselling popular titles in there as well as a smattering of classics and some poetry and non-fiction, but she obviously enjoyed a bit of escapism and why not?

'Noted and understood. I didn't mean to sound disparaging. No,' he corrected himself a little ruefully. 'I did, I was after a cheap joke. I'm sorry and won't again.'

'It's not Shakespeare as my father would pointedly say, but it still deals with love and growth and other universal themes. Both lead actors are hard-working and pretty down to earth and the director is really good at her job, so we are in luck there. Okay, so the heroine, Shelly, is an American who hates Christmas...'

'I thought all Americans loved Christmas?'

'Not this one because it's the anniversary of the day her parents split up. So, she's in London for a conference and has arranged her flight back on Christmas Day to avoid the festivities but before then she has booked a couple of days in a spa that promises Christmas-free time. Only her driver gets lost and instead of ending up at the spa she ends up at a Scottish castle belonging to our hero, Lachie, who has just inherited it and was wondering how he's going to keep it going.'

'I can have a word with him about an events business if you like? Hang on, how did her driver end up in Scotland?'

'The spa was there, keep up! Anyway, he offers her a bed for the night and she agrees but is horrified because the castle is over the top Christmas ready and it's all her worst nightmares, only she wakes up to find she is snowed in and can't escape. Meanwhile he is all grumpy because this might be the last Christmas in his family home if he has to sell and he doesn't know how to face telling his mother and sister.'

'Tricky. My advice is to enlist the mother and sister. Mine have all the best ideas.'

'His sister is only ten but okay. Anyway, cue snowball

fights and sledging and hot chocolate in front of fires and visits to the pub and a *let's put on the nativity right here even though we are all snowed in* moment with a real donkey and carols and everyone pulling together to make it the best Christmas ever, led by our very own hero and heroine and before you know it the snow has melted, and she can be on her way, but not before helping the hero discover a way to save the castle after all.'

'She sounds great, if I wasn't marrying Millie, I'd marry her myself.'

'A little moping from the hero before he realises with the help of his sister, his childhood best friend, and his best friend's love interest that he can't let her go and embarks on a mad dash to the airport and a happy ever after.'

'I can't wait to see it. Promise me there will be lots of beautiful shots of Glenmere looking like the perfect Scottish castle, and some walks through forests and around lochs?'

'Promise.'

'One small point, it'll still be October when you start filming, there won't be any snow for at least a month and these things can never be guaranteed, even in the Cairngorms.'

'All taken care of.'

'Intriguing. You'll have to let me know your secret. Weather on cue is every event professional and every farmer's dream. Do you enjoy it?'

'The fake snow? Not as much as the real thing. No good for sledging or snowball flights…' She stopped abruptly and looking over Charlie saw a tinge of red on her cheeks and he was irresistibly drawn to the memory of the last time he had indulged in a snowball fight with her. He quickly carried on the conversation.

'Not the snow, the job. You don't miss being in front of the camera or on-stage? You were good, as far as my limited knowledge goes. I took Tabby to see you when you were in that musical. Not my kind of thing but you had something, that was obvious even then.'

'My dad always said I was the most talented of the lot of us.' Her colour increased. 'That must sound really big-headed, I don't mean it that way, but in a family like ours...'

'No, not at all. It's a fact, and talent is a thing to celebrate. Tabby is always quick to point out I'm not heir because I am any better than her, just older and with a y chromosome.'

'She may have mentioned that to me once or twice,' Liberty said drily and Charlie laughed.

'I bet she has. I am very grateful she has so far used her considerable talents for the good of the family estate but I don't take them or her for granted.'

'If you and Millie have a daughter first would you break the entail?'

'If me and...?' Charlie remembered his position as a happily engaged man with a jolt. Concentrating on the road, on the two months ahead, enjoying chatting to Liberty, he had, somehow, forgotten his new status. 'We haven't talked... I don't know what Dad...' He stopped and pulled himself together. After all, this putative eldest child was the entire reason for the engagement. 'The problem is that we can't change the title. So, if we break the entail, which I quite agree is old-fashioned beyond belief, sexist and, as Tabby points out, wrong-headed because the matrilineal line is the only one to guarantee continuity...'

'Yes, I have heard her mention that too. Once or twice.'

'Times a hundred? She's right, but although Parliament has acted on the royal line of succession they haven't on hereditary titles. So we can break the entail and then risk separating the estate and title, or we carve the estate up which for the next generation might be fine but in one hundred years might mean it's in pieces too small to support the houses or to make farming worthwhile, hence the need for the entail in the first place.'

'Climate change might mean we are not even here in one hundred years, or a meteorite might have crashed into us or anything.'

'Cheerful point well made.'

'And does anyone actually need an estate like yours in the twenty-first century let alone the twenty-second? After all, you have the entire family working on keeping it solvent.'

'Another good point, but is it better that we keep the houses in good condition and generally accessible to the public or let them fall into private hands? So much expensive real estate now belongs to people who visit once or twice a year at most. There are the tenants, the farmers, the conservation areas to think of… I'm not saying you don't have a valid argument but it's not quite as easy as just selling it all on or carving it up between all the Howard heirs worldwide. So, for now I'll carry on as we are and look at the entail if it becomes an issue, I suppose.'

'Did you ever mind? Having your future decided for you like this?'

Charlie concentrated on the road ahead. No one had ever asked him that before, assuming that the title and the prestige made up for the lack of autonomy.

'Lots of people in my position spend some years in the city building up their fortune before taking the reins.

Giles has been very successful doing just that but it never appealed to me,' he said after a while. 'I'm lucky I guess, there was never anything else I wanted to do. I like the land. I like the opportunities I get to farm or build or wield a chainsaw or dig a ditch. I am proud of the communities we help foster. The people we employ. The business my mother started as a young bride which is now a substantial part of our income. I'm not a natural event planner like Tabby but I can do it if I need to, I'm not a born farmer like so many of our tenants but I am learning all the time, and I trust their expertise. I know I am lucky so, no, I don't hanker over what might have been if I had been born plain Charlie Howard of 10 something road. But how did we get onto me? Nice deflection, Gray.'

Liberty hadn't consciously chosen to move the conversation from her career to Charlie, she was genuinely interested. So much of what she knew of him, thought of him, was coloured by Tabby who didn't go in for subtlety. She liked that he wasn't instantly defensive about his title and privilege but thoughtful about what they represented and meant, the love for the estate he stood to inherit shining through.

'Do I have any regrets? No is the short answer. Not a single one. I always had disgusting stage fright, hate having my photo taken, and find a lot of acting boring.' She laughed at the surprise on Charlie's face. 'This is why my dad says my talent is wasted on me. No, I always preferred backstage, finding out how it all worked, spending time with props or costume or lighting, seeing a play or film come together behind the scenes. I like *doing*, keeping busy. There is a lot of hanging around on film sets, I want to be running around with a clipboard and an earpiece problem-solving, not sitting in a trailer having my make-up touched up, not having started work at 10am despite a 5am call.'

'Sounds reasonable to me. And if the star did get taken ill you could always step in.'

'Unlikely. I'd be too busy placating the anxious property owner, or I'd be one hundred miles away organising the next location shot.'

Liberty's phone rang and she answered it with a murmured apology, noting that Charlie immediately turned the radio down and kept it down as she continued to work throughout the long journey, though he often sang along in a surprisingly decent voice. Tabby, as she knew all too well, was completely tone-deaf but an enthusiastic karaoke partaker regardless.

Charlie's powerful car ate up the miles and they had only had one comfort and coffee break when they reached Newcastle where, instead of following the A1 up the gorgeous coastline Charlie followed the road inland up to Edinburgh. The scenery was magnificent, getting more beautiful with every mile north but, as it took at least four hours from Newcastle to Glenmere which was situated at the bottom of the Cairngorms, it was a relief when they stopped at a pub in Melrose to stretch their legs and grab a sandwich before the final push.

Seeing Glenmere for the first time was always a breathtaking experience. It seemed to just appear on the horizon, magicked up from the mountains, graceful grey spires surrounded by trees, snow-capped peaks framing the whole. As the car neared other details came into view; the loch, blue and mysterious, the seemingly never-ending pine forests. It was like a scene from a child's storybook, and, she thought with relief, it would look *glorious* on film.

Soon the clocks would change and the nights draw in early, which meant the director would want as many outside shots as possible first, and as Charlie pulled up in the small car park to the side of the castle, she was already calculating where she would recommend they shoot the snow scenes. For the backdrop shots they would use CGI, but for close-ups they would need fake snow, a biodegradable vegetable starch concoction.

Before Charlie had had a chance to switch the engine off a welcoming committee appeared to meet them, and Charlie jumped out of the car to greet the small group with hugs and handshakes, displaying the natural warm affability that had always characterised him. There was nothing of the heir about him, there never had been. Charlie had a gift for friendship, for putting people at their ease, it was one of the things she had always been drawn to. She got out of the car and joined him, returning the warm smiles with relief. Returning to Glenmere was like coming home.

Charlie indicated a fifty-something woman with a no-nonsense expression and kind eyes. 'Mrs McGregor, you remember Liberty, don't you?'

'Of course,' Mrs McGregor replied in her soft Highlands accent. 'Welcome, my dear. It's good to see you back. Now, Charlie, the family apartment is all ready, but I didn't know where anyone else will be staying and although everything is decorated and furnished there is still a lot to do. You did say I could bring in help from the village…'

'Liberty will be sleeping in the family apartments so no need to worry about anything else for a week at least, but then I am afraid we will be going from nought to hundred. We'll probably need every bed in the castle and all the cottages and lodges. Get all the staff you need, but this is just the start I hope, Mrs M. After this we will be ready for business so start with temps if you must but get recruiting everyone you need.'

The older woman nodded. 'And food? Will the restaurant be open?'

'We haven't employed a chef yet. This has rather caught us on the hop but…'

'There will be catering vans offering three meals and snacks to the cast and crew, so you don't need to worry about that,' Liberty interceded and Charlie nodded.

'But let's get recruiting anyway and if you could find it in your heart to make one of your famous breakfasts now and then you will have my undying love.'

'Oh, get away with you.' But Mrs McGregor couldn't hide her pleasure at the compliment.

'Let Liberty and I have a day to sort out requirements for the next ten weeks or so and then you and I need to look further ahead. But for now, let's get inside where I am sincerely hoping there is tea and maybe some scones awaiting us.' Another flash of that boyish grin.

'Tea and scones indeed. As if I didn't have enough to do with the short notice.' But they were led straight into the library where, despite the mildness of the day, a fire roared and a fresh-looking pot of tea sat on the coffee table next to a plate heaped with still warm buttered scones.

Charlie laughed. 'How do you do it, Mrs M? You must be a witch.'

'Witch indeed. My sister, you remember Morag? She saw you drive by and texted me.'

'I prefer the old days when an owl would deliver the message.' Charlie looked around with a contented sigh. 'Oh it's good to be back.'

'You were only here a month ago,' the housekeeper pointed out.

'True, but a lifetime has passed in that month. You know, when I am in Norfolk, I think there is no more glorious place. The sea and those endless skies. But then I come here to the sheer majesty of the landscape and I think this is the most beautiful place on earth. Have a scone, Liberty, and then I'll show you to your room and give you a quick tour while the daylight lasts. I'm looking forward to seeing what they've done since I was last here. Video calls are all very well but nothing beats seeing it in person.'

'Can I get you anything else?' the housekeeper asked and when, through a mouthful of scone, Charlie assured her that he had everything he wanted and more, she stood for a moment.

'I hope you don't mind me saying how pleased the staff and I, the villagers as well, were to hear about your engagement. Miss Millie is a lovely young woman and we hope you will be very happy.'

For a moment Charlie looked startled, as if he had no idea what Mrs McGregor was taking about, but he quickly recovered himself. 'Thank you. I'm sure she'll be up to visit very soon.'

'It's a long time to be away from her, especially so soon after the engagement,' Liberty said as the housekeeper left them alone with the scones and the fire. 'You must miss her.'

'We both have busy lives so we're used to it. Scone?'

It was definitely a shutdown of the subject. Liberty

took one of the temptingly smelling scones and forgot her questions as she took a bite. But once the crumbs were cleared, the tea drunk and their bags carried to their room, she couldn't help reflect that Charlie was behaving less like a newly engaged man and more like a man who had forgotten he had a fiancée at all. He didn't mention Millie every other sentence, wasn't constantly calling her, didn't smile at the mention of her name. It was all very strange, but it was also, she told herself firmly, absolutely none of her business.

CHAPTER SEVEN

LIBERTY WAS RELIEVED that there were enough hours of light left to do a quick tour; she was keen to stretch her legs after the long drive, especially after spending the whole of the previous day at her dining room table. Charlie suggested that he show her one of the newly refurbished cottages so that she could make sure it had everything her crew needed, picking one less than a mile from the castle for the tour.

The air was colder than it had been in London but immeasurably fresher and Liberty took in great lungfuls as she walked along the wide gravel paths, filling her eyes and mind with the landscape, the colours and natural beauty. Not for the first time, she wondered if it was time to leave London. But where would she go? Most of her friends lived in the city and she had no family she would want to settle near.

'I hope the distance isn't going to be a problem,' she said as they walked. 'I know it's just a mile to this one but the lodges and other cottages are a little further away and when people have 5am calls they don't tend to be in the mood for a nice nature walk.'

'I have several golf buggies for getting around the estate, we can get everyone collected, I'll show you the route to the other cottages tomorrow,' Charlie assured her. 'Then you can check out the lodges as well, before we go into the village to discuss rooms with Angus at The Leaping Salmon, although he's already put them all on reserve for you. There are a few hikers and tourists booked in but he's arranged a transfer with the hotel further around the loch at your expense, so hopefully that will be okay.'

'That's very accommodating of him, I'll have to let him know how grateful I am.'

'It's eight weeks' full income versus a night here and there plus the drinks and any food you lot buy. Angus isn't going to let that slip away! Okay, all the cottages are decorated in a sort of modernish but traditional style...'

'Interesting description.'

'Tabby would know the correct terms, but you know what I mean. Anyway, the lodges are a little more modern as they are all newly built, the tree-houses properly traditional with a lot of leather and wood, and the domes super modern, but they all incorporate the same themes using the family colours. You're the first person who's not local or from the estate to see them so I am really interested in your thoughts.'

'And if I hate them?' she teased. 'Will you rip it all out and start again?'

'It was all approved by Tabby and my mother so take it up with them.'

'I wouldn't dare. I am sure I'll love it; anything has to be better than all that oppressive dark wood and that Victorian deep red they were before.'

'Hopefully. Okay, here we are. This one is a two-bed cottage.'

Liberty had always liked the traditional tartan the Howards had adopted from the Scottish three-times-great-grandmother who had bequeathed them the castle, a soft mix of warm greens, misty greys and heathery purples which reflected the Glenmere landscape. As Charlie had promised the cottage took its inspiration from the family colours, the walls a light grey, the sofa upholstered in the tartan with the comfortable looking brown leather chairs heaped with matching cushions. The bedrooms were decorated in a soothing sage-green, the furniture a warm, polished oak, the bathroom luxuriously appointed. Liberty breathed a sigh of relief. Her crew would be more than comfortable here.

'It's gorgeous. I could move in and never leave.'

'Tabs was in charge of briefing the interior designers. Even I have to admit she's done a pretty good job. But you know, cosy as it is, the views are what really makes it stand out.' Charlie gestured towards the sliding glass doors at the back, overlooking a deck with views through the trees to the loch-side. 'Imagine waking up to that.'

'Yes,' Liberty murmured, looking at his profile. 'Imagine.'

There was also time for a tour of the refurbished castle before dinner, the strong patterns and heavy dark mahogany furniture favoured by Charlie's grandmother stripped away once again for the more muted family colours teamed with warm oak. Dinner was taken in the bar rather than the dining room on a small table next to the fire, and they spent the delicious meal discussing the timetable for the next two weeks. Liberty had now spent so much time one-on-one with Charlie that any shyness or anxiety about being alone with him had ebbed away and she found herself falling into the old easy manner. Even sharing an apartment was going to be okay, the space allotted to the family taking up three floors with her bedroom on the first and his on the second, both with en suites, and she would be too busy to use the communal areas much anyway.

But as she drifted off to sleep that night, she couldn't help but reflect again that it was odd how little Charlie mentioned Millie. He wasn't avoiding the topic, her name was mentioned in passing, with affection but not with the kind of intensity she would expect from such a whirlwind romance. He didn't smile goofily when he texted her or disappear off for long intimate conversations. It was all a little odd but it made no difference. He was engaged and out-of-bounds and that suited her just fine.

The next two weeks flew by. Liberty was so busy that, after the full site tour and trip into the village on their first full day, she saw very little of Charlie.

The producer had decided to fly in early, quickly followed by the director, and to her relief both were charmed by the castle. The production designer, key grip and assistant director also arrived earlier than planned, with the rest of the crew due the next day, followed by the cast three days later. It was somewhat of a relief. No more intimate conversations with Charlie, no more analysing his expression as he replied to texts from Millie, no more avoiding a certain walk and a certain tree and certain memories.

She barely saw him in the apartment either. Charlie had arranged with Mrs McGregor that she would supply breakfast and dinner for everyone staying in the castle; the catering vans supplemented by the pub and the self-catering facilities for those staying in lodges and cottages would more than do for everyone else. Charlie had also suggested turning the restaurant into a cafeteria, with the catering vans parked as close as possible with permanent inside coffee and snack stations. 'From what I remember films run on caffeine,' he said. 'And it's soon going to get too cold for people to want to eat outside.' But he usually ate separately in the apartment or at the pub while she dined with the rest of the senior crew.

Not only were their rooms on separate floors but he also had taken to using the study in the turret in his spare time, spending his days travelling around the estate and village, his evenings, she assumed, on paperwork—or binging on reality shows or sport or reading—she never ventured up there to check. She'd gradually taken over the bright, comfortable sitting room as her workspace, her never-ending to-do lists spread over the coffee table. She'd almost forgotten she had a flatmate at all. Almost.

Liberty enjoyed being back at Glenmere. She loved being busy, absorbed in the minutiae of her job, and the change in location meant many extra-long days, working with the director to scope out the best places for outdoor scenes and the scenery, directory and props leads to refit the interior, moving a few rooms around to fit their vision and the need to accommodate cameras and crew. Wires had already been neatly trailed through the house, most of the Howard belongings carefully boxed away with just a few mishaps, and the props for the film hung on the walls. Today, they had started decorating for Christmas. And that must be why she had been aware of a certain melancholy all day. One that seemed to intensify the more garlands and baubles and lights that were hung.

Liberty wasn't a huge fan of Christmas. It was a time when she was always very conscious of not having a home of her own. Oh, she had the flat and she was eternally grateful for that, but Christmas was about returning to familiar places and traditions, about family, and her own lack of all those things felt very stark as December approached. She could go to her mother's, she was always, if not exactly welcome, accepted, but she felt like a stranger there. She wanted to be the bigger person but she found it hard to see the traditions that excluded her, the effort made for this new family that had never been part of her childhood, the matching stockings for each of her siblings, the Christmas Eve boxes, the Boxing Day party, events in which she was an onlooker, not a participant.

She often spent Christmas with Tabby, but this year was Charlie's wedding and not only did she not expect an invite, she didn't want to be around it at all. She told herself that she no longer had a crush on Charlie but couldn't deny that she was still far too drawn to him. So better to keep her distance.

It was a good plan and one she had implemented almost effortlessly thanks to their busy timetables and, she suspected, because he was avoiding her as assiduously as she was avoiding him. So, it was a surprise to head into the boot room that evening on a mission to get some fresh air, and to immediately trip over an outstretched foot. She would have gone headlong if Charlie hadn't caught her, his hands strong on her arms as he broke her fall and set her upright.

'Steady. Do you always hurtle into a room like that?' His blue eyes laughed at her.

'I didn't expect a great big foot to be in my way,' she retorted, aware of his hands still lightly clasping her, the lack of distance between them. She was so close they were nearly touching and she hurriedly took a step back, nearly tripping again.

'Been at the whisky?'

'Ha very ha.' Liberty pulled her scarf firmly around her neck, shoving her hands into her gilet pockets.

Damn it, did he have to be so attractive? Did his eyes have to be so warm and so very blue? Did his hair have to tousle adorably? Did he always have to look as if he was pleased to see her? Did he have to suit autumnal country wear as if he were made for it—although to be fair with his heritage he was. She felt a little like she was playing dress-up in wellies, but Charlie rocked a wax jacket and sturdy boots like the sometime farmer he was. The posh sometime farmer.

'I just fancied some air. It's been an intense couple of weeks, and it's just going to get more intense. You?'

'The final tweaks to the last tree-house were finished today and I wanted to take a look.' He paused. 'Want to come with me or was this a solo mission?'

Liberty glanced at him, trying to gauge if he really wanted her company or was just being polite. She hadn't accompanied Charlie on any of his tours of the estate since the first couple of days; she'd been too busy, plus, there was the whole keeping her distance plan. But she was intrigued by the four tree-houses, whimsical structures hidden in the depths of the Glenmere forest, like something from a fairy tale suspended high above the floor. 'I might even throw in a trip to the domes,' he added. 'It's going to be a clear night and I haven't tested them properly yet.'

'I haven't even seen the domes,' she said, intrigued. 'Where are they?'

'The other side of the loch. Fancy it?'

Liberty bit her lip. What harm could an evening sight-seeing do? Besides, Tabby was bound to demand a review of all the new facilities. 'I'd love to,' she said. 'Let me get my shoes on.'

She followed Charlie round to the car park where he headed for one of several neatly parked golf carts. Liberty climbed into the passenger side and he took off with practised ease.

'I was planning to walk,' he said. 'But if we are getting to see the domes as well then we need some speed. It's always a shock when we get to this time of year and realise daylight isn't a limitless resource.'

Sure enough, the sky was beginning to pinken, the sun low in the sky. 'With sunsets like the ones we've had recently we can't complain,' Liberty pointed out and Charlie nodded.

'Agreed.'

To Liberty's surprise it took less than ten minutes to arrive at the tree-house. For all its air of seclusion it was close to one of the narrow roads which criss-crossed the estate, within a fifteen-minute walk of the village and pub. A twisty spiral staircase descended from the porch two storeys high and Charlie gestured for her to go first.

'Go on, I am really interested in your reaction.'

'Okay.' She was a little nervous as she ascended the staircase but for all its air of fragility it was sturdy with wide planks under her feet. She emerged onto a large wraparound porch that extended across several trees, high railings making it feel safe despite the height. 'Oh, Charlie, this is incredible! The views alone are worth whatever extortionate amount you are charging.' She looked around at the porch swing, the outdoor sofa heaped with blankets, the lanterns creating an intimate glow, the hot tub and outside bar area. 'Is that a sauna?'

'Yup, and the whole place is completely private.' He

produced a key and swung the arched door open. 'Come and take a look inside.'

She didn't need a second invitation and stepped in, aware that Charlie was close by her side, watching for her reaction. She didn't have to feign how impressive she found it, the inside as beautiful as the out with its rug-covered wooden floors, high arched ceilings, the way it was luxuriously and sympathetically kitted out from the central stove to the clever circular seating. Throws, cushions and large paintings brightened the room, relieving the polished wood.

'Oh, Charlie, it's amazing. I want to sink down onto that lounger, light the stove, grab a blanket and a glass of wine and never leave. How many bedrooms are there?'

He couldn't hide his pleasure at her reaction, his smile broad. 'This one has two. We have a smaller one-bedroom especially for couples, two of these and the fourth is a four-bed for larger families or groups of friends. This is the master...' He opened a door to a circular chamber, dominated by a large comfortable-looking bed. An ajar door led into the en suite, a huge bath in the window, a skylight above. 'You can literally bathe surrounded by the forest.'

'Let me move in. Don't we need my room for someone else? I am happy to slum it here. This is gorgeous, Charlie. It's going to be a real draw.'

He rubbed a hand across his face. 'I hope so. I think I said that we went all out here. Glenmere has been a substantial investment. While my grandmother was alive, she didn't want anything changed. The only income was a handful of old-fashioned cottages and forestry and with an estate of this size it just wasn't enough. Of course we could have opened up with just a lick of paint and a refresh, but branching out into full on hospitality beyond a couple of cottages here and there is a new venture for us. We wanted to do it right from the start.'

'I think you can tick that off your list. This is going to sell out, I am sure of it.'

'Let's hope you're right. The photographer is coming next week, and I have a travel marketing expert coming too to advise on the website and PR. It's a good thing I am based up here for now after all. Launching all of this properly is a full-time job. More Tab's expertise than mine but she's happy to boss me from London.'

'I'll bet she is.'

Charlie had a list of things to check, and he busied himself while Liberty looked around, glorying in all the hidden details, the clever workmanship, the effortless-looking luxury, and was sorry when Charlie announced he was done.

'Go without me. I am going to move in, didn't I mention it?'

'I thought you wanted to see the domes?'

'Are they as cool as this?'

'Some might think even cooler...'

'In that case I guess I could tear myself away,' she said reluctantly.

'So it's safe to assume you like the tree-houses?' he asked as he locked the door behind them.

'Love them, want them, wish you had had them when I was a teenager. Can you imagine the fun Tabby and I could have had up here?'

'I shudder to think. Carnage, absolute carnage.'

They walked back to the golf cart and this time Charlie took the passenger seat. 'Do you want to drive?'

'I don't know where we are going,' but she was tempted.

'Just follow the path round.'

Liberty hopped in and turned the key. 'So the plan is Glenmere will be more of a traditional holiday destination not just an event hire. Is this a new thing for all your properties or just here?'

'Just here for now, and it will hopefully be a combination of both. The pub and the villagers who work on the estate need more than just a few weddings and photo shoots. There were a lot of meetings, a lot of discussion, a lot of ideas between the village, staff and family. We even considered making the castle a hotel, but decided to keep it for private lets and events, but open up the grounds by adding more luxury accommodation. It's providing jobs, will hopefully do wonders for the economy and attract people to this beautiful corner of Scotland. That's the plan anyway.' His mouth twisted into a rueful smile. 'Otherwise, it's just a hideously expensive folly.'

'I hadn't really thought about it, that you need to innovate and change as you go. Just starting the events business must have felt like such a big thing to do back when your parents married.'

'The hardest part was convincing my grandparents, but it was definitely the right thing to do. We have to remember that we are just the custodians of the land whether that's here or Norfolk. It belongs to nature, to the people who live here through generations. My role is to sustain that in as many ways as I can. It can be a burden sometimes, but then there is an evening like this and it's an absolute joy.'

The sun was really low now, the sky a kaleidoscope of orange and purple and pink lighting up the mountains and reflecting on the lake. With increasing confidence Liberty drove them around the top of the loch until Charlie directed her off onto a narrow path which led to a small clearing by the loch empty apart from a futuristic-looking clear dome with a raised terrace at the front and an enclosed cabin at the back. Liberty pulled up outside it and killed the engine, turning to stare at it fascinated. 'It's not going to take off, is it? It looks like a spaceship. Are you sure you're not an alien and this isn't an abduction?'

'Not that I am aware of. Want to risk going inside?'

'Only if you promise not to take me to Mars.'

'Promise. I know it looks a little odd but there's no artificial light this side of the loch, so the idea is when you are in one of these domes with the lights off there is no light pollution and, on a clear night, like this promises to be, the stars should be incredible.'

Liberty looked around. 'Where's the other one?'

'About half a mile away. We'll start with two and then if they're popular we'll add more. We only use this side for walks and forestry, so it was just a case of using the natural clearings, improving the access roads and actually building the things. Oh, and installing the domes.'

'Only.'

'Simpler than a tree-house anyway, but equally cool I think. Come take a look.'

Inside the domes were cosy, two deep chairs overlooking the terrace which was complete with a wood-fired hot tub and outdoor wooden sofa. The rest of the dome was dominated by a huge bed, heaped with cushions and blankets. The whole dome was transparent apart from the back wall in which two doors were set, one at each side, leading into a fully kitted-out kitchen on one side, complete with a breakfast bar, and a luxurious bathroom on the other.

It was nearly dark now, a clear night, the first stars peeping out, clearly visible through the glass. 'Wow!' Liberty stared up at the ceiling transfixed. 'This is going to be incredible later on.'

'We can wait for a while if you want?' Charlie offered. 'It's perfect conditions for stargazing.'

Liberty hesitated. There were two chairs, and a comfortable-looking chaise on one side, but it couldn't be denied that there was a love nest vibe about the dome, the bed the dominant feature.

'Or do you have yet another dinner meeting?' Charlie must have noticed her hesitation. 'Do you need to get straight back?'

Get yourself together, Liberty. It's just a bed! 'Not tonight. Simone and Ted have gone to Edinburgh for the evening, the rest of the crew are staying in a hotel there and will be arriving on-site tomorrow so there's a prep session there.' She sank down onto one of the chairs. 'It would be lovely to stay and see the stars.'

'Great, I'll text Mrs M and ask her to put some food in the warmer. You don't mind eating a little later?'

'Last night it was after nine before we got round to eating. To say it's been busy doesn't come close to describing how insane it has been but I am very grateful to you, Charlie, we all are, and in many ways Glenmere is a better fit for us than the original location.' She laughed. 'Thanks to the renovation it's definitely a lot more luxurious. The crew are going to be delighted with the five-star vibes. But condensing three months of work into two weeks has been a challenge I would have been happier not to have taken on.'

Charlie took the chair next to hers, long legs stretching out. 'It suits you. I can tell you enjoy the adrenaline.
You've looked, I don't know, fired up.'

'I have enjoyed it, in a way,' she admitted, both pleased
and a little embarrassed that Charlie had noticed. 'But
I would prefer most shoots to be more straightforward.'
She leaned back and looked up at the sky, now a deep
purple, and sighed with satisfaction. 'I love it up here as
well, the air is so fresh it completely re-energised me.
Obviously, London is great, being able to get out to the
best bars and restaurants, to go to the theatre on a whim
and stuff like that.'

Charlie grinned. 'And how often do you take advantage of that?'

'Well, hardly ever,' she admitted. 'Ugh. I am twenty-
six and single and I am a workaholic. You're right, I could
live anywhere. The two evenings I spent at the local pub
here were the most frivolity I have enjoyed for months,
except when your sister drags me out.'

'Tabby never lets anything get in the way of her social
schedule,' her fond brother agreed.

'She's an inspiration. I know I am lucky to live in such
an amazing area, everything walkable or on my doorstep,
good transport links, Regent's Park just a stroll away...'

'The zoo.'

'The zoo. Not that I have been there since school, but
I could.'

'If you weren't such a workaholic.'

'Exactly. If I lived somewhere like this, I like to think
I'd go hiking at weekends, swim in the loch.'

'Now you're romanticising, that loch is icy even in the
middle of summer.'

She ignored him. 'Be part of the village community. If

it wasn't for Tabby, London would be a little, oh I don't know, lonely I guess. I love my flat, don't get me wrong, but it's easy to be lost in the crowd, and everyone else always looks like they have it sussed. But you're right. I am romanticising. I've been here a fortnight and not managed even one hike. Workaholics are going to work, I guess.'

'How about relationships? Or do you want to follow the template of your film, move to a small town and marry the local laird?'

'Seeing as you're the local laird and off the market it's a good thing that's not my plan.' She felt her cheeks heat. She had meant to make a light joking comment, but instead it had sounded almost wistful. 'One thing the city *is* good for is dating, especially if you're not after anything serious. Which I'm not,' she added firmly. 'Work comes first. Dating is purely a recreational activity.' She told herself that she preferred her love life short, sweet and uncomplicated but she knew part of her was scared to explore anything more meaningful. That rejection felt inevitable, especially from those who should love her, and she had to do all she could to shield herself from it.

'I don't know how you and Tab do it. I enjoy being in the city, for all the reasons you mentioned, I like the buzz of it, and I am lucky to have a central base when I am there, but give me Norfolk and its horizons any time, or here with air that makes you feel alive and landscapes that fill your spirits.'

Their eyes caught and held and Liberty was acutely aware of him, the lock of hair falling over his forehead, the pulse in his neck, the curve of his mouth. She knew them as well as she knew her own face, was attuned to his every shifting mood. She had, after all, fallen in love with him when she was twelve and he had been carelessly kind to her in a way her lonely heart had soaked up.

And she couldn't help but wonder, despite all the many good reasons not to be, whether she was still in love with him.

But she knew better than to think that love equalled a happy ever after.

And he wasn't free.

'Where will you and Millie live?' she blurted out, needing Millie between them, like a shield. 'Norfolk? Or would you settle here, do you think?'

He blinked, as if waking up from an enchantment. 'Live? You know, we haven't really discussed it. Her business is between Norfolk and London so either would work I suppose. I guess I just thought we would move into my apartments there but of course my parents are on-site, as are Aunt Flic and Millie's mum. That's a lot of close relatives to start married life with, even...' He stopped. 'Here would be amazing, but she has a whole business, a client list, I don't think she could be so cut off.'

They hadn't even discussed it. Whirlwind was one thing, but this was the oddest engagement she had ever come across—and she couldn't help thinking that Charlie was hiding something from her. Charlie's love life had nothing to do with her but every instinct told her something wasn't right.

CHAPTER EIGHT

NOW WHY ON earth had he asked Liberty about her love life? Things had been working out just the way Charlie had planned. He had been busy, Liberty had been busy, they had barely seen each other the last couple of weeks and that was exactly how he wanted it. Only here he was and here she was, the stars lighting up the sky above them, in an intimate venue orchestrated for romance and rather than keep the conversation to innocuous topics he'd got as up close and personal as possible. Why was he so interested in her personal life? Why did he want to know what made her tick? To be the one to make her eyes light up with laughter, to make her smile, to feel the connection between them?

Because there was a connection. An undeniable palpable connection. Charlie was still attracted to her, and that attraction seemed to deepen every day. But he couldn't act on it, *mustn't* act on it. Millie might have given him a get-out-of-jail card but it couldn't include Liberty. She was too close. There was history between them. There was emotion. And none of that added up to a last-minute fling but to mess and drama and everything he didn't want and she didn't deserve.

Liberty leaned back, staring up at the roof. The chairs were designed so users could stare up at the domed roof and out at the stars. There were more now, he saw as he tilted his head up, so much brighter than ever seen in London or even at Howard Hall.

The lighting in the dome was low, to enable the stars to be seen, a dull light strip along the bottom of the walls made it possible for occupants to make their way around the room without bumping into furniture or each other. Cast just enough light for him to see Liberty's elegant outline, the fall of her hair, the curve of her body, but not her expression.

'Tabby is so happy for you,' she said, almost wistfully. There had always been a wistful quality to Liberty. On the surface she had it all, money, famous parents, looks, talent, but he would see her at games nights, at Christmas, watching their family interactions, her eyes sad, loneliness running through her. It made him want to pull her close, to assure she was wanted, loved, but of course it wasn't his place. His mother, he knew, had and did. She even called her *her other daughter*, a joke but one with truth behind it.

'I think she's convinced herself it's all down to her?'

Liberty's laugh was bell-like, clear and warm. 'How exactly?'

'Details are not forthcoming. Apparently, she had a feeling that Millie and I were perfect together and that was enough for her to claim full credit.'

'Sounds like Tab.' She paused. 'How about you? When did you know? I didn't see…at the wedding…but of course you…'

'You mean when did Millie and I…' Charlie wanted to say *fall in love* but he couldn't form the words. 'Hold on, I just want to check something.'

It really was dim now and Charlie was grateful for

the low lighting as he edged his way around what really was an all-dominating bed—had he created romantic stargazing pods or just giant shag palaces—and into the kitchen. All accommodation would be supplied with hampers and any additional requests whilst being prepared, but he had suggested that they were kept stocked with staples which should include...he opened the fridge. Oh yes! Champagne. For one moment he wondered if adding alcohol into the already overwrought mix was a good idea, but he pushed the thought away. Champagne was always a good idea. The cupboard yielded up a large bag of locally made gourmet crisps and he tipped them into a bowl, grabbed two glasses, put the bottle into an already frozen ice bucket and made his way back to the front of the pod.

'I thought you might be in need of refreshment seeing as we are delaying dinner.'

'Oooh, champagne. As diversion techniques go this is a good one.'

'Diversion technique?' As if he didn't know. Charlie opened the bottle and poured two generous glasses before setting the ice bucket on the table between them and handing her a glass.

'Cheers. To *Jingle Bell Highlander.*'

'To happy cast and crew, good ratings and sticking to our schedule.' Liberty took a sip and eyed him from over the top of her glass. 'By diversion technique I mean you don't talk much about the wedding, or the engagement or even Millie.'

Charlie didn't answer for a long moment. Coming to Scotland, burying himself with all the work on the estate, was a way of escaping. He had no regrets about his decision to marry Millie, he still knew it was the right thing to do, but the subterfuge didn't come naturally to him. It would all be easier once they were settled into married life, with none of the expectations that came with a whirlwind engagement.

'I guess that's because my relationship with Octavia seemed to dominate every occasion, every conversation. I don't want to make the same mistake twice. Some things are better off private.'

It was Liberty's turn to fall silent. 'I'm sorry,' she said after a while. 'I didn't mean to pry.'

Damn it. Now he had upset her. 'I'm still getting used to it,' he said honestly. 'I didn't think we were going to announce it so soon, or to settle on a date and everything. But once Tabby got involved the whole thing turned into a runaway train and all I can do is cling on and hope to get to my destination intact.'

'That's Tabby! I won't go on, I promise. I get you want to keep part of it for yourself, but I just wanted to say I'm glad you're happy. I don't know Millie super well, but she's always seemed really nice. Genuine. And the two of you have always been so tight, Tabby is right, you are obviously made for each other.' There was that wistful note again, the one that made him want to sweep her into his arms and promise her that everything would be okay. Or maybe just sweep her into his arms. He took a hasty gulp of his drink.

'I first met Millie when I was about four and she must have been three. Her parents had just arrived at Howard Hall, and she was in the kitchen garden playing, her father was digging and keeping an eye on her. I swaggered up to her with all the dignity of an older boy and announced that the whole garden belonged to my daddy and one day it would belong to me too, and I waited for her to pay homage to me.'

'How very Henry the Eighth of you.'

'She put her little fists on her hips, tilted her chin and told me that her mother knew how to make fifty different types of cake and she had tried them all, and that her father could name every plant in the world. She then went back to her game and ignored me completely for about one minute which lasted a lifetime, then asked if I wanted to play. That was it. We were best friends and stayed that way even when I went to boarding school and then university, even with Octavia always jealous as hell that I was such close friends with another female.'

'Did she have any reason to be?'

'Jealous?' Charlie laughed, forgetting for a moment his status as a head-over-heels fiancé. 'Not at all, Millie and I never had as much as a moment.'

'Until now?' There was a slightly questioning note in her voice. God, he was bad at this! It was a good thing he was hundreds of miles away from his mother and sister.

'Until now.' He still felt uncomfortable about the thought of any kind of *moment*. It was something he needed to get over fast. The wedding was barely two months away, and Millie deserved a groom who showed some enthusiasm, not embarrassment.

'Do you think if you and Octavia hadn't got together, you and Millie might have done so earlier?'

The honest answer was no. Maybe they might have had a drunken fumble at some point, although he doubted it. But this was a time when honesty definitely wasn't the best policy. Especially as the only relationship he regretted not having the opportunity to pursue was with the woman sitting opposite him, a mere shadow now in the starlit dark. He caught himself. Regret? Was *that* what he felt? He liked Liberty, of course he did. He couldn't deny the attraction he felt for her. Couldn't deny the guilt he felt, the way it must have seemed that he had used her although his only thought back then had been to protect her. But did that mean that he wished he had chosen differently? Wondered what life would have looked like if he'd taken that path?

'It's impossible to say. For better or worse, Octavia is my past.' He hesitated. There was something he had wanted to say for a long time but never had. 'I owe you an apology.'

'Me? Why?' Liberty sounded wary.

'For that New Year's Eve.'

'Oh, Charlie, that was a lifetime ago. It was a drunken kiss. I'd finished school, was all grown up, you have nothing to apologise for.'

'I'm not apologising for the kiss. It was…' He knew he shouldn't say the next words but somehow they were out before he could recall them. 'It was one of the loveliest kisses of my life. I can still see you, in the snow and moonlight…' She was very still, her body tilted towards him. 'No, it's what happened after I need to apologise for. I had no idea Octavia would just turn up. I mean, who heads from London to Scotland on Hogmanay evening like that?' It was a rhetorical question and Liberty didn't answer. She still hadn't moved, even her breathing had slowed. 'But I shouldn't have left you as if that moment, as if you had meant nothing. But Octavia was jealous, could be vindictive. I didn't want her turning her sights onto you.'

'If she hadn't married Layton would you two have

ended up getting married instead? You were engaged, after all.'

'No.'

'You sound very sure.'

'I am.' Charlie hesitated. There were things about Octavia he had never told anyone, not even Millie. 'The thing about Octavia... She's more vulnerable than she lets on. In her family looks, success, money, winning, they are the things that count. Happiness isn't even in the running. Once you understand that it's easy to understand her, to pity her even, although she would be horrified if she thought she was an object of pity. For a long time, I thought I could be the one to save her...' He picked up his glass and realised with some surprise it was empty. He reached for the bottle and topped up first his and then Liberty's. 'But she didn't want saving. She liked the games and the drama. And so, I ended it, this time for good.'

Finally, Liberty moved, a start of surprise. '*You* ended it? But I thought...'

'Everyone thought. Thinks.'

'You don't mind?'

'What difference does it make to me? I don't really care what people think. Besides, over the years she probably instigated more break-ups than I did, she liked me to win her back, so we are probably even. But Layton also likes the game. I'm not sure marrying Octavia would have been so sweet if he didn't think he'd won.'

'They deserve each other.'

'Maybe.' He stared out at the starlit darkness. 'It wasn't easy. I was so used to being in love with her, it felt like it defined me, she defined me. For a long time I really thought we crazy kids would be able to sort things out.

But one day I realised that was the last thing she wanted, and the only thing I could do was get free. To set her free to be whatever she wanted. Which wasn't settling down to take on the responsibilities of a huge estate and work in the family business.'

'At the wedding you seemed… I don't know, sad. Heartbroken. Was it all an act?'

'To start with, a little, but of *course* I was genuinely sad. I was saying goodbye to nearly fourteen years, to the future I had once envisioned, to the world in which we were Charlie and Octavia, for better and worse. I might have been the one to make the break but it still hurt. The booze didn't help either. Made me sentimental.' He grimaced. 'Still, it played into the narrative, didn't it? I was the love-lost swain and Layton the victor.'

'Yet all the time you and Millie were together. You are more devious than I gave you credit for.'

'Not all the time.' How much champagne had he drunk? He shouldn't be giving away clues like that. No wonder he hadn't been tapped by the Secret Service when he finished university. He tipped back and looked up. 'Look at the stars, Liberty. Aren't they glorious?'

'Yes.' Her voice was soft. 'They really are.'

They were, so bright it almost hurt. She reclined the chair the better to see them, all too aware of the huge bed just behind them, her mind sorting through his words looking for clues, she didn't know for what. Trying not to let her mind linger on the soft caress of his voice when he had said how lovely their kiss had been. Trying not to let herself think that it really had been the best kiss of her life.

'How does Millie feel about taking on the estate, producing a dozen mini-barons to carry on the family name?'

It was like poking a tongue in a hole in a tooth. Each time it twinged, but she needed to remind herself it was there. Had to remind herself that Charlie was engaged.

'Millie wants a large family so the mini-barons part will be fine. How she'll fit in with the estate, that's another thing TBC. I don't expect her to give up her business. She's worked too hard to build up her reputation. But she grew up at Howard Hall too, she knows what it takes to keep it going. She's coming into this with her eyes wide open.'

'Of course.' There was a *lot* still TBC for a wedding taking place so soon. Of course, the whole thing had been a whirlwind but it seemed like they had made no plans at all. Almost as if the engagement had taken them by surprise… They hadn't discussed living arrangements, jobs, had allowed Tabby to take over the wedding, although to be fair nobody could stop Tabby once she had set her sights on something. Charlie barely seemed to even remember Millie, let alone miss her. Liberty couldn't shake the feeling that she was missing something, something important.

Not that it was any of her business.

She raised her glass. 'To you and Millie. To drama-free happiness.'

Keep saying it and she might mean it. No, she did mean it, she really wished them both well. She just couldn't wrap her head around them as a couple.

'And here's to you, Liberty Gray. To…what is it you want?'

'We already toasted to that, a smooth shoot, no over-running, a happy cast and crew and great ratings.'

'No, that's the film, what do *you* want?'

How could she answer that? The truth was she tried

hard not to want anything. That way she wasn't disappointed. 'Travel, adventures, fabulous wealth and many exotic love affairs with dangerous men, of course.'

'You don't have to pretend with me, Liberty.'

I'm not pretending... but the words wouldn't come. Instead, she blurted, 'To come first. For someone to put me first.'

'That should be a given. It's the least you deserve.'

'Maybe. I doubt I am even top five with either of my parents, barely register with my siblings...there's Tab of course, but she has her family, other friends, her dates. One day one of those will turn into something more serious...' She stopped. No more. 'Listen to me being all emo. I'm in this beautiful place, doing a job I adore. I have no right to moan about anything. But talking of jobs, I've another busy day tomorrow. I'd better get back, eat dinner and get some sleep.'

'Of course. Leave those,' as she made a move to pick up the glass and bottle. 'I'll swing by tomorrow to tidy and replace the crisps and champagne. Can you see okay?'

'Fine, thank you.'

Charlie stood up and stood back to let her go past. The space was small, and she had no choice but to brush past him, her body tingling at the brief touch. She stopped and looked back. 'Thank you, by the way.'

'For what?'

'For the apology. I know I said you didn't need to say anything, but I really appreciated it. And for saying that the kiss was lovely. I thought it was but I was quite a naïve eighteen-year-old for all I thought I knew it all. I was a naïve eighteen-year-old with a huge crush, and the kiss meant something to me, although I knew it shouldn't, that it didn't mean anything to you.' Oh. God. *Stop talking, Liberty.*

'I never said it didn't mean anything.' His voice was very low, reverberating straight through her. What she should do was walk through the door and insist she needed some night air and to walk the five kilometres around the loch and back to the castle. What she should do was keep her distance from Charlie Howard for the rest of his natural born life. But her feet wouldn't move. She stood still, acutely aware of him behind her, breathing a little faster, every nerve alive in the dark, starlit space.

She waited.

'It was lovely. It was the sweetest, most genuine kiss I had ever experienced. Have ever experienced. And if Octavia hadn't turned up when she did…'

'Yes?'

'I have often wondered just where that kiss would have taken us.' His voice was silk, wrapping around her senses. 'Would we have stepped apart and pretended it had never happened?'

'It was too cold to go much further where we were.'

'Oh I don't know, we were generating enough heat.'

Walk away, Liberty. Don't turn around.

But of course she was going to turn around. It was easier in the dark, his features hidden, hers equally inscrutable to him. He wouldn't be able to see the need and want that were surely blazing in her eyes, and in the dark she could pretend that he was hers, put her scruples to one side for just a few moments. One step and she was close to him, looking up at him as his hand unerringly found hers, his fingers slipping through hers as if he were made to fit her.

'Liberty Gray,' he murmured. Just two words but there was want in those syllables. Hunger. Need. Feelings that were as intoxicating to her as her own yearning for him thrumming through her body with every increasingly fast beat of her heart. Her whole body was aware of him, the touch of his hand on hers radiating out, creating sweet aches low in her belly, in her breasts, her thighs, aches that intensified as his other hand came to rest on her hip, possessive and yet light.

It wasn't too late. She could, she should still walk away. It was the right thing to do. But couldn't she, just once, do something just for her? What harm could one little kiss do? Liberty had no idea who moved first, but less than a second later his mouth was on hers, Charlie Howard was kissing her for the second time in her life and it was just as glorious as she had remembered.

The amount of tension in the room might have culminated in some kind of passionate explosion, a fierce, all-encompassing kiss, but instead Charlie kissed her like they had all the time in the world, slow, sweet, reverent. Like she meant something. His hand stayed entwined with hers, his fingers caressing the back of her hand in a way that made her knees weaken, and she pressed close to him, holding onto his shoulders like he was all that stopped her being swept away, acutely aware of his other hand resting so lightly on her hip, so tantalisingly close to all the parts of her aching for him. She pressed closer still, glorying in the hard planes of his body next to hers, allowing her hands to wander over his shoulders, his neck, to tangle into his hair, feeling his own clasp on her tighten as he pulled her into position, as he finally moved his hand from her hip, cupping her bottom, pressing her closer until they were both gasping.

The bed was right there. Inviting, romantic, so very close. It wouldn't take much to move there, just a few steps, to sink onto it, to start pulling at clothing, exploring bodies, to touch and be touched, kiss and be kissed, to give in to what they both wanted...

But he wasn't hers to kiss. He wasn't hers to touch.

With a gasp Liberty tore herself away, instantly cold as she stepped back, her every instinct telling her to carry on, that he was hers for the taking, tonight at least.

'We shouldn't have done that.' Her voice was unsteady and she reached out to the wall for support.

'No.'

'I'm sorry.' She was glad she couldn't see his face, that he couldn't see hers, probably raw with need and sorrow.

'Don't be sorry, Liberty. I'm not.'

'But Millie! You're engaged!' She needed to remind herself as much as him.

'I know.' He sounded weary now. 'It's not...it's not quite what you think. I wish I could say more but...' He sighed. 'I think we should get back. Are you okay with the buggy in the dark? I might walk.'

'That might be better. I'll be fine.'

Keep saying it, keep thinking it and it might actually be true.

CHAPTER NINE

IT WAS IN many ways a relief that work didn't let up for either of them and that both Charlie and Liberty were so busy that over the next few weeks they barely had a chance to mumble a hurried and never not embarrassed greeting at each other. The film was in full swing, the castle transformed into either a Christmassy wonderland or kitsch overload depending on your taste. Charlie veered towards the latter, but as long as the Gainsborough was safely in storage in Edinburgh, no one sat on, slept in or did anything other than look at Queen Victoria's bed and all the damage was repaired, then he was happy.

No, happy was not quite the word. Perturbed might be more accurate, restless, guilty. Not because of Millie, although he couldn't decide whether he should mention the kiss to her. They had made an agreement after all, and he really wasn't bothered who she had been kissing over the last few weeks. In fact, he hoped she was kissing lots of people, in a safe and respectfully consensual way of course.

No, he felt guilty for once again dragging Liberty into his emotional dramas. He knew he needed to apologise but look where the last belated apology had got him, right back where they started. He wanted to blame the moment on the stars and the seclusion and the champagne but he knew none of those were the reason why they had kissed. It was because he was drawn to her, attracted to her, wanted her. And she deserved better. What had she said? She wanted to come first with someone. And all he could offer was a paltry second best. A last fling before he settled down. It was unthinkable.

So, it was a good thing she was busy and he equally so. Operation market the hell out of the castle had started in earnest. He'd had the foresight to get a photographer in before the set designers had turned the castle into their clichéd idea of a perfect Scottish castle and the crew had strewn the cottages and lodges with their belongings, and was busy working with web designers, marketing and advertising agencies to create the perfect website and booking experience, to decide which third parties to list with and to reassess the pricing strategy. In addition to all this he was taking advantage of his extended stay to work through the whole estate and forestry management plan. It all meant early mornings, long days and working late into the night. He fell exhausted into bed every night, but still found it hard to sleep. The memory of Liberty's body pressed to his, the feel of the curve of her hip, the taste of her, the way she had held onto him, kept him tossing and turning into the small hours. It didn't help that she was just a floor away. Sometimes he fancied he could hear her breathe, pictured her lying there, her auburn hair spread over the pillow before berating himself for being an idiot and opening his laptop to work some more and carry on with his grown-up plan to keep avoiding her.

The forecast was clear and bright for the next few days, if cold with the first frost of the year turning the air distinctly wintry. Now they were heading into November the leaves had fallen, leaving the trees bare against

the skyline and the director decided to take advantage
of the forecast to shoot some outside scenes. As Liberty
had said, most of the snow would be added later thanks
to green screens and other industry tricks Charlie didn't
really understand, but for the close-up scenes fake snow
was being generated in bulk. Some of the scenes in question involved several extras and to Charlie's horror, the
director had asked him to take part, making it clear she
thought she was bestowing a great honour.

'No, no, I am much happier behind the camera,' he had
protested but to no avail. He, most of the village children,
and several much more willing local amateur thespians
had been pulled into hair and make-up at an obscenely
early hour, kitted out in huge coats that were far too warm
for the actual temperature but would come in handy if he
ever embarked on an arctic trek, hats and scarves.

Being an extra meant a lot of waiting around and being
moved from spot to spot like a piece on the chessboard
but to his surprise Charlie quite enjoyed the experience.
It was fascinating to see how the leads changed the second the cameras started rolling, instantly becoming their
characters, the sincerity they gave their words. The first
scene involved the moment the lead actress realised she
was snowed in, the second an entire village enjoying
sledging followed by a snowball fight. The actual sledging was to be filmed off-site at an indoor slope on the
outskirts of Edinburgh, but there were plenty of shots of
children tumbling off sledges and the hero and heroine
looking into each other's eyes and laughing in a way that
made Charlie's chest ache.

Good grief, he was getting sentimental in his old age.

The fake snow was still on the ground when the crew
finally packed up, the children were sent back to the

village and the cast returned to their rooms to wash the
sticky stuff out of their hair. Charlie had gladly relin-
quished his borrowed coat and hat back to the wardrobe
department as he headed down the stairs, where the set
designers were indulging in yet more rearranging, including a few of the castle's own belongings they had
begged to be able to use. Charlie was about to remind
them to be extra careful with the large and particularly
hideous gold vase they were trying to place when his
phone rang. Giles.

Of course, he and Millie were at Howard Hall today to
discuss guest lists and Charlie really should have phoned
in. He didn't think being press-ganged into being an extra
would stand up as an acceptable excuse for missing such
an important wedding planning moment.

He accepted the call, leaning against the panelled wall,
his heart beating faster as he saw Liberty, elegant in jeans
and a cashmere green jumper, stop to talk to the set ad-
visers who were still tweaking the décor, including the
few Howard belongings Charlie hadn't had put into storage. 'How's it going?'

'I think we've managed to persuade your mother and
sister to keep the guest list under a thousand or so. But
you may now have a twelve-course tasting menu wedding
breakfast as a result.' Giles sounded exhausted. Not surprising after a negotiation with Charlie's mother and sister.
A negotiation Charlie really should have been involved in.

He groaned. 'Is Millie okay?'

'Your mother is talking to her about wedding gowns
and heirloom rings.'

Charlie closed his eyes. He had said he would handle
the rings and dresses were definitely not the groom's
family's territory. 'I should be there.'

'Trust me, I would definitely rather you were here than me,' Giles said. 'And I'm sure Millie would too.' His pause was so loaded Charlie could envision him, jaw set, eyes blazing with accusation. 'Why aren't you?'

'This movie, up here in Scotland, I need to be here. For the…antiques. Insurance purposes. You know?'

What *was* he babbling about? There were marketing considerations, estate business matters, recruitment too… and it could all be done from Norfolk. The truth was he *wanted* to be here.

In many ways his disappearing act had worked a little too well. He had definitely found it all too easy to put his impending nuptials and the huge changes that awaited him out of his mind most of the time, although every video call with Millie reminded him just how much of the burden she had ended up shouldering, just to add to his guilt. But the downside was he was painfully un-prepared for married life. It was November now, which meant his wedding was next month.

It felt so soon. Too soon. But his reasons for marrying Millie were still absolutely valid. He did need an heir, did crave stability and, he reminded himself, there were very good reasons why Millie needed him too. Besides, left to his own inclinations he couldn't be trusted not to let drama overwhelm his love life. Just look at what had happened in the dome.

And with that he was back where he started. Avoiding Liberty, keeping his calls to Millie brief and business-like and wondering what the hell was wrong with him. He had finally sorted his life out. Why was he so hell-bent on sabotage?

And now his other best friend was annoyed with him—and in turn he had guilt about Giles to add to his long list. When he had asked his friend to step in for him, he thought he might need to help with some cake eating here, maybe some wine tasting there; after all, Tabby and his mother had things under control. But it seemed that Millie was taking on far more of the organising than he had anticipated and Giles was by her side every step of the way. Without too many clashes either, despite their different characters, which was of course great, he'd always wanted his two best friends to get along. In fact, once Charlie had hoped that they might…but of course Giles was wedding averse and Millie was marrying *him*.

A sudden thought struck him, and his hand tightened on the phone. Was Millie sowing her wild oats with *Giles*? She'd been asking questions about him recently, about his background, his parents, the only time their conversation veered away from tulle and colour schemes. And Giles was being *particularly* abrupt. And he had been interested in Millie at Octavia's wedding.

Giles and Millie. It would complicate things. But surely one of them would have said if they were more than bride and best man. He was probably just imagining things. Projecting his own guilt over his attraction to Liberty.

'Right. Insurance.' Yep, there was definitely accusation in Giles's voice. He didn't buy Charlie's reasons for one minute and no wonder. It wasn't as if Charlie was stuck on the other side of the world. He could easily have got back for a day or two if he wanted.

'Tell Millie I'm really sorry she's having to do this alone.' Charlie was about to say more, to apologise again, when there was a shout, some swearing and the ominous sound of a crash behind him. He whirled around, to see his grandmother's favourite vase lying in pieces on the ground, the set designer, dresser and Liberty standing around it, all three staring at him in horror. 'Sorry, I'm going to have to go. Liberty!' He pocketed his phone and waited for an explanation from the guilty-looking group.

'Charlie, I am so sorry. We'll replace it.' Liberty looked tired, her hair pulled back into a ponytail, and there were deep shadows under her eyes.

'I doubt it.' He walked towards them. 'It's Victorian.'

'I know your grandmother loved it.'

'She did, she really did.' He looked down at the shards. 'It was really ugly though.' He smiled at the still horrified set designer. 'You have the insurers' details? Good, I'll let them sort it out.'

He headed for the door, only to turn as he heard footsteps hurry after him. He turned to see Liberty. 'I just wanted to say again how sorry I am. You entrusted us with your house. I know we shouldn't have moved that vase.'

'*I* should have put the vase in storage. The only person who liked it was Grandma and if she's planning to haunt us she will have started by now. She's probably so disgusted by all the renovations she hasn't wanted to hang around. So you can sleep safely.'

'I loved your grandmother. I would be very happy to be haunted by her.'

Charlie smiled. 'She was the best. Honestly, don't worry, Aunt Flic will be sad but we'll cope. We have many other hideous vases.'

One good thing about the toppling of the vase was that it had got him out of the call with Giles, although he did now need to call his mother and remind her that she was to leave rings to him and dresses to Millie. Which meant he needed to actually order the wedding rings as he had promised to do, although he was going to suggest that

Millie pick her own engagement ring if she didn't want any of the heirlooms—he didn't blame her if she didn't, hideous overly bling things most of them were. There was that art deco emerald, but it wasn't Millie somehow. Liberty now...

Liberty smiled. 'Thank you for being so understanding. Look, I'm glad I caught you.'

'You are?' *Please don't mention what happened because then I'll have to apologise and then it will be out there and there is a lot to be said for keeping things buried.*

She looked down at her feet and then seemed to square her shoulders. 'Erm, yes. I just wanted a chance to go over the shooting schedule with you, if you have a chance? We want to do the indoor scenes from next week, which means more upheaval, I appreciate. We're planning to finish as much of the outdoor over the next few days while the weather holds and then start with the castle, then the pub and finally the village hall.'

'Great.' Shooting schedules. Safe, professional, no lips involved. Excellent.

'So, do you want to see the schedule? They are very keen on shooting in Queen Victoria's room but have promised not to touch the bed, I just want to make sure there is nothing else we need to be careful of and check if there are any extra forms to sign.'

Charlie really shouldn't have thought about lips because now he was far too aware of the curve of Liberty's full mouth. He was dimly aware that she was waiting for an answer and managed to pull himself together. 'I think that room is fine but I'll take another look just to be on the safe side. And yes, probably makes sense to go through the schedule too.'

'Great, I was about to head over to The Leaping Salmon to check with Angus. Do you want to come and we can discuss there, or shall we meet later? You can tell me about your acting debut too. Simone said you were a natural.'

Charlie hesitated. Was heading to the pub with Liberty wise? But it was a public space, filled with crew and villagers. What harm could a drink and a chat do?

'Pub sounds great,' he said. 'Let me get my coat and I'll walk over with you.'

It was funny how, despite her vows to stay far away from Charlie and to be nothing but professional when she did see him, Liberty soon fell into her old comfortable way of being with him. It was because she *felt* comfortable with him. Too comfortable. That was why she kept forgetting herself. Getting too close.

But there was no constrained atmosphere as they walked the fifteen minutes across the estate to the pub. Charlie told her some amusing anecdotes about his day on set as an extra and she filled him in on the affair between the actress playing the best friend and the lead actor and the ongoing feud between the set designer and the lead prop designer. He laughed in all the right places, giving her his full attention in a way that warmed her through. It was so unusual these days when most people were connected to at least two devices even during a conversation; she was guilty of it herself, but not Charlie. He was always very present.

The pub, like the castle, was decorated in a set designer's idea of a Scottish Christmas, which meant huge red tartan bows and garlands over everything. At least, Angus said, he didn't need to bother redecorating and as they slipped into November, the decorations looked less odd and just extra.

The pub belonged to the Glenmere estate and, as compensation for the long renovation which had eaten into what little tourism they had, the Howard Estate had paid for a refurbishment of the pub. Nothing too drastic, Charlie told her that they hadn't wanted to incite a village revolt, but a clean-up and repaint, new scrubbed oak tables, reupholstering of benches and chairs, opening up the function room and redecorating the bedrooms. But the fire still crackled in the same 500-year-old hearth, the ceilings were still the same, low and beamed and white-washed, the same tempting array of single malts were displayed behind the bar. Liberty approved. She always felt at home here, no matter how much time elapsed between her visits.

'My favourite location manager,' Angus proclaimed as they walked in. 'Liberty, if you can bring me a booking like this every year I will be forever in your debt. February would be a good time. Let us recover from Hogmanay but help us manage over the quiet time.'

'I'll bear that in mind,' Liberty promised. She slid into the booth nearest the fire and sank onto one of the now comfortable benches. She might not like too much change but new upholstery was something she did approve of. 'And would you like to have a role in every one of these films?'

'I can't help it if the camera loves me,' he said with a grin. 'What will I get you?'

'Coffee for me, this is a work meeting,' she said firmly. She needed her wits about her if she was going to be dealing with Charlie. Busy and professional, that was the key. That way her mind wouldn't keep returning to the dome, to the secrets he had told her, secrets he hadn't even told his fiancée, to the way her body had swayed towards his, the kiss, even more magical than the first.

No thinking about kissing. He wasn't hers to kiss.

They went over the schedules in some detail, Liberty promising to make sure no more wires were trailing near valuable if ugly vases, before moving over to discuss the next week with Angus. She returned to the table where Charlie was glaring at his phone, and started to tick things off on her iPad.

'The hall is all ready for us to use for the nativity scene, the airport scenes were done before they got here…'

'I always find it odd how films are shot out of order,' Charlie said. 'They did the happy ever after before they had even met. At least with a play you start at A and end up at Z, a film is like alphabet spaghetti.'

'I know. Yesterday we filmed her arrival, today she got snowed in and fell in love, tomorrow she will leave, and then we do the bits in between. But the actors seem to manage.'

'What did you prefer, stage or film?'

'For acting? Stage for all the reasons you said, but I wanted to work on films because it gives me the opportunity to travel. I like spending a few weeks in different places.' She looked over at the fire and sighed in contentment. 'Although right now I feel like I could settle here forever. Sometimes I think Glenmere is the most beautiful place in the world.'

'You're not wrong. I might get a quote from you for the website.' His smile was too intimate and Liberty sat back, wanting some space between them.

'How's Millie?' It felt safer to deliberately bring the

conversation around to his fiancée. 'Were you on the phone to her earlier? How's the wedding planning going.'

Charlie looked over to the bar and signalled to Angus, and in just a few moment pints were set in front of them along with an assortment of crisps. Millie looked at Charlie in surprise.

'If we are going to talk weddings I need sustenance,' he explained.

'That bad? I suppose three months *is* a short time to organise a wedding in even with a confirmed venue and professional planners in the family.'

'Maybe I was being ridiculously naïve but I didn't think that I would be leaving Millie—and it turns out, Giles—with so much to do. In my head we were going to do something small and intimate, that we would just turn up at the local church, then head to The Fox and Duchess… *What?*'

Liberty set her pint down and stared at Charlie in amusement. 'The Fox and Duchess? Have you *met* your mother and sister?'

'They are not the ones getting married.'

'No, *you* are. Charles St Clare Howard, heir to one of the oldest baronies in the entire country and just as importantly CEO of a business that relies on showcasing just how ideal his properties are for events such as society weddings. As if they were going to let you get away with the local pub!'

'I said I was being a little naïve. Okay,' as Liberty raised her eyebrows meaningfully. 'A lot naïve. At least Giles helped Millie battle the guest list down from everyone my parents have ever met to something manageable, but they had to agree to a twelve-course tasting menu in return. If I had been there…'

His voice trailed off.

Of course, he wanted to be there, supporting his bride-to-be, not stuck in Scotland with his sister's best friend who pounced on him whenever she had the opportunity. If she was Millie, she would be furious that Charlie had disappeared for so long at such a crucial time. Liberty took a deep breath. 'Look, you being here is a huge help, but I didn't expect you to be on hand the *whole* time. I'm sure if you needed to head back for a few days or even longer, we could manage.'

'And leave you with the vases unattended?'

'I think you left that vase there on purpose. I'm serious, Charlie, if Millie needs you on hand, then of course you should go home.'

He rubbed his forehead. 'Truth is I had no idea how much Mills was going to take on. I thought she would leave it all to Tabby.'

'Tabby certainly has lots of ideas.' Ideas she sent to Liberty in exhausting detail.

'But it turns out Millie wants some control over the day.'

'And that's a surprise?'

'Under the circumstances…' He stopped, an appalled look on his face. 'Due to how short a time we have, I mean. And now Giles is involved, sending me reminders to pick out wedding rings, addressing the invitations for goodness' sake. It's all such a circus.'

'It's a wedding. It comes with the territory.'

'It wouldn't for you though. At Octavia's wedding you said you wanted something small and intimate.'

He'd remembered? She'd assumed he had been too drunk to remember much of anything they had discussed that night. But then again, he'd not been too drunk to get engaged.

She stared at her still untouched pint, a nagging sense that something didn't add up about his engagement resurfacing. 'Well, in the unlikely event I did get married the alternative would be all ten of my siblings as bridesmaids and groomsmen, Mum and Dad fighting over which magazine to sell the photos to, Dad walking me down the aisle as if he had been part of my life. Ugh.' She shuddered. 'But it's not my wedding. It's yours and Millie's.'

'Right now, it's Mother and Tabby's and Millie and Giles's wedding. Not that I am complaining, I appreciate Giles stepping in and I know the day means a lot to Mum and Tabs.'

She stared at him. 'And to Millie and to you.'

'Right.' He took a long drink. 'Right. I guess I do only get married once. Might as well do it right.'

'Charlie.' The words slipped out before she could stop them. 'Do you actually *want* to get married.'

He didn't answer for a long time. 'I want to settle down, to be married, to have a calm quiet life. I could do without the big day and all the fuss, but you're right. It's not just about me. It's about the title and the estate and the business...'

'And Millie.'

'Right, and Millie.'

If she hadn't kissed him, would she be so interested, so sure that there was a mystery here? She should leave well enough alone, get on with her job and count down the days until she returned to London and Charlie Howard was out of her life. She slid a glance over at Charlie, who was staring into his pint, forehead creased, looking less like an eager groom and more like a man with all the weight in the world weighing him down and knew, that sensible as walking away might be, she just couldn't. She had to find out what was going on.

'Charlie,' she said. 'Tell me to butt out, but the engagement was so quick, so unexpected that even Tabby had no idea it was on the cards. The day before you announced it you were mourning your relationship with Octavia but went straight home to propose to someone else. Then there's the fact you are here...' She didn't say *kissing me*, but the words hung there between them. 'Something doesn't add up. I'm worried about you.'

As soon as she said the last words, she wanted to snatch them back. Who was she to worry about Charles St Clare Howard? But he didn't look angry or outraged at her presumption. Instead, he downed his pint, picked up his coat and stood up.

'Not here.' And with those cryptic words he strode towards the door. Liberty sat and stared after him for one long moment, then leaving her own pint unfinished, slipped on her own jacket and followed him. It was time for answers.

CHAPTER TEN

CHARLIE WAS TORN between betraying Millie's confidence and the relief of unburdening himself. Usually when he was in any kind of trouble he would go to Millie or to Giles. But that was out of the question. The recent phone call showed that Giles was firmly team Millie right now. And he didn't want his parents or Tabby to know that he and Millie weren't a traditional romantic love match, for their marriage, or Millie herself, to be diminished in their eyes.

And he owed Liberty an apology, one that could only come with an explanation.

He set off down the small, narrow high street, lined with a handful of shops to serve the community and the tourists, the usual small supermarket, butcher's, baker's and ironmongers joined by gift shops and outdoor gear shops. Liberty fell in beside him. It was dusk now, the street lights on, lighting their way as they left the village heading towards the huge iron gates which guarded the castle.

'I need to get married,' he said suddenly and abruptly. 'The title and estate are entailed, Tabby can't inherit, and we can debate the rights and wrongs of that forever, but right now that's a fact. The nearest heir is a second cousin twice removed who has no interest in the estate or farming or learning. So, I need to get married, and I really need a son.'

'You're a man, you don't have the same kind of biological clock women do. Why the hurry?'

'No, but I could get knocked over tomorrow,' he pointed out as they turned into the gates. The wide sweeping driveway was also lit up by just enough for them to find their way, the castle silhouetted in the distance. 'I could get ill. And if neither of those things happen and I put it off then I don't want to end up having to marry someone years younger.'

'But there are no guarantees. You could have trouble conceiving or be as fertile as the Nile but only have daughters. I can't believe I just said *only*, damn the patriarchy.'

'I agree. And if that happens then that's when we take a serious look at that pesky entail. But for now I owe it to my parents and the estate to at least try and do things traditionally. The problem is I have only been in love once in my life and I picked poorly.' He sighed. 'I say that I assumed that Octavia and I would settle down, that she would get bored of all the breaking up and making up and we'd head into a happy ever after, but in reality it was never going to happen. She thrives on drama, on being adored, on being part of society, she was never going to want to become a Norfolk farmer's wife and work in the family business.'

'No.' He could hear a quiver of amusement in Liberty's voice. 'She wasn't.'

'But I spent my whole adult life with her. I grew up with her. Learned about love with her.' He had no idea how to explain but he really wanted her to understand. 'What if that, I don't know, hardwired a template of what love *is*? Taught me that that is how a relationship works? What if I make the same mistake again? The future of the estate relies on stability.'

'The thing about mistakes, Charlie, is that we learn from them.'

'Ideally yes, but I can't risk getting it wrong again. The family business is too important to let emotion derail all we've built. I hadn't made any big decisions, but I had started to think the most sensible thing to do would be to look for someone I liked, who liked me, who understood my world, who didn't want to be swept off their feet but did want to settle down.'

'Then you and Millie realised you had feelings for each other, and you went straight to being engaged? I assumed you'd been secretly dating for some time, but this makes more sense. There seems to be so much you haven't discussed yet.' She inhaled. 'Not that it's any of my business.'

He stopped, turned to look down at her. 'Liberty, I need you to promise that you will never breathe a word of what I am about to say to anyone, especially not Tabitha.'

Her eyes widened. 'That sounds intense. I promise unless, you're not ill, are you? I can't keep that from Tabby.'

God, he was making a pig's ear of this. Was it even necessary? Liberty was making a good job of pretending the kiss had never happened, he should do the same. For her it had probably meant nothing. For him? No, better not to go there.

'No. I'm not ill. Look, I think you deserve some honesty from me, but some of this isn't mine to share which is why I don't want my parents or Tabby to know. The truth is that Millie…' He hesitated, trying to find the right words. 'She wants a big family, always has. And she would be—will be—a great mother. But time might not be on her side and if she wants to make sure she has that family she needs to get started pretty much straight away.'

'I see.'

'But she's not dated anyone for a long time, her ex screwed her over in a bad way and it has taken her some time to get over that. So there we are, neither of us is looking for romance, we both just want to be married and settled. We have the same goals. More importantly we love each other, respect each other, know each other better than ourselves in many ways…'

'But you're not *in* love with each other.' It was a statement not a question.

'Being in love is just about pheromones, chemicals. Something in your body reacts to something in someone else's body and that's it. It can lead you astray. But the end goal is to get to where Milly and I are now, we're just bypassing the messy, emotional phases. But I know my parents, her mum, Tabby, they'll be horrified, think of our marriage as less, not real in some ways. It's better for everyone that they think this is a whirlwind courtship between best friends. Do you understand?'

Liberty didn't reply, just resumed walking, her shoulders hunched against the wind, and Charlie had an urge to put his arm around her to shield her. Instead, he handed her his scarf and after a startled glance she took it, wrapping it around her neck.

By unspoken accord they headed round the side of the castle to the discreet door which led into the family apartment and into the boot room where they stayed silent as they hung their jackets up and took off their shoes before heading into the hallway. Usually, Charlie would head straight up to the turret study he had taken as his own, minimising alone time with Liberty, but he sensed their conversation wasn't yet done, so instead he followed her into the kitchen diner and accepted the large glass of red wine she handed him before she took a seat at the kitchen table, nursing her own glass. He leaned against the island, watching her intently.

Finally, she spoke. 'Do you think Mrs M would mind if I ate here instead of in the main house? I'm not sure I am up to seeing people. It's been a long day, week, month...'

'I'm sure she won't.' He hesitated. Should he offer to leave her alone to eat in peace? But he usually ate here, she knew that. 'After all, my dinner will be plated up.' It was an opportunity for Liberty to excuse herself, one she didn't take.

Less than ten minutes later their food arrived, Charlie meeting the housekeeper at the internal door to collect a tray, telling her to get herself home and promising to return the washed dishes to the main house before morning.

'When I speak to Mrs M I feel like I am a naughty twelve-year-old trying to scrump a pastry out of her kitchen,' he said when he returned and Liberty managed a tired smile.

'She adores and spoils you.'

'Oh, I know, this dinner is proof of that. Steak pie and mash. She's a queen, I should have married her, if only it wasn't for Mr McGregor.'

The joke hung there in the balance for a long few seconds before Liberty laughed, the flash of her dimple warming him through. 'Now marrying for food like this I do understand!'

'But you don't understand marrying for compatibility and similar goals?' She hadn't said so, hadn't said anything yet, but he sensed it.

Liberty didn't answer as she set the table, and he laid the food out, her expression thoughtful. 'What do I know?' she said in the end. 'I've never had a relationship last more than a few months, by choice, and I haven't exactly had shining examples of long-lasting marriage from my parents. Running after romance and true love has only brought my father a lot of alimony and my mother a nice collection of engagement rings. If this feels right to you then that's all that matters.'

Charlie was aware of a faint feeling of disappointment. What had he wanted her to say?

'It does,' he said firmly. Too firmly. As if he was trying to convince himself as much as her. 'But I have to admit I have needed some space to absorb it. We didn't expect the wedding to be quite so soon.'

'Hence you hiding up here while Giles and Millie face your family?'

He winced. 'Look, my ancestors might have excelled in battle, but I can promise every lance-wielding one of them would have been sent into a disorganised retreat at the sight of Tabby with a mood board.'

Liberty took another drink of her wine. Her cheeks had regained their colour, her eyes their usual intelligent gleam. 'So how will it work?'

'Like any other marriage. We'll respect each other, be faithful to each other…'

'That's a good thing. My father's second marriage was an open marriage, it did *not* end well.'

Charlie took a large sip of wine. 'Once we are married, that is.'

Her eyebrows drew together. '*What* is?'

'Being faithful. Everything has happened so quickly. I want Millie to be sure that this is what she wants, and like I say, she has been single for a long time. I don't want her to have any regrets. So, I made it clear that if she wants some romance while I'm away she should go for it. We've made no vows, no promises yet.'

Liberty put her fork down. 'Charlie Howard, are you saying that you and Millie have given *carte blanches* to each other to have some kind of last fling? Why are you telling me this? Why are you even here? Is *that* why you kissed me in the dome? Am I the lucky second choice *again*? Because we have been here once before and *you* broke my teenage heart.'

Why on earth had she said that? 'Teenage hearts are fragile, melodramatic things,' she said quickly, wanting to wipe the appalled self-loathing look off Charlie's face, to regain some dignity. 'Twenty-something hearts are much more resilient. Don't worry. I'm not in love with you. It was just one kiss and I feel a hell of a lot better knowing it wasn't completely wrong of us. I would have appreciated knowing that before though, I've felt pretty rotten over the last couple of weeks. I like Millie.'

Charlie looked discomfited, not an expression she was used to seeing on him. 'I know and I am so sorry. Look, yes, Millie said the exclusion applied to me too, but I hadn't planned to…' He shook his head. 'I'm not going to lie to you, Liberty. It was another really lovely kiss.' His voice dropped, almost to a whisper. 'Really lovely. But I had, *have*, no intent of using that exemption. I don't need to. Millie and I will have a good marriage, I'm convinced of that. And the best thing for me is enter it with no regrets or ties. But you were right, you deserved an explanation.'

'Thank you for the honesty.' Liberty looked down at her still half-full plate but her appetite was gone. Well, she'd asked for Charlie to be tell her what was going on and she had full disclosure. It wasn't Charlie's fault that she didn't like the answer. That no matter what he said, once again, she'd been Charlie's consolation prize. What an absolute fool she was.

She pushed her plate away and got to her feet. 'Of course, I will respect your and Millie's privacy. I won't breathe a word to Tabby and I genuinely hope you and Millie will be very happy. But I'm not willing to be a bit player in your love life a second time, Charlie.'

'I didn't…'

She held up a hand to silence him. 'It's obvious that we are attracted to each other, and under the circumstances that's a little less reprehensible than it seems. But that exemption of yours changes nothing. You don't want to use it and that's fine, but even if you did, I wouldn't be interested. I'm not a romantic, and I'm not a starry-eyed teen, but I do expect the men I sleep with to be mine for the duration at least. So, I think it's better not to spend too much time together from now on.'

She left the room quickly before Charlie could say anything else and made it to her bedroom before she felt tears press hot and hard. She blinked, forcing them back. She didn't cry, *especially* over men. It had been a kiss, that was all. She had known he was engaged. What did the circumstances of that engagement matter?

She opened her laptop and started to scroll through her emails, needing, wanting a knotty problem to absorb her, not wanting to figure out why she felt so raw, so hurt. Charlie hadn't been cheating on Millie, she hadn't been the other woman, her conscience was clear, she should be pleased. Relieved.

But she *was* the other woman. She wasn't the woman

he was in love with, or the woman he wanted to make a life with. She was still the woman he kissed and left. Second best. Again. She bit her lip hard. What was wrong with her? Why did everyone walk away? Why did no one ever choose her?

This was why it was far better for her to set the rules. Easy, fun, time-limited relationships with no hard feelings when they came to their inevitable end.

But now she knew he wasn't in love with Millie, now she knew about their little pre-wedding clause she couldn't stop wondering what would have happened if they had stayed in the dome, if she had allowed him to back her onto that huge bed. What it would be like to touch him properly, for him to touch her. To make love to him?

The possibility of it hung in the air, tantalisingly close and possible. She could go downstairs right now and proposition him and for all his fine words about not intending to use the exemption she knew he would agree. In less than five minutes they could be naked, here in her bed, on the kitchen table, on the stairs...in all three places. Desire surged, hot and sweet and so tempting.

But no. She might be used to rejection, to being left behind, but she didn't need to search it out. She'd spent her adult life choosing her relationships carefully, making sure she was desired more than she desired, ending each one before her feelings came anywhere near to getting involved. And she was wise enough to know that Charlie Howard had always been her Achilles heel. That the only way to keep herself safe was to stay away. Far away.

And that was exactly what she going to do.

Liberty managed to keep her promise to herself as the shoot progressed. She didn't ignore Charlie, that would have made it obvious to a cast and crew finely attuned to tension on a set that something had happened, but she was never alone with him. There were no more late-night drinks, no walks around the grounds, no more visits to the pub. She missed the easy friendship they had built up, and she spent more nights than she cared to admit, lying in bed and reliving every second of that kiss. How he had looked, what he had said, the feel of his hands on hers, the ragged sound of his breath. But then she would switch on her bedside lamp and read a chapter of her book until she had—almost—banished every illicit thought.

The end of the shoot couldn't come soon enough, she told herself. But at the same time she didn't want to leave. Didn't want to head back to the city, to her lonely flat. To a world where Charlie would be out of reach forever.

The days and weeks flew past, despite the long, sleepless nights, the temperature dropping week by week until there was no denying winter had finally arrived along with December, but Liberty was finding it hard to summon up any festive spirit. December meant the end of the shoot, the end of her time at Glenmere. And of course it was the month of Charlie's wedding, impossible to ignore thanks to Tabby's constant messages and an invitation she had yet to RSVP for, thanks to her own racing mind still dwelling on all he had told her in an unguarded minute. The only possible cure was to work even harder, to ensure she had no idle moments, no time to think, taking on any task she could, including organising the wrap party with Brad, the set designer, and Angus who clearly was as keen the shoot carry on as long as possible as she was.

'I can't believe there's just a week before you all pack up and go,' he said, when she walked into The Leaping Salmon to meet with him and Brad to finalise the last details. All the villagers and estate workers were also invited to the ceilidh in the village hall on the last day of the shoot.

Liberty leaned on the bar. 'You're not looking forward to getting rid of us?'

'Are you kidding? I'm praying every day for fiction to become reality and you all to be snowed in and have to stay another week.' He heaved a huge sigh. 'At least it's Christmas now and Charlie has managed to let the castle and most of the cottages for the whole festive season, so fingers crossed the guests all enjoy a dram or two at the atmospheric local pub.'

'Who could resist great food, a roaring fire and the best whisky selection in the Highlands? It's great that Charlie has managed to get the castle let.' She'd had no idea, not that she would expect to. Not while she avoided all conversation with him.

'How about you, Liberty? Looking forward to returning to London?'

'Not at all, I'm with you, if I could be snowed in here for the rest of the winter, I would be quite happy. And I have so much to do here and for home—Christmas is in just three weeks and I have done *nothing*. I still need to get presents for the cast and crew and decide what I am actually doing for Christmas although right now I am thinking sleeping is the perfect answer. Time has run away with me again.'

The not sleeping didn't help. Why hadn't she used those wide-awake times constructively and done some shopping rather than frittering them away on a series of crime novels she'd chosen for the total lack of any romantic subplot. The last thing she needed while she was getting over Charlie was to indulge in any romantic fiction. No, give her a high body count and a borderline alcoholic grumpy investigator instead.

Someone joined her at the bar. 'Why don't you take the rest of the day off and get some of your shopping done?'

Liberty turned to see Ted, the producer. 'Oh, I'm fine! Honestly! There's still plenty of time.'

'Liberty, you look exhausted. Besides, you haven't had a day off in months. We're nearly done, we can spare you for a day. Go, have a walk round, do your shopping, remind yourself there's a world outside this film.'

A world outside Glenmere. Maybe that was what she needed. 'You know, maybe I will. It's not even midday, I could be in Perth by early afternoon if I can just get a lift to the train station.'

Normally she would have hired a car but as Charlie had driven her up and she'd stayed firmly on-site she hadn't bothered.

Angus put down the glass he was polishing. 'Don't worry about a train. Charlie is heading to Perth, I'm sure he'll give you a lift.'

No no no. The last thing she needed was to be stuck in a car with Charlie for a couple of hours.

'It's fine, I don't want to put him to any inconvenience…oh, hi, Charlie.'

How had she not seen him? How had her Spidey sense not sent out an alert that he was in the vicinity? Why was he looking so unfairly good in his battered old jeans and cashmere jumper and tousled hair while she was looking like a location manager existing on three hours sleep a night at the end of a shoot with hair that needed a good washing and a hole in her own *not* cashmere jumper?

'Hi.' She tried to ignore the warm intimacy in the smile he directed her way. 'How are you, Liberty?'

'Good. Fine. Fantastic. You?'

'Liberty has some shopping to do and didn't you say you were heading into Perth today?' Angus said cheerfully as if the tension wasn't so palpable it was practically visible.

Charlie's pause was so brief that if you weren't looking out for it you wouldn't know it was there. Liberty however, was attuned to his every mood and she heard it loud and clear.

'Of course. Can you be ready in half an hour?'

'Yes, but I can easily get the bus, honestly.'

'That seems unnecessary if we're going the same way at the same time. Meet you in the car park in thirty minutes?'

And what could she say but 'Great! See you then.'

Half an hour to Perth then half an hour back. She could manage that. It wasn't like just being in Charlie's close proximity meant she would launch herself at him. Probably.

CHAPTER ELEVEN

THIS LIFT WAS a good thing. The awkwardness between him and Liberty was intensifying with every week and Charlie knew his sister would pick up on it the second they were all in the same room. The drive was a chance to clear the air, to return to some kind of normalcy.

Besides, he and Liberty had both put their cards on the table. They were attracted to each other, fine, they were both young, healthy and romantically unattached even if Charlie was engaged. But neither of them wanted to act on that attraction. It was all good.

So, he wasn't going to react when Liberty climbed into his car, hair freshly brushed and shining like the dawn sun, changed into a soft green top that clung lovingly to her curves, a dark grey scarf wrapped around her elegant neck bringing out the colour of her eyes and highlighting the flush on her cheeks. No, he was going to smile as if she were anyone, greet her with a cheery. 'Ready?'

'As I'll ever be.'

'I feel that way about Christmas shopping too.'

'Is that what you are going in to do?'

'Christmas shopping and I just realised there are wedding gifts I need to bestow as well. If I had thought ahead I would never have agreed to getting married on Christmas Eve, it's doubled the amount of seasonal gift buying pain.' There, get the wedding mentioned and on the table straight away. No more secrets. Just a return to the old easy conversation.

'Are men really terrible at buying gifts or is it weaponised incompetence?' she asked sweetly and Charlie was shocked into laughter.

'Both,' he admitted. 'In my case anyway.'

'Christmas at least happens every year. It can't be that much of a shock.'

'True. But I usually buy Tabby whatever expensive item of clothing she sends me a link to, whisky for my dad, my mother gets whatever Tabby has chosen and wants me to go halves on, Aunt Flic new riding gloves or something like that. Only this year with the wedding Tabby has failed to send me any links or hints and so I am on my own. And that's the tricky part. According to Octavia I was absolutely useless although in my defence buying for her was a minefield. I set off more than a few explosions over the years.'

'What about Millie? What do you usually buy her?'

'Millie? Oh, Millie is easy, vouchers for a restaurant, tickets for a play or an exhibition, something like that. But this year we are spending Christmas as newlyweds with both our families. A voucher isn't going to cut it, is it?'

'No. Not nearly. And I guess for the wedding you need thank-you gifts, something for the bridesmaids and Giles, a thank-you for Tabby and both mothers.' She paused. 'A bridal gift for Millie.'

'That's it, all of the above. Basically, Christmas two days in a row. How about you, do you like buying presents?'

'I like the idea of it more than the reality I guess.' She looked down at her hands. 'The problem is not only do most of my siblings pretty much have everything, I don't know any of them well enough to buy something special, so it ends up being generic. Usually books.'

'You can't go wrong with books.'

'That's my motto.'

'You buy for all ten?'

'Yup. Not sure why, it's not always reciprocated and probably not appreciated, spot the one only child in the whole dysfunctional family.'

'If you want to put your present buying skills to good use you could always help me.'

'You want me to help you with your present buying?' She sounded uncertain.

'I'll throw in dinner as a thank-you.'

Now why had he said that? Why hadn't he made small talk about the landscape for half an hour then left her at the car park with a cheery *see you back here at five*?

Charlie knew why. It was because he had missed her. Because this time together was hurtling towards its end, and he wasn't ready to say goodbye yet.

Liberty stared out of the window, her body language unreadable before she clearly came to some kind of decision, her shoulders relaxing. 'Okay. But you can help me with mine in return.'

The sky was overcast, the clouds low and heavy and now they were so close to midwinter it already felt like it was getting dark, which made the cheerful lights of the pretty Christmas market very welcome. The scent of hot chocolate, mulled wine and roasting chestnuts mingled in a festive cocktail as they browsed the myriad stalls.

'I want to buy presents for the people I've worked with the most and also for the director and cast,' Liberty explained. 'The producers will have something for us and for all the villagers who helped, but we usually exchange personal gifts too. I've learned to buy extras just in case someone I didn't expect surprises me with one.'

She murmured to herself as they perused the stalls. 'Whisky? Not all of them drink. Haggis bites? No use for the Americans on the crew, doubt they'll get them through Customs. Oh! Charlie, what about these?'

These were pretty little glass snow domes, a castle that looked remarkably like Glenmere in perched on a tree-lined mountain. 'Don't you just love snow globes?' Liberty picked one up and shook it, her eyes huge as she watched the snow whirl in the fantasy wintry landscape. 'I used to collect them as a child, but when Mum split up from Jack, well. My things weren't a priority.' She stopped, and for a moment the hurt blazed through, before she visibly fought it back. 'What do you think?'

'I think they are perfect.' Charlie found it hard to focus on the snow globes when Liberty was more dazzling by far, her hair like burnished fire, her eyes huge and luminous, filled with a mixture of nostalgia, sadness and excitement.

'Aren't they? This is brilliant, all sorted by the third stall! I'm going to go for it.'

Liberty arranged for the globes to be delivered to the castle and left the stall with a spring in her step. 'Okay. What's on your list? Shall we do Christmas first for both of us before we think about the wedding?'

The market and small independent shops that surrounded it were a treasure trove, and Liberty the perfect personal shopper. Her instincts and taste were unerring as she purchased locally made cashmere gloves for all her adult siblings, a gorgeous scarf for Tabby in a vibrant red they both knew his sister would love, a tweed hat for her father 'to wear for photo shoots on his country estate' and some locally made organic skincare for her mother.

'I am going to continue the tradition of buying books for all the children,' she said as they passed an inviting independent bookshop. 'They get whatever the must-have toys are times a million. There's no point buying them any, they just get lost.'

Charlie followed her example and guidance, purchasing locally made tweed cardigans for his mother, aunt and Millie's mother, the usual single malt for his father, a cashmere dress for Tabby and a carefully chosen selection of books for Millie, including some local cookbooks and one on the flora of Scotland he knew she'd like.

'And jewellery,' Liberty said as they dropped their bags back at the car. 'You should give her jewellery too. First Christmas and all.'

'Really? I'm going to get her something for the day before...'

'Then something matching,' Liberty said firmly. 'Come on, there's a couple of lovely jewellers along here.'

Left to his own devices Charlie would have been utterly clueless. There were several shops filled with bright and shiny rings, necklaces and other baubles, in every conceivable stone. It was quite frankly overwhelming. But Liberty was calm and focused, picking out gorgeous brooches, one a sprig of heather and one a thistle, for his mother and Millie's mother as a thank-you for hosting the wedding.

'I doubt your mother and Tabby have allowed Mrs Myles much say and she'll be too aware of her position to push in where she belongs but much more tactful to pretend you don't know this,' she said wryly. She also picked out pretty silver charm bracelets for Millie's two small cousins who would be her bridesmaids and a beautiful bangle for Tabby, a complicated twist of silver his sister would adore, while he selected some smart cuff-links for Giles.

'He does actually use cuff-links,' he said defensively when Liberty muttered something about an original choice and she laughed.

'He's a posh boy who works in the city. Of course he does.'

That just left Millie. Charlie was hard-pressed to remember what jewellery he had seen her wear. He wasn't even sure if her ears were pierced to Liberty's ill-hidden disgust.

'I know this isn't the most conventional of marriages but you have been friends with her for over twenty-five years! How can you not know if her ears are pierced?'

'They are because I remember them getting infected,' Charlie said triumphantly as Liberty whispered something that sounded very much like a repeat of her charge of *weaponised incompetence*.

'I'm just not observant about details that have very little to do with me,' he said with as much dignity as he could muster. But he did know that Liberty had pierced her ears several times, that she wore tiny delicate studs up her ears, and larger hoops at the front. That she often wore an amethyst pendant, a gift from her grandmother, and favoured a selection of chunky silver rings.

'What kind of engagement ring did she choose in the end?' Liberty asked and Charlie scrolled through his phone until he found the picture of the vintage emerald-and-ruby ring she had selected. Liberty took his phone off him and zoomed in, nodding approvingly.

'That's *gorgeous*. Okay, she likes character and history rather than new and bling, that makes sense, fits in with what I know of her. And rubies and emeralds, she's not afraid of colour. I don't think she's a pearl kind of girl even if it is her wedding day. Aha, how about this?' She'd stopped at an antique shop with an array of jewellery in the window and pointed at a matching set of ruby earrings and necklace in a dark gold setting dating from the nineteen twenties. 'You could give her say the earrings on your wedding day and save the necklace for Christmas? Or, how about the whole set for Christmas and that platinum bracelet for your wedding gift? That one there? It's got a similar vibe to the ring?'

On the surface it was all so normal, so easy. Two people who had known each other for much of their lives, who were working together, out shopping. They could discuss the wedding and Millie with no hint of diffidence, Liberty clearly taking her personal shopper role seriously. But underneath Charlie was aware of a deep undercurrent. The ever-strong pull of attraction, a sense of loss and a knowledge that he would want to hold onto this time. That he didn't want this day to be over.

Everything was purchased and safely stowed in Liberty's bag as they returned to the main market to reward themselves for their industry with a hot chocolate, Liberty insisting they head for the stall with the biggest queue and, not coincidentally, the largest servings of lashings of whipped cream. The drink was indulgent and rich, warming him through. Charlie wished he could stop time, right here, just for a while.

'Oh look, Father Christmas!' Liberty came to an abrupt halt by an elaborate grotto, defined by a picket fence and covered in fake snow and some alarming looking reindeer automatons, the tinny sound of 'Rudolph the Red-

Nosed Reindeer' blasting out on repeat. It was noisy and bright but she was completely absorbed as she watched the queue of small bundled-up children corralled by anxious parents as the excitement neared fever pitch. Two cold-looking elves hovered at the front of the queue.

'Look how excited they are. I envy kids at Christmas, all that anticipation and magic. I can't imagine having children of my own but if I did...' The wistfulness in her large grey eyes was painful to see. 'If I did then I want every Christmas tradition going. Reindeer food and pantomimes and even the elf on the shelf...'

'The *what*?'

'You've not heard of the elf on the shelf? It's a naughty elf who lives in your house over Advent and every night he gets up to another bit of mischief for the children to find when they get up the next day.'

'Why? What's wrong with an Advent calendar and a bit of chocolate every morning?'

'No idea why, but we will do it. And nativities and carols and a carrot for the reindeer.' Her voice trailed off and then she looked up at the sky and her whole face lit up. 'Oh, Charlie! It's snowing at last!'

Liberty loved snow, and she especially loved snow that fell thick and fast, dizzying flakes quickly blanketing the ground. When you added a Christmas market, fairy lights strung through trees, the very smell of Christmas in the air, well then it was just pure magic.

She turned slowly, head tilted up to the sky, eyes half closed. 'It's so beautiful.'

'Yes,' Charlie said hoarsely but when she looked at him, he wasn't looking at the sky, he was looking at her.

All around people were exclaiming, small children

bending to pick up handfuls of the rapidly falling snow, the whole scene transforming into a winter wonderland before their eyes, but she barely took any of it in, her whole focus on Charlie. The last time she had stood in real snow with him, it had settled. They had been in the moonlit forest, taking part in a Hogmanay game of hide-and-seek, the world falling away, the voices of their friends fading in the distance. They had looked at each other just like this and then…

She had spent the last few weeks keeping her distance because she knew if she was alone with him then this would happen. That she would forget all the very many good reasons she should stay away and only remember how much she wanted him. How sure she was that he wanted her. That he was free for just a few short weeks, less. That it was now or never.

She really didn't want never.

Her breath hitched and before she knew what she was doing she took a step forward, her hands grasping his lapels as she looked steadily into his clear blue eyes.

'Liberty,' he said, half a whisper, half a prayer.

'I've been thinking about what you said.'

His mouth quirked into a half-smile. 'Which part?'

'All of it. I have no right to comment on your decisions. The kind of marriage you and Millie have chosen wouldn't work for me. If I was going to get married I would want all or nothing.' But then again, she was so scared of the *all* she opted for the *nothing*. After all, wasn't true love her parents' aim? And they didn't mind how many marriages it took to get there. How much damage they inflicted on those around. How could she ever be sure she got it right. Nothing was infinitely safer. 'But I get it. I do.'

'Thank you.'

'I've also been thinking about the other part, about the opportunity you gave Millie. I've been asking myself why you don't want it for yourself?'

His gaze didn't waver. She could see the heat in his eyes, knew he was holding onto his control by a thread. 'Because I knew the only woman I would want to sleep with was you, and I dragged you into my dramas once before. I swore never again, Liberty.'

'Very chivalrous. But do you know what would be the most gentlemanly thing to do?'

His raised eyebrows were a query.

'To let me decide for myself. I had a crush on you when I was twelve, Charles St Clare Howard, when you barely even registered my existence. I am too old and wise for crushes now, but I do still fancy you, and I don't want to spend the rest of my life wondering…'

'Wondering what?'

'Just how good we might have been.'

Charlie took her hands in his, his clasp tight. 'Liberty, I can't offer more than a few nights and you deserve more than that. But I have made a promise to Millie. I won't break that.'

'I know. I'm not asking you to.'

'I don't want you to get hurt.'

'I don't want to get hurt either. But I would like to enjoy a night, or two, or even a week of no strings sex with someone I find attractive and who finds me attractive. It's been a while.'

You don't let me in, her last boyfriend had complained, a sign it was time she ended it.

Well, here was someone who wouldn't want to be let

in. Who would need all intimacy to be physical only.
What could be more perfect?

Only the fact it was snowing and that the someone in
question was Charlie.

'Charlie. I know you want me and you know I want
you and we both know you are a free man right now. No
one will get hurt but we could have a very nice time. But
it's just a proposition. If you don't want to then let's go
back to the car and I promise never to speak of it again.'

She did her best to sound like it was nothing to her.
To make sure he didn't know how breathless she was as
she waited for his reply.

'And if I do want to?' The words sounded dragged
from him.

Her smile was slow. 'Snow is falling pretty fast and
you don't have your winter tyres on. You should sort that,
but I doubt any garage is open now...'

She liked the light of mischief in his eyes. 'It is falling fast. It's probably not safe to drive back tonight.' He'd
swayed closer, his breath warm on her cheek.

'Probably not. Guess we're stuck here for the night.
What shall we do?'

'What any two travellers stuck in a storm do? Look
for a friendly inn?'

'But what if they only have one room?'

His mouth curved into a wicked grin and her insides
melted. 'Now that I am counting on.'

Was she really doing this? Had she really thrown cau-
tion and sense aside and propositioned Charlie despite
several weeks telling herself how bad an idea it was?

Reality seemed blurred, dreamlike as she and Charlie walked decorously side by side until they found an
anonymous if up-market chain hotel and Charlie checked

them in, with the easy confidence and manner that defined him. Of course they were upgraded to a suite, and of course he suggested champagne, and actually it was all so easy. A shower, a few emails to say they had decided to make sure it was safe to travel and so would head back in the morning. Champagne and a few mouthfuls of room service, both wrapped in the huge hotel robes, light conversation, laughter, until it stilled, and the air became heated, charged, and she couldn't eat any more, drink any more.

With unspoken accord, they both stood at the same moment and then his mouth was on hers and he was loosening the belt of her robe as he backed her towards the bed, and it felt so right. She allowed herself to get lost in him, in the moment in a way Liberty had never been lost before. Kisses went from sweetly seductive to darkly intoxicating, she shivered at every touch, responding with an ardency and need that would have shocked her if she'd been able to form any coherent thoughts. His eyes blazed with passion as he held her gaze and she gloried in the way his breath quickened as she explored him, the gasps and sighs and moans. The rightness. There could be no regrets, no if onlys, they'd been granted this night and she was going to make the most of every second.

CHAPTER TWELVE

THE VILLAGE HALL was filled to capacity with villagers, cast and crew all whirling with various degrees of competency and knowledge to the local ceilidh band who had filled the space with their fast-paced music. Angus, smart in his kilt, microphone in his hand, stood next to them on the stage, clearly in his element as the caller.

Charlie bowed to his partner and stepped aside, realising he had ended up next to Liberty. It was as if there was a gravitational pull between them. No matter who he danced with, where he was, he was aware of her every step.

'Having fun?'

'So much. I love a ceilidh anyway and this band is brilliant. Isn't Angus a natural entertainer? He's wasted in a country pub.'

'He certainly made the most of the three lines you gave him in the film.' Charlie leaned against the wall and tried to focus on the dancers reforming into sets, not on Liberty, gorgeous in a green silk slip dress, her hair cascading down her back.

It had been a week since their trip to Perth. Any thoughts that their lovemaking was a one-night-only deal had been dispelled their first night back in the apartment. After all, what was the point of Liberty sleeping alone in one room and Charlie in another, missing each other, when they could just share a bed? And, as Liberty said, it made sense for them to make sure they had really got each other out of their system before Christmas Eve. It had been a suggestion Charlie had only been too happy to oblige.

But the problem was he was by no means sure he was anywhere near getting Liberty Gray out of his mind or his thoughts or any system at all. The opposite in fact. The more he touched her, the more he wanted her. Just standing next to her, watching the dancers, he couldn't believe that no one knew about them; he felt as if there was a neon sign over their heads, that the pull between them was visible. But Angus, and Ryan, the actor playing the lead, and the main cameraman kept flirting with Liberty and he kept fielding off questions about his very much impending nuptials which meant the pair of them were pretty good actors indeed.

Angus called a Duke of Perth and the sets reshuffled as couples took their places. The village and film cast and crew were intermingled, the villagers patiently helping coach the film folk through the steps, although some had a more natural affinity than others. Liberty and Charlie both knew most of the dances and had joined the villagers in taking on the newbies, changing partners each time.

Charlie held out a hand to Liberty. 'Dance with me?'

She flushed. 'Should we?'

'It would look more suspicious if we didn't. Besides, it's a ceilidh not a waltz. More's the pity.'

'You fancy that, do you? A candle-lit ballroom, you in skintight breeches and a cravat, leading your lady into a scandalous dance.'

'Depends on the lady.'

Liberty took his hand and allowed him to lead her onto the floor to join three other couples in search of a fourth. She leaned in just before they were within hearing distance. 'Maybe we can role-play later.'

'I'll dig out my breeches.'

'Promises, promises.'

Charlie followed the instructions almost mechanically. On the surface he was laughing, exchanging breathless comments with their set partners, listening to Angus as they went through the intricate steps. He loved ceilidhs, the fun, the exertion, the music, the way everyone could join in whether they had learned the steps at school or were trying for the first time. But right now, he would prefer a darkened dance floor and hidden corners he could whisk Liberty into.

The film crew had packed up. Tomorrow they would all be gone. He didn't know when Liberty was planning to leave but he could see no reason for her to stay much longer.

Which meant there was no reason for him to stay. A general manager had been appointed and had already moved into the rooms set aside for her, the events manager was starting after Christmas. Mrs McGregor had the staff she needed to get the castle and cottages ready for the festive season, full-time bar staff and waiting staff had been employed and a new chef was expected the next day.

Glenmere Castle was launched. His job was done. Only one vase had been broken over the last two months, the insurers were happy, the accountants were happy. He could walk away knowing he had done a good job.

Back to normality. Normality with a twist. Because in less than two weeks' time he would be married.

And once they left Scotland he and Liberty would be over.

The reel came to an end and the dancers whooped their approval as Angus announced a break. Charlie scooped two glasses of wine and handed one to Liberty.

'I could do with some air,' he said.

'Me too.'

They weren't the only ones. The porch and car park were filled with hot revellers taking the opportunity to cool down, even though the temperature was below freezing and snow still covered the ground. 'I can't believe this is the last night,' Liberty said. 'It's been a great shoot. I've loved working with them all. That's the problem with freelancing, you get into a rhythm and then onto the next.'

'Do you have another job lined up?'

'In January. I think I might take a few weeks off, properly off I mean, go away. I don't have Christmas plans so some sunshine sounds in order. I just need to book something.'

'You're not coming to Howard Hall for Christmas.'

'With the wedding the last thing any of you need is extra people for Christmas and besides, it all feels too soon. I want us to be friends, Charlie. I don't have many close friends for one reason or another, and Tabby is like a sister to me. I would hate what has happened to ruin that, for us to be awkward with each other, but time is probably a good thing. We will need to readjust and you need to concentrate on Millie.'

She was right. 'Are you heading back tomorrow? I should know this,' he added.

Her smile was pure wickedness. 'Not necessarily, we

haven't done much talking recently. No, I need to go through the house with Mrs M and make sure we have stuck to the contract, check any damage, help put everything back to how it was etc., so I'm planning on staying on for about a week. Which is a good thing because I really need to fix my flight back. I am usually much more organised than this!'

'I am planning to stay on for a bit as well.' Charlie had planned for just a couple of days, but now he thought about it a week made sense. Professionally and personally. 'I want to meet the chef tomorrow, help them settle in and make sure Mrs M and the newer staff have all they need for Christmas. In fact, why don't I drive you back?'

'You don't need to do that, Charlie.'

'I want to. Full circle.'

'Okay. But if you change your mind…'

'I'll make sure you get on a plane. But I won't.'

Charlie wasn't lying, he did want to meet the chef again and show him around; the general manager was new in post and Mrs McGregor had more than enough to do without settling in new staff, but he also knew that arriving home less than a week before the wedding would raise some eyebrows.

Let them be raised.

'Come on,' he said. 'I think they're starting up again. Another?'

'Absolutely but I am afraid I am promised to another.' Her voice dropped. 'But that's okay, we can dance later. You promised me a waltz, I believe.'

Their gazes caught, held and for one long moment everything fell away but her. What would have happened, be happening if things were different? If Millie hadn't accompanied him to the wedding? If there was no engagement, no fast-approaching wedding of his own? Instead of wringing every second out of this too short-term fling would they be looking into the future? Making plans to meet in London, to keep their liaison secret over Christmas so Tabby didn't guess because it would still be such early days?

Or was Liberty here because he wasn't free? Because this could only be short and sweet then over. Tabby often bemoaned her friend's self-fulfilling prophecy when it came to relationships.

'She thinks they won't work out so they don't work out,' she had said. 'Either she picks the absolute worst, or, if she allows anyone vaguely decent in then she bins them before they get too close. Rejects before she gets rejected. It's infuriating. I wouldn't mind if she was happy.'

Charlie didn't think he was the absolute worst, he hoped not anyway, but he could see how the time limit imposed on their relationship made him safe. Made her safe. And who could say that if he was free that things would work out between them? He had allowed love and passion to dominate his teens and twenties and it had been a complete disaster. He wasn't marrying Millie just because they both wanted children and because time wasn't on her side but because she offered him safety from that, a sanctuary. With Millie he was guaranteed not to make the same mistakes again. Whereas Liberty had plenty of demons of her own, demons he wasn't sure she even *wanted* to conquer. Any relationship with her was bound to hit obstacles, to naturally have the kind of drama and emotional baggage he had sworn to avoid.

He had made Millie a promise. He couldn't let her down. Especially not when the alternative was so uncertain.

No, it was better this way, but as he followed Liberty back into the overheated hall he wished it wasn't. That he could take her hand in front of everyone, whirl her into the dance, into the future; instead it was a few more furtive nights and a goodbye.

Just over two months ago there had been a real danger this film wouldn't happen, and now it was all over. Most of the cast and crew were gone, just a handful left to return Glenmere Castle to its restored glory.

It was a different place to the one she had driven to in the autumn. There were more staff, the whole estate filled with purpose as they prepared for the lucrative Christmas season. Everywhere Liberty walked she could see activity, windows washed, pathways cleared, Christmas decorations put up, lights strung through trees. The general manager had finally moved into her apartment, the chef had arrived and was making the kitchen his own. There was an air of new adventures, a new era. And it didn't include her. Her time here was done, her time with Charlie was done.

Liberty looked around. She had walked with no destination in mind, trying to clear her head, and yet it was no surprise that she had ended up here, where it had all begun nearly eight years ago. A snow-covered glade, the weak wintry sun peeping through the pines on the nearby slopes, bare trees, their spindly branches heavy with snow. It had been that oak there. Her back against it, glad of the support because her knees refused to hold her up, her whole body on fire, aching, wanting. It was more than she had ever felt, imagined, and so very right. It was every book; he was every hero and she was playing the central role for the first time in her life. Dreams did come true. Charlie Howard had not just noticed her, but he wanted her too.

Her mind had flashed forward, Charlie visiting her at university, walking hand in hand by the river, Christmases like this where she wasn't just Tabby's poor friend, *it's very sad you know, lovely girl but she has nowhere to go. Her parents, well...*no, she would be part of the family.

And then he had unzipped her jacket, and his hands were under her top and his mouth was so hungry and demanding and yet so sweet she wanted to be absorbed into him. She was so glad she had waited, hadn't succumbed to the pleas of her handful of school and university boyfriends. She must have known that this moment awaited her.

But then footsteps, a laugh, a well-bred drawl. And five minutes later she was alone, her jacket still undone, lips still swollen...

She inhaled shakily, horrified to find tears brimming in her eyes. She was glad of that night, glad of the lessons it had taught her, the walls it had helped her erect around her heart, the way the memory kept her safe. Even now.

She had to hold onto that, remember to keep herself safe. After all, no one else would.

She had said at the ceilidh that she didn't want things to change. That she needed his friendship. But she had been fooling herself. She needed a lot more than that and she could never have it.

It was ironic, she'd spent her life indulging in short-term relationships, she'd thought she was well equipped to handle this. That she would be able to walk away untouched. She should have known better.

The only question now was how she disentangled herself with her pride intact.

'Hey, I've been looking for you.'

Of course Charlie had found her. She blinked again, forcing a smile onto her face as she turned to face him. God, he was everything she wanted him to be. Still that storybook hero of her teenage dreams. But a hero with feet of clay.

'Back to where it all began.'

He closed his eyes briefly, regret and pain flitting across his face. 'I am so sorry...'

'No.' She shook her head. 'We've been over this. There is no need.' Once she would have lapped up his apology, wanted the validation it gave her, but no more. Her heart gave a painful jolt at the sight of him, hair falling over his face, tall, eyes creased in concern, hoping she was okay. Charlie Howard always wanted everyone to be okay. He was the perfect brother, son, employer and friend. Look at him riding to Millie's rescue with no thought of the consequences. It was what he did. That was why he'd been the perfect boyfriend for a messed-up party girl, thinking he could save Octavia although the last thing she wanted was to be saved.

The one person he had never tried to save was her. She wasn't going to let him start now.

'You know,' she said. 'There's a tree over there that holds rather good memories for me.' She ignored the fact that some of her darkest memories were also associated with this spot. 'Want to make some more?' She held his gaze as she walked slowly to the tree, leaning against it provocatively.

'There's a warm, comfortable bed just ten minutes' walk away.'

'Just a kiss, Charlie, then we can discuss that bed.'

He held her gaze, his own smouldering, and her body responded the way it always did, immediately hungry for him. She leaned back further, tilting her head towards him. This would look a lot more seductive in a dress rather than leggings and a puffer jacket, but the look on Charlie's face showed that the clothes were no barrier to his imagination.

He finally reached her and put one hand on the tree by her head, leaning in until their faces were just millimetres apart, still holding her gaze. The intent mixed with the space between them was dangerously seductive, and Liberty's breath started to speed up in line with her pulse. It was dangerous how addictive he was.

'Are you just going to look at me or are you planning to kiss me any time soon?' She had meant to sound seductive but to her horror the words hitched in her throat, came out more as a plea than a challenge. His eyes darkened to navy, his mouth an irresistible curve.

'Oh I am planning to kiss you all right.'

Her knees weakened so much that if she hadn't had the tree for support, she was sure she would have staggered.

'Promises, promises.'

How could eyes say so much? Want and desire and need mingled with appreciation and humour—and regret. They both knew this was near its end. But only Liberty knew when. She wasn't prepared to have her life decided by someone else's timetable. Being the one to walk away was the only power she had.

'Patience,' he murmured, but Liberty was setting the rules. She cupped his cheek and leaned right back into him, folding her body into his, satisfaction filling her as he groaned. Leg against leg, hip against hip, her body as moulded to his as the layers allowed, she snaked an arm around his neck so she could angle him just where she wanted him.

'I'm done with patience.'

She felt his rumble of amusement reverberate through her, the shift in her balance as he took back control, pushing her back against the tree and now he was cupping her face as he finally, finally kissed her. Tantalisingly sweet, tantalisingly slow, a gradual increasing pressure. She was boneless, surrendering to him. *His.* The thought hung there, shocking and stark until she pushed it away, not wanting anything to mar the moment. Instead she unzipped his jacket, slipping her hands under his shirt, tugging at buttons, wanting to feel and be felt despite the snow all around. There was no more talk of beds or moving, Charlie responding to the change in pace, the urgency in kind.

Time stopped. There was only this. The kiss, that ratcheted up from sensual and teasing to urgent in seconds, hands exploring, kisses hard and hot, her hands working at his jeans, his hand inside her leggings as she impatiently slid them down. This is what she had wanted eight years ago, her inexperienced heart and body leading her towards this claiming, but who was claiming who she still didn't know. The tree was rough against her back and head, the air cold on exposed skin, the angle awkward, but she didn't care as he pressed closer, harder, his touch everywhere she needed it to be, his clever fingers making her gasp out loud, and cling to him, her own hands digging into his shoulders, her leg wrapping around him as he finally entered her. She buried her face in his neck, kissing, nipping, gasping, both glorying in the moment and mourning the moment they would both be spent.

Liberty had no idea how long they were there, but she gradually returned to herself, Charlie heavy against her. Slowly, without words, they disentangled themselves, redoing buttons and zips with cold hands.

'You were right,' Charlie said, pulling her close. 'We didn't need a bed. But you must be freezing, why don't we go warm up? I have some ideas on how we can do that…'

It was tempting, so very tempting. Liberty allowed herself to touch his cheek, to run a finger along his cheekbone and across his mouth before standing on tiptoes for one last lingering kiss. 'That sounds amazing but I need a quick shower. My lift leaves in half an hour.'

'Your what?'

'To the airport. I'm getting a lift with Bill.'

'But…' His eyebrows drew together. 'I thought you were coming back with me tomorrow. What's the hurry?'

'I think it's better we have a clean break, don't you?' Slowly, almost painfully, she disentangled herself, standing back, immediately cold, the inches between them a chasm.

'Yes, but why now when we still could have tonight?' His gaze sharpened. 'What's going on, Liberty?'

'Nothing.' She started walking back to the castle and after a second's hesitation he fell in beside her. 'I just have a chance to get back today and took it. No big deal.' She inhaled. It was time to take that control she had promised herself. 'Look, Charlie, the rules were clear from the start. We were here to have some fun. We've done that. What we did just now ticked off a little teenage fantasy of mine, it feels like the perfect way to finish, full circle, don't you agree?' She sounded as unconcerned as she could. As if the words, the sex, him, meant nothing.

'If that's what you want then of course.' Typical Charlie, always the gentleman. 'But I still don't get why so sudden. Is there something more going on?'

'You'd like that, wouldn't you?' She hadn't meant to say that but she couldn't stop herself. 'Then you could try and fix me.'

'What are you talking about?'

'You genuinely don't see that I am quite happy with how things are. To you I am poor, damaged Liberty, another entry on your roster of ladies in distress.'

'What?' Shock reverberated through his voice.

'Come on, Charlie. You thrive on riding to the rescue, the more doomed the better. You should have lived a thousand years ago and had some nice dragons to slay.'

'I have no idea what you're talking about.'

'No? Tell me, Charlie, did you never dream of another life? A city career like Giles, surrounded by your tribe as you make money. A tech startup, an office filled with boy toys and a real ale bar on Fridays? Acting, travelling, politics, anything?'

'No. Never.' The words were curt. He was getting angry. Good. She needed that anger, it made everything easier.

'No, because you had to take over the family business, nobly and selflessly. The perfect son and heir, the perfect brother, the perfect boyfriend, loyal to your lady no matter how undeserving. Anyone with half a brain could see Octavia didn't want or need saving, but how much more romantic the narrative if she did. You even let her win in the end, like a true knight would. Now you have ridden to Millie's rescue, but before that you couldn't help but detour to me. Trying to assuage your guilt over one kiss years ago that meant nothing. God, Charlie, do you really think my heart was broken back then? That I was so weak? I just told you what I knew you wanted to hear.'

It felt good, to say the bitter words, to see the anger growing on his face. Good, and yet at the same time they tore her apart.

His face was set into hard lines. 'Do you think I don't know what's going on here?'

'I'm sure you think you do.'

'Liberty Gray pushing me away, just as she pushes everyone. So scared of getting hurt, she would rather sabotage first.'

Good point and well made. It was a tactic that had kept her safe over the years. She just normally wasn't this obvious—or cruel. But these weren't normal circumstances. She didn't normally feel this vulnerable, this needy. She didn't normally wonder if her heart was actually engaged this time, and that's why it felt like it might just be cracking, fault lines running through it widening and shattering.

'Maybe I am, maybe I am just being honest. We both knew the rules, Charlie, so let's not make this something it's not. You have a wedding to go to. I hope you'll both be very happy.'

Charlie stopped, his hands in his pockets, his face a mixture of incredulity, anger, sorrow and a pity that tore at her and enraged her in equal measure. 'I'm not doing this, Liberty,' he said. 'Look. Let's go back to the apartment, talk properly there.'

'There's nothing more to say. Besides, my plane ticket is booked.'

'Okay then. If this is really what you want. But, Liberty. Stop pushing people away, they might just surprise you. And I am sorry, I didn't mean to hurt you.'

Her smile was as careless as she could make it. 'You didn't.'

'That's good.' She hated the disbelief in his voice.

He turned and started to walk away from the castle, towards the loch, head held high. She should have kept walking, but she couldn't move, had to watch him walk out of her life for good. He hadn't made it ten paces before he stopped and turned to look at her. 'Do you think I'm making a mistake?'

Of all the questions at all the times. 'It doesn't matter what I think, Charlie. You'll do what you think is right. Just like you always do.' And then she did walk away, knowing she was leaving part of her heart behind her.

CHAPTER THIRTEEN

IT WAS THE day before Christmas Eve. The day before his wedding and Charlie felt completely numb. He just needed to see Millie, to remind himself of all the reasons this marriage with guaranteed calm and happiness was the right thing to do. He'd hoped to see her before now, but he had been flat out catching up with all the hands-on work he hadn't been able to do whilst in Scotland, and Millie herself seemed too busy to come to him or to do more than exchange a few quick messages. Giles had been equally elusive.

He'd deliberated calling Liberty, but in the end hadn't even messaged. She'd made her feelings very clear and he had to respect that. Besides, he would only be calling to assuage his own conscience.

He'd known getting involved with her was a bad idea. He'd never had a no strings feelings-free fling in his life. Sex to Charlie meant something. He'd been kidding himself when he'd thought he could walk away unscathed. And here he was, on the eve of his wedding, thinking about another woman.

'Here you are! I've been looking for you everywhere. What are you doing on the roof?' Tabby. He'd been avoiding her, sure she would see the guilt in his eyes.

'Getting some air, thinking.'

His sister came and joined him. 'Remember when we were absolutely forbidden to come up here?'

'I'm not sure that ban was ever lifted.' Accessible from an attic window, the flat area, flanked by two vast chimney-stacks, had been an irresistible draw at every age. 'I love how you can see almost the whole estate from here, the sea and the horizon. Tabs?'

'Hmm?'

'Do you think I have a saviour complex?'

'Do I think you have a *what*?' She slanted a keen look at him. 'Is this about Octavia? Because a, that was a mug complex if anything and b, tomorrow you are marrying a wonderful woman who we all love and Octavia should be at the very end of a long list of things on your mind.'

'She is! Don't worry. There won't be three of us in this marriage.' At least, he didn't want there to be, but it wasn't Octavia's icy elegance that haunted his dreams but Liberty's burnished gold vibrancy. 'No, it was something Liberty said.' Just saying her name felt dangerous. 'Like, I never considered another career, I did exactly what was expected of me...'

'And that's a problem because? Look at what you inherit, Charlie.' She waved her arm dramatically. 'And you love it, you know you do.'

He exhaled. 'I do, it's just...and yes, Octavia. All those years I put up with her drama and all the rest because I thought I was the only one who could...' He grimaced. 'You're right, I was a mug.'

'Charlie, are you getting cold feet? Because Mum and I have put a lot of work into this wedding. But your happiness is more important, obviously,' she finished more than a little doubtfully.

'No.' He meant it. He'd given his word and this marriage made sense, he just needed to remind himself why. 'I just need to see Millie, that's all.'

'You're in luck. That's her car there just turning up the drive? Giles's car anyway, he's giving her a lift. Come on, stop philosophising on the roof and come and see your bride.'

It was a good plan, and Charlie was desperate to see Millie. But as they edged their way back to the large open attic window he couldn't help but ask. 'Have you heard from Liberty since she got back to London?'

'Not much. I've been so busy with all the last-minute wedding plans and she usually needs some decompression time after a shoot. I was hoping she would come for Christmas Day even though she couldn't make the wedding...' Liberty had been invited to the wedding? She had never said. 'But she says she is heading off somewhere. She was looking for a last-minute flight.'

'Good, that's good.' How could he have made his vows knowing she was listening, watching, that she knew the truth?

And then he was on the stairs and Millie was walking in, looking a little diffident, nervous, but her own glorious, welcoming, safe self and he was hugging her.

'Everything okay?' There was a hint of strain around her eyes.

'It's all going to be fine now,' she said, leaning in tight. Charlie's conscience smote him. He'd left her to do everything. While he was off adjusting and forgetting and dallying she had been organising and planning. He didn't deserve her. But he was going to make her happy, just as they had planned. No matter what it took.

* * *

Vow made, Charlie just wanted to get on and get married already. But there was a timetable to follow, starting with a rehearsal in the family chapel. He felt more like an actor than a groom as he stood in the small, sacred space, practising his lines, Giles looking unusually solemn next to him. Once that was done his duties continued with a formal rehearsal dinner in the dining room. Charlie knew exactly what was expected of him as host and heir on these occasions and so he made polite small talk before officially welcoming the guests who were staying overnight to Howard Hall and his wedding, complimenting Millie with a few lines that made her blush. It wasn't hard, she looked sensational in a green silk dress.

But he still wasn't attracted to her.

He was very proud of her though. She wasn't used to these occasions but her nerves didn't show as she made her own speech at the end of the meal, an elegant and heartfelt thanks to everyone who had helped.

'Finally,' she said. 'I want to say a special thank-you to Charlie's best friend and best man, Giles. When Charlie's work dragged him away, Giles stepped up and helped me organise all sorts of wedding-related things—from invitations to flowers and rings. And I can tell you, he can now put together a pretty impressive festive wreath, too! Seriously, though. Thank you, Giles, for everything.'

Millie looked across at Giles as she said this and he looked steadily back and for one moment his heart was in his eyes. Charlie sat there frozen. *Giles was in love with Millie?* Surely not. Attracted to, yes, but in love? He *had* been very protective of her. And wreath-making? That didn't fall into best man duties.

Besides, that look…it was unmistakable.

His best friend in love with his bride. Was she in love with him too?

Sleep was always going to be difficult but the revelation at the dinner made it impossible. He needed air and he needed a drink. Charlie grabbed a bottle of champagne and despite the temperature, headed outside to the ruined folly that had once been Millie's and his hideout.

He sat on the wall and took a swig from the opened bottle, thinking over what he had seen. *Was* Millie in love with Giles? If so, what did that mean. Giles was so adamantly anti marriage or commitment and a family, and those things were so important to Millie.

But how could she marry him if she was in love with someone else? Neither of them had planned for that contingency. Although as far as Millie was concerned, he still had feelings for Octavia. No wonder, he had allowed her to think that.

And yet it was so far from the truth it was laughable. He had barely thought about Octavia in months.

If he was in love with anyone, it was Liberty.

Love. Liberty.

Was this love? How was he expected to know when he had got it so very wrong before? He did want to protect her, help her, not because of some saviour complex but because he cared, because her happiness mattered to him. He desired her, enjoyed her company, loved to see her at work, hair tucked behind her ears, nose screwed in concentration. Liked her humour. Her directness. She'd made her feelings very plain, but Charlie knew her well enough to suspect that she had been masking. Pushing him away so she was the one to leave. Knew how vulnerable she was to rejection.

He heard footsteps and looked up to see a small figure

walking towards him, wrapped in a big coat over pyjamas and wellies at least a size too large. 'Millie?'

'Who else? Did you bring a second glass for me?' She joined him on the wall.

'I didn't even bring one for me.' He handed the bottle to her. 'I wasn't really expecting company.'

'Why not? We always used to meet here as kids. And teens, for that matter.'

'Yeah, but…everything's different now, isn't it?' And that was the last thing he wanted.

'I suppose. But if we're really getting married tomorrow, I don't *want* it to be different. I want it to be like it always was between us. Don't you?'

And there it was. '*If* we're getting married? Having doubts?'

'No,' she countered. 'Why, are you?'

Was he? She was Millie. He loved her. All his reasons for marrying her were unchanged. Whereas Liberty…he wanted her, desired her, but she unsettled him. And the way things had ended were reminiscent of Octavia at her worst. He had a good thing here; he shouldn't sabotage it. And hurting Millie was unthinkable. If she really wanted to go ahead then there was no other path. 'Of course not.'

She leaned against him and neither spoke for a while, Charlie's mind whirling. The look in Liberty's eyes as she deliberately set out to hurt him. She hadn't looked bored or amused or contemptuous, she had been defensive. The look in Giles's eyes when Millie made her toast. The rawness, he had never seen Giles like that before. He couldn't just ignore it.

'So… Giles. He really was a help? I know you two haven't always got on so well, and I really did feel bad about having to go away and leave it all to you two, but—'

Smooth, Charlie. Very smooth.

'No. He was great. He… I couldn't have done it all without him.'

'Good.' He could leave it, maybe he should. But at the same time… 'Only…the way he was watching you at the dinner. I wondered if…maybe something had happened between you two?'

Millie let out a groan. 'Were we that obvious?'

'You weren't but he was. To me, anyway.'

'I'm sorry.' She sounded mortified. 'We didn't mean for it to happen. It was just—'

'It's fine.' The last thing he deserved was an apology. 'We both agreed that if we wanted to have a last few weeks of freedom, we should. And at least it was Giles. I don't have to worry about his stealing you away and marrying you before I can.' It was a shame Giles was so opposed to marriage; the irony was that he would make a great husband, kind and conscientious underneath that charming exterior. But if even Millie couldn't change his mind, then his friend really was set on living life alone. And that meant Charlie's promise to Millie stood. He couldn't let her down, not if she wanted to go ahead.

'Right. What about you? Did you find someone to… sow those last wild oats with in Scotland, while you were away?' He shifted uncomfortably. 'You did! Who was she?'

She'd been honest with him, he needed to be in turn. There was no point starting marriage with a lie. 'You should know I didn't intend to, but I think there was always unfinished business between Liberty and me. I made it very clear I was committed to you, and she made it very clear she wasn't interested in anything serious, and like I said, unfinished business. But it's done, now,' he said as earnestly as he could, meaning every word. It *was* done, and whatever he felt about that, about Liberty, had to be locked away and never thought of again. 'And I'm here. I'm committed to you, Mills. I won't let you down, I promise.'

'I know.' She took the bottle from him and held it up. 'To us.'

'To us.' And he meant it. At least, he really wanted to mean it. And that was a good start.

Liberty stared at the clothes tossed on her bed. Thermals and jumpers and all the things she had taken to Scotland on one side, bikinis, flip-flops and little dresses on the other, a now empty suitcase between them. Her flight was booked. Like the heroine in *Jingle Bell Highlander*, she was avoiding Christmas by taking off. By the time she landed in Thailand it would be Boxing Day. She fully intended to lose track of time in an orgy of sunbathing, sleeping and reading.

She just had to get through the rest of Christmas Eve. She had hoped to sleep through it but no such luck. It had been a fitful night and she had ended up getting up before six to search out coffee from the early-opening café down the road, throwing a coat over her pyjamas so she could take it straight back to bed.

She wasn't a fan of Christmas Eve at the best of times. Christmas Eve as Charlie's wedding day felt infinitely worse. A reminder in every way of just how lonely she was.

Thanks to Tabby she knew every carefully timetabled moment from the wedding rehearsal yesterday followed by a formal meal, to the pre-wedding drinks and the timing of the service itself. Roll on the moment it would all be over, and she would be free.

Only free to *what*? Work as much as possible so she didn't get the opportunity to feel? Free to look for relationships that had *short-term* tattooed all over them? Free to keep her heart locked away? It was existence, not really freedom.

What would have happened if she had played it differently? If she had told Charlie she was falling for him? Had fallen for him. That the crush which had never quite gone away had crystallized into something real. If she had been honest when he asked her what he should do? She felt flayed at the thought of making herself so vulnerable, putting herself up for rejection. But without vulnerability how could she ever move on, have a fulfilling life, a proper relationship, a family?

She had been so scathing of Charlie's white knight tendencies but she still had wanted him to fight for her, for them. She was still poised for the bell to ring, to see him there at her front door, in his wedding suit, to tell her it had been her all along. To tell her he understood why she had pushed him away. That he loved her. That it had always been her.

Liberty sat on the bed and took a deep breath, pushing back the threatened tears. She hadn't cried over Charlie Howard for eight years, she wasn't going to start now. Instead, she was going to force herself back into the real world, pack her bag and then find a way to occupy herself until her flight finally took off in just under twenty-four hours' time.

She still had her mother's present to wrap and give along with her half-siblings and stepfather's gifts. She'd sent her presents to everyone on her father's side from

Scotland, with no expectation of seeing any of them over the festive period, but she usually tried to hand her mother's over in person. She could take a trip out to the Edwardian house backing onto Richmond Park. There would be a scrupulous timetable of festive activities of course, but surely there would be a thirty-minute slot available she could fit in to? The journey to and from Richmond would nicely fill several hours.

Not that her mother had asked if she was planning to visit or suggested that she did but if Liberty waited for an invitation, she would never see her.

Liberty retrieved the tote bag filled with the still un-wrapped presents that Charlie had helped her choose. The books for her siblings. *The Dark is Rising* quintet for the oldest, a selection of Diana Wynne Jones for the next and several illustrated books of myths for the youngest. The carefully chosen organic skincare for her mother. The history books for her stepfather. And a wrapped parcel. What was this? She hadn't put it there. She eased it out. It was a box, wrapped in red paper.

'What on earth?' She couldn't see a tag, but there was a scrap of Sellotape as if one had been attached at some point, and sure enough, when she shook the bag out, a glitter-covered cardboard rectangle fell onto the bed.

Dear Liberty. Time to restart the collection? Happy Christmas. All my love, Charlie xxx

All my love. It was the kind of thing people wrote all the time, it didn't mean anything.

But he had bought her a gift and hidden it. Surely that did.

With slightly shaking hands she undid the Sellotape and carefully peeled the paper back, revealing a card-board box. She opened it up and there, nestled on strips of paper packed in tight to keep them safe, were three snow globes of differing sizes. The smallest was the same as the ones she had handed out as gifts, the wintry scene resembling Glenmere, the second a Victorian London scene, the largest a fantasy of mountains and trees, a sleigh flying through the air. She swallowed, remembering the brief conversation in Perth. *I used to collect them as a child*, she had said, and then stopped. Tried to hide her hurt at her mother's casual attitude to her belongings, but Charlie had seen. He had seen her.

She put the box down, her mind whirling, her heart speeding up, her emotions a kaleidoscope. She loved Charlie, there was no point pretending otherwise, and if there was any chance he felt the same way then she had to tell him, preferably before the wedding which was in… oh, God, it was in five hours. She was still not dressed, in London and she had to get to Norfolk on one of the busiest travel days of the year.

Charlie Howard might not be charging in on his white horse to save her but that was fine. She was a modern woman. She could save him instead. As soon as she was dressed and could figure out how to get there, that was.

CHAPTER FOURTEEN

CHARLIE HAD BARELY drunk at the rehearsal dinner, and they hadn't finished the champagne, so why did he feel in the grips of the worst hangover ever? He couldn't stop his hands from shaking.

Last night, at the folly, things had made sense again. He, Millie. Stability. But once he had gone to bed, it all got jumbled up again. Instead of Millie's warm familiar smile he could only see the wistfulness in Liberty's eyes, relive the moment she had gone on the offensive. Hurting him so that he couldn't hurt her first. Retreating before she was rejected. All she wanted was for someone to put her first. Charlie knew that and yet he had still used her and justified it to himself. Fooled himself.

He could be wrong, of course. Liberty might have meant every bitter word, but he didn't think he was. He knew her, every mercurial shift in mood.

He loved Millie, he always would. But he couldn't ignore that he was *in* love with Liberty any longer. And whatever he did today would hurt one of them, possibly irrevocably.

He leaned on the windowsill, breathing slowly, trying to calm his nerves, wishing Giles would stop hovering ominously and just say whatever was on his mind.

'Charlie... Millie told me, about why the two of you decided to get married so fast.'

There it was. Charlie glanced back at him. 'The way she tells it, that's not the only thing the two of you shared while I was away.'

'I didn't know she... She said that you told her to have a last fling before the ring, if she wanted.'

He attempted a laugh but it fell flat. 'I did, God help me. I thought it would help us both reconcile ourselves to marriage.'

Giles tensed. 'If you're having second thoughts about this wedding, you need to tell Millie.'

Giles was lecturing *him* on *marriage*? On Millie? *Giles* who was too scared to even consider commitment? Who was exactly who Millie didn't need in her life. And yet Charlie had pushed the two of them together and no matter what Millie had said last night she clearly had feelings for his friend.

What kind of marriage would this be when she had fallen for Giles just as he had fallen for Liberty?

But right now, and more importantly how dare Giles break Millie's heart? 'I'm *not* having second thoughts!' He turned round and faced his best man. 'Millie is one of the best people I know, and I love her. She needs this, and I'd never let her down like that. She wants a family, a happy ever after, and if no one else is going to give it to her,' he added pointedly, 'then I'm damn well going to make sure she gets it, because she deserves *everything*.'

'I know,' Giles said quietly. Too quietly. Charlie stared at his friend and saw the same look he had seen at the rehearsal dinner last night, loss and regret and love.

If so, what was Giles waiting for? 'And what about

you, Giles?' he pushed. Now he had started he couldn't stop. His worry about the wedding, his love for Millie, his confusion around Liberty whirling round and round. 'So quick with the advice for others, but what do *you* want? I thought it really was just a fling before the ring between you and Millie, like we agreed. But looking at you now I'm not so sure.'

Giles paled. 'I'll stay away once you're married, Charlie. You know I'd never betray you that way. Millie and I ended everything before we came here. You know I can't give her what she wants.'

Couldn't he? The only thing stopping Giles, that had ever stopped him, were his own doubts and fears. It was so clear—why couldn't Giles see that? 'But you wish you could, don't you?'

His friend turned away, fussing with the tray of buttonholes refusing to answer.

'You're here asking what *I* want, but have you thought about what *you* want?' Charlie was in Giles's space, forcing his friend to concentrate, to listen. 'Or have you spent so long focussing on what you *don't* want—on *not* falling in love, *not* getting married, *not* ending up like your parents, or your sister, or chained to a money pit of a house because of history and society and expectations—that you've forgotten to even *think* about what *you* want?'

For a moment Charlie feared he had gone too far. Giles just stood staring at him, his face so pale it was grey.

But Charlie had to make him see. There was no way he was putting Millie through the humiliation of an abandoned wedding if something, someone better wasn't waiting for her. But how could he marry her knowing she and Giles had feelings for each other?

A saviour complex, Liberty had said. That wasn't always a bad thing and if he could help his two best friends see that they were right for each other then maybe it was actually a very good thing indeed. He was going to tell Liberty that, just as soon as he had sorted these two lovesick fools out. He grinned at Giles, the tension falling away, as the farcical nature of the situation hit him. They just needed French doors and an Edwardian drawing room and they could be characters in a Noel Coward play.

'So. When exactly did you fall in love with my fiancée? And just what are you going to do about it?'

Giles blinked rapidly. 'I need to talk to Millie.'

'I agree, but I think I should speak to her first.' Charlie looked at his watch. The timing couldn't be worse. Guests would be arriving for welcome drinks at any time before heading to the chapel. The last thing any of them needed was his mother or Tabby to suspect anything was wrong before they had sorted it out amongst themselves. 'Go to the chapel as arranged so that Tabby doesn't start panicking. And while you're there, I suggest you start figuring out how you are going to tell my best friend that you love her.'

Charlie wished he felt as confident as he sounded. Breaking off an engagement was tricky at the best of times, even when you were sure the bride didn't want to marry you. Doing it literally minutes before the wedding was filled with pitfalls. What if he didn't find Millie in time and had to add a chapel scene to the play? But luck was with him, he had no sooner headed into the main house than he saw her coming down the stairs, her face lighting up with relief when she saw him. He made his way through the brightly dressed crowd to meet her.

'Want to get out of here for a moment?'

She nodded, and, aware that any moment someone would notice Millie, especially as she was the one in a long white dress, he led the way back upstairs and into a small storage room where they kept his great-grandmother's fur coats.

'You aren't supposed to see me in my wedding dress before the ceremony,' Millie said.

'I think that only counts if the wedding is actually going to take place.' Just saying the words lessened a burden he hadn't realised he was carrying. 'Is it?'

Charlie watched Millie's expression change, from surprise to a slow-dawning relief. 'I... I don't think it can. I'm sorry, Charlie. I can't marry you.'

'Because you're in love with Giles.' He couldn't keep the grin off his face as Millie stared at him wide-eyed.

'You're not...angry?'

How could she think that? He shook his head, injecting as much love and sincerity into his voice as he could. 'I'm not angry. I'm... Honestly, right at this moment, I'm not sure what I am. Except your best friend. I'll always be that.'

'How did we end up here?' Millie asked. "I mean... really?!'

It was amazing to be able to hug her and know they were back to what they had always been, two people who loved and cared about each other deeply. 'I think we both wanted to make each other happy. And maybe we would have done. But it would only ever have been a sort of...' He tried to find the right word.

'Contentment. We'd have been content, I think. Except

now we both know there's something more out there, and it's hard to settle for contentment after that.'

'It is.' Charlie kissed the top of her head, before stepping away. 'So I think we'd both better get out there and demand what we *really* want from life. Don't you?'

Charlie did his best to insist that he be the one to go to the chapel and tell the guests that the wedding was off, but Millie was having none of it. 'I'll go,' she said firmly. 'This is a joint decision after all.' Charlie started to argue, but then stopped. It was already mid-afternoon and he had no idea when Liberty was leaving for the airport. He had to get to London as soon as possible to tell her the wedding was off. To tell her he loved her. What happened next was up to her, but he didn't want to leave it a second longer, especially as Tabby was bound to start spreading the news quickly.

'Good luck. With everything,' he said meaningfully, kissing Millie's cheek, then watched her gather up her dress and sprint down the stairs to go and deliver the news and, more importantly, find Giles.

By the time Charlie got downstairs it was empty. If all the guests were at the chapel then Charlie was supposed to be there too, Tabby would be having kittens. Sure enough, when he checked his phone there were several missed calls and texts, the latter all in caps with many exclamation marks. He pocketed his phone and half turned towards the kitchen to get his car keys but stopped as a figure appeared at the front door.

'Am I too late?' Liberty said. 'I want to object.'

Liberty was trembling, but she did her best to hide it. She was about to make herself the most vulnerable she had ever been. Just because she had fallen in love with Charlie didn't mean it was reciprocated. And if it *was* reciprocated that didn't mean he wasn't going to go ahead and get married. This was the man, after all, who allowed the world to think his ex had jilted him to spare her feelings. How likely was he to humiliate his best friend by calling off the wedding?

Talking of whom, why had Millie only just left the house, running down the path, white dress hitched up, too focused to see Liberty? Had she been with Charlie? Surely the groom shouldn't see the bride before the wedding? Whatever they *had* been doing, both were glowing; neither looked like they were exactly being dragged to the altar.

Liberty was suddenly cold. Had she got this very wrong after all? What was she *doing*? The certainty that had propelled her to Euston, over the two hours on the train willing it on and in the taxi from Kings Lynn to Howard Hall began to ebb away.

She finally found her voice. 'What's going on?'

'Millie has gone to tell everyone that the wedding is off.'

'Is it?' She was suddenly light-headed, her voice husky, half formed. 'When did you decide that?'

'About five minutes ago.' Charlie's gaze was direct, but there was a heat in his blue eyes that warmed her through. 'We decided that there was a clear impediment and better to decide now rather than at the altar, even if it's less dramatic.'

She swallowed. 'What was it? The impediment.'

'The small matter that we are both in love with some-

one else. Turns out Giles was standing in for me in more
ways than one. I just wish he had said something earlier
but then I can't really talk, can I? Look at how long it took
me to figure things out.' He glanced towards the door.
'Soon this place is going to be full of wedding guests
enjoying drinks and food even though there was no ceremony, and amongst them will be my mother and sister
and I don't know about you but I'm not quite ready to
face them. Fancy a walk?'

A *what*? Liberty was still grappling with that casual
in love with someone else.

Liberty had barely nodded before Charlie took her
hand and tugged her through the house to the huge boot
room, filled with a collection of old coats, boots, hats,
scarves and gloves, grabbing a coat and scarf to put on
over his suit, then after checking whether she wanted to
borrow anything, out the door and through the gardens.
'At least the path to the beach doesn't take us anywhere
near the chapel,' he said.

'Why the beach?' It was like being in some kind of
surrealist dream, Alice following the white rabbit. Was
she really here or still in bed? Would she wake up and
find it was the morning of Christmas Eve and she still
had the whole day to endure? But no, she could feel the
winter chill on her face, Charlie was beside her, real and
solid, his hand holding hers tightly, as if he didn't dare
to let her go as he headed to the discreet path which led
through the woods towards the sea.

'Because no one will disturb us there.' He checked his
watch. 'I can guarantee the house will be filled in less
than five minutes and at least half those people will be
demanding an explanation from me. That reminds me.'

He fished his phone out of his pocket and switched it off without looking at it. 'Let's not make it easy for them. I did wonder about just driving somewhere but I need to face my parents and Tabby at some point. It's not fair to leave this up to Millie and Giles to do alone along with everything else. Besides, there's a twelve-course tasting menu to sample, who wants to miss out on that?'

It sounded rather like he was babbling. Was Charlie *nervous*? The thought gave her strength.

'So, Liberty Gray. I have to ask,' he continued. 'If you hadn't got to the house on time, were you planning to do your objecting in the church?'

'I don't know.' Her stomach swooped at the thought of how very close she had actually come to having to decide. Would she have found the courage to burst in and stop the wedding or would she have bottled it? 'Maybe.'

'I hope you would have waited to the persons here present part,' Charlie said. 'Timing and traditions are so important. But the real question is,' he went on almost conversationally, 'what you wanted to object *to*. Christmas? I know you're not a fan. The very notion of a twelve-course meal? Hereditary titles? I thought,' he added, 'that you were going on holiday.'

He was *definitely* babbling, his conversation jumping all over the place. 'Tomorrow. Thailand.'

'Very nice.' They had finally reached the small, locked gate which led directly from the Howard estate onto the sand dunes. Charlie entered a code and the gate swung open so they could walk through. They were still holding hands, she realised, his fingers firm around hers. He took a deep breath. 'But can any beach beat Norfolk in winter? Just look at those skies.'

Liberty also inhaled, the fresh sea air filling her lungs, and found the courage to say what she had come here to say, with just the gulls and waves as her witness. 'I was going to object to you entering into a marriage with your head not your heart. I was going to tell everyone that I hoped you were in love with me, because I am in love with you. I was going to say that marriage is hard enough without going in with such low expectations and that both you and Millie deserve more.'

They had climbed to the top of the dunes while she was speaking and Charlie halted. The wind was whipping her hair into a tangle, her shoes were covered in sand and her coat inadequate for the wind, but she didn't care, because Charlie's eyes were blazing with love and affection. Love and affection for her. 'That sounds like quite an objection. I think it would have been pretty compelling. It almost makes me wish we'd waited. I almost did,' he said ruefully, cupping her face with his gloved hand. 'I almost left it too late. I knew you were pushing me away, I knew why, but I didn't trust in my own instincts. And I didn't want to let Millie down. Especially not here, in front of my family and friends, knowing how out of place she feels sometimes. But I couldn't ignore the feeling in my gut, the one telling me I was making a colossal mistake. The one telling me that you are worth fighting for and I would be a fool to walk away again. Knowing Giles and Millie have developed feelings for each other made it easier, but I would have called the wedding off this morning regardless. There is only one woman I want to make vows to and she is standing right here.'

'Charlie,' she half whispered.

'I love you, Liberty. I love your courage and kindness.

I love your spirit. I love your sense of humour and your intelligence. I love the way you make me feel and the man you make me want to be. I want to date you, properly. To take it slow. To spend time with you with no end date or expectations, but because it's what we both want. I want to hold hands in the street and kiss you on corners, to take you for meals out and spend evenings in, enjoy long lazy days on the beach and long phone calls at night when we're working away. Some of them,' he added, a glint in his eye, 'X-rated. I want all your Christmases and birthdays, to fall more in love with you every day. No more sneaking around, no more pretence. I want honesty.'

Liberty trembled and his hands tightened on hers. 'I know that scares you. Honestly, it scares me too. For me, before, being that vulnerable meant conceding power. Weakness. But love should make us stronger. It took knowing you to realise that.'

'It does scare me,' she admitted. 'But coming here today scared me and here I am. Because I want all that too. I want it with you. I love you, Charlie Howard, I've loved you for over half my life and if you're with me I'm willing to try.'

He kissed her then, fierce and sweet and she clung to him. 'You're shivering,' he said, taking off his scarf and wrapping it around her neck. 'And I need to go in and face my family. I won't think any less of you if you want to go back to London and avoid all the fallout. You've got a much-deserved holiday to pack for after all.'

'Why don't I postpone the flight for a couple of days? I could always see if I can book another seat, if you wanted to come with me?' she suggested. 'If you don't mind, I think I would like to take Tabby up on her offer of spending Christmas here after all.'

'That sounds like the best Christmas present ever.' He kissed her again. 'Happy Christmas, Liberty. Let this be the first of many.'

'I like the idea of that.' And as they walked back towards the estate, Liberty realised that she was looking forward to Christmas for the first time she could remember, because she had everything she wanted, right here.

EPILOGUE

One year later

'CHARLIE, YOU LOOK so handsome.'

Charlie turned and looked at his sister. 'What's happened? Is Liberty okay?'

Tabby shook her head. 'Honestly, that's your first thought? Not "Thank you, Tabby, you look beautiful too"?'

'You do look beautiful,' he said quickly. She did, of course, in her long silk dress of dull gold teamed with a cream faux fur cape, her hair piled up on top of her head, small gold stars holding it in place.

'That's better. Liberty is having some photos taken so I thought I would check in on you. Make sure you are okay—that you are still planning on turning up for *this* wedding.'

'Very funny.' He felt suddenly cold. 'Liberty isn't having second thoughts, is she?'

'No, panic not. Where are Millie and Giles? Shouldn't they be looking after you?'

'Millie is resting before the ceremony and you know what Giles is like. He doesn't like her to be alone for too long.'

'The devoted father-to-be, who would have thought it? And who would have thought that my big brother would be marrying my best friend? I hope you know I will always take her side in arguments.'

'I wouldn't expect anything less.' Charlie smiled at his sister. 'Thank you. Organising one wedding for me was one thing but to organise a second just one year later...'

'And with even less notice,' Tabby said meaningfully. 'I actually did this for Liberty. I didn't see why she should suffer for your sins. Besides, it's so small, and everything is in place at Glenmere so there was hardly anything to do.'

This time Charlie had been involved every step of the way, making sure the wedding was exactly what Liberty wanted. They were holding it at Glenmere of course, the place where it had all begun, a pared-down guest list, just a handful of friends each, his immediate family, and, those of hers who had accepted. In the end she had invited them all, and to her amazement most had accepted even without the inducement of magazine coverage. Both Giles and Millie were acting as best man, Tabby as maid of honour, the bridesmaids Liberty's youngest siblings. No twelve-course tasting menu, no ostentation, just as simple as a wedding in a castle could be. It was small, quiet and utterly perfect.

'No nerves?' Tabby asked.

'Only that she'll change her mind. I think a third failed engagement would be more than I can live down.'

His sister grinned. 'Third time lucky. Don't worry, Charlie. This time you've managed to propose to the right bride. She'll be there.'

The chapel at Glenmere had been transformed thanks to Millie's clever work, cream and gold garlands brightening the rather austere grey walls and simple pews, the same colours repeated in the large floral arrangements on the altar and at every corner of the chapel. Liberty smoothed down her cream silk skirt and adjusted her veil. She wasn't nervous, to her surprise, just eager to be married.

The guests were all seated, waiting, apart from Giles and Millie who stood with Charlie by the altar. Charlie was nervous, she could tell by the way he fidgeted, the quirk in his mouth, how pale he was. On one side were his family and friends, on the other hers, and she still couldn't believe how many had made the effort to be here on New Year's Eve, even Orlando flying in from LA for the occasion. She would never have a normal family, but Charlie had helped her accept the one she had, given her the courage to reach out to them. Which was why her father stood by her side and her father's twins and her sisters on her mother's side were clustered around Tabitha, in cream dresses with gold sashes. She had let Felix off the role of pageboy, he had looked so appalled at the suggestion.

'Ready?' her father asked and she nodded.

'Absolutely.'

She'd been ready since Charlie Howard had smiled at her the first time she had visited his house, since all those times when he had been kind to his sister's lonely friend, since that first kiss.

He had kept his word and wooed her patiently and slowly for most of the last year until Liberty had decided enough was enough, taken him to Paris and proposed to him. She would have been happy with an elopement, but they had already decided on a family Christmas and New Year's at Glenmere. Combining the festive season with their wedding made sense. Only not Christmas, she had said, especially as that was the anniversary of his last wedding. New Year's Eve was where it had begun for them. It was the perfect day to start their next step.

The music started and her sisters started their solemn march down the short aisle, the twins holding their posies tightly, then Tabby sauntered down as if it was a catwalk, winking at Orlando as she went. And then it was time. The small congregation were on their feet, everyone turning to watch her, phones out and recording, but all she could see was Charlie, smiling at her, his face alive with love.

'Hi,' Charlie whispered. 'You look beautiful.'

She grinned back, taking his outstretched hand. 'You showed up.'

'Always and forever,' he promised.

As they turned to face the vicar, she knew that he had made the most important vow already. There were no guarantees in life but with Charlie by her side she could face anything and she couldn't wait to get started.

* * * * *

If you missed the previous story in the Blame It on the Mistletoe duet, then check out

Christmas Bride's Stand-In Groom
by Sophie Pembroke

And if you enjoyed this story, check out these other great reads from Jessica Gilmore

It Started with a Vegas Wedding
Christmas with His Ballerina
The Princess and the Single Dad

All available now!

MILLS & BOON®

Coming next month

BEAUTY AND THE BROODING CEO
Juliette Hyland

The candlelight caressed her features. This was another painting. All the walls in the closed-off wing were going to be Cora. His masterpieces. Memories of her.

'May I have this dance?' He offered a small bow, enjoying the grin spreading on her face.

'I feel like Beauty in the fairy tale.' She put her hand in his and he wrapped his other arm around her waist.

'Does that make me the Beast?' He spun them in a wide circle.

'You are not a beast.' Cora ran her hand down his cheek. Her fingers brushed his scar but she didn't recoil.

'In your arms I feel like that might actually be true.' Everett skimmed his hand up her back, pulling her a little closer.

'Everett.'

This time it was his turn to silence her rather than touch the uncomfortable subject. He bent his head, capturing her lips. She let out a little moan, pressing her hips against his as they moved in sync around the room.

When the song shifted to a faster beat, neither pulled away or adjusted the dance's speed. He simply held her. Reveled in the moment, the majesty.

Continue reading

BEAUTY AND THE BROODING CEO
Juliette Hyland

Available next month
millsandboon.co.uk

COMING SOON!

We really hope you enjoyed reading this book.
If you're looking for more romance
be sure to head to the shops when
new books are available on

Thursday 19th December

To see which titles are coming soon, please visit
millsandboon.co.uk/nextmonth

MILLS & BOON

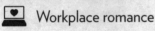

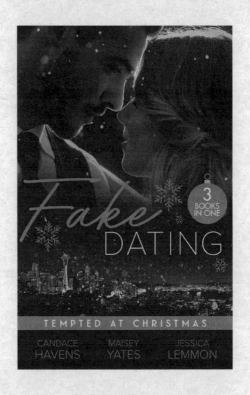

LET'S TALK

Romance

For exclusive extracts, competitions and special offers, find us online:

f MillsandBoon

X @MillsandBoon

◉ @MillsandBoonUK

♪ @MillsandBoonUK

Get in touch on 01413 063 232